the wood wife

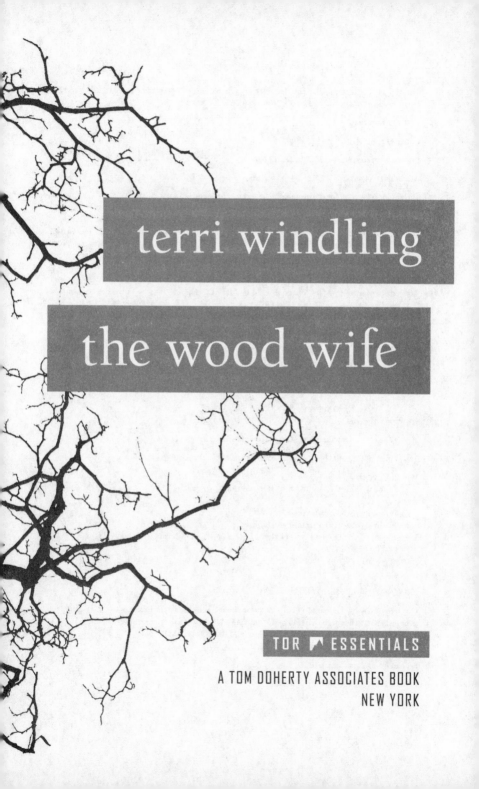

terri windling

the wood wife

TOR ▶ ESSENTIALS

A TOM DOHERTY ASSOCIATES BOOK
NEW YORK

THE WOOD WIFE

Edited by Patrick Nielsen Hayden

A Tor Essentials Book
Published by Tom Doherty Associates
120 Broadway
New York, NY 10271

www.tor-forge.com

Tor® is a registered trademark of Macmillan Publishing Group, LLC.

The Library of Congress has cataloged the first trade paperback edition as follows:

Windling, Terri.
    The wood wife / by Terri Windling.—First edition.
        p. cm.
    "A Tom Doherty Associates book."
    ISBN 978-0-7653-0293-9 (trade paperback)
1. Poets—Fiction. 2. Biographers—Fiction. 3. Arizona—Fiction. 4. Fantasy fiction—Fiction. I. Title.
PS3573.I5175 W66 1996
813'.54—dc23

                                                                                          96016113

ISBN 978-1-250-23755-2 (trade paperback)

Our books may be purchased in bulk for promotional, educational, or business use. Please contact your local bookseller or the Macmillan Corporate and Premium Sales Department at 1-800-221-7945, extension 5442, or by email at MacmillanSpecialMarkets@macmillan.com.

First Edition: October 1996
Second Trade Paperback Edition: January 2021

Printed in the United States of America

0 9 8 7 6 5 4 3 2 1

introduction
by Delia Sherman

When Maggie Black, the East Coast poet and journalist who conducts us through the first pages of *The Wood Wife*, arrives in Tucson, she finds it bleak and difficult.

> *Everything here had spines or thorns. The sky was too vast; the light was too clear. There was nothing soft or hidden in the land, and it made her feel raw, overexposed, like a photograph left in the sun.*

When I started going to Arizona in the 1990s, my initial reaction to the desert was pretty much the same. Everything looked brown and grey, low, spiky, and absolutely unwelcoming. There seemed to be an unnecessary amount of dust and strip malls and thorny plants. But Terri Windling lived there, and Terri was my partner Ellen Kushner's best friend and was becoming one of mine, and I loved the dry, warm fall and the sunsets and the conversation, so we kept going back.

I didn't know, at first, that Terri was writing a desert book. Terri doesn't talk about her fiction much—she's reticent about her stories until they're complete. This one, I found out later, had been meant to be the final volume of a series of novellas based on Brian Froud's fairy paintings. When the publisher decided that the time was not yet ripe for stand-alone novellas, Terri's sketch-draft was free to grow into the subtle, complex novel the desert demanded.

In the meantime, everything in Terri's life reflected her love of this beautiful, demanding, uplifting country. The walls of her house were hung with paintings and sketches of the beauty she'd found in what

seemed to be a barren land—not landscapes, but soulscapes, alive
with spirits of tree and plant, animal and bird. She painted women
with branching hair or drooping rabbit's ears, troops of children with
feet like birds and wings hanging in tatters from their shoulders,
narrow-faced men with long black hair who reminded me of birds
or animals or wind or the occasional desert storms of pelting rain
that drummed on the roof of the camper we slept in when we visited.
Journey by journey, image by image, they persuaded me that the Sonoran desert was not only beautiful, but very much alive.

In *The Wood Wife,* Terri gives her images voice and movement:
they not only are, they act. If the desert is a study in contradictions
and interdependencies, where heat and poisonous snakes and flash
floods are inseparable from the clarity of the air and the glory of the
mountains at sunset, the desert spirits Terri shows us are both beautiful and dangerous, faithful and capricious, inhuman and fascinated
by the habits of humanity. Their actions and tastes are mysteries, as
incomprehensible to us as ours are to them. Where they live, mystery
is everywhere.

It makes sense, then, that a genuine mystery lies at the center of
The Wood Wife. Every page bristles with questions: Why did Davis
Cooper leave his house to a woman he had never met? Was he the
father of the young man who lives on his property? What drove his
painter lover from the desert she loved? How in the world could he
have drowned in a dry riverbed?

As a mystery must, *The Wood Wife* answers these human questions, satisfying and delighting us in the process. But those answers
lead us to more questions, questions that cannot be so easily answered, about myth and the nature of reality and time and love and
home and art.

As a writer, one of the things I have always loved about *The Wood
Wife* is its examination of artists and their relationship with their
art, with their muses, with each other. Each artist she mentions—
remembered, present, historical, invented—wrestles with the knowledge that their art is never really going to match their inspiration. I
don't think I've ever read a contemporary novel in which artists play

such a central role. Maggie is a poet, Davis Cooper is a poet: both try (or give up on trying) to catch the inexpressible in words, trap the universe in type on a page. Cooper's lover, Anna Naverra, is a painter, as is Maggie's neighbor Juan. But other characters make it clear that painting and writing, dancing and music are not the only arts that can build a bridge to the spirit world. In Terri's world, gardening and building, cooking and healing, rescuing wounded animals and living intensely and beautifully are arts as well, with their own skills and frustrations.

For me, then, *The Wood Wife* is a book about how fantasy grows out of myth and how myth grows out of the land; how not all mysteries should be explained; how anyone who creates beauty and order is an artist. For others, *The Wood Wife* might be a different book. Like myth itself—like the desert or the moors or the mountains or the ocean—we see in *The Wood Wife* what we need and take from it what we can. This book—and Terri's paintings—have opened my eyes to the possibilities of magic, encouraged me to listen with attention and to be aware of the messages inherent in the scents and textures and tastes of the world. It has informed the way I approach the new places I visit and the way I write about places I know. It has changed other people's lives. Perhaps it will change yours.

The Wood Wife *is for*
Brian, Wendy, and Toby Froud,
with love.

And in memory of Herbert Emil Rasmussen
(1916–1994), who is greatly missed.

Who wants to understand the poem
Must go to the land of poetry.

—Johann Wolfgang von Goethe

prologue

On the night that Davis Cooper died, coyotes came down from the hills to the town in the desert valley below. They came from the Santa Rita Mountains in the south. From the Tucson Mountains in the west. From the Catalinas in the north. From the Rincons, where the sun would rise over the dead man's body.

They entered the sleeping city, shadows traveling stealthily through a network of dry riverbeds, slipping through the streets, through parking lots, through drainage tunnels and alleyways. There was one small boy who saw them pass, his nose pressed to the window glass as four, ten, twenty coyotes drifted through suburban yards, headed for some wilder place where the child longed to follow. Later his mother would tell him it was only a dream, and he would believe her.

The place where the coyotes gathered—by the hundreds, a sea of silver fur beneath a moon like a bright new coin—was not a place that one would easily find on any city map. Davis Cooper had known that place. One other had found it, and returned. Now she ignored the calling song. She shut the window, sat down at her kitchen table, lit another cigarette. She was free now. Free. The word tasted sour. Her heart was as heavy as a stone.

Johnny Foxxe made a camp among the trees at Deer Head Springs, high in the Rincon Mountains. In the city below on the desert floor the spring night had been soft and warm, but here it was sharp, biting through his denim jacket and the flannel shirt beneath. He gathered deadfall for a fire. The wood was dry and lit easily. The smoke streamed upward to the stars and marked his presence, if anyone watched.

He breathed in familiar mountain smells and bent down at the lip of *the springs to taste the sweetness of the water. Deer Head Springs was on a trail so steep that few ever climbed it except the animals who had given it its name: the small, shy desert mule deer, and the elusive white stag whom he'd glimpsed only twice in all his years on the mountain.*

The first time he had seen the stag had been by Red Springs, many years before. The second time had been right here, two months ago, on the day he'd left the mountain. He smiled. Now he was back again. It was several miles by mountain trails to the Red Springs house where he'd been born, but the entire length of the Rincon range was home to Johnny Foxxe. Each time he left it, it summoned him back. He'd never been able to resist its call. No woman, no job, no other ties had ever bound him so securely.

In several days he would make the long hike to the canyon where the old house stood. But now he had a job to do. His smile vanished. He sat down by the fire and arranged his tools beside him. A copal flute, a deerskin drum. A hunting knife and a sharpening stone. He sat and bided his time until the water trapped the image of the moon. He fed live oak branches into the fire, waiting, preparing himself.

Dora del Río woke from a deep sleep in the middle of the night. Something was howling outside the bedroom window—a strange, feral, ferocious sound, neither quite human nor animal. She reached for Juan, but he wasn't there asleep in the bed beside her. She turned on the light. The cats were curled and stretched among the bedclothes. She counted all four. The cats were all right. The dog was snoring on the rug below, but Juan was gone and the bed was cold. The clock read 1:15 in the morning.

Outside the howling stopped abruptly. She got up, shivering, and reached for her shawl. Through the window, she could see lights on in the barn where Juan had his studio. She stopped to put on dusty boots beneath her long white nightdress, and then she stepped out into the dark and crossed the stable yard.

The doors to the barn were flung open. Inside, Juan stood in the center of the room, a hunting knife clutched in his hand. Ten years' worth of paintings hung in tatters, the frames shattered, the canvases slashed.

Clay sculptures littered the room in pieces. Carvings smouldered on the wooden floor, threatening to torch the whole barn.

Dora stood and stared at him. Then she ran to fetch a bucket. Juan watched, impassive and glassy-eyed, until she doused the flames with water. Then he wrenched the bucket from her hands and struck her, hard, across the jaw. He had never hit his wife before and even in this wild state the action seemed to startle him; he stopped and looked at her, wide-eyed. And then he made that howling sound, an animal sound, a sound of pain, wrenched from deep in the gut.

He pushed past Dora and out the open door. She fetched another bucket of water and thoroughly drenched the piled wood. Then she dropped the bucket and ran to the door. Juan had already disappeared. The night was quiet. The moon was bright. Blood spattered the cobbled yard. She stopped in the house just long enough to put on a sweater and gloves, and call the dog. Then she snatched a flashlight and went out to follow her husband up the mountainside.

She sent the dog first and followed after, hoping the dog would follow Juan. The hills sounded strangely quiet now; the birds were still, the coyotes as silent as though they all had disappeared. She climbed for many hours that night, farther and farther up the mountain slope. Her jaw ached where Juan had struck her, a thing he'd vowed he would never do. Dora shivered and she continued to climb, looking for signs of his passage. She saw jackrabbits, a pair of deer, a huge white owl passing overhead, but she did not see any sign of Juan and at last she admitted defeat. She whistled for the dog and circled back toward the house nestled in the hills below. Beyond were the distant lights of the city farther down on the desert floor.

She found him on the way back home, at the place where Redwater Creek cut through the granite to form deep bathing pools. He was curled up, naked, fast asleep on the flat boulders at the water's edge. He had marked himself with oil paint: jagged white lines, green snake curves, blue spiral patterns and slashes of red. There was paint in his hair, blood on his chin. He had cut himself above one cheek; any closer and he would have lost the eye.

She touched him gently. "Juan?" she said.

He opened his eyes and smiled at her. Then tears began to fall, mixing with blood, oil paint and dirt. "I want to go home," he whispered to Dora.

"All right, my love. Here, take my hand."

He rose to his feet unsteadily, leaning heavily on her smaller frame. His feet were bare. His legs were bruised. His skin was cold and his eyes confused. She led him down the steep mountain path, the dog trailing silent behind.

The saguaro cactus were straight and slim, standing ten and twelve feet tall, bathed in the silver moonlight. They clustered on the rocky slope, silent guardians of the low foothills, their arms upraised as if in prayer, or preparation for flight.

At their feet was Davis Cooper. The dead man lay facedown in the dirt, his body sprawled in the bottom of a dried-out riverbed. The old man's lungs were filled with water, although no water had run through that wash for forty years. His skin was stained with smears of paint; the fingers of one hand were curled as though he had held on to something tightly—but whatever it had been was gone. Only the poet's body remained, circled by a single pair of footprints lightly pressed into the ground and soon scattered by the desert wind.

Tomás stared into the fire, aware of the other fire that burned that night several miles away. The flames leapt high into the dark. The mesquite wood burned quick and hot. He could feel a rhythm, a pulse, a drum, sounding deep in the rock below.

He poured kinnikinnick from a pouch into the scarred palm of one hand, then tossed a mixture of herbs and tobacco into the dancing flames. The voice of the fire spoke to him. And the voice of the wind in the mesquite wood. Of the stone people, and of the water flowing there at the canyon's heart.

It has ended, *these voices told him.* It has ended, and it has just begun.

The hills call in a tongue
only the language-haunted hear,
and lead us back again
into the place where we have started.
—The Wood Wife, *Davis Cooper*

Nigel came down the street toward her, his face shadowed with annoyance. Her heart, that traitorous organ, still leapt when she saw her ex-husband through the window glass. She knew then why she'd run back to Los Angeles, away from the nice man up north who said he loved her; Nigel was a hard act to follow. He entered the cafe, his irritation and his energy like a cloud that entered with him, changing the weather of the entire room. And reminding her of why she'd once run away from Nigel too.

He looked around the cafe with displeasure. Maggie had picked the place, a little Czech bakery popular with film students and would-be poets half her age. She imagined that he would have preferred some trendy new restaurant where he could make a point of paying the extravagant bill. But this was her turf, not his, for once in their lives. She needed every advantage she could get. And he'd be mollified once he tasted the pastry. Good food, in Nigel's book, always won out over ambiance.

"For god's sake, there you are." Nigel threaded his way through the students to her table in the corner. She stood for his embrace. In her boots with the heels she was even taller than he was. He kissed her on both cheeks, the European way, and said, "You're looking well. Fantastic, in fact."

Maggie shrugged off the compliment as lightly as it was given. Unbidden came the image of Nigel's current wife, a skinny young Parisian fashion model.

"How are you, Nige? You look . . . tired," she said.

He sighed as he sat, rested his chin on his hand, and gave the grin that had won her heart years ago. "What day is this? Thursday? Still Wednesday for me. I never got home to bed last night. We play Toronto this weekend, Chicago on Tuesday, my alto is sick and my percussionist has just discovered his wife is sleeping with the soundman. So what's good here?"

"The coffee. The strudel. Any of the unpronounceable Czech pastries. The French ones will disappoint you."

He signalled the waitress, a young woman with hair dyed an alarming shade of magenta wearing a "Kafka in Prague" T-shirt covered with paint. Nigel ordered for both of them without consulting Maggie, a habit she'd never been able to get him to break. He remembered this too late, and gave her a guilty smile. "Is there something else you wanted? I'll call her back."

Maggie shook her head. "So long as there's coffee and lots of it. Look, Nige, I can't stay that long. I've got a plane to catch at four."

"*Today*?" he said, genuinely taken aback. "I thought you'd be in L.A. a while."

"This is just a stopover. To pick up a few things. And see you." She rolled a fork across the table nervously. "Actually, I'm headed for Tucson."

"*Tucson*? As in Arizona? Whatever for?" He leaned back in the chair and asked the question casually, but she knew that she had rattled him. His transatlantic accent shifted back to his native British whenever he was feeling out of sorts.

Despite her nervousness, she took a certain malicious pleasure in telling him, "I'm going to live there for a while. I found another tenant for the house here; I told that piano player of yours he could have it. He's made an offer to buy it, and I think we should consider it. I can't honestly imagine coming back to Los Angeles."

Nigel sat still, with the ominous quiet he sunk into whenever something displeased him. She envied him that. She always spoke first and thought after—and usually regretted it.

The waitress brought their order as Maggie waited for the inevitable barrage of questions. She picked up the coffee cup gratefully, letting its warmth dispel her anxiety. She didn't need Nigel's permission or blessing. She needn't have told Nigel any of this at all. So why did she feel nervous as a cat on a griddle, as her granddaddy in West Virginia used to say?

For all Nigel's attempts at cool British reserve, his emotions were as tangible in the static field around him as if the air had changed color. Surprise shaded into suspicion and anger. It was not that he needed her here in L.A. But he didn't like things happening outside of his control. They still co-owned the little house by Venice Beach where she'd lived for several years after the divorce, and it was his plan that she should come back to it. They prided themselves on a "friendly divorce." She went to his concerts and he went to her book signings, the former considerably more frequent and star-studded than the latter; she was seen in the better L.A. restaurants in the company of Nigel and his current wife, Nicole.

But for the last two years she'd been renting out the beach house, determined to stay away from L.A. and the circle of friends who still thought of her as half of the Nigel-and-Maggie Show. First she'd gone up to San Francisco, living on a boat owned by an actor friend of Nigel's who was filming abroad for the winter. Then farther up the coast to Inverness, and then even farther to Mendocino. Each time, although the destination had been her choice, the way had been comfortably paved by Nigel. Accommodations had miraculously appeared which she never could have afforded on her own—always "on loan" from some friend of his but subsidized, she suspected, by Nigel's wealth.

It was still odd to think of her ex-husband as wealthy, although he had always assumed he would be. The popular and financial success of the medieval music group he directed had taken everyone but arrogant Nigel by surprise; whereas the fact that she was barely making it on a writer's income came as a surprise to no one. It was not that she worked less hard than he did, or that she was any less well known in her field; but sales on poetry and essay collections, along with the occasional teaching gig, rarely earned enough to pay all the bills. Too often it was Nigel who paid them.

Nigel picked up his pastry and took a bite. His expression was bland, but there was thunder in the air. Then he pinned her with those lovely blue eyes that she'd never been able to withstand. "Why on earth Tucson, Arizona? I played a concert there once. There's nothing in that city but two-stepping cowboys and retired old dears from Long Island. Have you looked at the map? There's no ocean in Tucson. It's the desert, and hotter than bloody hell."

"Do you remember Davis Cooper?"

He nodded. "The cranky old dodger whose poetry you're so enamored of. I know he's dead. I saw it in the papers—what was it, last spring?"

"Yes. Six months ago."

"Awfully sorry about that, Puck. You were still corresponding with him, weren't you? You know, I hadn't realized he'd won the Pulitzer 'til I read it in the obit."

"I've inherited his house. In Tucson."

For the second time that day she had the sweet pleasure of startling her ex-husband. He choked down his pastry and said, "Good lord, why? I thought you'd never actually met him."

She shrugged. "I hadn't. To be honest, it was just as much a shock to me. We've been writing for years now, but he always put me off when I suggested a visit. I wanted to write a book on him, remember? No one's done a definitive biography of Davis Cooper. He said 'no' flat out, but then he kept writing and we got to be friends. Of a sort. He's left me his house, and his papers. I assume this is his way of letting me do the book now that he's gone."

"What about his family? Wife? Children?"

She shook her head. "His ex-wife is dead; his lover is dead; neither had any children. There's just an elderly housekeeper, and he's left the rest of what he has to her. Not that there's much. The royalties on his books, some of which are still in print. A small life insurance policy. Some other bits of property in Tucson."

"Arizona is a damned odd place for an Englishman like Cooper to have ended up," Nigel said testily. "It's a long way from Dartmoor to the desert."

"His lover was Mexican, remember? Anna Naverra—the painter. He met her down in Mexico, then they moved over the border to Tucson. Naverra died a few years later, but he never left the desert again."

"As I recall," Nigel said, interest warring with his anger and interest winning, "there was some mystery surrounding Naverra's death. And now your Cooper has died under mysterious circumstances as well, hasn't he?"

"He drowned. Isn't that strange? In the middle of the desert, with no water anywhere nearby. Murder, definitely. But no one knows why. His house was ransacked, and yet everything of value seemed to be untouched. The police never found out who did it. Poor old Davis. What an awful way to go."

She stared down at her coffee cup, swallowing her anger. Death had touched her life before, but nothing so brutal as murder. It maddened her that Davis had died when the streets outside were full of people who would never give anything half so fine back to the world they lived in. Why on earth would anyone want to murder an elderly poet?

"Hey Puck," Nigel said, leaning forward and encircling her wrist with his hand. "I'm real sorry. I know you admired old Cooper. I still remember when you did your master's thesis on *The Wood Wife*. You had a copy of the book under your arm the day we met."

"You remember that?" She looked up and smiled. It was a detail Maggie had forgotten herself. She remembered the scene, in an artist's studio in a bad but trendy part of London. The artist had been her good friend, Tat. Nigel had been her good friend's lover. The electricity between them had been immediate although it was two years, two lovers, and two cities later before they finally got together.

"I remember everything about you," Nigel said, giving her a look calculated to melt bones.

"You're married. Stop it." She smiled as she said it, but she withdrew her hand and picked up her cup.

"And whose fault is that?" he countered.

Whose fault? His as much as hers, surely. She might have been the one to end the marriage over his protestations, but the Parisian fashion model, and any number of other lovers, each more beautiful and empty-headed than the last, had preceded the divorce, not followed it. "I've a weakness for stupid women," he'd told her at the time, "they're just so restful. But you're my life."

"Well, your life is walking out the door," she'd snapped. Out of the door but not out of his orbit. She was moon to his sun, still trying to break free; and never quite certain it was freedom she desired.

"So it's research you'll be doing," Nigel was saying, framing her departure in more comfortable terms. "All right. I understand now. You'll probably get a good book out of this, even if Davis Cooper isn't exactly canon anymore. Second-rate Yeats, they called him at Oxford; too fairy-taley I suppose. But still, a Pulitzer . . ."

"For his war poems. Not *The Wood Wife*. The critics savaged that one."

"Ah, well that explains it. Look, you should talk to Jennifer, my editor friend at HarperCollins. A book like this would be right up her street. Give me your phone number in Tucson and I'll have her get in touch."

"Nigel, wait," she said as he flipped a leather-bound notepad out of the pocket of his Armani suit jacket, identical to her own jacket. They'd bought them together a couple of years ago; she always wore men's clothes, in basic black. "I don't know what I'm walking into," she explained. "I don't know what I'm going to write, or when. I'm just going down to check it all out."

"But nonetheless you want to sell our house in Venice Beach," he said, looking at her sharply. "It sounds to me like you intend to be there a while."

She made a helpless gesture with her hands. Unlike Nigel's other women, she knew herself to be neither beautiful nor stupid; so why did he always make her feel like an incompetent child? "I don't know where I want to be yet. Maybe New York or Boston for a while. Maybe back to Europe. I'll spend some time in Arizona, go over Davis Cooper's papers, and try to figure out my next move. The only thing I know at this point is I don't want to come back to Los Angeles. There's nothing for me here now."

"That's not true, and you know it," said Nigel, his voice seductive, pinning her eyes with his own.

"Stop it," she said, and this time she did not smile.

He sighed. "All right, I won't call Jennifer for you. But I'll send you her number, just in case. Give me your address, Puck. I'll send you silly postcards from Toronto. You weren't planning to disappear into the desert altogether, were you?"

Irrationally, she didn't want to give it to him. But of course he had to have it. They were friends, weren't they? They still moved in the same circles; he still had her cat, an arthritic Abyssinian who loved Nigel more than the air she breathed and pined when parted from him.

He claimed her address, then restrained himself from asking after her affairs again. Instead he regaled her with stories set in his international Early Music world, courting her with his wit and his brilliance, nuggets of gold from his glittering life, clearly intended to remind Maggie Black of just what she had given up.

He succeeded. By the time she boarded the plane from LAX to Tucson, it was Nigel's parting embrace she carried with her, hot as heat rash upon her skin, and not the embrace of the perfectly adequate man she'd been dating up north. She watched the sprawl of L.A. diminish as the plane leapt up into the clouds.

"Goddamn you, Nigel," she said to herself as the city faded from her sight.

Fox sat on the steps of his adobe cabin breathing in the intoxicating smell of the desert after the rain: the pungent scents of creosote and sage, and the spicy scent of mesquite wood burning in a house farther up the mountain. The rains had brought autumn wildflowers to the rock-strewn mountain slopes. Yellow brittlebush blanketed the hillside and orange globe mallow lined the sides of the wash. The small oval leaves of the cottonwood trees were turning autumnal gold. In the stillness of early evening he could hear the call of the mourning doves, a lone coyote high in the hills, and the sound of someone approaching, tires sliding on the old dirt road. An engine revved, revved again, then silence. A string of steady curses.

Grinning, Fox got to his feet and ambled down the path to his truck. Someone was stuck in the wash again. He wondered who it was this time. Dora, he wagered with himself. In Juan's new jeep, looking guilty as sin.

He got in his truck and drove down to the wash. The vehicle that was stuck was unfamiliar, a small Toyota with rental car plates, totally unsuitable for mountain terrain. The car had gotten halfway through the wash bed, then stuck in the sand on the eastern bank. A stranger emerged from the driver's seat, a tall, dark-haired woman with a thin, unusual face. She looked up as his truck approached, her expression a mixture of worry and embarrassment.

He backed his pickup close to the Toyota, parked, and took the chains from the bed. "Don't feel so bad," he said to the woman. "It happens all the time."

She followed him as he hooked the chains to her car, looking as rattled by the unrequested rescue as she was by the car sunk in water and mud. "I saw the sign," she said, pointing at it: DO NOT ENTER WHEN FLOODED. "But I thought it looked so shallow. . . ."

"I know. The water's just rain runoff. By morning the streambed will be bone dry. Right now, there's no traction under there; you ought to pay attention to the signs." He grinned. "But we all ignore them half the time. I don't want to tell you how many times I've been stuck myself. Go get in your car now and put her in drive."

The woman got back into the Toyota. Fox couldn't quite peg her. The clothes—a loose and mannish black suit over a casual white T-shirt—were pure New York or Los Angeles, her short haircut was artsy and European, but the accent was something altogether different. Kentucky? Virginia? He couldn't tell. He knew who the woman was, however. She'd come to live in Cooper's house and write a book about him. He'd pictured someone older and more stereotypically librarian-ish. Not a tall, dark woman with a voice like Kentucky bourbon. He shook his head as he started up the truck. That son of a gun, Cooper; six months dead and he was still full of surprises. The truck protested the weight on its tail, but it slowly pulled the Toyota up out of the water and onto dry land.

He parked under the paloverde trees and unhooked the car behind him. The woman rolled down the window. "I'm looking for Redwater Road."

"This is it," he said. "You've found it. It runs for another three quarters of a mile and then stops at the Red Springs trailhead."

She got out of the car and looked around at the valley wedged between two mountain slopes. The road had wound through the lower slope, a ridge topped with boulders, populated by tall cactus. On the far side of the canyon, Mica Mountain rose from the desert floor to a height of fifty-five hundred feet, a part of the Rincon Mountain range that stretched across the eastern horizon.

To the north, the Catalina Mountains dominated the sky and local imagination. Most hikers, horse riders and climbers favored the taller Catalinas, or the Tucson Mountains at the city's western edge, leaving the Rincon range in the east to the deer, the mountain lions, the botanists and the rangers who fought off the lightning fires each summer. The Rincons were a secretive range; there were no roads up to the heart of it. To learn its secrets, one went on foot, climbing hour after hot weary hour, through cactus and scrub at the base of the mountain, up through gnarled groves of live oak, to the forests of pine at the peak.

Although designated as a federal wilderness, there were still a few places in the Rincons where old land claims permitted people to live, removed from the sprawl of city life below: the cattle ranches of Reddington Pass and along the Happy Valley Road, and the dude ranch in Red Springs Canyon, nestled in the northern slopes. The ranch had been built in 1912 out of oak, mesquite, adobe, and stone. Its buildings were scattered across the small valley, connected by footpaths and one rutted road. The dude ranch had flourished for a handful of years; a hunting club had owned the property for several more; and then the land had been broken up, the buildings sold off one by one. Each cabin had its own history now of owners and tenants who had come and gone; yet together they still formed a loose community close to, but separate from, Tucson.

Fox prided himself that he knew damn near everything there was to know about the history of the canyon; after growing up here, he knew these mountain trails far better than the city streets below. To him, this was a beautiful land, dramatic, surprising and mysterious. But he could tell by the look in the woman's eyes that she was not One of Them, as Dora would say. One of Them, with desert heat in her heart and a desert wind singing in her bones. She looked around at the loose, dry soil, the spiny cactus and ocotillo thorns, with an edgy, city-bred wariness as thought it was an alien moon.

She turned that wary look on Fox, appraised him, then stuck out her hand. "I'm Marguerita Black," she said. Her grip on his hand was firm.

"Johnny Foxxe. Or just Fox. You're Cooper's friend."

"That's right. I'm looking for his house. If you're Johnny Foxxe, you're the son of Davis's housekeeper—and the man who has my key."

He acknowledged that he was the keeper of the keys, and turned back to his cabin to fetch them. He was conscious of her eyes on his back until he stepped through the cabin door. He found the woman disconcerting; there was something too direct for comfort about her manner and her level gaze. He reckoned she was older than him, five years at least, maybe even ten; she had streaks of silver in her dark hair, and a sexy air of worldliness. He glanced out the window as he reached for Cooper's keys on the hook by the kitchen sink. She stood looking up at the Catalina crags, watching them turn the color of old violet glass in the setting sun.

She clearly hadn't expected to find the place so isolated and rough—a reasonable enough assumption on her part, Fox had to admit. Cooper's address merely said Tucson, and Tucson was a modern enough city with a population of over half a million; you had to know the town to realize it had these wild pockets as well. He grinned, imagining what she must have thought as the roads took her farther and farther from civilization. She didn't seem entirely pleased by the place. But she also wasn't scared off. Yet.

He went back outside and handed over Cooper's keys: the heavy iron key to the house and the smaller one to the generator shed. "I'll take you over and turn on the water. We ought to check the flue as well before you light a fire there—I think something is nesting in the chimney."

"Thank you. That's very kind of you."

He waved away her thanks. "It's my job. Didn't anyone tell you that? You own my cabin. And all this land from here, up the wash, to the third bend in the road. I take care of all the house repairs instead of paying rent. Don't look alarmed. I'm not a nuisance, and old adobes need a lot of work. I'm patching Cooper's roof at the moment. You'd best be glad you have me around or it would flood come the winter rains." The woman looked at Fox warily. Too bad. He came along with the house. He'd claimed that cabin long before and wasn't going to let go of it now. "There's another cabin on your land, up there, just beyond that ridge. Tomás lives there. He's an auto mechanic. He doesn't pay rent either, but he'll keep your car running, and he'll bring you good game during the hunting season."

"I'm a vegetarian," the woman said flatly.

Fox grinned. "Take Tomás's vegetables then. And his eggs. You eat eggs? He's got a big garden. And chickens. And a bunch of goats."

"What can possibly grow up here, in this soil?" she asked him curiously, looking around at the rocky expanse of mica-flecked granite and quartz.

"You'd be surprised," Fox told her as he climbed, uninvited, into her car. He waited expectantly until she joined him. "Follow the road on this side of the wash," he directed as she shifted into gear. The sun was passing behind the outer ridge, casting the valley into shadow.

"How many houses are there in the canyon?" she asked him, pulling back onto the road.

"Six."

"Just six?" She sounded surprised. He was right. She hadn't expected the isolation.

"Just six. Cooper used to own five—our local land baron," he told her. "There's your house, and its two cabins. There's my mother's house—but it's so run down that no one really lives there now. I've turned the most functional part of it into a carpentry workshop. Then there's the old stable, which Cooper sold to Juan and Dora del Río a couple of years ago. And there's the Alders in the Big House, down where the road dead-ends."

"The Big House?"

"It was the main guest hall when this was still a dude ranch. You'll like John and Lillian Alder. They're retired now; all their kids are grown so it's just the two of them rattling around the place. The house was in Lillian's family; she's been on the mountain even longer than Cooper."

"And I'd venture a guess that John Alder is the reason you go by Fox and not Johnny, am I right?"

"You got it. John Alder and John Alder Junior. We got divided into John, J.J., and Fox fairly early on."

"Well, it suits," she said, leaving him to ponder just what she meant by that.

She steered the car through a mesquite grove of small, crooked trees, roots fed by a stream that ran through Red Springs Canyon and then disappeared underground. On the other side of the grove was a clearing where a simple, rustic adobe house stood, shaded by an old cottonwood tree, and guarded by three tall saguaro cactus with many heavy arms. A wide wooden porch ran entirely around the low, square building the color of wet sand. On the front porch, two weathered Mission rockers and a Mexican bench stood to either side of a heavy wood door painted indigo blue. A wisteria vine as old as the house arched over the porch with twisted, woody growth. Beside it a tall bougainvillea was weighted down with bright scarlet blooms. The flowers glowed like flames in the dusk, brightening the gloom of the approaching night. The woman cut the car's engine, and the wind in the mesquite grew still.

They sat for a moment, in silence, for no reason he could fathom. Then he swung his long legs from the cramped little car, waited while she did the same, and followed her to Copper's door. The porch light was busted. Another thing to fix. She fumbled with the heavy key, and finally it clicked open. He reached past her to turn on the light, and a blur of darkness came at him. Fox heard a sharp intake of breath, felt feathers brush against his skin. Something hit his shoulder hard, pushing him away from the door. A huge white owl swooped from the house, through the porch, and out into the trees. It must have measured a full five feet from outstretched wingtip to wingtip.

"My god," she said in that low whiskey voice that sent a shiver through the core of him. Her eyes were wide, alarmed. "I've never seen a bird that big. How long has it been in the house? Has the place been empty since . . ."

Since Cooper was murdered, Fox finished the sentence silently. The old man had died some miles away, but he doubted that distance was comforting to her. Six months had passed since Cooper's death, and the police had no clue who had killed him.

"I've been in and out of the house, doing repairs," Fox assured her, "and I've never seen that owl before. It must have just gotten in somehow. There's probably a broken window. I'll take a look. Right now, I'm going to go turn on the water. If you go through the door there, into the kitchen, you'll find a light switch to the left."

He left her in the kitchen, looking curiously around her new home. It was strange to think of Cooper's house that way . . . but the old man must have had his reasons for leaving his house to a lady friend he'd never even mentioned.

He stepped back out onto the porch and looked down the road toward the mesquite wood. The white horned owl had disappeared. He knew what Tomás would say about that. An owl was bad luck, a sudden death, or the ghost of someone who had died. Fox had lied to the woman. He had seen it before. Six months ago, over Deer Head Springs, on the night Davis Cooper was killed.

He stood on the porch for a few moments more, but the huge white owl did not reappear. He stood and listened to the song of the lone coyote somewhere farther up the canyon. He'd often seen its skinny figure skulking near the house since Cooper had died, smaller than the others in the hills, one eye white and blind. Fox yipped back to his four-legged friend, whose answer came an octave above. Then he headed back to the water pipes at the rear of his father's house.

Dora put a tape on the tape deck as she maneuvered through the evening traffic on Speedway. R. Carlos Nakai's Navajo flute filled the truck with haunting music soft as water on stone, a whisper of feathers, the wind in a high mountain pass. Nakai was a Tucson man, and his music perfectly suited the underlying rhythms of the desert land.

Outside the Bronco's windows, however, the desert was decidedly less tranquil. The city's traffic was beginning to swell with the autumn migration of college students and snowbirds—as the locals called winter residents—escaping cold northern climes. She was glad that the fierce summer heat had passed and the city was coming back to life, but she already missed the quiet of the season when only hardcore desert dwellers remained.

The day had been far from quiet at the Book Arts Gallery where she worked downtown. Two important collectors had come down from Santa Fe, purchasing several pricey handmade books between them. Then there were the chatty tourists from Des Moines, book lovers who spent an hour among the shelves, asking a million questions. Then twenty students from the Book Arts class at the university—all dressed, despite the Tucson heat, in the black uniform of art students everywhere—crowded into the gallery's small storefront for a lecture on hand-binding methods. After the slow, sweet summer months, Dora had to learn to deal with people again, to put her thoughts and her troubles aside and smile when the gallery door opened.

It was a relief when her boss closed the door for the night and there was only the gauntlet of rush-hour traffic between her and the silence of the mountains. The traffic thinned out on Tanque Verde at the easternmost edge of the city, and then disappeared altogether when she crossed to the Reddington Road. The road snaked into sage-green hills backed by the blue of the Rincon slopes. The pavement ended. Dora shifted into four-wheel drive and began to climb.

The dirt road wound upward into the mountains, past Lower Tan-

que Verde Falls, past the Upper Falls as well and over the top of a
cactus-spiked ridge surrounded by acres of sky. A narrow, pitted,
unmarked road led back to Red Springs Canyon—at least when the
summer monsoons or winter rains didn't wash it out. Then Dora
stayed downtown with her in-laws until the floods had passed.

Thank the Lord it wasn't flood season. She needed her own house
around her. She wanted a fire, some Mexican beer, the patchwork
quilt draped over her feet, and the four cats over her lap. The days
were still hot at the end of September, but the nights were brisk, especially up here. She hoped that Juan had made something warm like
soup or chili for dinner. She hoped he'd remembered to make anything at all—all too often these days he hadn't.

Dora sighed. She'd never really minded being the breadwinner
for the two of them before. She believed in her husband's artwork and
his need for the time to paint. Up until the last six months he'd also
worked restoring the house; he'd sold a bit of his art, and taken on the
odd commission. But lately . . . Dora turned firmly away from that
depressing line of thought. Juan needed her now. And so she needed
these two jobs. There was no point in dwelling on the inequity of it—
for what was she going to do, up and leave? There was nothing in Dora's blood and bones that would permit her to let a loved one down.

As she approached the wash she saw water in it, turned to silver
by her headlights. She ignored the flood signs, gunned her engine,
went through the standing water at a steady speed and made it safely
up the other bank. She followed the road deep into the canyon, not-
ing that there were lights on in Cooper's place. A line of smoke came
from Cooper's chimney, and another one from farther up the road in
the direction of her own house. Juan, dear heart, had already lit a fire.
She smiled as she pulled in beside his jeep and climbed down from
the truck.

The house had been a stable that she and Juan had converted
themselves—or more accurately, were in the process of converting.
The big main room was cozy and complete, with a kitchen at one end
of it, but the bedrooms were little more than sheetrock shells await-
ing their plaster walls. An old stone barn stood next to the stable,

built for barn dances in the dude-ranch days. It made a good-sized studio for Juan. Her own workspace would be in its upper loft when Juan got around to reinforcing the floor; meanwhile her desk was in a corner of the kitchen surrounded by stacks of papers, books, and the inevitable clutter of a building site.

She entered the wide stable door into the house, which smelled of apples baking. She and Tomás had picked them in Wilcox last week, and Juan had apparently made one of his famous pies. Dora let out a small breath of relief as she hung up her beaded Indian jacket, kicked off her cowboy boots. She clung to these signs of normalcy, added them all together each day to convince herself Juan was all right.

"Juan?" she called. He wasn't in the kitchen, he wasn't in the bedroom. She crossed the courtyard to the barn, but that was empty too. A single light was lit over his work table; the rest of the studio was dark and cold. The doors had been left wide open. Outside, a movement caught her eye. Four shapes—coyotes?—dashed across the yard, headed toward Cooper's house.

She stepped farther into her husband's studio. The floor was cold beneath her feet. On Juan's table was a sculpted figure that he had been working on all week, the image of a local cowboy hero. It was the kind of schmaltzy commission he loathed but used to accept anyway just for the work. Now he turned these jobs away; he would have turned this one down as well only this time she'd clipped the overdue electric bill to the client's request.

Dora stood in front of the table and looked at the work before her in alarm. The cowboy's blandly handsome features had changed: his eyes were thinned to narrow slits, his nose was hooked, his cheekbones high, and stag horns were growing from his forehead. Beside it, a bucket of plaster was overturned, its contents puddled on the table and the floor. Juan's favorite cup was smashed and coffee was stained across the wall.

She could feel the rapid beating of her heart as she crossed the room to the open doors. "Juan?" she called into the night. Silence and darkness answered her. *He's all right*, Dora told herself firmly. *He just got a little frustrated and now he's gone for a walk, that's all.*

She turned off the lights, shut the doors, and crossed the yard to the kitchen's warmth. But even sitting beside the fire, a warm quilt wrapped around her, Dora found herself shivering as she waited for her husband to return.

Crow climbed the funnel of rock that led to the top of Rincon Peak. The rock was sharp beneath his bare feet. A strong wind whipped his long, black hair. When he reached the top, he sat under a star-filled sky and waited. At last he heard the boy approach, a rush of air, footsteps on stone.

"The man is dead," the boy told him, angry, daring him to deny this.

"Yes," Crow replied mildly. "It's been six months since you've been gone."

The boy ignored this quiet reproof. Time, as yet, meant nothing to him. "Then who stands guard over the east?"

"Not I. Not you. The stars still watch. The rocks still sleep. Nothing has changed, my deario."

"You lie. He's dead. He's gone. And you lie."

Crow shrugged. "And what if I do? You know who I am, and what I'm like. All things must be true to their nature. Even the dead. Especially the dead."

The boy laughed. And laughing, flung himself right over the mountain's edge.

Crow shuddered. And then he laughed himself.

The boy had left a white feather behind. Crow picked it up, tied it into his hair, then began the long descent.

DAVIS COOPER
Redwater Road
Tucson, Arizona

H. Miller
Big Sur, California

October 5, 1947

Henry, you old bugger,

You are entirely wrong about deMontillo's latest. How you can get excited about that self-serving puffery disguised as poetry is completely beyond me—all that pathetic he-man verbiage about the terrible beauty of battle *when we all know he spent the war safe in his mistress's villa, waited on hand and foot by sloe-eyed Moroccan girls (or was it boys?). This sudden critical appetite for deMonty the Perpetual Dilettante is bewildering, and you, at least, ought to have better sense.*

By now you'll have read about the floods. Our land remained dry, of course, being so far up in the mountains here, but we were cut off from the valley for several weeks. Redwater and Tanque Verde creeks flooded over, entirely washing the roads away. I tell you, I was beginning to go stir-crazy, cut off from the mails and the news of the world—but Anna was in her element. I swear she wishes it would flood again. It's gotten so she doesn't want to see anyone with the single exception of yours truly, and on some days barely that. She is obsessed with these new paintings of hers, and they are, indeed, magnificent so how can I complain when the washing piles up and dinner is beans on toast again? I want to get a girl up here to do the work, but Anna won't have it. She's shy of her creations now—she won't paint if anyone else is around.

She has taken to roaming the mountain by night and it's no good trying to stop her with tales of rattlesnakes or wolves or mountain lions, let me tell you. She's meeting her muse out in those hills. When she returns there is a fire in her eyes and she works like a woman possessed by spirits until she drops in exhaustion. She is strong and brown, and so terribly thin. She has never looked more beautiful to me. I am frightened of this intensity, and yet I am stirred and fascinated. The process

THE WOOD WIFE35

of creation seems to pour directly from the ground through her small body into the paint.

My own work, it comes . . . in bits and pieces, dribs and drabs, it comes, it comes. I am nearly done with Exile Songs and count myself an exile indeed, from Europe, from Paris, from the cafe life which the war has stolen from us all. Perhaps when this collection of poems is done I'll be able to lay those ghosts to rest and resign myself to this raw, brash land; but so long as I work, I am back there again, sitting in the Paris streets with you and Fred and Brassai and the rest. Then I leave the page and I leave the desk and I find myself here, on a mountainside, in the desert, the far side of Nowhere. In truth, Nowhere is as good a place to be as any other—it doesn't matter where I am so long as I can do my work and live on the streets of Memory.

Yet for Anna, in her own exile, place has become the crux of her being, the source that now feeds her art in a way that I am still trying to grasp. The Red Springs is just water to me, not the well of inspiration it is for Anna; I see no salmon swimming in its depths, no hazelnuts falling from the trees. I have no muse. I struggle on my own. Every word, every line is chiseled with great effort from the hard white block of language.

Exile Songs will be published next spring. And then deMontillo better watch his ass.

Yours as ever,
Cooper

The hills call in a tongue
I cannot speak, a constant murmuring,
calling the rain from my dry bones,
and syllables from the marrow.
—**The Wood Wife,** *Davis Cooper*

Maggie woke early, with a wrenching sense of dislocation. She stared at the water-stained ceiling above her and tried to recall just where she was. On a mountainside, in Davis Cooper's house. The sky outside was a shade of violet that she'd never quite seen before.

She got up, washed, put her bathrobe on and padded into the kitchen. She'd always been an early riser; she felt cheated if she slept too late and missed the rising sun. She cherished the silver morning light, the stillness, the morning rituals: water in the kettle, bitter coffee grounds, a warm mug held between cold hands, the scent of a day unfolding before her, pungent with possibility.

As the water heated, Maggie unpacked the bag of provisions she'd brought along: dark Dutch coffee, bread, muesli, vegetables, garlic, a bottle of wine. In the small refrigerator were eggs, cheese, fresh pasta from Los Angeles, green corn tamales from downtown Tucson. The only strange thing about the un-familiarity of this kitchen was the knowledge that it was hers now, these pans, these plates, this old dented kettle, this mug decorated with petroglyph paintings. For years she'd been traveling light and making herself at home in other people's houses. Having an entire house of her own was going to take some getting used to.

She made the coffee, grilled some toast, and sat down at the kitchen table with yesterday's edition of the *Arizona Daily Star*, too unsettled to actually read it. Davis's kitchen was the heart of the house, with a rough wood table in the center that could have easily seated a family of twelve and not just one elderly poet. The kitchen hearth held a woodstove—the winter nights were probably cold up here. Fat wicker rockers were pulled close to it, covered by faded old serapes. The walls were a mottled tea-colored adobe with shades of some brighter tone showing through and wainscotting up to waist-height stained or aged to a woodsy green. The window frames were painted violet, the doors were a rich but weathered shade of blue. Mexican saints in beaten tin frames hung among Davis's pots and pans; folk art and dusty tin *milagros* hung among strings of red chili peppers, garlic, and desert herbs. The windowsills were crowded with stones, geodes, fossils, clumps of smoky quartz, and Indian pottery shards.

The rest of the house was less colorful and cluttered, with plain adobe walls and simple, old Mission furniture made of oak. There was a small living room with a beehive fireplace and an old-style ceiling of saguaro ribs; the side bedroom where Maggie had slept on a lumpy feather bed with a tarnished brass frame; Davis's study in the front of the house; and one other room at the back of the house that seemed to be firmly locked. The wood plank floors were strewn with Navajo rugs in patterns of brown, black and red. Every straight wall held bookcases packed with books in English, Spanish and French. Indian drums hung over one case, a Rincon trail map over another, but otherwise the walls were bare, studded with nails as though recently pictures had hung there and been removed.

The electricity, Johnny Foxxe had told her, came from a generator she shared with her neighbors. The water was from her own underground spring and tasted of rust. She wondered if her phone was hooked up yet. As she got up to test it, it began to ring. It was probably Nigel. Who else would phone her before dawn?

"Hey Puck," he said, "how's life in the desert?"

"Nigel, I've been in Tucson for exactly," she looked at her watch, "twelve hours. It's a little soon for a progress report."

"So what's it like? Is it hot there? Did you meet any cowboys or Indians yet?"

"Not unless you count the kid who rescued my car from a ditch. He had a snazzy pair of cowboy boots on, but no chaps or spurs, I'm sorry to disappoint you. It's early, Nigel. Go away. I'll call you when you get back next week."

"Car? Ditch? Did you have an accident?"

"No, Mother. I'm hanging up now. Have a good time up in Ottawa."

"Toronto," he said as she hung up the receiver.

She poured herself another cup of coffee and ignored the phone when it rang again.

It rang and rang and eventually stopped as she stood in the door of Davis's study. She had peered into the room last night, but had hesitated to enter it. It had been a disturbing room by moonlight: the desk with the poet's papers still on it, as though he had just stepped away. If the old man's ghost was haunting the house, this was where it would be.

The room was now bathed in blue pre-dawn light filtered through the French doors and two small windows set deep in the adobe wall. Through the glass of the doors was a view of the Three Graces (as he had once named the three tall saguaro cactus in a letter to her) and a yard full of ground-hugging prickly pear, scrubby wildflowers and hard-packed earth. In the distance, beyond the long dirt drive, was the wash, a fugitive river that ran only after the heaviest rains. Its banks were edged by cottonwoods with the mountains looming behind them, black against the purple sky. It was a dramatic land-scape, harsh and vivid. She did not find the desert beautiful. The air felt parched; her skin felt dry; the color of the sky looked unnatural. Already she missed the deep and abundant green of the Pacific coast.

She sighed, turned on the lamp by the desk, and sat in Davis's desk chair. She picked up an ink-stained Montblanc pen, covered with a thin layer of dust. In the unfinished letter below it he'd been declining a request for an interview, in the acerbic epistolary prose that Maggie had known so well. The rest of the house was a stranger's house, but here was the man Maggie knew: in the pictures pinned above his desk; in the calligraphic handwriting; in the books on the shelves—books that he'd discussed in his long, cranky, occasionally drunken and often hilarious letters.

The desktop was full of letters and envelopes postmarked around the world. This had been his work these last years, this voluminous correspondence. There were no poems on the old man's desk, except the poems other writers had sent. Davis Cooper had not published a book, or a single poem, in over thirty years. Instead he drank. Legend had it that it was alcohol that had fueled his early brilliance, and alcohol that had destroyed it. An occupational hazard, he had called it; in his day, it was normal, almost expected.

Maggie picked up a pipe from the corner of the desk and breathed the scent of stale tobacco, trying to catch the lingering essence of a man she would never meet. Goddamn him, he'd kept putting her visits off and off until it was too late. It was absurd to be angry with a dead man, but she was angry with Davis nonetheless—and at the same time overwhelmed by his last unexpected gift: the chance to finally know the man, to understand the life he'd led. The study was crammed full of notes, letters, journals, marked-up manuscripts; an entire life sat in these pages, was filed away in trunks and drawers. He'd been a reclusive, secretive man. But he'd trusted her with all this.

The task before her was daunting. She wondered how and where she should begin. By living here, she answered herself. By sleeping where he slept, eating where he ate, walking this raw, uncomfortable land and trying to learn what kept him here, away from all his colleagues and friends back in Europe and New York. Were the demons that drove him still in this place, or had he taken them with him to his grave? Had he ever written poetry again? It was Maggie's belief that he had.

His letters weren't the work of a retired man, but of an artist still struggling with his craft and his muse. His study confirmed that impression. This was a working writer's room. The walls were filled with poetry, other poets' work as well as his own, written in brown ink right on the walls in that distinctive calligraphic hand: Blake, Shake-

speare, Yeats, Pound, Stevens, Neruda, Adrienne Rich. Quotes from
sources as diverse as popular fiction, science texts and the Bible. He'd
written on the walls in other rooms too; she'd come across poems in
surprising places (Keats by the john, Borges by the sugar tin, a line
from one of her own poems on the back of the bedroom door) but
here he'd covered the walls with them, a collage of words, in four lan-
guages: his own English, his adopted Spanish and French, and Rilke
in German.

Above his desk was a line from Homer:

Sing heavenly muse.

Under that were the last words of Michaelangelo upon his deathbed,
to his apprentice:

Draw, Antonio, draw, Antonio,
draw and do not waste time.

The first was written in faded ink; the second quote was fresh and
new, written in a slanted, urgent hand. Why would a man who had
given up his craft write out those particular words? She was certain
that somewhere in this room she would find evidence that he'd been
writing still, writing up to the very end. But if so, why had he kept it a
secret? And would the work be any good?

She looked long at the bulletin board hanging above Homer's
exhortation. Old photographs were pinned to it and she recognized
her friend from the photos printed in biographies of other poets: the
young Davis, fair-haired and clean-featured, in the square-shouldered
suits of New York in the forties; a more weathered face in the fifties
in the harsher Arizona light. Here was one taken with T. S. Eliot in
London, another with Pablo Neruda. A grainy snapshot of Anaïs Nin
and Henry Miller had been taken in Paris before the war. There were
several photographs of Anna Naverra, the Surrealist painter he'd become involved with when he fled his brief marriage to a New York
socialite and ended up in Mexico. All the photographs were black-

and-white; there were none more recent than thirty years before. As though his life had then ground to a halt, like the poetry did.

She examined the other items pinned to the board: A grocery list. A phone list. A list of book titles—all nonfiction. A list of what seemed like place names. A list of the titles of Maggie's early poems. A list of words with no obvious connection between them at all.

Three small pictures tacked to the board were the only images of art in the room. One was an old, faded postcard from London's V & A Museum: "The Moon's Betrothed," by the English Pre-Raphaelite painter Charles Endicott Bete. The second postcard, from a Tucson gallery, was a contemporary painting by Holly Roberts: the abstracted figure of a man with stag horns rendered in greys and blues. Below that card was a larger reproduction of a painting by Brian Froud, an English artist the poet admired and with whom, she knew, he had corresponded. Froud lived on Dartmoor, the wild corner of Britain where Davis himself had been born. The painting was of a mysterious woman in a mask of leaves and crowned with horns. The figure could have easily stepped from the pages of Davis's "Wood Wife" poems. She wondered if it illustrated the poems, or simply grew from the same rocky soil—the landscape she had always assumed inspired the poems. Until she came here.

Tucked behind the Froud picture was an envelope, a thick one, of heavy starched paper. Maggie pulled it out and looked at it, startled. It was addressed hastily in Davis's hand to "Black Maggie"—his name for her. The envelope was sealed with wax and covered with thick, grimy layers of dust. Whoever had cleaned the house since then—Johnny Foxxe or his mother, she supposed—had not discovered the envelope, or had left it there undisturbed.

As she stood holding it in her hands—half-eager, half-afraid to open it—the phone began to ring again. Nigel, she thought to herself crossly as she pocketed the envelope and headed back to the kitchen.

It was not Nigel, it was her best friend, Tat, calling her from London and blithely unaware of how early it was on this side of the world.

"Hey, Tat!" Maggie said, ridiculously glad to hear her voice again. She and Tat had known each other for half their lives, ever since their university days at Exeter, in the west of England—not far from where Cooper had been born, and where she'd discovered his work.

"I've been trying to reach you all week," Tat said. "What happened with what's-his-name in Mendocino? When I called, he said you'd left him and he wouldn't say where you'd gone. I had to track down Nigel to get your number. Where is it I'm calling, anyway?"

"Tucson."

"Tucson?"

"Why does everybody say it that way? It's not the end of the earth."

"No, but it's surely next door to it. You must be at Davis Cooper's house. How long are you going to be there? When are you coming home?"

Home to Tat was London, just as to Nigel it was L.A. Neither could imagine anyone actually choosing to remain in any other place. For Maggie, it was the idea of "home" that was hard for her to imagine. Itchy feet, her granddaddy always said. She'd moved between half a dozen countries, trailing friends, lovers, possessions in her wake, and all of those places were home, and none of them. She wasn't quite sure what "home" meant.

"I don't know where I'm going next," she told Tat, just as she'd told Nigel yesterday. "I expect I'll be in Tucson for a while. Davis's house is in the mountains, not the city—rather more isolated than I'd imagined. But I'll have a nice warm winter here and plenty of work to keep me busy. If I'm going to give this book a go, there's a hell of a lot of research ahead."

"So gather up the papers and bring them to London. You're going to have to travel anyway, aren't you? To interview the people who knew him? Most of his old colleagues must be in New York or over here."

"Or dead," Maggie said with a sigh. "But I'm nowhere near the interview stage yet. First I've got five decades worth of papers to go through. And there's something else," Maggie added, struggling to find the words to express it. "He wrote those poems *here*, Tat. About *this* land. *These* mountains. I haven't been here a full day yet, and I've already realized that everything I thought about his poetry is wrong.

That thesis I wrote years ago is nonsense. I thought *The Wood Wife* was rooted in his memories of rural England. But he wrote it in a landscape that's like nothing else I've ever seen. If I can't understand this place, or what Cooper found so compelling here, then I'll never really understand his work. Does that make sense to you?"

"It does," Tat conceded. "Which is a pity, because I really wanted to talk you into coming over here. I miss you, girl. Well, maybe I'll try to get over there instead. It will have to be after my show in November; I've still got too many prints to finish. London is horrid in the winter, anyway. It would be good to escape the rain. If I come to visit you in the wild west, do you promise me sunshine, art supply stores, and handsome western lads to go dancing with?"

"Will you settle for sunshine and art supplies? There's a handsome western lad next door, but he's too young, and probably too aware of just how handsome he is."

"Ummmm, just my type. The ones that have 'Trouble' written all over them. You know I have a weakness for those sexy American accents."

"You're the only Brit I know who does. Everyone else winces when we open our mouths. Will you really come, Tat?"

"Girl, I'll book the flight today. What do you want me to bring you?"

"Single malt from the Highlands and the latest on Di."

"You're on," Tat said. "Now it's back to the drawing board for me. Ring me if you get lonely. Cheers."

Maggie hung up the phone slowly. She hadn't felt particularly lonely before, but she suddenly felt so now. The house was too empty. The mountain was quiet but for an astonishing racket of birds. The sun was still just a glow on the hills but the sky had paled to lavender. The wash had dried out during the night, and now was just a broad expanse of sand.

She saw something lurking out in the yard, on the far side of the cottonwood tree. She stepped closer to the window. It was a coyote, standing motionless. She'd never seen one close up before. It was the size of a German shepherd, but tawny colored, bushy tailed, with the ears and pointed muzzle of a fox. The coyote was skinny, its ribs sticking out, and an eye was damaged, filmed over. It stared at her through its one good eye, and she stared back, feeling strangely moved. It was beautiful in its wildness. Then it turned silently and trotted away, heading through the trees to the bed of the wash. Maggie let out the breath she'd been holding as she watched it disappear.

She went outside onto the porch and sat down in a rocking chair. The air still held the nighttime's chill and she was glad for her bathrobe's warmth. It was one she had pinched off Nigel long ago, and still held the memories of their best days together. Now the robe's flannel was faded and threadbare, but its touch was a familiar comfort in this unfamiliar place. In the pocket was Davis's envelope. Maggie pulled it out, stared at it, then she broke the thick wax seal.

My dear Marguerita, if you find this note, then I fear that I have failed once more. I pray to God that I will not—but prayers are worth little on a gin-sodden tongue, and my God has long turned a deaf ear.

Yes, more secrets, even now. I dare not tell you more. Words have power, remember that, woman. Even written on a page. Letters. Runes. Alphabets. The stars, the stones, the very trees reveal the language of the earth.

I am leaving you my house, and everything that's in it. My books. Anna's paintings. My journals, and my notes for poems—do with them as you will. Did you guess that I've been writing poems? "The Saguaro Forest" is my last work. I wrote it for the mountain. Someday you'll understand.

Until we meet again,
Davis Cooper

April the 16th,
the Night of the Dark Stone

Maggie read the letter over twice more. It made no more sense than the first time. She was right—he'd been writing again, that was clear. But what did all the rest of it mean? And why did he write that he'd meet her *again* when he'd never met her at all?

April 16th was the night he had died. The Night of the Dark Stone—whatever that was. The night he'd been left dead out in the desert, his "gin-sodden tongue" silenced forever.

She folded up the letter again and sat there simply holding it. Sorrow was a rock lodged in her chest. She wished she was a woman who could cry. She wished she could wail and howl with grief—not just for what the world of poetry had lost, but for what she had lost and would not have again: the man whose work had inspired her; whose unexpected friendship had been so conditional, yet so necessary; whose long and supportive letters had followed her halfway around the world. But she never cried. Not once, in all the long years since death had claimed her parents. Back then she had cried enough tears that perhaps she simply had none left now.

She had a history of losing the ones she loved. She was seven when a car crash took her parents; her only grandmother died not long thereafter. For years she used to watch Nigel while he slept, certain that she'd lose him too. When Tat flew over, Maggie would not rest until the plane safely reached the ground. She called her granddaddy in West Virginia once a week, to be certain he was still there.

In the hills the coyotes knew her pain, gave voice to the tears the woman would not shed. One called to her; another added his voice; then another; and another. Their eerie song filled up the canyon. The half-blind, lone coyote heard them; and Dora's cats; and Tomás, in the hills. But Maggie, like Davis Cooper's God, was deaf to the language of their call.

Dora sat feeding mesquite branches to the fire. Her face was pale, her eyes were red; the cats were huddled close to her side, sensing her distress. Beyond the circle of warmth from the hearth, the early morning was cold, and still. The sun hovered behind Rincon Peak, preparing to start the day. Juan was somewhere out on the hundreds of trails that crisscrossed the mountains. Or had fallen down some steep ravine, or had stepped on a rattlesnake in the dark, and now lay helpless, waiting for day to come and someone to find him.

She rose stiffly from the chair. The cats jumped down to wind around her feet and herd her into the kitchen. She opened up the cat food tins, feeling dazed by lack of sleep. This was the third time he'd gone off this week. But he'd always returned long before dawn—except for that once, six months ago. She shuddered, and reached for her sweater. It was cold at this end of the room.

Dora put four cat food bowls on the floor, one for each cat so they would not fight, then she took the dog's water dish to the sink. The dog had disappeared as well, and she hoped Bandido, their big old mutt, was in the mountains looking after Juan. As she looked out the window over the sink she saw two shadows approaching the house, a smaller shadow trailing behind. She set down the bowl and it shattered, knifing a gash through the palm of her hand.

Dora grabbed a dishrag, staunched the gush of blood, and rushed to open the door. Outside, Fox was crossing the cobbled stable yard, half carrying Juan as he limped along. Juan's feet were bare, his chest was bare, and his lips were blue with cold. Dark red paint was crusted on his fingers and streaked his skin.

"Where was he?" she asked, her voice cracking.

Fox looked at her, his eyes flat and dark. "By Red Springs. He's freezing. Help me get him inside."

"Juan?" Dora said as she took his other arm. His eyes slid across her face and away. "Come inside now. Lean on me. It's nice and warm by the fire," she said, hearing herself speak in the soothing voice that she usually used for the cats.

She turned and whistled for Bandido del Corazón—but the creature who lurked at the edge of the yard was coyote, not a dog. It regarded her with steady eyes, and then disappeared through the creosote. Bandido emerged from under the couch where he had been hiding all night.

They sat Juan down in the chair by the hearth. She wrapped the quilt around him. His feet were torn and bloody, as though he had walked a long, long way. She tucked a pillow under his head, and Bandido settled in close by his feet. Juan's eyes were closed, his breath even; he was already fast asleep.

She looked up at Fox, who stood holding a cat, gazing into the fire.

"Have tea with me, Johnny?" Dora whispered. He nodded and followed her to the kitchen.

Fox sat down at the table he'd built for her and Juan last year, made out of mesquite wood polished to a smooth, rich red-brown surface. The cat slid from Fox's arms to his lap, and two of her littermates joined her; the fourth sat purring on Fox's boot with a silly grin on her face. He'd always had a gift for charming cats, and dogs . . . and women too, Dora thought, as she put the kettle on the stove. He was a good-looking devil, long and lanky, with skin tanned deep by the desert sun, his brown hair as perpetually dishevelled as his rumpled flannel shirts and his dusty jeans. His smile was an endearing one, revealing a chipped front tooth. Dora placed a mug in front of him, and washed another one for herself. Then she sat down at the table, all her energy draining in a rush.

Fox touched her hand, wrapped with the bloody rag. "What's going on?" he asked her.

She shook her head. "I don't know," she admitted. "Juan has been like that since—well, for a while now. He takes off at night, and when he comes back he's dazed or half asleep. Then when he wakes up again, he says he doesn't remember."

"He just gets up and starts roaming in the middle of the night?" Fox asked. "Has he seen a doctor?"

"He won't go. He says there's nothing wrong with him. He used to walk in his sleep when he was a boy, and he says there's nothing harmful in it, but—I don't know. There's more to it than that. Juan won't talk to me about it."

She wished he would offer to talk to Juan himself. But she couldn't ask Fox; the code of etiquette among men was different than that among women friends. If she poured out her fears about Juan to Johnny Foxxe, was she supporting her husband or betraying him?

"Have you tried locking the door?" Fox asked her.

"What good would it do? He's awake when he leaves. I can't keep him locked inside the house. He's my husband, not one of my cats."

"He could get hurt out there at night."

"I know. But how can I stop him?"

"Look, Dora, there's some fool with a gun out there, ignoring all the no hunting signs. Tomás and I have both seen him roaming around, down there by the creek. You tell Juan he'd best be more careful. The idiot will think he's a deer."

Dora swallowed. "I will. I'll tell him that."

They sat in uncomfortable silence then until the kettle whistled loudly and Fox rose to make the tea.

He measured sticks of Mormon tea into the pot, filled it with hot water, and said in a conversational tone, "That woman has come. Did you know that? The one who'll live in Cooper's house. Marguerita Black."

"The writer?" asked Dora with surprise.

"Yeah, I reckon she must be a writer. She's supposed to be writing a book on Cooper. You heard of her?"

"Darn right I have. And so have you, you know. Remember I loaned you *The Maid on the Shore*? That book of essays about the California coast?"

"Oh yeah? Didn't Annie Dillard write that? That was Marguerita Black? No wonder the name sounded familiar. I thought I must have heard it from Cooper."

Dora shook her head, grateful for the change of subject from Juan. "I would have remembered if Cooper had ever talked about Maguerita Black. I've been reading her work since I was in college. She used to publish these travelogue kind of pieces in *Harper's* and *The New Yorker*: very urban, cosmopolitan stuff, full of people who were always dashing off between London and Rome and Amsterdam, you know what I mean? I ate it up. I used to fantasize about living that kind of life someday. But the sad truth, Johnny," she said with a wry smile, "is that now I want my own house around me, a comfy chair, a cup of tea and a good travel book instead."

"Are we talking about the same writer? *The Maid on the Shore* is—"

"Quieter. More down to earth. It surprised me when it came out . . . but I think I like it the best of all. What a kick that she'll be living next door, huh? Have you met her? What's she like?"

"Like you said," he replied carefully. "Urban, cosmopolitan. Like someone who wrote for *The New Yorker,* not like someone who wrote *The Maid on the Shore.*"

"Hmmm. That's interesting," she said. "Now wait 'til I tell Juan." But at the mention of Juan's name the animation drained from Dora's pale face. She cast a wary look toward her husband where he sat by the fire, sleeping soundly. His own face was clear and untroubled, his cheeks flushed from the heat of the flames.

She rose, her tea untouched. "I ought to go get Juan into bed."

"You need some sleep yourself," Fox pointed out, spilling cats from his lap as he stood. He cooled his tea with tap water, and then drained it in three long gulps.

"I wish." Dora gave him a weary smile and stood on tiptoe to kiss his cheek.

She stood at the door as Fox left the house and watched him amble down the road. A shadow darted at his heels. The small coyote was still out there, its fur matted, its ribs distinct. She watched it weave its way through the trees—almost as if it were following the man but dared not approach too close to him. She was glad the cats were safe inside the house; they'd make a good breakfast for a hungry coyote, and that one looked like it could use a square meal. A whole coyote pack was singing in the hills; there seemed to be a lot of them around. Today she'd keep the cats locked in and send Bandido out to mark their turf.

The sun was rising above the mountains now, bringing its heat back to the canyon. She still had time for a bath and some breakfast before she headed into town and opened up the gallery again. Juan was sleeping so peacefully that she wouldn't try to move him after all. She envied him that untroubled sleep. For her, it was going to be another long day. She picked up her cup of tea and went to run the bathwater with four cats trailing along behind. As she did so, she realized she'd never asked Fox what he'd been doing in the mountains himself, up before the crack of dawn. Like Juan that night, six months ago. She frowned.

No, she wasn't going to think about that. She was going to put one foot in front of her at a time, take a bath, get dressed, get into her truck, and drive off this mountain into town. When she got back home, if she wasn't too tired, she'd try to talk to Juan again. Somehow, it was going to be all right. It had to be, that was all.

She sat in the shadows of the mesquite grove, crouched among the tree roots, her long and sensitive rabbit ears twitching as the wind above her changed direction. The voice of the wind was a rustle in the leaves, speaking in a language she'd once known and had forgotten. She did not have a name. She had not earned one yet. Or perhaps she had, and had forgotten that too. She was not old, as her kind reckoned age; and she was old, old as the granite hills. Old as Time, which spiralled like the tattoos on a shape-shifter's skin.

She put a pale, human hand to her mouth, licked it, and washed her face with it, smoothing back the soft grey fur. She knew she must sit and wait in this place. She didn't know what she was waiting for. No matter. The day was warming up; her heart was light; her belly was full. She stretched out on her back and rolled among the leaves, delighted with herself.

When the coyotes howled she ignored them. It was other meat they hunted now—the coyotes, and the Hounds of the Dark Hunter's pack. She wondered which of them would reach their prey first. Did it matter?

She seemed to remember that it did, but she'd forgotten why it mattered. Or what it had to do with her.

DAVIS COOPER
Redwater Road
Tucson, Arizona

M. Tippetts
New York City

March 9, 1948

Dear Maisie,

I agree completely. A trip to New York is exactly what we need. We have been buried alive out here these last months and the heat that descends on us in June is more than mortal man was meant to bear. I tell you, I think Anna needs a change of scene as much as I do. If you can persuade her to make this trip, I'd be most grateful—as would Riddley, at the gallery.

Our Anna has become a different creature out here; she is turning into a desert woman. Strip away that Mexico City gloss of urban civilization and the granddaughter of an Indian bruja lies beneath. She is a wonder to me, brown as the stones, fierce as a she-wolf, graceful as the deer. She is something other than woman in this place, she is earth and fire and sky as well. It is all in the paintings. Riddley has a shock in store when he sees the new work.

But she is too much alone, out in the hills. She rebels at visitors, at seeing old friends. She wants only me and the companionship of these creatures she paints—has she spoken of this? I don't know what to think. I accept the fact that our Anna has . . . visions; she is after all a woman, a witch, a lapsed Catholic, a painter, a Surrealist. I am but a war-scarred cynic myself, and perhaps my own vision is thus limited; it is only through the canvas that I can see the world as Anna describes it.

And yet . . . even I have begun to think that perhaps there is something in these hills. I can't see it, but I can almost hear it. A low drumbeat. A murmur of language. There are poems in these trees, in the rock underfoot. I resist it, this slow seduction. The land itself fought against Exile Songs, saying: "Write our poems, Cooper, not yours. . . ."

*And I shut the door and I closed the curtains and I finished the book
nonetheless.*

*Yes, I must come to the city again—or I shall be lost to the language
of this land and forget my own native tongue. Gotham Book Mart has
offered to host a publication party when* Exile Songs *comes out in June.
If we can pull our desert woman from her mountains, even for just a
few short weeks, I shall wire them and tell them we are coming. Even
Anna must long to escape the damn heat.*

Help me, Maisie. She'll listen to you.

Yours as ever,
Davis Cooper

three

And by whose grace did I arrive here, set down
in this place where moonlight kills, and
dreams leave blood and leaves
upon the twisted sheets of dawn?
—The Wood Wife, *Davis Cooper*

Maggie wiped the sweat from her brow, grateful that evening would fall soon, bringing its chill to the mountain. The midday sun had been fierce, and even though it was cooler in the house she'd had to strip down to her undershirt to work. She didn't have the proper clothes for this place, or the proper car, or the proper frame of mind. She found herself cursing the heat, the dust, and the pitiless landscape outside.

There seemed to be no kind of order at all to any of Davis's papers. The old man had been meticulous enough to make copies of all his correspondence—and then had shoved those papers away into any random corner or drawer. Insurance bills were filed with letters; old galley proof pages were wedged among his books. She'd found notes and roughs of his unpublished poems, but nothing close to a final manuscript. If "The Saguaro Forest" was still in this room, it was not in any obvious place.

The other place to look, of course, was behind the locked door in the back of the house. She'd tried a nail file on the lock, but the door was good and firmly shut. She wondered if Johnny Foxxe had a key, or could pry it open for her. She decided she'd go out for a walk, and stop by the handyman's cabin on the way. The sun was sinking low in the hills; it was high time to take a break.

She put on a shirt, one of Davis's hats, and laced on her English walking boots. As she stepped on the porch, she saw that someone had left her a basket of apples. Perhaps it had been her other tenant, the mechanic. What was his name?

She picked up an apple, rubbed it on her thigh, and bit into it as she crossed the yard. Birds sat on the Three Graces' arms, scolding noisily as she passed. A jackrabbit crouched in the shade beneath the black trunk of a mesquite tree. A herd of small deer leapt through the wash and into the brush on the other side. She hadn't expected deer on this land. She watched them vanish with a frown.

The desert wasn't as she'd imagined it at all: a Sahara landscape of sand and dunes. Rather, it was a Japanese garden made of stone, a sage-green land of low, gnarled trees, creosote bushes and cactus. The cactus came in a lush abundance of sizes and shapes, all alien to her. Everything here had spines or thorns. The sky was too vast; the light was too clear. There was nothing soft or hidden in the land, and it made her feel raw, overexposed, like a photograph left in the sun.

She followed a trail through the mesquite grove that stood between the house and the handyman's cabin. Here there were bits of grass underfoot and wildflowers, small purple blooms against the dark mesquite trunks. A low rattling sound puzzled her until she spied a wind chime in a tree. It was made of stones with holes in them ("hagstones" she remembered they were called, Davis had used the word in a poem) and bits of something white, like bone, suspended from long waxy threads. There were several of them hanging in the grove, clacking drily in the wind.

She emerged from the grove by Fox's house. His pickup truck was parked out front, and the door was open, but no one was within. He was probably at his workshop on the other side of the wash. She peered through the doorway curiously. The cabin was rustic, sparsely furnished, and neat as a pin, which surprised her. The kitchen and living room were one open space with a sleeping loft above it. The walls were hung with tools, horse-riding tack, and musical instruments: a collection of Indian flutes and drums, an acoustic guitar, an accordion. A single painting hung near the beehive hearth; it looked like an Anna Naverra. On a low table before the hearth was a red clay bowl filled with some green herb, Indian rattles made from two round gourds, smooth grey stones arranged in a circle and a long brown pinion feather. Beside them a sharp-looking hunting knife lay open on its leather sheath.

Maggie backed away from the door. What if he caught her here looking? And yet, apparently she owned this cabin; perhaps she'd every right to look. The lawyer for the estate hadn't mentioned cabins or tenants—or maybe she had and Maggie hadn't paid attention. It didn't matter. She wasn't going to change Davis's arrangements or try to kick anyone out. This mountainside was their world, not hers. She felt like a guest on Davis's land, waiting for her host to return.

There was a path at the back of the cabin running up the slope into the hills. Another path went down the slope. She chose the upper one and climbed. The path snaked up the mountainside, looping back and forth across it. She climbed steadily on a well-worn trail that led her up and over a ridge. When she reached the crest she paused. The trail dipped slightly down again into a long half-moon of land tucked into a fold of the cliffs. A population of saguaro grew there, from knee-height up to ten feet tall. Behind them was a small cabin with its back up against the rock.

The cabin was much like the one Fox lived in: made of flour-colored adobe with rounded edges and a stone chimney built into the shortest end. This one had outbuildings as well, and a small ramada made of untrimmed mesquite branches holding up the woody growth of a tombstone rose. Beneath the ramada was a battered formica table and a couple of kitchen chairs. A dish of apples on the outdoor table and a half-dozen chickens in a fenced-in yard were the only signs of life up here. A narrow road led up to the cabin but no vehicle was parked out front.

The trail led through the saguaros and past the cabin, then began to climb upward again. Above her a bird rode the wind in circles, too far away for her to make out what it was. It was dark, like a crow, but large—perhaps a buzzard or local species of hawk. The bird was hunting its supper, no doubt. It would circle lazily until it spied movement below and then it would attack. She stood and watched its elegant flight, and then she turned back to the climb. The path was hard to negotiate, full of loose stones that shifted underfoot and went skittering down the dry hill.

The bird had gone and she was breathing hard by the time she reached the top of the trail. She sat on a boulder to catch her breath. The peak was a rounded outcrop of stone, adorned with prickly pear cactus and yellow flowers clustered on brittle grey leaves. Sun-bleached boulders made her a seat surrounded by mountains and sky. In the distance she could see the lights of Tucson spreading out from the Rincons' feet. Beyond it, the Tucson Mountains' silhouette had the sinking sun balanced on its jagged edge. The sky was a blue she'd seen before only in the Mediterranean, streaked with an improbable shade of scarlet fading into mauves and pinks. Even after years of Pacific sunsets, Maggie admitted that she was impressed. The sky was as vast as an ocean and the mountain was an island in its midst.

"Sky islands, that's what we call them."

Her heart leapt, startled by the voice and the man who had read her mind. He was not breathing hard from his climb up the trail. His feet were bare on the sharp stones. He greeted her with an intimate smile, although she'd never seen him before.

"You've found the best place for the sunset already," he said with distinct approval. "This is where I often come to see it too, so you'll have to share."

She found she had lost the power of speech. She stared at him, but he didn't seem to mind this evident rudeness. He stood engrossed in the setting sun's gaudy technicolor display, standing braced against an evening wind that pushed long, dark hair from his shoulders.

He was not a tall man, not so tall as Maggie, but fit and lean, and beautiful. He was dressed oddly in a plain buckskin shirt held closed at the throat with what looked like long thorns. His jeans were tied with long buckskin strips around the shins and ankles. He looked part Native American, with that rich black hair, a white feather tied in it; but his face had a European cast as well, and his eyes were a deep moss green. He wore several thongs around his neck hung with hagstones, turquoise, a little leather bag and a silver disk with a Celtic design. Copper bands encircled one wrist, etched with an intricate spiral pattern. The same spirals were drawn around his other wrist, or else it was a tattoo.

She wanted to introduce herself, and ask his name and if he lived below. Instead Maggie said nothing at all, feeling herself grow younger, shyer, struck dumb by his physical beauty; turning, in an instant, back into the tongue-tied teenager she'd been many years before: too tall, too bookish, too altogether odd for those small-town West Virginia boys. She didn't like feeling that way again. She reminded herself she was forty years old and that was all far in the past now. . . .

Yet she watched the sun sinking lower in silence. Her companion never sat; he stood quite still, close behind her on the narrow perch. So close she could smell the musky scent of sweat and woodsmoke on his skin—and something more which she couldn't name, teasingly half-familiar. The moon was rising, round and pale and melancholy in the darkening sky. The coyotes began their evensong. For some reason this made the stranger laugh.

She found her voice at last and asked him, "This is your particular sunset place then?"

He looked at her and cocked his head. She saw that he had lines lightly drawn across the high bones of his cheeks—odd, but not unattractive. He did not answer the question she'd asked but the one that lay underneath it.

"We'll meet again," he answered her, with the gravity of a promise. She was chilled by the echo of Davis's words, and yet unaccountably pleased by this. She nodded in acknowledgment, masking the confusion she felt.

He gave her a smile she couldn't read—there was amusement in it, flirtatiousness, and a glimpse of something lost and sad. Then he left, abruptly, stepping easily down the steepest side of the mountain slope. He did not follow the trail she'd used; he struck off on an unmarked route. The coyotes' song grew louder as he went, sounding to her like laughter. It reminded her of his.

She sat still while the sun disappeared, her heart beating loudly in her chest. Her heart seemed to beat to a rhythm that was pulsing in the stones, in the ground beneath her feet. The night was filled with scents and sounds that were strange to her, and heady. There was something primal about this land, a language spoken by the stones and the wind. What had Davis's letter said? *The stars, the stones, the very trees reveal the language of the earth.*

Maggie stood finally to begin her descent, knowing she should have done so long since, while there was light left in the sky. The canyon below was a black river. She could just make out the tops of the trees. A truck was traveling toward Redwater Road, its headlights piercing the dark.

She was wary, almost frightened, as she picked her way down the treacherous slope. The night was very black up here. The stars hung so low and close it seemed she could brush her head on them. Below, the lights of Tucson spread an impossible distance away. She was closer to the stars than she was to the world, but it was to the world that she must return. She could barely see the path she walked, edged by sharp cactus on either side. The saguaro loomed tall and ghostly as she passed through their ranks by the upper cabin. There were no lights on inside the cabin. Below, Fox's place was dark as well.

She reached the bottom of the trail at last and skirted Fox's house on the way to her own. The chimes rattled loudly in the mesquite wood, and something small skittered close by her feet. The truck was coming up the road now. It turned and she was caught in its lights. She stared at it, blinded, as it came up her drive. The engine stopped and the headlights went out.

A young woman climbed down from the truck and extended a bandaged hand to Maggie. "I'm Dora del Río. My husband and I live in that old stable up the road. I don't mean to disturb you. Just wanted to stop by and say welcome."

"Thanks for stopping," Maggie said a bit breathlessly, glad after her trip down the dark mountainside for this simple human interaction. "It's nice to meet you. My name's Maggie Black."

"I know." Dora flushed. "I mean, I know your work. I loved *The Maid on the Shore*."

"That's kind of you." Maggie smiled at Dora. The younger woman was small and pretty in a delicate, almost childlike way, the kind of woman that always made Maggie feel like a leggy giraffe. She had thick red-gold curls pulled back with a velvet band, clear brown eyes and a heart-shaped face. Maggie instantly liked the look of her; her eccentric dress sense reminded her of Tat: a vintage fifties' flowered skirt over purple leggings and green cowboy boots. Her suede jacket was beaded and fringed, and underneath it was an edge of lace. "Come in for a cup of tea?" Maggie offered.

The other woman looked nervously up the road in the direction of her own house. "I should let my husband know I'm home first."

"Why don't you bring him over too? I've got a bottle of wine if you'd rather. Or I could make margueritas."

"I vote for margueritas," said Dora, climbing back into her battered truck. "I'll fetch Juan and be back in a sec. It's not very far to our place—down the wash on the left, past the bend." She shifted gear, gave a jaunty wave, and backed the truck from Davis's drive; then she gunned the engine and headed up the dirt track, dust flying behind her.

Maggie laughed as she watched Dora go. The woman drove like Tat as well, as though the internal combustion engine ran on raw enthusiasm instead of gas. She watched the truck bounce over the rutted road. No wonder it was so banged up.

She turned and walked back toward the house, her fear of the darkened mountain dispelled. She'd remember to take a flashlight with her the next time she went walking at dusk. No doubt she'd feel less jumpy here if she had some friends just up the road—someone beside ol' Johnny Foxxe, and that disturbing man on the hill.

Maggie wondered then if Dora's husband was the beautiful man she'd met up there. It would probably be just as well, she decided, if he was attached to someone else. The very last thing that she needed in her life was a schoolgirl crush on a total stranger. Or worse, another half-baked romance—like the last one, in Mendocino. Romance, unlike friendship, was not a skill she seemed to practice with any great success. She'd written Tat just a few days ago that she planned to swear off men for a while. She'd be an "art nun," as Tat laughingly described those solitary stretches. That is, if her life could be called solitary with Nigel always on the phone. And with Davis Cooper's ornery presence, even now that the man was dead.

Maggie reached the porch, and stared at it. The French doors to Davis's study were open. The blue front door was standing ajar even though she was certain she'd locked it. She stepped into the hall and turned on the light. There were muddy prints leading into the kitchen, and the trace of an acrid, unpleasant smell.

She looked into the kitchen, appalled. The heavy wood table had been knocked over, glasses smashed on the hardwood floor. Mud and leaves were everywhere, and animal prints were tracked in the dirt. Before the hearth was a pile of vomit containing the bones and half-digested organs of some rodent or bird. Something had spattered the front of the woodstove, a rusty color like blood.

The living room was in better shape, although the couch had been overturned and one tall bookcase lay facedown, its volumes scattered across the floor. Davis's bedroom had been spared. The door to the back room remained safely locked. The door itself had been clawed and battered; deep gouges marred the length of it. The worst of the stench came from Davis's office. She flicked on the overhead light with dread. The poet's desktop had been swept clear, its papers strewn across the rug. The floor was thick with mud and puddled urine and piles of shit.

Maggie took a deep and steadying breath. Then she turned the light back off again. She went outside, shut the front door and sat down, shivering, on the porch steps. Soon Dora and her husband would come. Maybe they could make sense of this. Maybe they could explain what the hell had just been inside Davis Cooper's house.

Juan took a rag to the canvas, wiping away an hour's worth of paint and work. It wasn't right. The rhythm wasn't there. The paint didn't sing, it sat there, so much lifeless pigment in linseed oil, blended into shades of mud.

He threw down the cloth, disgusted. He could feel the rhythm pulsing in his hands, see the colors dancing behind his eyes. Why couldn't he translate that insistent pulse into paint or plaster or clay? It wasn't right, it just wasn't right. Nothing had been right for months. He knew what he saw when he closed his eyes, he just couldn't put it onto canvas.

He left his easel and sat down at the drawing board instead, picking up a charcoal stick, opening a hardbound sketchbook. He sharpened the stub of charcoal and began to draw random shapes and patterns. Spirals, linked together in intricate designs like a Celtic knot. Patterns that seemed to pour from his hands, bypassing conscious thought. It was the only work that pleased him now. The only thing that satisfied. The rest was skill, empty of art—the paintings he'd made for all these years. He had painted surface shadows only, the skin of the earth without the bones, flayed from the organism beneath. The shape of the mountains without their voice—oh, Cooper had been right about that.

And look where being right got him, said a calmer, steadier voice in Juan's head. The practical voice. The Dora voice. All right, so he wouldn't go out tonight. His feet were raw and painful anyway; his muscles ached. He'd stay indoors. He'd already shut the windows tight, locked the big doors of the barn. Tonight he would watch television with Dora and ignore the singing of the stars.

Bandido stirred and lumbered to his feet. Juan put down the drawing charcoal. The old mutt always knew when Dora was approaching, long before he could possibly hear her truck coming down the road. Juan switched off his work light, wiped his hands and headed for the kitchen. He had a pot of chili cooking and brown bread rising, ready for the oven. He was resolved to be a more satisfactory husband to Dora tonight.

As he stepped into the house he tried to avoid looking closely at the pictures on the wall, his old ones, which Dora insisted on hanging. He wanted to burn them, or paint them all over, but she would be furious with him if he did. He focused instead on the pictures by other artists (conscious of the failure of his own, hanging there, nagging him like an itch he could not scratch): the obligatory Georgia O'Keefe poster; the Froud reproductions that Dora had arranged in a row over her worktable; and the smaller canvas hanging in the place of honor above the fireplace.

The canvas was an original Mexican Surrealist painting, by Anna Naverra. It showed a pale and white-haired girl holding water cupped in her small hands against a desert night filled with Escher-like towers, white moths, an antique clock. It was titled *The Mage and the Midnight Hour,* although the clock read 1:15 in the morning. Cooper had given it to them last year, on Dora's twenty-fifth birthday. It had been a generous, astonishing gift. As if he'd known he'd soon be gone and it would be his last.

Juan stood before the painting now; he never got tired of looking at it. Rendered in the vivid and painstaking style of the Surrealists, its rich colors were luminous; the figure glowed as if with an inner fire against the dark background. He sighed. If he could paint like this . . . Portray that light, that heart of flame. . . . He'd tried. He'd studied Naverra's art, and that of the other painters who worked in Mexico after the Second World War. Frida Kahlo. Remedios Varo. Leonora Carrington. He'd never paid much attention to them before he moved next door to Cooper; the art history he'd learned at school was largely French, English, and Italian, despite his own hispanic roots. Now he couldn't get enough of Mexican painting, Anna Naverra especially. What secrets had Naverra known? What witchery had she conjured here? And had those secrets destroyed her, as they'd destroyed old Cooper in the end? Juan's eyes traced spiral patterns woven into the canvas, into the paint, into the smoke of the pale girl's breath, losing himself in a draught of dark desert night brewed from wind and stars.

Bandido barked and the cats looked up as the Bronco pulled into the driveway, Juan roused himself from Naverra's painting and went back into the kitchen. The chili was fine. He turned off the flame; it was too early to eat dinner now. Dora would want to relax, have a beer. He'd make a salad, and for dessert there was the apple pie that sat on the counter. Why hadn't they eaten it last night, he wondered, while it was still warm from the oven? He shook his head. He couldn't remember. He'd probably been locked away working again. And Dora was probably still angry about it. She always seemed angry lately. Well, tonight he'd make it up to her. "Mr. House-husband rises again," he said, picking up the chopping knife.

Through the window he saw her jump from the truck—a tiny woman, doll-like in her stature but with a will the size of the Rincons. Watching her now as she walked to the door, her face tired, her eyes shadowed, her copper-colored curls escaping from a velvet band, he felt a sudden rush of love for her. The first he'd felt in quite a long while. Not that he loved her any the less, he silently defended himself; but love, like the other habits of daily life, was pushed to the corners of his consciousness. The urgency of the colors, the rhythms, the visions he sought on the mountain's trails left little room for anything else but the raw desire to paint. Wasn't this what true artists felt? He'd never felt such compulsion before; it thrilled him, it frightened him, it made him hope that at last he'd do good work.

If only he could explain that to Dora. That it wasn't the marriage that had changed, but him. His work. And something he couldn't name, as necessary now as the air he breathed, out there somewhere in the hills. Dora would never understand. His wife was not Anna Naverra, not a witch woman with a heart of flame, she was a woman of earth: granite and quartz. Her love was reserved for human things: her family, her husband, Bandido and the cats, for the simple daily magic of food on the table, friends close by, a warm body in the dark. These were the things that mattered to Dora. They used to matter to him.

Juan looked at his reflection in the dark window glass as Dora came up behind him. A young Chicano man stared back, eyes both dark and bright with visions. He didn't recognize that man. He had changed. Was changing. Shedding one snake skin and finding another skin beneath. He was turning into someone else. Now he turned, and he embraced his wife. He breathed in Dora's sharp, sweet scent, holding tightly on to love, remembering, for that moment, that it was precious.

Dora held the storm lamp that lit their path through the dry wash bed. Juan held her other hand, his calloused fingers warm around hers, as they made their way on foot down the sandy bank to Cooper's house. Maggie Black's house, she corrected herself. She could see it through the cottonwood trees, the yellow light over the door of the porch. Maggie herself was sitting outside on the steps as they walked up the drive.

As she introduced Juan to their new neighbor Dora registered the look on the other woman's face. "Good god, what is it? What's wrong? You look like you've seen a ghost," she said. Then she bit her tongue. What a stupid thing to come out with at a dead man's house.

"Something has been inside the house," Maggie said, speaking perfectly calmly in that low and husky voice of hers. But her eyes, dark and wide, and the pallor of her face betrayed the fact that she was alarmed. "I was out for a while walking in the hills. I came back and the door was unlocked."

"Some*thing* or some*one*?" Juan asked her, eyes narrowed.

"Come look for yourself," Maggie replied. She led them through the door and into the hallway, stepping over leaves and mud.

Dora sucked in her breath when she entered the kitchen behind her husband and saw what they'd done. What *something* had done— for Maggie was right. There were animal tracks, and no human ones. The mud was particularly curious. Outside, the wash was dry as a bone.

Juan sniffed. "What is that smell?" he asked.

"It's in the study," Maggie said flatly. They followed her to Cooper's office.

"Shit," Dora said.

Maggie smiled wryly. "My sentiments exactly."

Juan stepped carefully over the puddles of urine and squatted in the center of the room. "This is animal scat. Coyote I think. Lots of coyotes, and pretty fresh. They must have gotten into the house somehow. I'll be damned. They're not usually so bold as this." He looked up at them, his face containing more puzzlement than alarm. "Perhaps the doors blew open and they came in looking for some food?" he conjectured. "Or chased a rabbit into the house. That's the only scenario I can think of that would account for their coming in here. Perhaps a whole hunting pack of them. Are you absolutely sure the doors were locked?"

"I think so. But no, I'm not absolutely sure. I must not have locked them after all. I didn't know coyotes could be such a problem. I saw one in the yard just this morning. He was so beautiful, it never occurred to me to wonder if he was dangerous."

Dora said, "*I've* never known them to be. Except to mice and rabbits and cats. But I've never seen anything like this before either."

"They're wild animals, don't forget," said Juan. "They look like dogs, but they're closer to wolves. When exactly did this happen, Maggie?"

The woman frowned, considering. "I went out walking just before sunset. I was coming back when Dora stopped me—so sometime in the last couple of hours. I heard coyotes when I was out there. Back in the hills, not near the house. But come to think of it, yesterday Fox and I startled a huge owl nesting in here. Perhaps the local wildlife have gotten used to this house being empty."

"In just six months?" Juan said skeptically. "Animals are generally more wary of human habitats than that."

"They weren't wary of this one, were they? It looks like they had the whole pack in here, having a party. I wonder if they're likely to come back? And what they'd do if they found me here?"

"They'd run, I should think," said Dora. "Fox always says they have better reason to be scared of us than we do of them."

Juan said, "We should give Fox a call. Maybe he can make head or tail of this."

"The phone's in the kitchen," Maggie told him. "And that bottle of tequila I promised you. I'm going to open it. I don't know about you all, but I seriously need a drink."

Maggie fetched the tequila bottle and made up a pitcher of strong margueritas, while Dora searched for some unbroken glasses and Juan got Fox on the phone.

"I don't think anything's been stolen," Dora heard Juan tell him. "I think she just had animals in here. You come look, and then you tell me. All right. We'll see you in five."

He turned around and said to Maggie, "Fox is coming right over. Now listen, why don't you have supper with us, and spend the night at our place? We should clean up whatever stinks right away, but I'd say leave the rest for the morning. You're tired now, and things have a way of looking worse at night."

Maggie gave Juan a grateful smile. "I'd love to stay at your house tonight. I don't think I'd sleep, staying here."

"I've a day off work tomorrow," Dora told her, "and I can help you clean this up. Not much of a welcome to the mountain is it? Don't worry. It's not usually like this. It's usually quiet and peaceful up here. You'll love it when you get to know it."

"Well, Davis loved it," she said dubiously. Clearly it wasn't an opinion Maggie shared.

But then, she hadn't been here long; it hadn't yet gotten into her bones. Dora hadn't liked the desert herself when she'd first come here, trailing after Juan. But the desert had claimed her, entering her heart and marking her there as one of its own. Now she was like her desert-born husband: unfit to live anywhere else.

She heard Fox's boots crunching over the yard, the creak of the porch floor under his step. He gave a low whistle as he came through the door, his eyes surveying the damage. He crouched down and looked closely at the prints, his knees poking through the holes in his jeans. "Animals all right. Maybe coyotes. Doesn't make a lick of sense though." He straightened, frowning. "Are you all right?" he asked Maggie with concern.

Maggie nodded. "Just a bit shook up. This doesn't happen in California," she answered with a dry smile. "Breaking-and-entering is generally committed by animals of the two-legged kind."

"I'd rather take my chances with coyotes. I've never heard tell of them harming anyone." Fox picked up a kitchen chair and set it on its feet again. Then he gave Maggie a long, thoughtful look. "I think you should talk to John Alder about this—up the road in the Big House. He's a bit of a wildlife expert. I can take you up there in the morning."

"Let's call John now," Dora suggested.

Fox shook his head. "He's not home. He's down at Tanque Verde Falls. Just got back from there myself."

It was only then that Dora noted Fox had climbing gear clipped to his belt. "You've been out with Mountain Search and Rescue again? Has anyone been hurt?"

"Yeah," he confirmed, his voice edged with his disgust, "another drunk high school kid and his buddies, messing around down there. Idiot kid nearly drowned." He sighed and turned to Maggie. "You've seen those signs for Upper Falls? In Reddington Pass, as you come up the hill? It's beautiful there, but treacherous. Seems like damn near every week we're pulling some fool kid from the canyon. This one broke his leg down there and had to be airlifted out. He's lucky. People have died there. The water is stronger than it looks, and flash floods come out of nowhere if its been raining farther up the hills. But you can't keep people away from a bit of water in the desert."

Fox sat down at the kitchen table, looking completely exhausted. He shook his head at Maggie's offer of a drink. She didn't know he never touched the stuff, not after watching Cooper's slow self-destruction with whiskey and gin.

Maggie refilled her own empty glass, and Juan's, and topped up Dora's. Her expression was thoughtful. "I never imagined there would be creeks in dry land like this." She paused, then added hesitantly, "Is that where they found Davis, then? His lawyer told me he'd been drowned. But I couldn't understand how he'd been drowned in the middle of the desert."

Fox shook his head. "No one understands it. He was a good mile from Tanque Verde Creek, or any other water. His body was left in an old wash bed, one that's been dried out for years. The police don't know where it was he drowned, but wherever it was, it wasn't where he was found. That means somebody put him there. That's how they know it was murder."

"But who would possibly have done that?" she asked. Dora could hear a mix of confusion, anger and grief in the woman's low voice. "He didn't have any enemies, did he? Other than the usual literary kind. And those old feuds, with deMontillo and that critic . . . what's his name . . . St. Johns? Those are decades past. He doesn't seem to have owned much of value, if robbery was the motive."

"The land. And Anna's paintings," said Fox. "But if anyone had a motive to kill him for that," he added with an odd, small grin, "well, I reckon it would have been you."

Maggie shook her head. "I didn't even know I was in his will," she told him.

"No? Well, I'll be damned," Fox said, looking startled by this.

Dora looked around, suddenly realizing just what was missing from Cooper's house. "Where are all of Anna's paintings now?"

Fox looked at Maggie and, at her blank response, he ventured, "Cooper's lawyer must have had them put somewhere for safekeeping. They're fairly valuable now, you know. He was always getting letters from museums that wanted to buy them, or even just exhibit a few. But you know Cooper, he'd throw the letters out. The old man couldn't be bothered."

"He'd promised Anna the paintings wouldn't leave the mountain," Dora corrected him. "At least that's what he said to me. I had to promise I'd never take the one he gave me away from here."

"The lawyer wouldn't take them away," said Juan, "without informing Maggie. And the cops would have noticed if they were missing. They must be here somewhere."

Maggie said, "I haven't seen any paintings. But there's one room here that's all locked up; my guess is that they'd be in there." She looked at Fox. "I meant to ask you for the key to it."

"I haven't got a key," Fox said. "That door has been locked since I was a boy. The mystery room. My sisters and I always wondered what the hell was in there."

"Surely someone opened up the room for the police investigation."

"Maybe they did. I don't know." Fox shrugged.

"Hmmm." Maggie smiled suddenly. "Well, here's your chance to find out what's inside. Let's just break through the lock."

"Maybe the cops still have the key," said Fox. "Maybe you should give them a call before we break down Cooper's door."

"It's Maggie's door now," Dora pointed out.

"I'm not protesting," said Fox. "Believe me, there's no one more curious than I am. I can bring my tool box over in the morning and work on the door after we see John." He grinned suddenly at Maggie. "I admit, I've been sorely tempted to break in myself since Cooper's death. If I were less honest, or maybe just less superstitious, I probably would have. Lord, how we used to scheme to get in when my sisters and I were growing up. But the windows were nailed, the lock couldn't be jimmied, and old man Cooper never budged. We couldn't even talk to him about it—he'd go all funny on us."

Maggie gave him a thoughtful look. "It's strange to hear you talk about him that way. I never pictured Davis with children around. He seemed so solitary."

"He *was* solitary. He was living all alone up here after Anna died, drunk as a skunk."

"When did your mother come up here, then?"

"Sometime in the early fifties, I think; several years before I was born. Cooper was living at the bottom of a bottle and he needed looking after. He said he put an ad in the paper and my mother answered it."

"And your father?"

Fox met her gaze steadily. "Truth is, my mother never married. According to Cooper, our father was some local cowboy Mama went out with from time to time; he came and went, and finally went for good, leaving her with three kids to raise."

"You were born here, in the mountains? Then you must have known Cooper quite well," Maggie said to him with interest.

"Well sure. I was raised in the house across the wash. The canyon was even more remote back then; we almost never went downtown. My sisters and I got 'homeschooled' by Cooper—which mostly meant we ran wild on the mountain . . . and recited a lot of poetry."

Dora listened to this, fascinated. She'd never heard Fox say more than two words about his past before.

Maggie said, "Would you and your mother and your sisters be willing to talk to me about Davis for the biography of him I'm writing?"

Fox looked dubious. "I reckon I could. But Cooper and me, we didn't exactly see eye to eye, I have to warn you. My sisters don't come back here much—I never really know when they'll turn up. And my mother, she's a sweet old lady, but she's spent a lifetime in the mountains. It's made her extremely shy of anyone that she doesn't know. Mama has always been closemouthed about the past—the way old people are sometimes, particularly when there are things in their lives that they'd just as soon forget."

"Still, I'd like to try talking to her."

Fox shrugged. "I'll take you over there, then. She lives out on the west side of town, on a bit of property Cooper left her. She didn't want to be in the mountains anymore after he died. I think she might have left long ago, except that Cooper needed her here. She worshipped the ground he walked on no matter how drunk or crazy he got."

"Crazy?" Maggie picked up on the word.

Fox grinned at her. "Well, that's my opinion. You ought to take it with a grain of salt since we didn't get along these last few years. He said I was too much of a drifter, would never amount to anything. And I thought that was pretty rich coming from a drunk. Even a Pulitzer Prize–winning drunk. Lillian—that's John Alder's wife—said we were just doing the Antler Dance. You know, the male territorial thing. Maybe she was right." Fox shrugged again, and then he suddenly stood, having obviously decided he'd revealed enough confidences for one night. His movements were so eloquent of closure that Dora saw Maggie shut her mouth on whatever her next question was going to be.

Fox got up and crossed the room. He produced a small plastic container from the cabinet below the sink. "I'd like to take some of that animal scat from Cooper's study, for John to look at."

"Be my guest," said Maggie magnanimously. "You're welcome to it. Take all the crap you want."

Juan laughed, and stood. "Well then, we've put if off long enough," he said. "Let's go get that shit out of there. Have you got some buckets? And a shovel?"

"I know where they are," Fox told him.

They gathered mops, buckets, detergent, and a couple of short-handled shovels. Dora and Maggie set to work washing puddled urine from the rug as Juan and Fox shovelled animal droppings out into the mesquite wood.

When they were finished the study, unlike the kitchen, was clean and tidy. Too tidy, thought Dora. There was something terribly sad about the room without the poet himself in it, smoking like a chimney, surrounded by papers, books, dirty clothes, half-drunk cups of tea, bits of scavenged desert flora, the inevitable bottles of gin. It was seeing that room, empty of life, that finally convinced Dora the old man was gone and would not be returning. She was glad when they finished up and left, locking the doors carefully behind.

They parted with Fox at the path through the mesquite wood leading back to his cabin. Juan lit the lamp to light their trail, although it was unnecessary. The moon was very bright tonight, pouring silver into the wash. At the end of the drive Dora looked back at the house, sitting dark and empty. It was missing Cooper, Dora thought. Not just the house, the land itself. The three tall saguaro, the cottonwood tree, the mountain beneath her feet. A single coyote sang up in the hills, a thin, high-pitched and lonesome sound. She shivered. Juan put an arm around her and she leaned into his warmth.

She crept from out of her hiding place, trembling, licking the blood from her fur. The Hounds were hunting indeed tonight, but they'd found no satisfaction. The trail was cold. The lock had held. There were still strong old protections here. Moonlight spun to flesh, the Hounds had left the marks of their displeasure. And nearly had her own sweet red life's-blood in consolation.

She sat in the silver moonlight, her breath fast, her heart still pounding, her long, silky jackrabbit ears twitching at every sound. Her eyes were dark in a pale, human face. The Hounds had run her to exhaustion. But she must not sleep, for she had promised that she would watch over this land tonight. Who was it she had promised? The Spine Witch, or the Woodmage, or perhaps even the One-Who-Sleeps—she was going to have to remember now. To resist the pull of the animal-self and be present in this place and time, walking that linear human path that went so against her nature.

She fled into the shadows again as a rumbling sound came to her, carried through the rock below and the wind in the mesquite trees. A truck on the road. *Truck. Road.* She knew those words—yes, she could do this. She could remember how to be in this place. She concentrated, and the features of her face grew even more human in appearance, except for the ears; the round, unblinking eyes; and a nose colored rabbit pink. She watched the truck approach and stop, shadowed by the limbs of the cottonwood tree. The man inside was the one called Fox. She had nothing to fear from *him.* He just sat there inside the truck, a blanket wrapped around him. Did he know that she was out here? Were his eyes so sharp, his nose so keen?

No, he didn't know that there were two of them there to guard the house, to watch through the long and moonlit night. It didn't matter. She was glad of his presence. She curled herself into the hollow in the ground between the three saguaro, and she waited, shivering, long ears cocked, listening for the baying of the Hounds.

DAVIS COOPER
c/o F. M. Martino
New York, New York

H. Miller
Big Sur, California

June 15, 1948

So Henry,

    Anaïs tells me you're strapped again. I've enclosed a check—just add it to the tab and pay me back when you're a filthy rich celebrity. I've sold the property I inherited in England, so Anna and I are fine for a while, and it costs us very little to live in the desert. Even a poet can survive out there.

    You know, you're already a cause celebre in an underground way here in New York. Half the young poets who showed up for my signing last night were more interested in the fact that I knew you, you bastard, than in Exile Songs. I can't quite get used to being the older generation at thirty-five—hardly an old man yet. These kids all want to re-create the cafe life we lived in Paris before the war. Impossible here. New York is too fast, too slick, and too jazzed up for that. Where can you linger over coffee or wine, trade books and ideas, argue, make love? You eat, you drink, you vacate your table or the waiter will throw you out.

    I'll tell you, after arguing with Anna about coming, I find I don't want to be here after all. I'm in Frank's old rooms on 13th Street, just down the block from Hugo and Anaïs. My plan was to stay in the city three weeks, head on out to Caresse's place—where Dalí and his wretched wife are staying—then back to Tucson next month. But after a week of New York I am ready to catch any train headed west. I want silence again, and vast blue skies. I want the heat, honest earth underfoot. I can't sleep here. I don't think I'll sleep till I reach the mountains and Anna.

    Where is the man I used to be? All those things I've missed, the crowded streets, the talk, the advertising cant, all worthless now. There is poetry in this man-made place, but its language is stilted, its vision is grey, it holds no interest for me anymore. I see now that it is not only Anna that Red Springs Canyon has claimed after all. I need the wild. I need the source. I need a land where sun and wind will strip a man down to the soul and bleach his dying bones. I want to speak the language of stones, even if there is no one but Anna to hear, and patient old friends like you, Henry, and Pablo, and Anaïs.

Frank is angry. I've cancelled two signings in order to get out of here. Exile Songs is having the success I've always craved, but I no longer care. It feels odd to sit signing copies of the book when I'm no longer the man who wrote it. I hung onto that man just long enough to finish the poems, correct the proofs. The war is over. It's time to go on with the lives we are making now. I've agreed to stay in Manhattan through Friday and go to lunch with Pat Clarke from Scribners, if only to mollify Frank—or else, he threatens, I'll need a new agent.

Did you hear that Anna has six paintings hung at the Wallace Gallery this month? My entire trip has been worth it just to see them shining like small, perfect jewels in that grey city box of a place. When you come through Tucson, you'll see her new work. Her vision is witchy, disturbing, uncomfortable—and beautiful. Bring your own paints when you come, old boy. There's nothing like the desert light.

Yours as ever,
Cooper

four

Tonight they have won.
Dusk is hard to breathe, it catches
in my throat, and I am less a man
than a hunger. Waiting.
—The Wood Wife, *Davis Cooper*

Waking up in Dora's house, Maggie felt none of the sense of dislocation she'd had her first morning at Cooper's. She woke to the homey smell of bacon frying; the sound of bathwater running; the warmth of a plump tuxedo cat draped across her stomach. The guest room was still under construction, so they'd bedded her down on the couch instead, in a cozy living room of fat thirties chairs, hooked rugs and patchwork quilts. The beautiful desert morning light streamed through curtains of old ivory lace.

But for all of its charm, the room was an absolute mess, filled with lumber, tiles, tools, art supplies, books and papers piled on every available surface. Maggie pushed away the urge to tidy it all up—that streak of the Puritan in her that her granddaddy said must have come from her granny, since he was a slob himself. She smiled, thinking of her grandfather. She'd give him a call later in the day. She eased herself out from under the cat and the cat continued to purr.

Dora looked up from the stove at the other end of the L-shaped room. She was wearing a bathrobe covered with pictures of cowboys and cartoon cactus; her long copper-colored hair was loose and tousled, hanging in Botticelli curls. "Coffee?" she asked.

"Bless you," Maggie said, coming to take the mug from her hand.

"This is a wonderful old building you've got. How long have you been working on it?"

"Oh, off and on for a couple of years, whenever a chunk of money comes in. Which isn't very often these days," Dora confided cheerfully, "so at this rate we may never finish. Which is exactly what happened with the place we were renovating before this, downtown in the Barrio. We're setting a new style: the construction-site look. Don't you think its *trés chic*?"

"Oh indeed."

Dora switched the radio on to the local public radio station. The music of Pycard's *Gloria* filled the room with rich choral voices. Maggie listened closely. It was not her ex-husband's recording of the piece but some other, and the tension left her shoulders. Sometimes it seemed she could never go far enough to escape from Nigel.

She sat down at the table, pushing aside piled lumber, laundry, and two wrestling cats. She cradled the coffee mug in her hands, enjoying the music, the chaos of Dora's kitchen, the smells of breakfast to come. Sunlight streamed through vines over the windows, heavy with clusters of purple blooms. Between the windows hung a large framed drawing depicting a very different view: birch trees in a field of snow, rendered in charcoal on white rag paper in an angular, abstracted style. It was an attractive piece of work, if not quite exceptional.

"Is this your drawing?" she asked Dora.

"That's Juan's, that one, and the paintings on the wall to the left of the fireplace."

Maggie crossed the room to look at the paintings. They were all paintings of northern woods.

"Vermont," Dora explained to her. "That's where I'm from. And where we met. Juan did a painting residency at Bennington College, when I was a student. But you can't keep a desert boy from the desert. I knew when I married him I'd have to pull up stakes and come down here."

"This is lovely work," Maggie said. "But why no paintings of the Southwest?"

Dora shrugged. "Beats me. He spent years painting the desert. Here. Texas. New Mexico. Even down in Sonora. Now he doesn't like those paintings anymore. I don't know why. They're beautiful. But he just doesn't like them all of a sudden. Do you ever feel like that with your writing?"

"All too goddamn often," Maggie said with sympathy.

Below the paintings, a framed photograph stood perched on top of a table's clutter. She picked it up. It was a wedding picture: Dora in an antique dress, Juan in a tux, and what seemed to be one huge extended Mexican-American family crowded in behind them. Dora had not only married a desert man, she'd married a clan.

"Yep, those are all del Ríos," Dora confirmed. "It's an old, old family in these parts. And huge! I still can't keep all the names straight. Half of them live in Tucson, and the other half over the border. They've all been really sweet to me since I moved down here with Juan."

Maggie put the picture down again. She asked, "So what do you do here? Are you an artist too?"

"Me? No, I work in a gallery downtown. Typing and filing and watching the shop, mind you; nothing glamorous. And I tend bar in a hotel three nights a week. You know the kind: a kitschy border motif and we all have to wear fruit on our heads. The tourists seem to think that's Mexican." Dora rolled her eyes. She turned back to the stove. "I've always liked to hang around with artists, though. The boyfriend before Juan was a painter too. And the one before that called himself an artist, although he liked the pose more than the work."

Maggie laughed, commiserating. "I had one of those myself, in my misbegotten youth. He was totally romantic, and totally a mess."

"You got it. Mine was Mr. Romance: bedroom eyes, and those nice strong hands that sculptors always have . . . ummmm. I'm a sucker for that. He gave me the best two weeks of my life, and then the *worst* two years." She flipped the bacon out of the pan and onto a plate. "Do you eat meat? Never mind. I'm making pancakes too. I'd better make extra for Fox. He always turns up hungry."

Maggie was still exploring the room with her usual curiosity, which she liked to blame on her journalist training although she'd al-

ways been that way. Above a crowded desk in the corner were several
prints in simple wood frames, images of fairy tale creatures formed
out of tree roots, limbs, and leaves. "Are these by Brian Froud?" she
asked, and Dora turned and nodded. "I like them. His work has the
spirit of Cooper's poems—the later ones, I mean. In *The Wood Wife*."

"That's why I have them there," Dora said. "To tell you the truth, I
like Froud's work much better than Anna Naverra's—but I don't dare
say that in front of Juan! Cooper gave me these reproductions. He has
one in his study."

"I saw it." Maggie looked down and picked a book up off the desk.
The Spine Witch, by Dora del Río. It was a small edition, barely bigger than Maggie's hand, printed on beautiful creamy paper, the type
letterset in the blackest of inks. The frontispiece was an etching by
Juan. The publisher was Rincon Press. Maggie looked up at Dora. "So
you're a writer," she said.

Dora flushed. "Not like you are. I just make up my own books. Little
limited editions like that one. The Spine Witch is an image from one of
Davis Cooper's poems—well, you know that. He gave me permission
to write a story about her. It's kind of a children's story."

Maggie took the book over to the table. "What do you mean, you're
not a writer like I am? A writer is a writer. What's Rincon Press?"

"Oh that. That's me as well. They have an old letter press at the
back of the gallery that I use to set the books. I learned about print-
ing and hand-binding from a class at the university. I even made the
paper—it's got bits of cactus spines embedded in it, see?"

"And you don't think you're an artist? Girl, you've got a modesty
problem. This is lovely work."

Dora shrugged, turning her back to Maggie as she cooked. "It's
just . . . well, you know how it is. We've been concentrating on getting
Juan's painting career off the ground. When that happens, then I'll
have the time to do a few things myself." She turned suddenly. "That
sounds terrible doesn't it? Like I've no life or ambition of my own.
But I honestly enjoy supporting what Juan is doing. When I look at
his paintings and then at my little books, the books just don't seem as
important. He's a very gifted painter."

"I used to think that way," Maggie told her. "I supported my ex-husband all through the lean years at the beginning of his career. I stopped writing poetry and hustled my butt getting every magazine assignment I could. Cooper was furious with me but I wouldn't listen; I was in love, and ready to join that long tradition of the little woman behind the great man, god help me."

"Then what happened?" Dora asked her over the hiss of batter hitting the grill.

"I think I had this romantic vision of being The Artist's Muse—but instead I was just The Hardworking Wife. And the muses were all the ladies that my husband had on the side. The ones that didn't fuss about electric bills. We broke up right before he made it big."

"Oh yeah?"

"Nigel Vanderlin; have you ever heard of him? He's the director of Estampie."

"What's a stampy?" Dora said, the spoon in her hand dribbling batter onto the floor.

"An Early Music group. It's been quite successful. Who would have thought that medieval music would end up on the Billboard charts? Not me, anyway. I thought Nigel would be like all my poet friends: known by a handful of people who care for the stuff, and thoroughly ignored by all the rest."

"So he made it big, and then he went and left you? What a rat," said Dora with disgust.

Maggie shook her head. "Nigel's not so bad. Leaving the marriage was my idea. And ever since he came into money he's been trying his best to help me out. But the thing is, I hate it. I don't know why. He considers it perfectly reasonable to give something back after living off me, but it makes me uncomfortable all the same. There's freedom in earning your own living."

"If he's not a rat, then why did you leave?" Dora asked her curiously. "The ladies on the side, I suppose?"

"For a lot of different reasons, really. One of them was that he was unfaithful, but that was only part of it—the easiest thing to pin it on," she answered Dora honestly. "The truth is more complex than that. Our unspoken assumption that Nigel was the 'real artist' in the family was at the core of what went wrong between us. So you be careful of that, you hear?"

"I hear you," Dora said with a smile. "And I'll think about what you've said."

Maggie smiled back at the younger woman. She had that feeling one got on rare occasions that here was a friend returned from a long absence instead of stranger newly met, and one could plunge right into real conversation without the months of small talk first. When it happened this way, these were the friendships she found she tended to keep—unlike the other kind, the fleeting ones that came and went like the ocean tide, dependent on such transient things as a shared neighborhood, a class, a job; chance meetings in foreign cafes; the rolling dice of circumstance.

Juan came out of the bathroom then, his dark hair wet, smelling of soap, tucking the tails of his paint-streaked denim shirt into his jeans. He kissed Dora on the top of the head and poured himself a cup of coffee.

"Good morning," he said to Maggie. "Did you sleep all right on the couch?"

"Just fine. I had a furry foot warmer all night. I've missed having cats around; my own cat is still back in L.A."

"Well, take some of ours," Juan said magnanimously, ignoring the murderous look Dora shot him. "We used to have just one, fat old Moose there. Then she had kittens and somehow we never gave any of them away. I suppose we should be grateful Moose didn't have a dozen."

"Ignore him," said Dora. "He makes out he doesn't want them, but he's the one we have to blindfold every time we pass a FREE KITTENS sign. I wanted to leave Moose with my sister in Vermont because of all the coyotes around here. *He's* the one who wouldn't leave her behind."

"She's an excellent mouser," Juan protested.

"So are the coyotes," said Dora.

"And she'd miss us," said Juan, in a smaller voice.

Dora smiled. "Admit it. It's you who would miss her, not the other way around. Moose loved those woods in Vermont."

"Juan," Maggie said, "your paintings of Vermont are beautiful. I'd love to see your studio." She saw a wary look pass between Juan and Dora, and she added, "If that's all right?"

"Of course," Juan said a little too heartily. "You can take a quick look while we wait for Fox."

Dora looked troubled, and Maggie was sorry then that she had asked him. Perhaps his dissatisfaction with his old work extended to his new work as well.

She followed Juan over a cobbled yard to an old stone barn that reminded her of England—except here there was no green covering of thick ivy and old rose vines. Just the grey granite stones, the inevitable cactus, a scattering of red desert poppies. The morning air was crisp and fresh, but soon it would warm up again. A haze lay on the mountain peaks, promising another hot day.

Inside, the barn was spacious but the studio was crowded nonetheless, with tables, easels, shelves of fat art books, sketchbooks, pigments, sculpting tools, buckets of plaster and clay. Raw linen canvas was draped over the rafters; the floor was covered with bright splashes of paint. Walking into an art studio always gave Maggie pangs of jealousy. The tools of writing seem so much less romantic. Her computer. Her printer. A stack of fanfold paper. A legal pad of scribbled notes.

The room had a familiar turpentine smell that would always mean *Tat* and *London* to her. The walls were covered with drawings on large sheets of creamy paper: spiral designs and Celtic knotwork rendered in smudged black charcoal. Some were simple repetitions of patterns, others had images trapped inside: rabbits, deer, foxes, owls whose shapes were rendered as part of the overall pattern, tucked into the intricate designs. The entire effect, from one angle of the room, was a bit like Morris wallpaper. From another, it was simply obsessive, disturbing, although Maggie couldn't say why.

She looked instead at the canvas on the easel. It was streaked with pale ghosts of color. She realized its image had been wiped away by the paint-soaked rag discarded on the floor. The other canvases in the room were blank, or had their faces turned to the wall. On the table was a single sculpture, and Maggie moved closer to see it.

It was the image of a man with the horns of a stag, formed from some kind of plaster or clay of a terra-cotta color. Unlike the other work in the room, this was in fact a breathtaking piece. It, too, was disturbing, but compellingly so. The body was crudely rendered, a simple cylinder, roughly textured and wrapped with knotted leather cords from which hung hagstones, copper beads, and a single feather, pure white. A pattern of simple spirals ran around the figure's base. From the shoulders up, the figure had been more realistically sculpted, the slanted eyes, the thin, stern face with lines etched across the cheeks. Stag horns arced from the figure's brow, carved of mesquite wood.

She swallowed and found her voice again. "This is extraordinary, Juan."

But the sculptor frowned and shook his head. "It's still not right. I just can't get it right. I'll have to keep working on it."

"No," she said quickly, surprising herself by the vehemence in her voice. "Don't. Sometimes you just have to stop. This is finished, don't you see that?"

She wondered if he would take offense, but Juan frowned and considered this. "Who was it," he asked, "who said a work of art is never finished, merely abandoned? Maybe you're right. Maybe it's time for me to abandon it."

Relief flowed through her; she did not know why. Yet she knew that this work should not be changed. "Is it for sale?" she asked carefully.

Juan looked startled. "Why? Do you want it? Take it then. If it's here, I know that I'll keep messing with it. It would be good of you to take it away. Consider it a housewarming present."

"Are you certain? I don't—"

He cut off her protest. "I'm certain. But it's still drying, so you'll have to handle it carefully. And don't think you're getting it scot-free, mind you. Dora is going to make you sign every one of your books that she's got in the house—and probably ten for Christmas presents as well."

The young man smiled, his mood changing, as though a great weight had been lifted. The tension left his smooth, brown face; the smile he gave her was sweet, and teasing.

"It's a deal," she said. "And thank you. I promise to give your deer man a good home." At least for as long as she stayed here, she thought as she walked back to the kitchen with Juan. And then what on earth would she do with it? She was in the habit of traveling light. Well, she wasn't going to worry about that now; she was too pleased with the gift.

Fox's truck was parked in the yard, and the man himself was in the kitchen. He joined them for breakfast as Dora had predicted, downing more pancakes than Maggie would have thought possible considering his lanky physique. When they finished, Juan carefully packed the sculpture up and Fox put it in the back of his truck. Maggie signed copies of her books, surprised to find Dora even owned her old poetry editions. She borrowed a copy of Dora's *Spine Witch,* then she set off for the Alders' with Fox.

Maggie looked back at the stag man's box anxiously as they bumped along the heavily rutted road. She hoped it would survive the trip. It was a haunting creature, with those thin, scarred cheeks, those slanted eyes full of secrets. It reminded her of the man on the hill, whose beautiful face had carried similar lines. That man had turned up in her dreams last night, she remembered suddenly.

In the dream his chest had been painted with spirals that dipped to the curve of his belly, his hips, and the soft, paler skin above his groin. She felt her cheeks flush, remembering the heat of the dream, its stark eroticism. She could still taste his kisses, as though they had actually happened in waking life. Good lord. How would she meet him again without stammering with her embarrassment? She wondered who the stranger was and she put the question to Fox.

"Native American? Long black hair?"

"Well—part Native American anyway."

"Then you mean Tomás. Your other tenant."

"He's my tenant? The auto mechanic?"

"That's right. Your description sounds like him. Tomás is Tohono

O'odham on one side of the family; Navajo and Anglo on the other. You met him on that upper ridge on the trail that runs above his house?"

"Yes. Does he live all alone up there?"

Fox nodded. "He's got a married daughter in Flagstaff, and an ex-wife on the San Xavier Reservation. And other family all over the place. But he lives here on his own."

"He has a grown daughter? He didn't seem that old."

"Well, he was pretty young when he had her, I reckon. But I don't really know how old Tomás is. It's not the sort of thing you ask people. I wonder why? How old are you, then?"

"Me?" she said, startled. "I just turned forty."

"An excellent age," said Fox.

"So how old are you?" she asked, amused.

"Seventy-three going on six," he told her. "Or thirty-five. Take your pick."

"Thirty-five? I thought you were younger than that," she said, hanging on to the door of the truck as they flew up the rutted dirt road. In cowboy boots, an old flannel shirt, and jeans so ripped that his knees showed through, he could either pass for a college student or else a rock musician. He wore a silver Hopi bracelet on his arm, and a gold earring glinted in one ear.

"Hmmm," Fox said, "I don't think that's a compliment." He wheeled around a drainage ditch and then a fallen paloverde limb.

She shrugged. "But doesn't everyone want to look younger these days?"

"I guess. Damned if I know why. So you've got me figured for a callow youth, do you?"

She smiled. "I haven't got you figured at all."

"Good," he said. "A man of mystery. That's better than a callow youth."

The dirt road came to a sudden dead end where a forestry sign marked the beginning of the trail that ran along Redwater Creek. On the left of the road was a narrow drive that wound back deep into the hills. The drive crossed over Coyote Creek on a crumbling humpbacked bridge of stone. At the end of the drive was a white adobe wall with a single low wooden door. A brass bell hung by the door. Fox rang it, and they went inside.

Within the wall was a sprawling Hispanic ranch house of white-washed adobe. It had a red tiled roof and a peaceful courtyard shaded by a desert willow tree, with a crude wooden bench beneath. A delicate deer, barely bigger than a good-sized dog, sat in the shade of the tree. It regarded them calmly with wide, dark eyes as they crossed the yard, the wooden porch, and knocked on a rustic door.

The man who came in answer to their knock was tall and burly—a leathery old cowboy in dusty denims and a worn Stetson hat. "Come on through," John Alder said to them. "Lilli is in the back garden. We've got a sick raccoon back there she's trying to give medicine to."

As they crossed through the ranch house, Maggie got an impression of many large rooms with tiled floors, thick adobe walls, and high corbel ceilings—a tranquil place, shadowed and cool, old, and somewhat run-down. And then they were through the house and out the back door into another walled garden.

Here it seemed almost tropical. There were flowers growing in lush profusion and an oval pool of water reflecting the cottony morning clouds. A couple of dogs were dozing in the shade of a swaybacked mesquite tree. The whinny of horses sounded from somewhere behind the adobe garden wall. "Hi girls," Fox called, and Maggie heard the horses whinny again.

Lillian Alder was a wiry old woman, her grey hair pulled back into a braid, dressed in well-worn denims like her husband and fancy hand-tooled cowboy boots. She was not a small woman like Dora, but beside her huge husband she seemed as if she was. She held a tiny raccoon in her lap, and an eyedropper in her hand.

"He's falling asleep now," she said, nodding at the raccoon. "I don't want to rise and disturb him. John, can you fetch some iced tea for these kids?"

"I'll be right back," he said.

"What's wrong with him?" Maggie asked her.

"With John? Shoot, he's always been that way. *Loco.*" The older woman tapped her head. "Naw, I know, you mean Mr. Raccoon here. He lost a foot in a trap, is what. And now it's gone gotten infected. So you must be Maggie. Welcome to Tucson. How do you like the desert?"

"Well," Maggie said carefully as she sat down, "I'm not really sure yet. It's interesting. Very different from anything I'm used to."

"I was born and raised here, so this is the norm I compare everything else to. I feel closed in everywhere but the desert. So where is it you're from then, gal?"

"West Virginia, originally. But I haven't lived there for years. California is where I was last, and London is where I've spent the most time."

"London." The old woman's expression grew wistful. "I've always wanted to go to London to visit Kew Gardens, but shoot, the farthest east I ever got was Texas. Did you ever go to Kew Gardens?"

Maggie admitted she hadn't.

"Lillian used to be a botanist," said Fox.

"I'm retired, Fox, I'm not dead yet. Once a botanist, always a botanist. It's part of the hardwiring, like breathing."

"Do you work with desert plants? It must be an unusual environment to study," said Maggie.

"It's fascinating, really. The Sonoran desert is utterly unique. Take these big saguaro cactus. They don't grow anywhere else in the world but here. It takes them almost three hundred years to grow that tall."

"And it takes housing developers three minutes and a single bulldozer to bring them down," muttered Fox.

"Now, now," said Lillian, scowling at Fox, "I don't like what's happening in the valley any more than you do. But even developers don't knock down mature saguaro. It's highly illegal, and you know it."

"No," he conceded, "they dig them up and sell them to garden centers in L.A. And then they strip the rest of the land down to bare soil, and plant a goddamn lawn."

"I did see an awful lot of building going on when I was driving here from the airport," Maggie said. "Those horrible cookie-cutter housing developments, like the worst of southern California."

"That's no coincidence," said Fox. "A lot of these developers are from California. They come in from out of state because Tucson has been targeted as a 'good market.' They ruin our desert, pocket the money, and hightail it out again. Wiping out in a few months what took thousands of years to create."

Lillian said, "That's true, I'm afraid. I've spent over sixty years in Tucson, and I'll tell you Maggie, it's changed more in the last ten years than in the whole fifty before that. It makes me mad looking at those butt-ugly houses every time I drive into town. It only makes it worse remembering there used to be groves of mesquite and iron-wood there."

"And yet somebody's buying those houses," Fox said, leaning back in his lawn chair with his long legs crossed before him. One of the Alder dogs roused itself to come sit at Fox's knee. He scratched the dog behind the ears, and a grin spread across the canine face.

"Some people just don't know any better," Lillian said. "There ought to be some kind of test you have to take before you can live in the desert—to make sure you really want to live *here,* and not to turn it into New Jersey."

"Then I would have been stopped at the border," Maggie admitted. "I've always been an ocean lover, myself. This land is completely alien to me."

Lillian looked at her through narrow eyes. "Give it time. This mountain wanted you here," the older woman said cryptically.

Maggie, amused, just smiled.

"So," Lillian said, changing the subject and shifting the raccoon to her other knee, "Fox tells us you're a writer?"

"That's right. And did he tell you I'm planning to write a biography of Davis Cooper? Davis knew I wanted to, and now he's left all his papers to me. I'm assuming this means I have his blessing. You and your husband must have known him for many years. Would you be willing to talk to me about him?"

"I don't see why not. Leastwise, as it seems it's what Cooper would have wanted. But let me speak to John about it first. Today I gather you've come over here to talk about the man's favorite subject? Be careful. You get him started on coyotes and you may have to stay the night."

"I heard that," said John as he came out of the house with a tray of four glasses and a sweating glass pitcher. He set it on the table, pulled up a chair, and sat down beside his wife.

Fox reached over and handed him the plastic container of scat that he carried. "This is what we wanted to show you. Something got into Cooper's house last night. The tracks on the floor looked canine to me, but none of them were clear enough to identify precisely. Juan reckons something may have come in after some smaller animal—there was a bit of furniture knocked over, some scratching, a lot of leaves and debris. Then in Cooper's office there was urine, as if the territory had been marked. And a lot of this stuff. I mean *a lot*. Not just one or two animals in there."

John looked at the container, and sniffed it. "What did it smell like in the room?"

"Unpleasant." Fox shrugged.

"Just unpleasant?"

"Pungent. The way dog shit smells when it's fresh."

John looked at the container, puzzled. "Can I keep this? I hate to admit it since I'm an old hand at tracking, but I can't tell you what this is. I'd like to take it down to the university lab, see what they think. I can tell you what this isn't, though. It's not coyote scat."

"No?" Maggie said.

John shook his head. "You say there was a lot of urine? If it had been coyotes, the smell would have knocked you right out of your socks. It's like ammonia—completely overpowering. Besides which, coyotes don't behave like that. They're not going to go into a strange human habitat. We're their primary predator; they're much too smart, and too wary. At a guess I'd say you had someone's dogs in there. It wasn't our two; they're too old for that kind of mischief. I don't imagine it was Bandido either. Maybe someone came up the mountain with some dogs."

"That's an unsettling thought," said Fox. "Why would a stranger send dogs in there?"

John shrugged. "Maybe just some hunter's hounds, running game into the house and trying to flush it back out again."

"A hunter?" Fox said, his expression alert. "What about our young friend, that cretin I had the run-in with?"

"Well now, I *have* spotted him around—down there by Redwater Springs. But he doesn't run any dogs, does he? Still, you never can tell," said John.

"Is there hunting permitted here in the canyon?" Maggie asked.

"No there isn't, but that never stops a determined poacher," Lillian said with disgust. "So you be careful, back in the mountains."

"You know," Maggie told them, "I'm actually glad to hear it wasn't coyotes. I like seeing them around."

"So do we," said Lillian. "They're beautiful creatures, aren't they? God's Dog, that's what the Indians call them."

"And Trickster," said John. "In our local legends, they're sometimes the hero, sometimes the villain, and most often a kind of divine Fool."

Maggie said, "I saw one up close in the yard yesterday morning, right up beside the house."

"Skinny little fellow? With one bad eye?" John asked her. "I know the one. He's been around here too. He visits Cody, our tame coyote."

"You have a tame coyote?"

"Well, as tame as coyotes ever get, which isn't very," Lillian put in. "They're wild creatures. They're built to be alert and wary; too independent for domestication. But Cody's different. She's nervous of strangers but she's come to trust John and me, in her fashion."

"Would you like to meet her?" John asked Maggie.

"I sure would. If that's all right?"

"You go on, old man," said Lillian. "I'll stay here with the 'coon."

John led Fox and Maggie through a gate in the wall, past a stable and back to a series of outbuildings enclosed by fenced-in runs. The runs contained animals of various kinds, a pair of mule deer, a tiny kit fox, a pronghorn antelope with a splint on its leg, an eagle with only one wing.

"We belong to a wildlife rescue and rehabilitation group," John explained. "People call up with sick or injured critters on their land, our doc fixes them up, and then we supply four-star hotel service until they're ready to be reintroduced into the wild."

"This is their idea of a quiet retirement," Fox told Maggie, "hand-feeding wild animals, and fishing drunk teenagers out of the creek."

"Damn straight. What are we supposed to do? Put our feet up and watch the TV? Look here, this is our litter of bobcat kittens. Aren't they the prettiest little gals you ever saw? Some big brave idiot shot their mama. Trophy hunter. Just took the head and left the rest, including the kits. They were still trying to suckle. We've had them for a couple of weeks now—we lost the little male at the beginning but his sisters look like they're going to make it. They're so dern cute Lilli wants to bring them in the house—but of course we can't. I don't want them to get too comfortable with humans, seeing as what humans did to their mama."

While Fox slipped off to say hello to the horses, John led Maggie to a low shed at the end of the row of cages. The run behind it was so large that an entire mesquite tree was fenced inside.

"This is where Cody lives during the day," John said. "At night she comes into the house. Sleeps at the foot of the bed like a pup, along with the two dogs. She's crippled; she'll never make it back in the wild, so she's become part of the family."

At the sound of John's voice, a slim and golden coyote came up to the edge of the fence, then backed away nervously when Maggie approached, her amber eyes alarmed.

"It's all right, Cody," John told her, "Maggie's just come to tell you how pretty you are."

Cody kept wary eyes on Maggie, but she edged around closer to John, presenting her hind quarters for him to scratch through the wire fence. When he'd hit the right spot, an unmistakable expression of bliss covered her face. She would indeed have been a handsome animal, with soft, tawny fur and a pure white muzzle. But she hobbled along, dragging one lame leg, and her long fluffy tail had been bobbed.

"She's an unusual creature," John told Maggie. "You generally can't keep coyotes like a dog or even certain wolf breeds. They're too nervous. People take 'em in as pups, and then throw 'em out again when—surprise!—they grow up into wild animals."

"She is beautiful, isn't she? Despite the leg."

"In the wild they're gorgeous creatures. They run together in family groups, and generally have just one mate for life—they're enormously loyal creatures that way. Not like dogs, who'll mate with dern near anything that presents its backside. Sometimes at night what you're hearing is a male and a female singing together, just for the sheer pleasure of it. It's a different sound from their hunting cry. Makes me smile just to hear them."

Maggie watched with a bit of envy as the coyote rubbed against the big man with obvious affection. But when Maggie tried to step closer, Cody jumped back again, breathing hard.

Suddenly Cody spied Fox returning from the stable, and bounded over toward him. For all John's words about wild creatures, she looked exactly like an excited dog, wagging her bobbed tail and grinning broadly as Fox came near her run.

"She's always had a soft spot for Fox," John commented. "Animals love him, it's the damnedest thing. But Cody's smart. I reckon she knows that he's the one who saved her life."

Maggie watched the coyote greet Fox, raining kisses on his extended hand. "How did he do that?"

"Well now, some fool cowboy shot her in that leg there. Fox is the one who found her, and he got her to the doc in time."

"I watched her get shot," Fox said bitterly, coming over to stand beside them, the coyote trailing behind him on the other side of the fence. "I was watching two coyotes trotting down the wash, a pair that we've known around here for years. It was just after the heat had broke and they were all frisky, enjoying themselves. Then I saw a stranger pointing a gun. I yelled, and the other coyote got away but Cody here wasn't fast enough. She went down and I thought he'd killed her.

"I ran over, and found that she had taken the bullet in the leg. I was thinking I needed to find John, get some help, when I realized the stranger was coming over too. A young guy—brand new shotgun in his hand, laughing, a big smile on his face. He says 'Guess I showed that sonuvabitch, huh?' and slaps my back like he's some kind of hero. And before I can get a word out he's grabbed her tail and he's cut it off. She's not even dead and he's claiming his trophy." Fox's voice was clipped with anger. "When I yelled at him to get off our goddamn land, he backed off like *I* was the dangerous lunatic when *he* was the one carrying the gun. He left all right, but we've seen him around here several times since then."

"He's either PRC," John said, "or he's a poacher after the deer and the coyotes are target practice. Either way, he's got no business here."

"What's PRC?" Maggie asked him.

"Predator and Rodent Control. Your tax dollars at work. It's a federally funded agency—millions of bucks poured into it each year. Not into educating or feeding hungry youngsters, mind you," the old man growled, "but into wiping out whole species of animals because you can't make a profit on 'em like ranch stock or hunters' game."

John took off his Stetson, wiping the sweat from his brow. The morning sun was already growing strong, burning the haze from the mountaintop. When he put the hat back on again the coyote startled at the movement. She jumped back, eyed the three of them, then slowly edged back to the fence, her head held low as if embarrassed.

John squatted down to stroke the nervous animal. "I used to be a PRC man myself years ago," he said, looking up at Maggie. "I grew up on a cattle ranch in Wyoming and I should have known better than that. Coyotes never bothered healthy stock and they kept the rodent population in check. My daddy, and *his* daddy, raised us kids to treat 'em with respect. But there was good money working for PRC, so I chose to believe all the guff they spread: that coyotes kill off whole sheep herds, or will bring down healthy cows and deer. It was all a scam. No one ever cared about coyotes when PRC was after wolves. But the wolves were all killed off, so we needed another predator to holler about, otherwise the agency would have been shut down." He stood again. "When PRC killed coyotes and pups in a given area, we were always careful to leave at least one good breeding couple alone.

Because if sheep ranchers stopped spotting coyotes, we would all be out of a job."

Maggie looked at the rancher curiously. "You used to make a living killing coyotes?"

"Yes ma'am. And bobcats, and hawks, and eagles, and little kit foxes no bigger than a pussycat. American sheepmen pay a bounty for those things rather than hire shepherds to look after their stock like they goddamn ought to, 'scuse my French. Shoot, there's people who'll kill the critters in one state and drive them over to the next where fool ranchers pay good bounty money."

"And now you're doing wildlife rehabilitation? That's quite a transition, John. Seems to me there must be an interesting story there."

John stood and gave her a terse little smile. "Well maybe I'll tell you that story someday. But I warn you, it's not a pretty one. Or one that I'm very proud of."

The old man turned back to the house. Cody trailed him as far as she could on her side of the wire fence. Maggie looked thoughtfully at the mutilated coyote, dragging one lame leg in the dust. Then she followed after the rancher, Fox walking silent behind.

"They're an interesting couple," she said to Fox later, as he maneuvered his truck down the Alders' drive. On the seat between were several books about the desert and coyotes that she'd borrowed from John.

He shot her a look. "Do you always think like a journalist, then? Is everyone a potential story?"

She looked at him closely, trying to determine if this was criticism or no. "I've always been interested in people," she said a bit defensively. "In who they are and how they got that way. It didn't come from being a journalist, but it's a trait that helped when I was."

"You say that in the past tense."

"Well, it's been some years since I've worked for magazines. The books I've published since are nonfiction, but they're personal essays rather than journalism. Mind you, I'm not sure where exactly you draw the line between the two. Davis never did. As long as it wasn't poetry, it didn't count."

"Dora said you wrote poetry." Fox shot her another unreadable look.

"Wrote. Past tense. She's quite correct." Maggie said the words lightly, but felt tension in her shoulders nonetheless.

This time the look he gave her was thoughtful. "Do you prefer writing prose, then?"

"I'd prefer to be writing poetry, or both," Maggie answered him frankly. "But it's been twenty years since I was a 'rising young poet'—and that's an awful long time. I turned to magazines to make a living, and then I stopped thinking like a poet, I guess. As you said, I think like a journalist now. I'm still trying to determine if the condition is reversible."

Fox frowned. "Then do you share Cooper's view that being a poet is the only valid thing to be?"

"No," she said, shaking her head, "I'm proud of my books, no matter what he thought." She looked across at Fox, eyes narrowed. "What's your opinion? For someone who's not a journalist, you're good at asking personal questions."

"Me? I'm continuing an old argument," he told her with a self-mocking smile. "I'm still arguing with Cooper's ghost. But it's as stubborn as he always was. Nothing mattered but poetry to Cooper. Maybe painting, because that was Anna's art. Not people. He lived in his poems, not in the world, for the last forty years of his life."

Fox shifted gears, lurching over the ruts. His eyes were shadowed, his face serious.

"You know all those poems and quotes he wrote all over his office walls?" he asked her. "The day I left the mountain the last time, I came in when Cooper wasn't there and wrote another quote on his door. From Katherine Paterson. You've heard of her? She said: *'If we marvel at the artist who has written a great book, we must marvel more at those people whose lives are works of art and who don't even know it, who wouldn't believe it if they were told. However hard work good writing may be, it is easier than good living.'*"

Maggie said, "I saw that written on the door. I noticed it was a different handwriting."

"And did you notice what he'd written beneath it? No? Just one small word: *Touché*. The last word I ever had from Cooper. When I came back he was dead."

Maggie turned to look at him again and Fox gave her an unconvincing smile. He pulled the truck beside Maggie's car, parking in the shade of the cottonwood. He turned off the engine, and climbed from the truck, slamming the door behind him.

Fox took out his tools and began to remove the lock from the door of the back room. As he did so, Maggie and Dora set to work scrubbing the mud from the kitchen floor. Lillian turned up just a few minutes later, announcing she was there to help.

Fox paused for a moment in his work to listen to the women at theirs, laughter ringing through the dusty old house. He enjoyed the sound of women's voices, the effortless talk that bound them together. He'd grown up silent on the mountain; talk was a thing that had come hard to him. Words in his world had been scarce and precious, reserved for the poetry page.

His mother had been a reserved little woman, and his two sisters equally quiet and shy. He searched his memory and couldn't remember them gossiping together or laughing out loud. Theirs had been a hushed household. His sisters were like wild deer, like poems in motion on the mountainside. Fox was the one who had clattered and clumped and broke things and made all the noise.

The Alders had lived down in Tucson then, but they came up every weekend, filling the Big House with seven loud children and the tumult of normal family life. The six Alder daughters had frightened Fox; he'd hide from them, as shy as his sisters. Now he preferred strong, talkative women. If Lillian had been a generation younger he'd have fallen in love, John or no John; yet none of her daughters were quite her match. Emma, the youngest, had been his lover, but it was friendship between them now, nothing more.

The lock mechanism came apart at last. Fox looked thoughtfully at the scarred wood door, resisting the strong impulse to push it open. He went to help the women finish up, and only when the rest of the kitchen was put to rights did they gather around the back-room door.

"You go in," Maggie said, nudging Fox's shoulder. "Go on. Go in first. I haven't been waiting thirty years for this."

Fox took a deep breath. He pushed the door. It moved stiffly on the hinges, groaning. Inside, the air was stale, filled with dust. The room was dark, the windows heavily curtained. He found a light switch and turned it on. The bulbs were old, but they still worked, filling the room with an amber glow.

The room had been an art studio. Anna Naverra's, Fox realized. It looked like Cooper hadn't moved a thing in all the years since Anna had died. The long tables still held scattered sketchbooks and dusty tubes of dried-out paint. Brushes stood in jars with their stiff bristles down, adhered to the rust-colored residue caked at the bottom. Old postcards from art museums were curling away from their tacks on the walls. The small room was crowded with canvases, watercolor studies and smudged chalk sketches. Piled in one corner were the pictures that had hung for years on the walls of Cooper's house. But why had he moved them all right before he died, when his death was so sudden?

Lillian came into the room behind Maggie. "I thought that's what you'd find in here. I thought he would have kept her things. Cooper was a romantic at heart, and he fell apart when Anna died."

"Did you know her?" Maggie asked Lillian.

"Not very well. None of us did. Anna and Cooper kept to themselves. And I wasn't here much in those years. I was nineteen when they came to the mountain, and I'd just moved north to marry John. But what I remember is the change that had come over Cooper when I moved back here. This was after Anna was gone. Cooper was a different man then. Lost without her. But driven somehow. He was writing the 'Wood Wife' poems like there were devils hanging on his tail."

"*After* she died?" Maggie said. "I thought he wrote them when they lived together."

"Oh no," said the older woman firmly. "I remember when Cooper started working on them. I'd inherited the Big House by then, and John had come with me back down to Tucson. Why? Does it matter when he wrote them?"

"In terms of literary scholarship, yes. The assumption has always been that her pictures with the same imagery were illustrations of his poems."

"And not that the paintings may have come first. I see," said Lillian.

Dora said, "I can think of a lot of feminist scholars who would love to hear about that." She was bent down by a shelf of books. She pulled one out and opened it, biting her lip as she turned the pages. She looked up at Maggie. "There are journals here. Full of sketches, mostly, and notes for compositions. But there are also long hand-written blocks of text. Do you read Spanish, Maggie? Maybe when you've finished your book on Cooper you might do one on Anna Naverra."

Fox said to Dora, "Do you remember when that woman from the Tucson Art Museum was trying to get some of Anna's paintings to exhibit?"

"Yeah, and Cooper all but ran her off the mountain with a shotgun. There was something he was protecting in here."

"His reputation," Lillian muttered. "He won the Pulitzer for *The Wood Wife* and I don't recall Anna's name ever being mentioned."

"It was *Exile Songs* he won the Pulitzer for," Maggie corrected her. "His collection of poems about the war. People think it was for *The Wood Wife* because that's the book he became famous for. But it came out after *Exile Songs* and the critics didn't like it one bit. It was too full of fairy-tale allusions—and the popularity of it with the general public didn't help his credibility in poetry circles. In fact it was the kiss of death."

Fox said, "So whatever he was hiding here wasn't his reputation. Because by that time he didn't have as much of a critical reputation left to lose."

Dora stood, still holding the journal and looking flushed, excited. "It's going to be fascinating, don't you think, to pore through all of this and piece the truth of their lives back together? If you want help,

Maggie, just say so. My Spanish isn't as fluent as Juan's, but I'd give it a go."

"Thanks. I may take you up on that," she said, "since I don't speak Spanish myself." She was looking through the piled canvases, an expression of wonder on her face.

Dora came over to stand beside her. "Are you going to put the paintings back up in the house? It looks strange here without them."

"Which ones did he have up?" she asked.

Lillian said, "Never mind Cooper. This is your house now. You should hang the ones that you like best. Assuming you like Anna's work?"

"Heavens, yes," said Maggie. "I'm just a little stunned, that's all. I knew Cooper had left me his own work—I didn't realize till I got here that he'd also left me hers."

Fox crossed his arms and looked at the paintings, relieved to find that they were indeed here. It had frightened him to think they might be missing. They belonged on this mountain. Cooper had been right about that, although he couldn't say why. And there were more of them in storage here than Fox had ever expected. Anna had died young, and he'd never imagined that she'd been so prolific.

Fox moved to help Maggie pull more paintings down from a wooden storage loft. The paintings were beautiful, full of rich color, dreamlike images and juxtapositions rendered in the vivid detail that was typical of the Mexican Surrealist style. Owls, moths, clocks, towers, trees with leaves the color of silver coins, floors made of spiral-patterned tiles that dissolved into desert sand: these were common Naverra images that appeared again and again in her work. Maggie looked them over with evident pleasure. And then Fox heard her catch her breath.

The oil painting she held showed the figure of a man standing in the desert, surrounded by the faintly pencilled lines of a circle of slit-eyed coyotes, each holding the tail of the one before it in a mouth full of sharp canine teeth. The man was striking, with long black hair and eyes of an unusual shade of green. His cheeks were etched with pale blue lines. Spirals circled one outstretched wrist. He was pouring water onto the sand; where it hit the ground it burst into flame.

"What is it, Maggie?" Lillian asked. She came over to look at the painting. "Well I'll be," she said, looking startled herself. "I didn't know Anna had painted him. But no, she couldn't have. No, that doesn't make sense."

"Couldn't have painted who?" Fox said.

Lillian looked at him and hesitated. "It's just that he looks like a man I met here once. Years after Anna had died. Cooper introduced him as Mr. Foxxe. I believe he was your father."

"Your father?" said Maggie, and the confusion in her voice matched the feeling in Johnny Foxxe's heart.

He'd never really believed in Mr. Foxxe. He had come to believe that they were really Cooper's illegitimate children, and that Mr. Foxxe was just a story. Now suddenly he didn't know what to think. He could see his sisters in this man, maybe even his own bony face. But how had his father known Anna Naverra? His mother hadn't come up to the mountain until nine years after Naverra's death. Unless that had been the story, and Mr. Foxxe had been the truth.

Fox stared at the oil painting before him, trying to make sense of this image, this man. He looked into that half-familiar face, and was not comforted by what he saw.

They sat together by Redwater Creek, their white toes dangled in the water. A hiker passing by never noticed them. Their limbs were as white as a desert sycamore, their hair the silver-green of its leaves. The hiker looked in their direction, but all he saw were two young saplings clinging to the rocky bank.

Below, the water began to smoke. Flames licked the surface of the creek. They quickly pulled up their feet, and laughed. "You don't scare us," the eldest called. Then they put their feet back down again and the flames died out around them.

A woman's face was barely visible beneath the water's surface. Cold black eyes stared up at them. Then the eyes began to close. The water cleared. Now there was just the sandy bottom of Redwater Creek, and the slim, white feet of the two young women. Each had a spiral pattern drawn around the bones of the left ankle.

The eldest rose, and with her help the younger woman got to her feet. As they left the creek, the women changed. Silver-green hair turned gold, then brown; white limbs darkened, kissed by sun, red blood beating under the skin. One wore a white dress. The other's was red; then she changed her mind and was dressed in jeans. They crossed the road and followed the trail that led them through the dry wash bed, the youngest limping as she walked.

The lights went on in the old Foxxe house. Johnny Foxxe's sisters had come home.

DAVIS COOPER
Redwater Road
Tucson, Arizona

The Riddley Wallace Gallery
New York City

August 18, 1948

Dear Riddley,

I can assure you that you are wrong—Anna has not found another gallery. When we send the paintings out they will go only to you and to Veirdas in Mexico City, as always. But I must tell you that it is difficult, right now, for me to persuade her to part with them. The new work is quite . . . personal; and as such, it seems to be difficult for Anna to let the pictures go. After we sent the last crate off, I found her in the studio sobbing. Be patient, old boy. Artists are a sensitive breed and Anna, as you know, is strong-willed as well. She is in a highly nervous state now, and I don't want to push her too far.

The review you sent was interesting in many respects—who is this Richard St. Johns? We don't recognize the name. His ideas on the nature of the Surrealist movement are like a fresh wind in a room grown stale, but when it comes to Anna's work that gust of wind turns to mere hot air. The man is so busy explicating his theories that he has forgotten to look at the paintings.

I know for a fact that Anna has never seen those pieces by Max Ernst; she has never attempted to copy his style; she has never been romantically involved with the man, as Mr. St. Johns implies. (Leonora Carrington was a more formative influence and a better painter besides.) St. Johns disassembles Anna's paintings like so many jigsaw puzzle pieces—but this new work is not a game or intellectual exercise to its maker, I can assure you. Anna left Theories and Surrealist Manifestos behind in Mexico City. The work has changed. She is painting this land. She is obsessed with it. She is rooted in Arizona now as deeply, as firmly as any tenacious desert tree drawing sustenance from the hard, dry soil. When she told you her muse walks in these hills, she spoke the truth, more than you can know. She will not leave. She will not come east for the next show opening either. You must be content with the paintings, old boy. I'll see that she sends them. Be patient.

Yours as ever,
Davis Cooper

Stone, not skin, a face of ivory tattooed
by time, by paint, the
horns rising above his brow, the
steam rising with every step.
    —**The Wood Wife,** *Davis Cooper*

Maggie turned the stereo up loud to cover the banging on the roof. The music of Josquin de Pres filled the house with the sound of medieval instruments. Nigel used to say Josquin's music made him believe in the existence of angels. This was an early Estampie recording, and it was still one of her favorites.

She hummed along with harp and viol as she divided stacks of Davis's papers into Letters, Memos, Bills, Lists, Notes/Poems/Old, Notes/Poems/New. Stacks that had simply grown larger and no less overwhelming over the last two weeks. She paused, holding a phone bill in her hand dated March 1981. This music took her back as many years, when Estampie was still a loose group of musicians moonlighting from their more profitable gigs, gathering to practice in the kitchen of her Amsterdam flat.

She put down the papers suddenly, wondering what on earth she was doing here, on this mountain, in this dry, hard land. She wanted to be sitting in that little cafe at the corner of their old street, with a cup of strong coffee and a glass of cognac, canal boats bobbing gently in the water, tall punked-out Dutch students passing by, and Nigel across the table enthusing about some early-music instrument maker he'd just found.

The phone rang, interrupting these thoughts. Nigel always knew when she was thinking of him. She picked up the receiver and said "Good morning Nigel," and he didn't seem startled by the greeting. "How's New York?"

"I don't know. I'm in a hotel room," he said. "All right, don't be mad, but I just *happened* to be talking to Jennifer at HarperCollins this morning, and so I mentioned what you were up to. She's interested, babe. We're talking six figures here. They're into biography now in New York, and she thinks a book on Davis Cooper could really sell. It's the mystery of it, Cooper's death, and that old business with Naverra."

"Nigel, slow down," Maggie interrupted, feeling swept away by his strong current again. "And don't call me babe. It's Nicole who's babe. Call me that again and I'll break your face."

He sighed. "You're mad."

"Damn straight, I am. I asked you not to talk to Jennifer."

"You've got to strike while the fire is hot, Mags. You know New York. They might not be into biography six months from now."

"That's iron, Nigel."

"What?"

"Strike while the iron's hot. Never mind. I don't know why we're having this conversation. I'm not ready to talk to a publisher."

"Oh." Nigel paused. "Well, I'm afraid Jennifer's going to call you today. No, no, don't hang up on me, Puck. Look, I'm trying to help."

"I know, Nigel," she said, exasperated, tossing her sweet vision of Amsterdam cafes right out the kitchen window. She'd been forgetting the reality of life with Nigel. After enthusing about the instrument maker he would have proceeded to convince her she needed to give him a thousand bucks to buy a crumhorn or something. And then dashed off to meet his latest lover.

"Look," she said, "I know you mean well, but I'm still finding my feet here. And I'd like to do it without interference." *For once in my life,* she added silently. "So why don't you call Jennifer back and tell her I'll call when I'm ready."

"All right," he said in that contrite voice that always won her back again. "So how *is* it going? It must be strange living in a dead man's house."

"You know how it's going. You've called every day since I got here—nothing's changed. Though I'll tell you, it's interesting. Davis Cooper's life is like a jigsaw puzzle that you know probably has a fabulous picture on it—only too many of the pieces are missing. I'm just hoping if I keep at this long enough, I'll be able to fit together the pieces that are left."

"How long is long enough?" he said. "You've been away, what, two weeks now? How long are you going to be on that mountain?"

"I've no idea. But Nige, I meant it. I'm not coming back to L.A. You've got a life with Nicole now."

There was silence on the other end. Then he said, "Damn. You *are* mad. You never bring Nicole into it unless you're really pissed off at me."

"Oh, no worse than usual," she said with a smile. "So cheer up. You've got a concert to do."

It was half an hour later by the time she got off the phone with her ex-husband. The banging overhead had stopped, and Fox was sitting on her porch.

She stood in the doorway. "Do you always make it a habit to listen to phone conversations?"

He shrugged. "I can hear you just as well from the roof. What do you want me to do, go home whenever the phone rings? Or just pretend that I can't hear?"

She stepped onto the porch and sat beside him on the steps. "Sorry, it's my husband I'm irritated with. I shouldn't take it out on you."

"Husband?"

"Ex-husband I mean."

"Not so very ex from the sound of it."

"Not so ex as I'd like. No, I don't mean that. Nigel's a good pal. He just wants to run everybody else's life except his own. And that he hires managers for."

"What is he, some kind of big shot then?"

"Hmmm. Nigel Vanderlin. He's—"

"Estampie."

"That's the one." Maggie squinted at the sun slanting through the cottonwoods. "Look," she said, "there he is."

The skinny coyote trotted up the wash. It stopped to stare at them rakishly, then it leapt the other bank.

Fox said, "John and Lillian lost Cody, did you hear? Not long after we saw her. She got out of the pen, and she hasn't come back. I reckon she will—their ranch is her turf and she can't get far on that leg. But we should keep an eye out for her. I don't want that poacher turning up and finishing off the job."

Maggie nodded, thinking about Cody and wondering how long she would last in the wild. She was glad that this one had managed to survive, despite the loss of his eye. She watched until he disappeared in the brush on the other side of the wash. "Look, he's going in the direction of your mother's old house," she said.

"He's going to check out who's in there. My sisters are here. Angela and Isabella. They turned up again last night."

"Turned up? You weren't expecting them, then."

He shrugged. "I never know when they'll be back. That's just the way they are. They're dancers, with a flamenco troupe, and they spend most of their time on the road. Which is just as well, as that house isn't really fit for habitation. One of these days Mama's going to have to let me fix it up."

"Your sisters are flamenco dancers?"

"That's right. With a small local troupe. Believe me, you never heard of it. It's not the big league, like your ex-husband. Or you, for that matter. Or Cooper. None of us kids ever really wanted fame. Which Cooper never understood."

Maggie looked at him curiously. "Well, fame or no fame, I have to say it's a surprising crew you've got here in the canyon. Dancers. Artists. Wildlife experts. My ex assured me Tucson would be boring."

Fox leaned back against a porch post, shading himself from the midday sun. "In a place this remote, you're not going to find your average nine-to-five commuter types, are you? Dora is the only one who has to commute downtown to a job."

"How long have she and Juan lived here?"

He scratched his chin, thinking. "A couple of years now. Cooper met Dora down at the gallery. Have you been to Book Arts yet? They carry small press poetry editions, so it was one of the old man's favorite haunts. Cooper really hit it off with Dora, and who wouldn't when she's such a sweetheart? She and Juan lived in the Barrio then, and Dora was homesick for the East Coast. She liked the mountain though; maybe because she'd lived in mountains back in Vermont. So Cooper decided he'd sell them the stable. It was just a ruin before."

"What about Tomás? What's his story?" Maggie asked him then, with feigned casualness. She'd had another of those dreams last night. She couldn't quite stop thinking of the man. Fox grinned at her, and she added, "I know. I'm sounding like a journalist again."

"Tomás," said Fox. "Well, Cooper met him some years ago at an AA meeting. Did you know Cooper tried to stop drinking for a while? Tomás stayed clean and Cooper went back to the bottle, but they stayed friends all the same—and then Tomás moved into the upper cabin. The cabins were empty when I was growing up. I don't think Cooper ever used them before."

"According to his letters, he and Anna used to put their houseguests in the cabins. A lot of their European friends came to visit when they first moved here from Mexico City. All kinds of people have been in those cabins: Anaïs Nin, Dalí, Pablo Casals. . . ."

Fox squinted against the sunlight as he turned his head to look at her. "Houseguests? Cooper? I thought they'd always been reclusive—Cooper and Anna both."

Maggie shook her head. "Not at first. Cooper was a real gregarious guy in his youth, a dashing-young-man-about-town type. It was Anna who started turning their friends away after a couple of years in Arizona."

"When she went crazy," Fox said flatly, looking away again in the direction of the wash. The skinny coyote was back now, tracking something in the sandy soil.

Maggie asked, "Is that what Cooper told you?"

Fox frowned. "Cooper didn't talk about Anna. Not to us kids. But that's the impression I got from things other people said, that she went crazy, right? And then they had to lock her up."

Maggie shifted uncomfortably on the wooden step. "I don't know if she was crazy exactly. She had some kind of nervous breakdown, certainly. At which point her parents stepped in, and took her back to Mexico. She wasn't locked up though. She went to a convent—not taking the veil or anything, but living there in retreat from the world. She died a year later—officially of pneumonia, but there has always been speculation that she killed herself." Maggie looked at Fox curiously. "You haven't heard any of this before?"

"The way I heard it, she got very depressed, and then she committed suicide. No one ever really said why. Did Cooper tell you this, or are you finding it in his papers?"

"Neither. I did a profile of Maisie Tippetts years ago for *Harper's*. She'd been part of that circle of Europeans who fled to Mexico during World War II. Maisie had met Cooper in a detention camp in France— you didn't know about that either? That he'd been held by the Nazis?"

Fox shook his head emphatically. "No. In fact, he told me his asthma problems kept him out of the war."

"Well, it kept him out of the army at any rate, but he was living in Paris when the Germans came. Hitler was going after the Surrealists, and Cooper was very tight with that crowd. Maisie and Cooper were fortunate—an organization called the Emergency Rescue Committee got them and a number of other artists out of the camps and then out of the country, just in time. Some of their friends weren't so lucky, and didn't survive.

"Talking to Maisie was when I first had the idea of writing a biography of Cooper," Maggie told Fox. "She and Cooper had stayed friends after the war, and she'd also been very close to Anna. She told me about Anna's breakdown. I don't know what precipitated it, and I never had the nerve to ask Cooper about it. But there's nothing I'm finding now that contradicts the basic facts of what Maisie told me."

Fox groaned and put his head in his hands. In the wash, the coyote pounced suddenly, and then sprang backwards into the air. He held a small rodent in his mouth, which he devoured in one great gulp.

"Are you all right?"

"Ummm," Fox said. "It's just my head is reeling. You think you know someone, and then you turn around one day and everything you thought you knew is wrong. Or not wrong, exactly, but it's all got this color on it, blue, instead of yellow or pink. And so it all looks completely different."

"That's how I felt driving up this mountain," she said, commiserating. He raised his head and looked at her. "Well, I've studied Davis Cooper as an *English* poet. Born and raised in the West Country. So when I read his poems, I see English woods, I see the moor, and hedgerows, and walls of stone. And then I drive up here," she waved her hand at the dry land around them, "and I realize that these are the woods that he's been talking about all along. These hills. This sky. Now I'm reading a whole different set of poems when I look at Cooper's work." She frowned and sighed heavily. "The other ones, the ones I thought I knew, were just in my head."

"That bothers you, does it?" He narrowed his eyes. "I don't get it. What does it matter whose head those images came from? *'Poetry is a conversation not a monologue,'*" Fox quoted Cooper in a passable English accent. "A writer can only put the words on paper; the vision has to come from the reader, right? It's language, not paint, not film. That's the beauty of it to me. Why do your woods, or your Wood Wife, have to look precisely the same as Cooper's?"

"Well, in terms of Miller's work on Cooper—"

"We're not talking literary critique here. We're talking about *poems,* words on a page," Fox said, tapping his knee, "and what those words turn into when they slip inside your brain." He tapped his head. "It's magic; and magic disappears if you try too hard to pin it down."

"I can't leave it at that," Maggie said. "I want to know what Davis was seeing when he wrote those lines—not just what I see when I read them. I want to truly understand the poems."

"Ah," he said, stretching his long legs in front of him, "then you have to go to the land of poetry."

"Goethe," she said.

"That's right. I told you my sisters and I grew up on a steady diet of Cooper's poetry books. Christ, by the time I was ten I could recite Goethe and Wordsworth word for word, yet barely add or subtract. Look, Cooper's land of poetry was a place in his head, all mixed up of England, France, Mexico, Arizona—it was all part of him, and all part of the poems. I don't think he ever separated it: *In this poem I'm talking about the English woods, in this poem I'm talking about the Rincons.* It was like it was all one land for him. In a way he never left England. You'd think, listening to him sometimes, he could walk out his door and be there."

"That's what I can't get my head around. That he could love that and he could love this and the two are so very different. The new poems, the fragments I've found so far, are even more confusing. Time and distance is all broken up, the past and the future all jumbled together."

"Time is a spiral."

"What do you mean?"

"I don't know." He smiled. "I'm just repeating something Cooper used to tell me."

"*'Time is not a river; it flows in two directions,'*" she recited, from one of the *Wood Wife* poems. Maggie frowned, trying to remember it. "*'Time is the land I wander in, through smoke, through sage. A land carved in stone. . . .'*" She squinted at the distant peaks. She couldn't remember how the rest of it went. Then she looked at Fox closely. She said, "There was a critic, back in the fifties, who wrote an essay insisting that all of Cooper's surrealistic metaphors were actually literal descriptions of the hallucinations of a drunk. You said you thought Cooper was crazy yourself. Did you ever think that . . . well, that the 'land of poetry' was a real place to him? That maybe what he was doing was writing about things he'd seen—or thought he'd seen?"

Fox let out a deep exhalation. He hesitated, and seemed to be weighing his words. Then he said, "That's what they say about Anna, you know. That she believed what she painted was real."

"Who is they? Who says that?"

He shook his head. "Maybe my mother told me that. Or Lillian. I don't remember now. But Cooper was a bit like that as he got older. You have to remember, the man was an alcoholic; he could have been seeing little blue Martians and no one around here would have been surprised."

"I've gotten drunken letters from Davis. And I'll tell you, the bits of new poems I'm finding in his notes don't read like the work of a drunk. I still don't have the foggiest idea of why he wouldn't tell anyone he was writing them. And the further I get into his paperwork, the more I don't understand."

Fox gave her a wry look. "Well, join the club. I've been trying to understand that old man for thirty-five years. And all I've done is to find out just how little about him I ever knew." He stood up. "Look, you still want to meet my mother?"

"Yes, I do. Your sisters, too, if I could."

"I'm going to my mother's place today and I'll ask her whether she'll talk to you. I'll be out of here in another hour—then you can make all the phone calls you want."

As if on cue the phone rang again.

Maggie groaned. "That had better not be Nigel," she said as she rose to answer it. She paused. "Thanks, Fox. Talking like this, it helps me sort it out."

Fox smiled. *De nada.* He headed for the ladder to the roof as she stepped into the house.

It wasn't Nigel on the phone. It was Nigel's editor friend, Jennifer, calling from New York and eager to hear all about Cooper's biography. Which Nigel had neglected to mention wasn't even started yet.

In the end, Maggie found herself telling the woman all about the book as she envisioned it—as Nigel had clearly intended. As she did so, she heard Fox banging loudly on the roof over her head.

Fox turned up the radio as he drove down from the Rincons, singing along with Luka Bloom's "Diamond Mountain," slightly out of key. The truck bounced from dirt onto solid paved road, and he switched it out of four-wheel drive. He made the turn onto Wentworth, then followed Speedway into town, watching as the roadside changed from horse ranches and pecan groves into a depressing modern maze of new construction, builders' signs, and bulldozed ground barren of life where his beloved desert used to be. Every six months another piece was gone, and he would never get it back again.

Halfway into town the developments turned into used car lots, fast food joints, and shopping plazas standing half empty. But closer to the city's heart the street turned back into one he enjoyed, lined with old adobe houses, Mission-style and Mexican; houses meant for the desert and built on a smaller, more human scale. Fox maneuvered his truck through the tangled traffic around the university; past the second-generation hippies lingering on the sidewalks of 4th Avenue; under the tunnel and up to Congress Street in the city's small downtown core.

He parked in front of Cafe Magritte, and then walked up to Dora's gallery. He could see her through the plate-glass window, leaning on the counter, looking lovely but tired.

"What are you doing here?" she said as Fox came through the gallery door.

"Have you eaten? I've come to take you out. I'm headed out west to my mother's place and I thought I'd come and bother you first."

"Let me check with Dick and Marie if they can spare me for a while." Dora disappeared into the back while Fox lingered over the handmade book displays and illustrations on the wall. Dora returned a few minutes later, an embroidered velvet purse over her arm. She was dressed in typical Dora style, like some cowgirl Pre-Raphaelite, in a long, full skirt, an antique shirt, her steel-toed boots and a Zuni bolo tie. Fox had the urge to swoop her up and take her dancing just to see that long skirt swing.

He said, "Where do you want to go? Magritte? The Congress Hotel?"

She chose the latter, and they walked together up Congress past the other galleries and shops. The Congress Hotel had been built in the twenties and renovated in the last several years as part of the

Downtown Arts District that sprawled across several city blocks. The hotel was a wild-looking old place, its walls painted mauve and turquoise and covered with bright southwestern designs, its lobby full of old Mission couches and the tables of a small cafe. The bar beyond was a smokey affair filled with students, painters, musicians, and old cowboys. A dance club operated out of the bottom floor, and anyone who stayed overnight in the hotel was treated to wall-shaking music until the wee hours of the morning.

They parked themselves at a table in the lobby, which was nearly empty this late in the afternoon. The waiter was propping up the counter, an Anglo boy with Indian braids, so studiously laid-back he was nearly comatose. He finally deigned to notice them and sauntered over to take their order, as if he was doing the greatest of favors. His cowboy boots were a neon blue so bright they made Fox's wisdom teeth ache, and they looked like they pinched besides.

"Check out the quesadillas," Fox suggested. "They make them with Brie and mango and I know that sounds just too damn hip for words, but it's pretty good."

"Sounds great. Will you share some gazpacho with me?"

"You're on."

The waiter wrote the order down and sauntered slowly away again. It worried Fox that he was not sauntering in the direction of the kitchen.

"This is my treat, by the way," said Fox.

"What did you do, rob a bank?"

He smiled. "I've got a gig tonight. It's good for a few bucks."

"Which band this time?"

"I'm sitting in with Diamondback Rattlers, down at the Cushing Street Bar."

"What do they play?"

"A little bit of everything. Tex-Mex, worldbeat, chicken scratch. They've got a didj player sitting in too, so I reckon it could get interesting. You and Juan want to come?"

"I'm beat, Johnny. Next time you play, okay? Have you asked Maggie?"

Fox shook his head.

"Why not? The woman has barely been out of the mountains since she got to Tucson. I bet she'd love a night out on the town."

"Well, as much of a town as we've got around here." Fox hesitated, uncomfortable. "I don't think it would be her scene. . . . Look, she was married to Nigel Vanderlin. That man plays the viol like he was the one who invented it. I play the accordion, for chrissake." To his disgust he could feel his face going red. And Dora didn't miss that either.

"Fox," she said, "I've never seen you get shy around a woman before."

"Yeah, well, don't rub it in, okay? I'll get over it. Maggie Black's not going to be hanging 'round here all that long anyway."

"Now what makes you say that?"

"I'm just repeating what she says. That this is only a stopover, while she sorts out Cooper's papers. Then it's back to L.A., or maybe it's Europe. Or Timbuktu. . . ."

"But what about the house?"

"I don't know. Maybe she'll sell it," Fox answered moodily. "You think that lad took our order or has he just gone to take a nap?"

Dora looked around for the waiter and she didn't see him either. She shrugged. "Well, I hope you're wrong about Maggie. I think Cooper's house suits her. And I think she'd like Diamondback Rattlers. *And* I think it's cute that you're shy."

"Cute," Fox said, kicking her boot with his own. "Puppies are cute. Small children are cute. I want to be sexy and brilliant and devastating."

"You're just lazy. Every other woman falls at your feet like a gift-wrapped present with a nice big bow. And of course you fall for the one who doesn't."

"That's right. That's the only reason she interests me. It's not that she writes like an angel, or has a voice that makes me shiver to my toes, or that she lives her life with more sheer guts than any ten people put together. No, you're right. It's just her singular good taste in *not* falling for me."

"Not every woman falls like fruit out of a tree. Some of us take a while. You've known her now, what, a whole two weeks? Maybe you ought to work on it."

"Why? So I can be her townie boyfriend until she gets back to her real life in L.A.? No thanks. I've thought this all through already, Dora, and I'm staying clear of it."

"If you say so," she told him dubiously.

"I say so," Fox said firmly.

The waiter appeared, flung down a tray, and drifted out of the room again. Dora picked up her bottle of Dos Equis and looked at the food on her plate. "What is this?" she said.

"It looks like a chimichanga and, let's see—" Fox poked with a fork. "A bean burrito," he announced. He ate some. "It's not bad actually. It's got spinach and walnuts or something else weird inside."

"But Fox, it's not what we ordered."

"Darlin'," he said, "I count myself lucky that we got anything from that young man at all. Try it, it's good. Like life, you know? It doesn't always give you what you ask for, but usually it turns out fine just the same."

Dora gave him a disgusted look. "Thank you for that deep philosophy. Life doesn't give you a bill for it afterward."

"We're not going to get one either. He's forgotten about us already."

It was true. Their waiter was heading out the door and sauntering along up Congress Street. Now there was no one but them in the cafe or in the hotel lobby. They ate their meal, poured themselves some coffee from a pot they found behind the counter, and when they rose to leave again the waiter still hadn't returned.

Fox left a big tip on the table, and then he saw Dora's puzzled look. He said, "I reckon anyone that bad at their job is going to need the money more than me."

Dora smiled and put her arm through his as they walked together up Congress Street. "That's the screwiest logic I've ever heard. But things are always screwy when you're around, Johnny—why do you think that is?"

"It's a natural talent," he assured her.

She laughed. "Yeah, I reckon it is," she said, mimicking his drawling voice.

The sun set quietly that night, slinking behind the Tucsons with subdued whispers in blues and pinks, and then a long violet sigh. Maggie watched from her sunset place on the hill above the upper cabin. She'd been here every night this week. The dark-haired man had not shown up again—except, inexplicably, in a canvas painted over forty years ago. Each time she came here and found the hill empty there was relief mixed with her disappointment; and yet she continued to dream of him. Just the thought of those dreams brought the blood to her cheeks. She sighed, and turned away from the vast purple sky to climb back down the slope.

There were lights on in the upper cabin now, and a red Ford truck in the narrow drive. She saw someone was sitting at the outdoor table and her heart beat faster. But no, it was not the man from the hill. This man was older, stern-looking, with a barrel chest, copper skin, and black hair tied in a single braid. He sat very still, just watching her. His face was fierce, etched deep with lines of age around the eyes and mouth. If this was Tomás, then her tenant was not the man she'd met up on the peak.

Maggie took a breath and went on over to him. "I'm Marguerita Black. Thank you for the apples."

He smiled, and it transformed his face. She'd pegged him as an older man and now she hadn't any idea; he could be her age, or John Alder's, or anything in between. He was dressed in jeans and a denim jacket; he wore a string of beads at his neck, and a necklace of animals carved out of polished stone.

"Tomás Yazzie," he said in an accented voice. "You're the new landlady. Pleased to meet you."

"Likewise. But I don't feel like a landlady yet. I still feel more like a guest up here."

"My Dineh relatives call this land God's Backyard. So really we're all guests here."

She smiled at him. "I like that. But what's 'Dineh'?" she asked.

"Navajo, in our own language," he explained. Then he offered, "I've just made some coffee. Stay for a cup?"

"I've never been able to resist the offer of coffee in my entire life," she confided.

"A sensible woman. And here I thought all you California people were too healthy for that. Fox told me you're a vegetarian." He said it in tones that somebody else might say *a serial killer*.

"I am. But I still have a few vices left, and I cling to them tenaciously."

"Well I'm not going to ask you what the others are," he said as he led her to the house. They passed through a fenced garden area, where corn, beans, tomatoes and squash were growing in lush profusion. She stared, astonished by what the man had coaxed from the dry desert soil.

Maggie stepped into the mechanic's cabin. He turned from the stove, eyeing her suspiciously. "Now this isn't your fancy L.A. coffee. It's cowboy coffee. The grounds are boiled right here in the pot."

"That's the way my grandaddy always made it," she assured him. "He called it coalminer's coffee. He used to say coffee should be thick as mud and strong enough to put hair on your chest. Then I worried that he was right and it would."

He gave her that delightful smile again, and handed her her coffee in a blue tin mug. It was strong. It tasted like West Virginia and smelled of a decade long past.

Tomás's house was a simple place, one large room like the cabin below, with a kitchen, a couch, a big television. A small desk with a computer on it. A pine bed covered with a woven blanket. A Navajo rug hung over the couch and a single Indian flute over the bed. Before the hearth was a red clay bowl filled with herbs, like the one in Fox's house.

This cabin too had an Anna Naverra painting on one side of the rounded fireplace, and a small framed sketch on the other side that might have been Naverra's as well. Maggie stepped over to the wall, fascinated. The painting was of the huge granite boulders that topped the distant Catalina peaks, an ordinary landscape of wind-shaped rock and desert sky. Yet as Maggie stood and stared at it, a figure slowly emerged from the stone, a sleeping man, formed from the rock and the sepia tones of the earth. Three red slashes were painted on the back of one hand resting on the ground; the only bright color on the canvas, it drew the eye's attention. The figure was so subtly rendered that it seemed to waver in and out of her vision; one moment it was there, and in the next she was looking at a simple landscape again. The title was printed next to Anna's signature. "The One-Who-Sleeps," Maggie read, recognizing the phrase from one of Cooper's poems.

She moved over to the framed pencil drawing, lightly sketched on blue-grey paper with a few deft highlights of soft white chalk. The image was of a stag man, and Maggie wondered if it had been the inspiration behind the sculpture Juan had given her. But this creature, although it had the figure of a man, had the face of a stag, not a human face. The stag was pale, its eyes were dark, its rack of horns was heavy, and at the end of each point was a flame. The drawing was unsigned and untitled, but it was certainly by Naverra.

"Have you seen him?" Tomás said.

She turned around and stared. "Have I seen a stag man?"

He smiled once more. "I mean our big white buck who runs around the hills here. Haven't you seen him yet? He's enormous, not like our little mule deer. He's been here for years. It used to be a rare occurrence to see him; but now he comes out almost every night, drinking down there by Red Springs. Fox doesn't believe me. He's only even seen the buck twice himself. But Lillian Alder has seen him by the springs; and I wondered if you had too."

"No. But I've still never been to Red Springs," she admitted. "I'd like to. How would I get there?"

"Finish your coffee and I'll take you. If it's not too dark to see the trail."

She swallowed the dregs of her coffee quickly, before they lost the blue light of dusk. Maggie followed Tomás as he stepped from the cabin, making his way through the tall cactus to a path that she'd not noticed before. It was steep and rocky, leading down the mountain in the other direction from Fox's house. When they got to the bottom, she realized they were on the road between Cooper's place and Dora's. The pathway led them through the trees, across the wash, and up the other side. In the distance she could see lights glow in the house where Fox's sisters lived.

They skirted the bottom of another hill to the spot where the canyon narrowed; then the trail twisted up over boulders and roots along the bank of Redwater Creek. Tomás climbed it easily. For Maggie it was harder work; the footing was uneven, the sky was growing darker, Tomás was a silent shadow ahead. She found the man's lack of small talk alternately peaceful and unnerving.

And then the ground levelled into a circle of soft, grassy land embraced by stone. The canyon walls beyond were steep, saguaro and ocotillo clinging to the slopes. The spring itself was circled by a tumble of boulders, white granite striped with quartz, and tall white trees that seemed to glow luminescent in the thickening dusk.

"Desert sycamore," Tomás told her. They were beautiful, almost magical, as they arched over the water below. Their delicate leaves were green and gold, and trembled in the evening wind.

He put a hand on her arm, stopping her. She stood still and forgot to breathe. Against white trees and smooth white rock was the shape of a powerful seven-point buck, so white and still he could have been carved from a piece of the sun-bleached stone.

He looked at them. He knew they were there. And yet he didn't turn to flee. He stood poised above the mountain spring, and then he slowly bent down to drink. She was standing so close she could see the muscles rippling in the stag's strong neck.

Maggie let out her breath. The stag looked up, dripping water from his muzzle. Then he gathered himself and he leapt for the hills, crossing the water in one great lunge. His hooves seemed to spark flames where they struck, and something rattled down the mountainside.

She looked down. There was a trail of bright blue stones where the stag had been.

Tomás bent down and gathered several stones. "Turquoise," he said. He put them in her hand. "You keep them. Turquoise is for protection."

"What do I need to be protected from?" She looked at the raw chunks of blue rock in her palm.

"Ask him," said Tomás, nodding in the direction the stag had taken. "It's getting darker. We should go back, but now you can find your way here again."

She nodded, and followed him down the creek. Six blue stones made a bulge in her pocket. The seventh she clutched tightly in her hand.

She stood in the bedroom doorway, her long ears cocked, her nose twitching at the pungent, unfamiliar smells. If the Spine Witch hadn't been there beside her, she would have fled back into the night. Not from fear, as when the hounds had come. But from a sharp and deeply rooted shyness . . . of the house, of the woman, of the scent of humankind. She whimpered, standing with one foot inside the door. It was almost too much for her to bear.

The Spine Witch showed no such emotion, but only a cool curiosity as she looked at the woman fast asleep in Cooper's bed. She touched the dark hair and smooth, white cheek. She poked the warm flesh covered by sheets. The woman moved and the Witch jumped back, her useless, tattered wings fluttering and her long, boney feet splayed on the ground.

The stones were on a table by the bed. Seven blue stones, in a shallow yellow dish. The Spine Witch scooped them into her hands. Then she studied them, and she put one back. The rest she tucked into a flap of fur that covered her belly just like a pocket.

When the Spine Witch turned to go, the other one hissed and shook her head. "You took. You took. Now you give something back."

The Spine Witch paused. She'd forgotten that. She looked at the woman in Cooper's bed. She bent close and kissed one closed eyelid, and then she kissed the other. Then she looked at her small companion and grinned, flashing milky, sharp white teeth.

They crept out of the poet's house again, leaving the blue front door ajar behind them as they went.

DAVIS COOPER
Redwater Road
Tucson, Arizona

H. Miller
Big Sur, California

October 11, 1948

Henry,

I didn't send poems in the last letter because I have no poems to send you. I have not written a poem in half a year—not since Exile Songs. *It doesn't matter. I'm going to need a wordless time of gestation while the next poems slowly form.*

I don't yet know if I even have the skill to bring them to the page. The mountains have overwhelmed me, Henry. Their raw beauty has struck me dumb. Anna has learned to capture their essence in oil paint, and I must do the same with words but I don't yet know that I can.

I am reading, reading, devouring books. Natural history, the works of Jung. Myth, folklore, and fairy tales. I came across a story that my Irish granny used to tell: A midwife is summoned to a grand house to deliver a wealthy man's child. She's given a salve to put on the babe, but some of it gets into her left eye—and then she can see that the man and his wife and the child are faeries, all ragged and thin. Through her right eye she can see a big room, a four-poster bed, and white linen sheets. Through her left the room is just roots of a tree and the bed but a pile of leaves.

For Anna, the paint is a salve in her eye. I want to see as a painter sees. We spend whole days out in the hills. The nights are dark and growing cold. I am learning to wait, to watch, to listen. I have never been a patient man. I've never been so empty of words, and never felt so full.

Yours as ever,
Cooper

The year has turned. Slim girls are
shedding leaves, preparing for winter,
while I push backwards, shoulder hard
against the wheel. . . .
—The Wood Wife, *Davis Cooper*

Dora dumped the contents of the bottom dresser drawer onto the bed. "It's all sweaters in here," she said. "What do you want me to do with them?"

Maggie came out of the closet, carrying another armful. "Just box it up. I'll have Fox go through it in case there's anything he wants to keep. The rest I'm going to donate to a homeless shelter downtown. Make sure you check out all the pockets. Don't throw out any lists or notes."

"I won't," Dora promised, sorting through the clothes. She thought it was good that Maggie was finally making space for herself here. It was too creepy that the house still looked like Cooper might return any moment. But bits and pieces of Maggie were slowly appearing in the old man's rooms: Postcards from Europe clipped to the fridge. Juan's deer man sculpture in the living room. Photographs tucked in the bedroom mirror of her friends, her grandfather, the woods of England, and her ex-husband holding a cat.

The paintings she had chosen for the walls were different from the ones that Cooper had hung there. In the living room was a picture of a woman stitching the pages of a book into a blanket; a naked young man called *The Star Blower* hung on one wall in here. Above the bed was an abstract print that clearly belonged to Maggie, not Cooper.

Rich with luminous color and texture, it was a lush, exuberant piece of art, unlike the melancholy Naverras.

"That's lovely," Dora commented, nodding at the picture.

"My friend Tatiana Ludvik did that. It's of the light in a Tuscan hill town near Florence, where we spent one summer."

"You've been so many different places," Dora said to Maggie, her voice wistful. Then she smiled. "Well, I think it's good you're cleaning out and making this your home now."

Maggie deposited a box on the bedroom floor and sat on it, long-legged and lanky, wiping beads of sweat from her brow. She was wearing one of Cooper's undershirts, and her black trousers were rolled up to the shins. "To tell you the truth, what I'm doing is looking for a missing manuscript. I thought getting the house cleaned out would help. I don't know the half of what's in this place. Here. Look at this." She pushed another box toward Dora. "Old-fashioned women's clothes. They're Anna's, I guess. Ah, look at your face. Well, it's Christmas today. Just take anything you want."

Anna had been a small woman, and Dora was delighted. There were long linen skirts, lingerie of old lace, fringed shawls and a good pair of boots.

"You sure you don't want them?"

"Me?" Maggie made a face. "I'm happy with some of Cooper's old shirts."

"Do you always just wear men's clothes then?"

"I'm a menace around men's closets—I'm always pinching clothes off my boyfriends."

Dora grinned. "I had a boyfriend in college who used to pinch mine. I got rid of that one quick."

"I dunno, I think men look good in skirts. Like that gorgeous lad in *The Highlander.*"

"It wasn't my *skirts* he was after," Dora said drily, and Maggie laughed.

Maggie went into the closet and pulled down another box. "You know what I like?" she said as she emerged. "I like seeing so many men wearing jewelry here in the west, all that beautiful turquoise and silver. There's something so sexy about a bracelet on a strong, masculine arm."

Dora smiled to herself. Fox wore a bracelet; maybe there was hope for him yet. "Perhaps it's the combination of masculine and feminine together that's so devastating. I find men with long hair sexy for the same reason."

"Like the man in that painting," Maggie said casually, but there was something in her face that was not casual at all.

"What painting?"

"You know. The one that Lillian said looks like Fox's father."

Dora sat down on the bed among the clothes. "Shoot, wasn't that the oddest thing? I wonder if it really is Fox's father? If it is, he'd be Cooper's age by now; if he's even still alive, I mean. It must be weird for Fox not to know. I come from a family almost as big as Juan's, and I can't imagine what it's like not to have one. Oh no, I'm sorry. You don't have much family either, do you?"

"Sure I do," Maggie said cheerfully as she sorted through another box, "spread across half a dozen countries. Good friends, old lovers, Granddaddy Black. Just depends on how you define family."

Dora said, "Do you know that whenever you mention your grandfather the West Virginia twang gets deeper?"

"Hmmm. It's funny how a place stays in your bones."

"Like Cooper and England. He never lost the accent, you know? You could always tell he was an Englishman."

"But he never went back."

"He couldn't," she said.

Maggie put down a fedora hat and looked at her. "What do you mean by that?"

"He said that this was where the poetry was—the 'whisper of the stones' he called it. He said if he ever left, it would all be gone. He was really pretty superstitious about it. At least during the years I knew him."

"Did you know that he was still writing poems?"

"Well, yes, didn't you?"

"No. I don't think anyone did—I mean, in publishing circles. I suspected that he was, but I didn't know for sure until I got here."

"Is that the manuscript you're looking for?"

"That's right. There's supposed to be a whole new collection, called *The Saguaro Forest*. Did he talk to you about it?"

Dora put her arms around her knees. "Sure. A little bit. We'd talk about writing sometimes. He read me some of the poems."

"He did?" Maggie came over to sit down as well, resting her back against the headboard. "You know, I feel a little jealous. He never said a thing about them to me at all. And I thought we were good friends."

"Well, you were out in the world," Dora pointed out. "I was here in the Rincons. I think maybe he didn't want those poems to go off of the mountain any more than Anna's paintings."

"But why?"

She shrugged. "He was an eccentric old guy. Pissed on gin half of the time, you know. Who knows what was going through his head?"

"I want to show you a letter he left me." Maggie reached for an envelope on her bedside table, weighted down with a chunk of raw turquoise. She opened Cooper's letter from the stiff envelope and handed it to Dora.

Dora read it, perplexed. "April sixteenth. That's right before he died, isn't it?"

"The same day."

Dora shivered. "What's the 'Night of the Dark Stone'?"

"I don't know. Listen to this," she said, picking up a book. "It's from Pablo Neruda:

Return me, oh sun,
to my wild destiny,
rain of the ancient wood . . .
I want to go back to being what I have not been,
and learn to go back from such deeps
that amongst all natural things
I could live or not live; it does not matter,

to be one stone more, the dark stone,
the pure stone which the river bears away.

"He knew that poem, of course," Maggie continued. "He referred to it in a letter to me not long before he died. And he's written part of it here on the wall by the mirror, in ink that looks relatively fresh."

"*The dark stone, the pure stone which the river bears away,*" Dora repeated. "And then he up and died in some dried-out riverbed. That's either ironic or spooky, Maggie, I don't know which. Are you thinking maybe there's some kind of connection?"

"With Cooper there are always connections. His letters were often like that; you couldn't just read them, you had to mull over them, decipher them."

"Like his poems."

"That's right."

"*The dark stone,*" said Dora, musing. "Hmmm. Well here, take a look at this then." She handed Maggie a scrap of paper from the pile taken from the pockets of Cooper's clothes. "I found it in the green cardigan. He wore that sweater all the time."

Maggie read the words scribbled on the back of a grocery receipt out loud: "*It is ultimately stone in you and star.*"

"What do you suppose that could mean: 'stone in you and star'?"

"It's from Rilke. Let me find the poem." Maggie left the room and came back with a volume of the German poet's work. She read aloud in her lovely, husky voice:

The sky puts on the darkening blue coat
held for it by a row of ancient trees;
you watch: and the lands grow distant in your sight,
one journeying to heaven, one that falls;

and leave you, not at home in either one,
not quite so still and dark as the darkened houses,
not calling to eternity with the passion
of what becomes a star each night, and rises;

and leave you (inexpressibly to unravel)
your life, with its immensity and fear,
so that, now bounded, now immeasurable,
it is alternately stone in you and star.

She put down the volume, looking thoughtful.

Dora said softly, "That sounds like Cooper. God, I still miss him. Crankiness and all."

"But Cooper's poems are never that clear; he was always so damn clever and oblique. . . ."

"That's like Anna Naverra. Did you ever notice how the titles of her paintings are always puzzling and mysterious . . . like the punch line of a good story, without any of the rest?"

Maggie hesitated, then said, "There's something else I want to show you."

Dora followed her into Naverra's studio. The room had been scrubbed and swept; the curtains were gone, and the windows overlooked the back porch and the mesquite wood. Maggie's computer sat on one long table, with a notebook, a half-drunk cup of coffee, an arrangement of wildflowers in a jar. She seemed to have taken this as her office instead of moving into Cooper's more spacious one, but she shared it with the dead woman whose art, paints and distinctive presence still crowded the little room.

Maggie showed her a collection of unframed paintings that Dora had never seen before. They were small, like Naverra's canvases, but painted on thin panels of wood, with dark backgrounds and a rich, diffuse light that made Dora think of old Flemish masters. The paintings were portraits, of a sort. But the figures portrayed were not human ones—or rather, they were part human, and part something else, both beautiful and disturbing. The figures looked like personifications of the desert, root, rock, and thorn.

Dora said, "These almost look like Brian Froud's paintings, don't they? Not the same style, but . . . as though both of them were painting the same creatures, just filtered through a different . . . perception."

"Anna's vision is a darker one," Maggie pointed out. "As though she's frightened by what she sees, and yet is still compelled to record it. Look at this. This is the one I wanted to show you."

The portrait was dark, and so loosely rendered—unlike Naverra's usual work—that the woman's features were difficult to see. But Dora could make out her crouched figure, covered with slashes of paint, spiral lines. *Like Juan,* she thought. At the figure's feet was a dark oval shape, like an egg carved out of hematite or onyx. She felt her hands shaking and put the painting down, a sick feeling in her stomach.

Maggie picked the painting up and turned it over. Written in Anna Naverra's neat handwriting was the title: *The Night of the Dark Stone, April 16, 1949.*

"April sixteenth again," Dora said. "I don't understand what any of this means."

"Neither do I. But I think if we did understand, we'd know why Cooper died. And how. And why his manuscript is missing. And why other things are missing from the house."

"What other things?"

"Little things. Drafts of poems that I've found in Cooper's files that have since disappeared again. My Celtic knotwork brooch that I left on the dresser. Some stones I put on the night table. Don't tell me I'm just losing things, Dora. I'm not that absentminded. And even though I lock the door every night, it's always standing open in the morning."

Maggie's voice was even huskier than usual, and her face was looking tense and pale. Whatever was going on here had spooked her, no matter what she said. Dora shivered again. She thought about Juan, who was disappearing almost every night now. She couldn't believe her husband was actually breaking into their neighbor's house, but she also couldn't quite banish the thought. His fascination with the work of Anna Naverra trembled on the edge of obsession.

"Put a new lock on the door," she said firmly. "If someone has a key, then that will stop them. Maybe you shouldn't be staying here at all. Maybe you should call the police."

"And tell them what? Some stones are missing? A manuscript that I can't prove was ever here? But you're right about the door. I don't want to move out of here, so I'm going to have to lock the place up better." She attempted a grin. "I know this is the point in horror films where you want to shout at the idiot girl in the dark, 'Well just get out of the bloody house.' But whatever's going on, whoever's coming in, it doesn't feel . . . malign to me. Not like those animal tracks did. I know, I'm sounding as crazy now as Cooper. But that's the way it seems."

"But you'll get another lock?"

"I'll pick one up today when I go downtown for groceries," she promised. She began to stack the paintings against the wall and said, not looking at Dora, "Do you think it might be Fox coming in? He's used to having the run of the place."

Dora shook her head. "He wouldn't scare you like that."

Maggie looked at her. "But I'm not scared. I don't know why, but I'm not." She paused, framing her next question carefully. "Did Fox ever tell you people used to say that Anna believed in what she was painting? That it was real to her, not symbolic or metaphoric?"

"Well, I heard she went a bit loco out here. The canyon was pretty isolated. And I guess Anna must have been unstable to begin with, considering how she died."

"But you say Cooper was also superstitious. Do you think he believed in this world of Anna's too?"

Dora nodded slowly. "But I don't think I'd call it Anna's world. It's more concrete than that. It's the mountain."

"What do you mean?"

Dora was embarrassed suddenly. "Oh, I don't know," she said, "I've probably just read *The Wood Wife* one time too many."

"You're not comfortable talking about this, are you?"

"Not really," Dora admitted. "Talking about the things you secretly believe in is a bit like talking about sex, isn't it? It's a private thing. Words diminish it somehow. And I guess I worry that I'm crazy too, the things I feel about this land—or at any rate that someone else would think so."

"Like who for instance?"

"Like you for instance."

"Why me? Do I seem so narrow-minded to you?"

"No, it's not that. But what I feel about the mountain here isn't entirely . . . rational. I feel it with my belly," she placed a hand on her stomach, "not so much with my head. You're more . . . cosmopolitan than me. You've seen more; you know more. I just know what I feel."

"Yeah, that's me," Maggie said drily, "the original Cosmo Girl. Why do you think I wouldn't respect your perceptions? You're smart, you're sharp and you're hardly naive."

Dora bit her lip. "But not like you."

"What on earth do you mean, not like me? Look, Dora, I'm just a cracker from the middle of Nowhere, West Virginia. I grew up in the country. And I know it has a kind of . . . spirit to it, that you can't easily put into words. Unless you're Cooper. He did it. He used words like they were an incantation, a spell, a glamour—do you know what that old word used to mean? A glamour was a kind of spell or enchantment. Somehow Cooper learned to speak the 'language of the earth' while he was living up here."

"But those images in his poems: the Wood Wife, the Spine Witch, the boy with the owl's face, the drowned girl in the river. . . . Maggie, are you saying you think they're *real,* not symbolic?"

"Why can't they be both?" Then Maggie shrugged. "I don't know. I don't know what I think about anything anymore, to tell you the truth. Living in this house, on this land, has turned everything I thought upside down and back again twice over. But I can't dismiss Cooper as just a drunk, or crazy. The old man may have been both those things, but he was too smart to be *only* those things. There is something behind those poems and Anna's paintings, and I reckon Cooper expected me to find it or he wouldn't have left them to me."

"You reckon, huh?" Dora smiled. "Now you're beginning to sound like Fox."

"I am?" Maggie looked more startled by this than she was by any of Cooper's mysteries.

"This place is going to rub off on you yet," Dora warned the other woman as they put away Anna's paintings in the storage loft overhead. Maggie looked thoughtful. She closed the door of the studio behind them as they left, and as she did so Dora noticed Fox had installed another lock.

Dora returned to the bedroom while Maggie stopped to put music on the CD player. It sounded medieval. "Is that Estampie?" she asked when Maggie came back into the room.

"No, Symphonye," Maggie said. "But you're close—Nigel has recorded this too. I love this piece of music. It was written by Hildegard von Bingen, a twelfth-century abbess, and a mystic. She had visions—but she was able to reconcile them with her Catholicism."

"Unlike our poor Anna."

"That's right. That's what made me think of Hildegard just now."

"It's pretty," Dora said, although in fact she liked music with a little more kick. She boxed up clothes without seeing them, thinking about Anna's painting.

She was going to have to talk to Juan, breach that wall that was going up between them. Last night he hadn't even come to bed. He'd stayed out till well past midnight, and then he'd sacked out on the couch. She had woken up in an empty bed, wondering what had happened to their marriage. . . .

They finished packing Cooper's things, and then opened up two bottles of beer, taking them outside to the cool shade of the front porch. The day was a scorcher, more like summer heat than the middle of October. The ocotillo were blooming again, resembling wands in a tarot card deck, bursting into bright plumes at the top, brilliant red against the new green leaves.

Two figures walked down the road by the wash, kicking up the dust with long, boney feet. "Hey!" Dora called, waving her hand. The taller of the women waved back.

"Are those Fox's sisters?" Maggie asked with surprise. "They look so young."

"You haven't met them yet? Come on over then, I'll introduce you."

She called out again, and the women stopped and waited in the shade of a paloverde tree. They were slender and graceful, and looked very much alike. Each had brown hair loose to her waist, and eyes of a brown so dark it was almost black. Their faces were thin and delicate and their long noses ever-so-slightly hooked.

Each put a long, thin hand in Maggie's just briefly, and gave her a hesitant smile. Dora often wondered how they could perform when offstage they were so painfully shy. But she'd seen how the sisters transformed when they danced. They'd given an impromptu performance once at the Alders', at Cooper's seventy-eighth birthday party. They'd danced to Debussy, Lillian on piano and Fox on an Irish concertina. The magic of that evening was one she'd not forget—nor the sound of Debussy on a squeezebox.

"If you'd like to come over," Maggie was saying, "you're welcome, anytime."

Isabella cocked her head, with a strange little smile.

Angela was silent, her eyes very wide. Then she said, in her quiet, breathy voice, "And you must come to the place where we live. Mustn't she, Isabella?"

The other woman said, "My sister isn't well. She's had an injury and she needs to rest now."

"What's wrong?" asked Dora with concern.

"I can't dance," Angela told her. For a moment Dora saw a glint of anger in the woman's dark eyes.

"What happened?"

"She was hurt," Isabella told her simply, and the look on her face stopped the rest of Dora's questions. As they turned to go, Dora saw that Angela was limping, leaning on her sister's arm.

They crossed the wash in the direction of their house, identical from behind in their simple yellow shifts. Their feet were bare on the sand and stones, despite the danger of cactus spines, and each wore something circling the left ankle like a thin blue band. A small coyote, the half-blind one, was sitting on the opposite bank, looking as though he waited for them and panting in the midday heat. As the sisters approached, he didn't turn and run. He waited there, almost expectantly.

Maggie turned to walk back to her own house, but Dora lingered for a moment more. She watched as one sister stretched out her hand, and the coyote's pink tongue gave it a kiss.

Fox put another log on the fire. When the sun went down, the evening would chill and the warmth of the flames would be welcome, but now he was stripped down to his jeans and sweating as the fire grew hotter. His silver bracelet lay on the ground along with his shirt and a small suede bag, leaving only a thin cord of knotted leather tied loosely around his wrist.

Tomás sat and watched Fox work, silently smoking a cigarette. He too was stripped down to the waist, and his hair was loose upon his back. Small white scars puckered the skin across his broad copper chest.

"There's too much you're not telling me," Fox accused the older man crossly. He picked up an ax and brought it down hard on a long length of mesquite wood, splitting the log in two. He picked up one end to put on the fire, but Tomás got up and took it from him. He placed the wood on the fire himself, his movements careful and unhurried.

He turned to Fox. "If you tend the fire like that it will burn with your anger."

Fox dropped the ax, sat down, wiped his face. "I'm not angry," he said, "I'm frustrated. I want to know what's out in those hills."

"And you think I know?"

Fox was silent.

Tomás laughed. "You think I'm some shaman, white boy? Yeah, you think I'm some 'wise Injun medicine man,' like something you seen in a movie somewhere. Or read in some woo-woo book from California."

"And aren't you?" Fox asked. It was a question he'd never asked the other man before.

Tomás gave him a broad smile. "I'm just a man. I fix cars for a living, I watch TV, I go to Burger King like anyone else. I haven't got the secret of the universe. Don't make me out to be what I'm not."

"What is this you're teaching me then?"

"How to listen. To the fire. The water. The wind. Nothing more mystical than that," he said.

Fox sat and he considered this. "That seems mystical to me."

Tomás laughed again, at some joke of his own. "That's because you have only begun."

Maggie got back from town before dusk, and put her groceries away in the house. Then she stood out on the porch looking up the canyon, undecided. She could climb to the peak, watch the sun set and pretend she wasn't waiting for anyone there; or she could find her way to Red Springs and hope that the stag would appear once again.

She chose Red Springs, in a spirit of defiance. Why should she wait for that man to return? She'd been on the peak every night again this week. She was starting to feel like a fool.

She found the trail that Tomás had used, and followed it over the wash, up the hill, past the crumbling house where Fox had grown up, half buried in the creosote scrub. Far up the hill, she could make out the figure of Lillian Alder on an opposite trail. She called up and waved, but Lillian was bent over a plant and oblivious to her.

The sky overhead was turning deep blue, streaked with banners of orange, red, and pink. The desert was bathed in a golden light, each cactus, each small tree vivid, distinct. Its beauty stopped her on the path. Something had changed. Something was different ever since she woke up that morning. Her eyes seemed to have adjusted now to the subtler colors of the Sonoran palette. The desert was no longer an emptiness, an absence of water and dark northern greens, but an abundance: of sky, of silver and sage and sepia and indigo blue, of gold desert light, so pure, so clear she wanted to gather it up in her two cupped hands and drink it down.

She rubbed her eyes. Her vision kept changing. One moment it was the way it had been and the desert was just a dry, hostile land. In the next moment it was lovely again, a sentient presence beneath her feet, holding her like a stone in its hand. *To be one stone more . . . ,* she repeated to herself as she walked on into the tall blue hills, *Return me, oh sun, to my wild destiny. . . .*

She continued on toward the canyon's wild heart, toward the sycamore grove and the circle of the springs. The stag would be there.

She could almost feel his presence, drawing her closer. She blinked her eyes. Her vision kept wavering. Time felt stretched, as it did in dreams—perhaps she was home in bed dreaming now. *But home, where is that?* a voice whispered. Was that voice in her head, or in the land?

She reached Redwater Creek's rocky bank and then she stopped, her heart in her throat. He was there, by the creek, as though he'd been waiting. He wore only his jeans this time, his thick black hair unbound on his shoulders, his green eyes intent on her. She swallowed, and continued up the path. As she drew close to him he reached out his hand. She took it, and he pulled her up the bank. She was moving in the dreamtime now, although real rock lay underfoot and a real wind ruffled the back of her hair. Wasn't this why she had looked for him? Hadn't she been dreaming of him for weeks? His skin was cool and smooth against hers. She could almost hear the rhythm of his pulse, beating like an Indian drum, a sound that carried on the wind from somewhere farther down the canyon.

They walked hand in hand along the length of the trail, silent, until they reached the springs. The circle of tall white trees was empty. There was only white rock and water and wind. The stag wasn't there. Maggie let out a long, soft sigh of disappointment.

Her companion frowned. "So he was the one you were looking for here, not me." He touched her suddenly on one flushed cheek, then ran his finger down to her chin, down her throat to the skin of her breast.

She felt fire beneath the touch. But this was no dream, and time, which had slowed, was now moving too fast. She took his hand and lifted it away. "I don't even know your name."

"Call me Crow."

"Just Crow?"

"Just Crow," he said.

"Even Fox has more of a name than that. Fox, Crow. I feel like I'm living in the middle of *Aesop's Fables*."

He laughed, showing even white teeth against the sun-browned skin of his face. "Black Maggie," he named her. She caught her breath.

"How do you know that name?"

"Cooper, of course."

"You knew Cooper?"

"I knew Cooper better than he knew himself. Now stand very still."

"Why?" she said.

"Because your man is coming up the canyon now. He knows we're here, but a sudden movement might still startle him away again."

She turned slowly, and saw the great white stag pick its way up the rocks of the creek. His eyes were black as a starless night. His hide was velvet, his horns were ivory, he was made of more than flesh and bones. He gathered the dying light of the sky into his being, like a radiant star.

They watched as the stag approached the springs and slowly drank his fill there. When he was finished he turned and watched them. The stars seemed to swirl around his great horns. The earth was spinning beneath Maggie's feet; Crow placed his arm around Maggie's shoulder and she leaned back, grateful for his touch. But the stag's big head jerked upward, and he backed away from them, eyes wild.

He stopped when he reached the water's edge. Staring at Crow, he lowered his head until it touched the ground. Then he wheeled and ran, hooves striking the stones, disappearing from the canyon. He took the dying light with him, and now the hills were dark.

She moved away from Crow and stepped up to the springs. There was just one stone where the stag had stood, dark turquoise with veins of black. She picked it up, brought it over to Crow, and placed it in his palm.

"For protection," she repeated what Tomás had said.

But the stone crumbled into bits in his hand. He laughed, and blew the dust away. "You see, I can't be protected. I'm afraid it's much too late for that. Now I must give you something in return for the gift," Crow said.

He stepped closer to her, put his hand to her face—and did not touch it. They were of a height, although she could have sworn that she'd been the taller when last they met. His smile was tender, but also sad; there was loneliness in the lines of his face. His eyes looked very dark to her now, containing the whole of the mountains.

He said, "No, I won't touch you again, Black Maggie. Unless, of course, you ask me to."

Maggie smiled back at him. "In that case," she said, "I'm asking."

He put his two hands in Maggie's hair and his mouth came down on hers, hard and bruising. He tasted salty and he tasted sweet. He had tasted this way in her dreams. She sunk into the depths of his kiss, and then she rose and broke surface again. Her hands were hot where they rested on his hips. She took a breath, and raised her eyes.

The heat chilled to ice, for the man had gone. A woman held Maggie in her arms. The flushed face that looked back at her was the mirror image of her own. She stared at that familiar face, and it mimicked her confusion.

Maggie broke from the embrace, stumbling, rocks skittering beneath her boot heels. Her identical twin, her doppelganger, smiled then, and laughed at her. The voice, the laughter, was Crow's, not her own, and sharp with the cactus spines of mockery. Maggie felt her legs give way beneath her and she sat down hard by the edge of the creek. When she looked again it was Crow standing there—male once more, and beautiful, and painfully desirable, tossing back long blue-black hair the color of the darkened hills.

Perhaps she had imagined that other face; her vision was funny; she'd felt strange all day. But she hadn't imagined the laughter. He was standing and laughing at her still. His face held no passion or tenderness for her, just amusement. She felt her stomach turn.

"Who are you?" she asked him once again, her voice low with anger, shame, and disappointment.

Crow strode up to her and grabbed her arm, hard, pulling her to her feet. "Who are *you*?" he said close to her face. "Answer me that, and then you can ask me that question for a third time."

He let her go abruptly. Then he flung back his head, and he began to howl, an animal sound, filling the hills. The coyotes answered from the slopes all around. The drums in the night were insistent now. Crow laughed, as if he had just received a startling message in one of those sounds.

He left her then, as suddenly as he had come, and did not look back.

* * *

Crow stepped into the circle of the fire. Beyond there was only darkness. The sky was black and starless, merging with the black of the
hills below. One man sat in the fire circle, smoking a cigarette, talking
to the flames, although Crow could smell the presence of the other
who had departed not long before.

Crow sat down, cross-legged in the dirt, next to the drum that
had called him here. Tomás passed him the cigarette. Crow took it,
breathed in smoke and flame, and he passed it back again.

Tomás was silent, until he'd smoked the cigarette down to the very
end. He didn't look at Crow. It was a gesture of respect, and Crow was
pleased by this.

At length Tomás said, "Who comes to my fire? Man or spirit?"

Crow grinned. He rattled the copper on his wrist. He said, "Which
do you think?"

Tomás was silent.

Crow frowned at this. And then he smiled again. *"Today I stew
and then I'll bake, Tomorrow I shall the Queen's child take, Ah! how
famous is the game; there's nobody here who knows my name is Rumplestiltskin. . . ."*

But Tomás didn't know that story. He still sat silent, listening.

Crow grew annoyed. "You must guess," he growled. "It's a riddle.
You must guess my name."

Tomás stirred the embers of the fire with his usual careful, unhurried movements. "Brother," he named the other at last.

"Wrong." Crow laughed. "I'm no relative of yours."

"The fire is my brother. And the stones below, and the trees and
the cactus on this hill. You've entered the circle. You've smoked the
tobacco. And I name you Brother," Tomás said.

Crow's laughter stopped. His smile died. He looked at the other
uneasily. He rose, took off a copper band, and flung it down before
the other man. Then he disappeared, melting into the dark of the
night and the mountainside.

DAVIS COOPER
Redwater Road
Tucson, Arizona

M. Tippetts
New York, New York

May 9, 1949

Dear Maisie,

I no longer know what to do. Anna has gone away from me, into some private grief of her own. What has happened? Can you tell me this? Anna won't tell me. The paintings won't tell me. The stones are strangely silent now. All I know is this: There was a night when Anna did not come home at all. I roamed the hills, calling her name, knowing that on the vast mountainside I had no prayer of finding her. At dawn I stumbled home again. She was sitting there in the shadows of the porch, clothes torn to rags, breasts bared, spirals of blood and red oil paint on her skin. A man sat beside her—with long black hair, a womanly face, tattoos on his cheeks. He smiled, and his teeth were sharp— like a predatory animal.

Anna looked at me sadly. She did not speak. She rose, she took my hands, and collapsed. I carried her into the house; when I looked back, the man, her creature, was gone. I bathed her, put her to bed . . . and in the morning she laughed the whole thing away. But something changed that night, I am certain. She does not leave the studio now; she no longer walks in her beloved hills. For the first time since we came to this dream-haunted place, I fear for her sanity. I am at my wit's end. She won't speak of this. She wants nothing now but to paint.

Maisie, I know she has written to you. You must tell me, will Anna be all right?

Cooper

I do not fear the dark, or sleep, or death.
The knife. The teeth of hounds.
I only fear the fool in the wood,
the water, the mirror glass. . . .
    —**The Wood Wife,** *Davis Cooper*

Maggie stepped from the bathtub, dried herself off, and put on an old white shirt of Cooper's, a big black sweater that used to be Nigel's, a pair of tight black jeans. She'd slept late, after a night of heated dreams that she'd rather not think about now. The sun was already peeking over the distant purple hills. Soon heat would fill the canyon again, but now the house was cold and the bathwater steamed in the chilly morning air.

She brushed wet hair back from her face, put on ivory earrings shaped like little dangling hands, and a silver ring with an amber stone. She'd had the ring since she was a child; the earrings had been a gift last year from the man she'd been seeing in Mendocino. A guilty look crossed over her face in the old-fashioned bathroom mirror. She hadn't called Mendocino, or sent a card or even, she admitted, thought about him all that much since the day of her hasty retreat. Instead of heartache, all she felt about the end of that chapter of her life was guilty relief.

It was possible he was feeling the same way, she reflected as she put on her socks and then her new black cowboy boots. It was hard to imagine he'd found her to be a satisfactory person to love. No one had claimed her heart since Nigel. She'd tried to be with men since then, but no one else quite touched the place that Nigel had reached so effortlessly. She tried, but sooner or later she always started feeling those "itchy feet" again.

She sighed as she went into the kitchen. Romance was definitely not her forte. Last night, with Crow by Redwater Creek, was proof again of that—as if she needed more proof. She swung open the refrigerator and took out two of Tomás's eggs, hot salsa, and flour tortillas. As she heated oil in a frying pan to make huevos rancheros, she made herself think about the meeting with Crow instead of flinching from it in her mind.

She touched on those thoughts gingerly, like a sore tooth, waiting for the sting to come. And it came. She was angry with the man, yes, but just as angry with herself, for she'd been acting like some naive schoolgirl. All he'd been doing was amusing himself, and she'd gone right along with it, obsessed with a man she didn't even know just because he was so lovely to look at. And because, she admitted to herself, it was romantic, and wild, like Cooper's poems. She shuddered, remembering the dreams she'd had, so starkly erotic. Thank god things had never gotten that far in real life. If they had . . . She didn't finish the thought.

She broke the eggs into the pan and made herself think of less mortifying scenarios. All right, so she got a bit carried away, but she wasn't a total fool. She thought instead about the queer vision she'd had of her own face staring back at her. And all the strange things that he'd said to her. And the oddest thing of all, which was the fact that Crow seemed to have stepped from one of Anna's paintings.

So many of the paintings had their counterparts in Cooper's later poetry, but there was no man named Crow in the "Wood Wife" poems, or any of Cooper's other work. And yet there were images that reminded her of him. The mythical Trickster, wild and unpredictable. Compelling in one breath, sinister the next—wise and foolish both at once. Puck was a Trickster in English folklore; Hermes or Loki in Europe. She recalled there were Tricksters in both Mexican and Native American legendry, and she resolved to look through Cooper's library today to see what she could find. . . .

Maggie took her breakfast to the table, laughing at the route her thoughts had taken. She poured some coffee. Dora was right. The mountain was rubbing off on her. She was becoming as loco as the rest of them here. She had come to do biographical research, and now she was chasing down fairy tales, half-convinced that Cooper or Anna had conjured Crow from the desert air. "It's just a metaphor," she said out loud, but she didn't really believe this.

Then you've been seduced by a metaphor, said an ornery, contrary voice in Maggie's head. She recognized that voice; it sounded like Cooper's. It made her smile to herself.

"That's right," Maggie said aloud to the empty room. "And it won't be the first time either."

She finished her breakfast and went back to the study she'd made in Anna's studio. She had all of Cooper's collections in there, and what notes she could find toward the unpublished poems. She'd just found another of his notebooks wedged between two Victorian fairy-tale books: *The Moon Wife* and *The Moon Wife's Daughter,* two volumes that Cooper had loved. She opened the notebook and began to read, skipping old memos and grocery lists. In between these things were notes for poems, phrases, lines, an occasional whole verse—nothing complete, just enough tantalizing information to let her know what she was missing. She read the calligraphic handwriting with pleasure, and a bit of envy for the old man's imagination. Perhaps she could go over these notes with Dora; there might be something here that the other woman would recognize. Then she found something she recognized herself, and it jolted her to the bone:

NOTE. *Remember that A. handed him stone. Jade? Lapis? No, turquoise. "For protection," she told him. Turns to powder in his hand.*

C: "I can't be protected. It's too late for that. But now I must give you a gift in return."

There is always a return, a cycle, a gift exchange. The breath in, the breath out. This is what I'd forgotten. Did she? Would that have made a difference? This question seems important. This is the question the poem must answer.

Maggie sat and stared at the words on the page. The notebook was dated 1958. How could Cooper have forseen her own experience in words written over thirty years before? But it was not Maggie he wrote about at all; it was "A."—probably Anna—and "C."—another C., or was it Crow?—saying the very same words to each other. Perhaps she had read these words before somewhere, and then unconsciously repeated them?

She quickly flipped through the other pages. More lists. Phone numbers. Car parts information. More notes for poems, but none about C., or turquoise, or gifts again. One poem was about the mountain, simple and naturalistic. In the second, an old man thinks about death. The third was about birth. She read this note twice, and then she read it over once more, bent over the water-stained page, chewing the end of her pencil.

<u>NOTE</u>. *She would not leave the mountain, even now. It is the midnight hour. The air is cold but she is warm, even hot to the touch. The river, dry. Moon, full. Image: she lies in the sand of the wash, silver light, legs spread. There is no blood. This disturbs me. I am frightened. But the baby slips from her legs like a stone through water, and into my hands. Cold. Crying. Tiny, but alive. At last she is persuaded to go back into the house. She will not tell me the father's Christian name. She will not name the baby. He is only The Baby for many months, but a child must have a name I tell her. She is surprised. I have begun calling the boy after Gutiérrez, and she accepts this.*

Gutiérrez. The name was half-familiar to Maggie. She looked it up on her computer, where she had been making notes of Cooper's references. She quickly found the name in her file: Johnny Gutiérrez, of the Emergency Rescue Committee. The man who had gotten Cooper out of France during the war, and saved his life. She could double-check that with Maisie Tippetts, she thought. She wrote a note to herself: Johnny—

Johnny. She repeated the name and sat back in her chair, eyes narrowed as realization dawned. Cooper had written, or had been planning to write, a poem about Johnny Foxxe's birth; the woman in labor on the mountain was clearly Cooper's pregnant housekeeper. Unless it was Anna who . . . No, Maggie answered the half-completed thought. Anna left the mountain in 1949. Johnny Foxxe was born in—hmmmm. Maggie did a rapid calculation. He was thirty-five years old. Yes. 1958, the date of this notebook.

A knock at the front door interrupted her conjectures. Perhaps, she thought, it was Fox himself. She looked at her watch. It was much too early for Fox. He was going to take her to meet his mother, but not until later in the day.

When she reached the door she found the mailman, late with delivery this morning. The man looked like an overgrown Boy Scout in his little blue uniform shorts and knee socks, driving a U.S. Mail jeep. She had a bulky package to sign for, along with letters with foreign postmarks, an invitation to Tat's upcoming show, and a campy postcard from Nigel. His card gave a name and an L.A. phone number and read: *Film interest. Call him.*

She took the mail into the kitchen, and put Tat's invitation on the refrigerator with a howling-coyote magnet. She put Nigel's card in the rubbish bin, then repented and fetched it back out again. The package, she discovered, was from Maisie Tippetts, postmarked New York City. Maggie had contacted the playwright again, hoping for another interview and help in tracking down Cooper's old friends. In response Maisie had sent her a parcel of letters from Anna Naverra.

The letters, written in fluent English, covered a five-year period, in Mexico City and Tucson. At the bottom of the box was a slim copper bracelet. She looked at it closely. It had spiral designs. It was similar, if not identical to, the copper bracelet Crow wore on his wrist. A note in the box read simply,

My dear Marguerita,
These are all I have left of Anna, aside from a handful of paintings. I thought you should have the letters, and this bracelet she once gave

*to me. If you can ever be persuaded to part with any of her artwork, I
hope you will tell me. I'll pay any price. But I'll understand if you, like
Anna and Cooper, feel it shouldn't leave the mountains Anna loved.*

With warm regards,
Maisie Tippetts

Maggie held Maisie's note and looked at the well-worn bundle of Anna's correspondence. Then she poured herself another cup of coffee,
and took all the letters into her study. She laid them out on Anna's
desk in chronological order. She made a new file on her computer: *A.
Naverra to M. Tippetts, February 1944–April 1949.*

April. She picked up the last of the envelopes that Maisie had received. It was postmarked in Tucson on April 24th. Seven days after
the Night of the Dark Stone. She resisted the strong urge to open it
right up, and she began properly at the beginning.

When Fox arrived for her several hours later, she barely heard the
knock on the door.

Maggie seemed distracted when Fox came over to drive her to his
mother's place. Her dark hair was dishevelled and there was a smudge
of pencil lead on her cheek. She said, "I'll follow you in my car, okay?"

"I thought you were coming in my truck?"

"I have to stop at the grocery store after," she explained. "I forgot
half the things I needed yesterday. I'm a city girl. I haven't got the
knack of stocking up."

"So we'll stop. You can't take that," he said dismissively, nodding
at the small rental car. "If you think the road up here is bad, wait 'til
you see my mother's."

"Oh, I see. All right then." She picked up her bag. "I ought to get
rid of that car anyway, if I stay up here much longer. Buy a cheap
truck or something."

"Ask Tomás," Fox advised. "He'll find you something, and keep it
running for you."

"Is he good then?"

"Best damn mechanic I know. Tomás says machines talk to him," Fox told her as she climbed into the pickup.

For a city girl, she was looking rather western today. She still wore men's clothes in black and white, but now it was black jeans over Tony Lamas boots, and a white cotton shirt rolled up at the sleeves. Yet there was still something about her, beyond the artsy haircut, that subtly marked her as different. Different, and special, Fox said to himself, although perhaps she didn't see it that way. People generally just wanted to fit in, and Maggie wasn't the type who ever would.

He whistled to the music that was on the tape deck as he rolled the truck back from the drive; Tex-Mex music, with Mexican guitars and songs in both English and Spanish. "Do you mind this?" he asked her. "Or would you rather listen to something else?"

"No, it's good. What is it?"

"Tish Hinojosa. You like this? This is Border music. You'll hear a lot of it here." Maybe Dora was right. Maybe she would have liked Diamondback Rattlers after all.

They bounced down the mountain to Tanque Verde, then on to the traffic of Sabino Canyon. He picked up River Road, which meandered through the city but still had the flavor of an older Tucson, lined with farms, horse corrals, a few old adobe houses. He pointed out the little road signs that marked specimens of desert flora: Agave. Prickly pear. Teddy bear cholla. At the sign for desert broom, some wag had planted a straw kitchen broom, upside down. Maggie laughed and he loved the way that it sounded, low in the throat, thoroughly wicked.

The music ended, and Fox said, "Choose another tape. There's a box of them on the floor there."

Maggie picked up the box and set it on her lap, looking through his tapes with interest. "Blues. Reggae. Pearl Jam. Vaughan Williams. Sioux Ceremonial Songs," she read aloud. "You can always tell a lot about a person from their music collection, don't you think?"

"Maybe a journalist can," he teased her. "What does that tell you except my taste is eclectic?"

"Well, let's see now. Here's tapes of Irish and Hopi flute, three different solo accordion recordings—not exactly Top Ten is it? I could cleverly deduce that you play those instruments yourself—but in fact I saw them hanging in your cabin, so I reckon that wouldn't be fair."

Fox smiled. "You reckon, do you?"

Maggie picked up another handful of cassettes. "BeauSoleil—a Cajun band. Here's Peter Rowan's latest. Two Estampie tapes, one Gothic Voices. June Tabor. A harp duo from Scotland—and this is interesting, the price tag on it is in sterling. Hmmm, here's some European folk music and the tapes were clearly bought over there. Either you're well traveled, Fox, or you have nice friends who send you things."

"A little bit of both," he admitted.

"So you've been to Europe by the looks of this. And Mexico, no big surprise. And, whoa, Africa?"

"Africa," he confirmed.

"But not Asia. Or else you don't like Asian music."

"I do. I haven't gotten there yet."

"You see?" said Maggie smugly. "That's more than I knew about you before."

"You're right," he conceded with amusement. "Someday you'll have to show me your collection. Now how about choosing a tape to listen to?"

She looked through the box again. "We're spoiled for choice here. What about . . . This looks interesting. Desert Wind, music for flute, percussion and didjeridoo." She looked more closely. "By Wood, Begay and Foxxe. Hey, this is you."

"That *was* me. Five years ago. Begay and I still play together sometimes, but Wood's moved back to Australia."

"I didn't know you played professionally, Fox."

He laughed. "That's because I don't. That recording is from a little local company, now defunct; it sold six copies, to us and our mothers. Begay still has a garage full of them."

"Have you recorded anything else?"

Fox shook his head.

"Well why not? Look, my first book didn't sell many copies, or even the one after that. It was only with *Low Life* and *The Maid on the Shore* that anyone paid attention. But you have to believe in your work anyway. Keep putting yourself out there. Go after what you want."

"And that's what you've done? You've gone after what you wanted?"

"Yes." Maggie looked uncomfortable. "Well, kind of." She did not elaborate.

Fox glanced at her as he turned off River and onto a busy road running north. "But you assume that what I want is what you would want: Success. Recognition. I'm not like you. I'm not like Cooper. That's not what a good life means to me. Playing music is a high, for sure—but there's other things that I like just as much. Carpentry, for instance; it's honest work, it's solid, it's real, it pays a living wage. And the Mentor Program, that's another kind of high."

"What's that?"

"I give free music lessons to kids—in the barrio, and on the reservations. I like having time for things like that. And time for my friends. And for myself. I don't want to spend all my time hustling music. Just want to play it, enjoy it, and have a life."

Fox braked abruptly, turning toward the interstate. Then he glanced over at Maggie again, and saw that she was smiling.

He said, "Sorry for that diatribe. You pushed some old buttons, that's all."

"You're arguing with Cooper's ghost again, aren't you?"

Then he smiled himself. "I reckon I am."

Maggie said, "You're right, though. I am like Cooper. Art is the thing that matters to me. It's not the desire for fame that drives me, but to do good work, the best that I can. When I was married, it was as if my energy was in hock—to Nigel, to the magazines, to anyone who asked for it loudly enough. Now I'm more single-minded, I admit it. I want to leave something good behind me when I go, something that will last."

"There's the difference between us then. Immortality means nothing to me. I'm a desert boy. *'I have learned to walk lightly on this land, and to leave no trace behind.'*"

"Ghalad Keller's 'Stone Canyon'?" she guessed.

He was pleased that she recognized it. "'*The mountains reach into heaven,*'" Fox said. "'*And a man, so small. And a man, so small.*'"

As they climbed the ramp to the interstate, the city stretched around them, filling the valley from the mountains in the east to the mountains in the west. The sky was a clear, deep blue above them, the rich color of old Bisbee turquoise. The sound of flute and drums filled the truck, masking the traffic's noise.

The traffic was light on the highway as soon as they left the city center. It disappeared almost altogether when they turned off the interstate again, heading west into low hills. Fox's mother lived north and west of the city, between the Tucson and Tortolita Mountains. The desert here was drier, scrubbier than the land below the Rincon range. The Tucsons were volcanic plugs with the jagged profile seen in a hundred cowboy movies. It was a land of saguaro and ironwood trees, unique in Sonoran ecology. Builders' signs were everywhere on it, announcing high-density developments to come.

The imminent construction disappeared as the road beneath them turned to dirt. There were still houses here, but individually built and tucked into the low desert scrub. The desert was peaceful, but arid and rough. The sky made a vast blue dome overhead. The heat shimmered in waves just above the dusty road they travelled on.

He turned suddenly onto a narrow track that bumped its way along a dry creek bed. Maggie grabbed for the dashboard as the truck hit a rock. "My god, what kind of a road is this?"

"We're on Cooper's land. Well, it's my mother's land now. Two hundred acres, going up into the Tortilitas. These last ten years he was buying up what he could, one step ahead of the developers. Cooper's version of the National Trust. It was one thing we could agree on."

"How does your mother get in and out?"

"She doesn't. She doesn't like to leave it. There's a Mexican family that lives over that way." He gestured vaguely to the north. "They look after things and look after Mama. The eldest of the Hernández boys dates one of my sisters."

"What do I call your mother?"

"Her name is María Rosa."

"Ms. Rosa?"

"Just call her María. That's what everyone else does." He ran the pickup through another wash, over a hill, and into a little hollow. He stopped the truck. The tape deck switched off, and the desert seemed suddenly very quiet. He could hear many birds and the steady hum of traffic, although the rise of the land hid the interstate from view.

There wasn't much to his mother's place. A small trailer, with a porch that he'd built for her out of lengths of Rincon mesquite. An outdoor oven. And the remains of a corral that hadn't seen a horse in years. The trailer was parked in a semicircle of tall saguaro cactus, nestled beneath their protective arms. At their base was a scattering of wildflowers, tall, slender stems of pink penstemon and the smaller, fluffy fairy dusters.

"There are so many saguaro here," said Maggie with wonder as she stepped from the truck. "Do you suppose this is where Cooper got the inspiration for the name *The Saguaro Forest*? It's an odd name, don't you think?"

"That's what this is called, a saguaro forest."

"Really? I thought he'd made that up. I thought a forest had to have trees."

"When I was a boy, my mother used to tell me that at night the saguaro all dance together. That's why they look the way they do—with all their arms raised high. They won't move while you're watching them, they wait until you fall asleep. And then at dawn they all have to rush to get back into place again. She used to say to me, 'Close your eyes, *mijo;* the saguraro are waiting for you to sleep so they can run off to dance. . . .'"

Maggie looked enchanted, holding her arms up like a saguaro ready for a waltz. "I can almost see it. Aren't they wonderful? Almost like they're human too."

"That's what the Tohono O'odom say. They call them 'Aunt' and 'Uncle.'"

He stepped up to the little trailer and called out to his mother, but no one answered him. Fox opened the unlocked door and stepped inside. The air was sour with old cigarette smoke, the place dusty, abandoned-looking. It often looked that way when he came to visit— as though his mother had decided she'd cleaned up houses for too many years and simply wasn't going to do it again. He usually spent time with a bucket and mop before he left.

He stepped outside and said to Maggie, "She's either out in the desert, as usual, or she's gone over to the Hernández place."

"Did she know we were coming?"

"I told her last week. But she's a forgetful old woman. She likes to keep the phone unplugged so I have no way to remind her. Come on. Let's take a walk."

He led Maggie on the narrow path that skirted the hills to the Hernández spread. They could see the Hernández house in the distance, a low wooden building, a couple of stables, and several empty horse corrals. The land here was dotted with ironwood trees, growing hand in hand with the saguaro. They were small trees, but strong, and tough—like his mother. Halfway down the trail they found her. She was gathering wild desert plants in a flat-bottomed basket hung over one brown arm. She was a tiny old lady, small as Dora, her face covered with a fine network of wrinkles. She wore a shapeless, faded cotton dress that looked exactly like every other dress she'd ever worn. A red bandana tied back silver-grey hair, and on her feet were dusty socks and sandals. Fox couldn't even imagine what Maggie Black was going to make of his mother.

A smile lit up the wrinkled face when María Rosa saw them. She waved her hand at them like a child, and then waited in an ironwood's meager shade while Maggie and Fox approached. Fox leaned down and kissed her cheek. He introduced Maggie, glad that he had warned her that his mother was the shyest old woman on God's green earth.

But now María was beaming at Maggie, and the two women were soon chatting up a storm as his mother took them on a circular path, pointing out the desert flora. Fox scratched his head as he trailed along behind. There was just no predicting his mama, he reckoned.

"Creosote," María was instructing Maggie. "A little branch under your pillow every night, you'll never have trouble with arthritis. Or in a salve, it's good if you cut yourself. Now this, this agave. A tincture of this, very good for colic or indigestion. This sage here, dry it out, make a tea—you have a sore throat? You gargle with it. White sage, that you smudge with, you know? Good for purification. This here, sagebrush—not sage. Good for diaper rash. Ocotillo here, you make a tincture of the bark, put in the bath, good for fatigue."

This lecture continued all the way back to the trailer, but Maggie seemed completely fascinated. Fox had heard all this many times before, and he wasn't sure why Maggie needed to hear it now, but he knew better than to question his mother. He'd never get a straight answer anyway.

The women sat down at a picnic table in the small bit of shade provided by the porch. His mama pulled out her tobacco pouch and rolled herself a cigarette—a habit she knew Fox worried about as her voice grew raspier with each passing year. She gave him a little smile as she lit up, half guilty and half devil-may-care. He rolled his eyes and he went inside to brew a pot of tea.

Outside, the lecture continued. "Now these prickly pear cactus, you must carefully cut off the spines and the skin, and then you have a poultice for bad burns. Leave it right on for several hours; it will draw the fluid out."

"What about the saguaro?" he heard Maggie ask as he put three mugs on a battered tin tray.

"Ah, make wine from the fruit. Drink till you puke," the old woman answered and the two women laughed. "Very good purgative."

He carried the pot of tea to the porch. His mama stubbed out her cigarette as Maggie took a notebook from her bag. "María," the younger woman said, "what I'd really like to talk to you about is Davis Cooper. Fox told you I'm here to write a book about Cooper, didn't he? It would be very helpful, and I'd be grateful, if you could tell me some stories about your life with him."

His mother folded her hands on her lap, looking like a good little schoolgirl. She nodded, her eyes round and dark in her face. She didn't volunteer anything.

Maggie shot Fox a look.

"Mama, what if Maggie just asks you some questions?"

She nodded again, retreating back into the shyness she usually presented to strangers.

Maggie took a breath. "All right. For instance, when did you first meet Cooper?"

"Oh," María said, in a hesitant little voice, "years ago it must have been."

"Where, Mama?" Fox prompted.

"Oh," she said, "on the mountain."

Maggie said, "Now, what I've been told is that Cooper advertised for a housekeeper, and you saw the ad and you answered it. Is that right? Is that what happened?"

Her head bobbed.

"Well, when would that have been? What year?"

"Umm. Nineteen seventy-three?" María guessed, as though she were reaching for an answer on an exam she hadn't studied for.

"Mama, I was born in fifty-eight. It was the year I was born, wasn't it?"

"Yes!" she said, and a smile lit her face.

"But where were you before then?"

The smile left. She looked confused. "Well, I was here."

"Here, where?"

She sketched the air with her hand. She could have meant this spot, she could have meant Tucson, she could have meant the United States.

Maggie tried another tack. "When I was reading Cooper's work today, I came across some notes for his poems. Perhaps you've seen this one before? He wrote it in 1959. I think it must be about Fox."

María looked at the notebook. She sat very still. Then she put her two hands on the page, and touched the letters gently, a strange expression on her round, wrinkled face. A look of wonder, and tenderness. Then she rose abruptly, and she went into the trailer, and shut the door behind her. She did not come out again.

"Oh dear," said Maggie. "I'm not doing very well at this at all, am I?"

"It's not you. It's my mother. She never talks about the past like this. Or to people she doesn't know. Actually you've done rather well."

"Have I upset her?"

"Not exactly. But she won't come out again now, I'm afraid."

But Fox was wrong. When they finished their tea and got back into his pickup truck, the trailer door opened and María came out, a lidded basket under her arm. She came to the window and gave it to Maggie. Maggie opened the lid. There were herbs inside.

"Thank you," said Maggie. She sounded touched. "May I give something to you then?"

The old woman gave her a shy, delighted smile. Maggie took a turquoise stone from her pocket and put it in his mother's palm. María clutched it tightly with the sweetest of expressions breaking over the sun-browned face. She waved at them as Fox turned the truck around, and then she struck out into the desert. As the truck pulled away, she was bent down in the dirt, absorbed in her plants once again. Fox knew from past experience that she'd soon forget all about them.

"Your mother is a doll," Maggie commented. "She and Lillian must get along famously."

"You bet," Fox said as he steered the truck back over the broken trail.

He turned onto the graded dirt road, and headed east for the interstate. The afternoon sun was a blaze of light behind them, throwing long shadows.

Fox looked at Maggie. "So what was that page of Cooper's you showed my mother, anyway?"

She turned to him, her eyes opaque. When she spoke, her voice was hesitant. "I think it might be about your birth." She read the passage to him.

Fox was quiet for a long while.

Then he said, "She told me I was born on the mountain. I knew that part of it before—that she didn't go to a hospital. I knew Cooper or someone had to have been there. But to tell you the truth," he added, swiftly braking for a pair of coyotes crossing the road, "I always thought Cooper was our father, and those two would never admit it."

"*Cooper?*" Maggie's voice was startled.

"Well, not that he ever acted like he was. But it made a kind of sense—more sense than Mama's story. Now it turns out Lillian actually met my father. And here's Cooper wondering about his Christian name. It seems," he said with remarkable calm, "that Mr. Foxxe was a real man after all." He put the truck back into gear, stepping hard on the accelerator.

She said quietly, "I've seen a man who looks like him. Like the man in Anna's painting. I've seen him in the Rincons, wandering around the hills."

"The man in that painting would have to be as old as Davis Cooper now," Fox pointed out.

"I know," she said, her voice husky. He could not read her expression.

"You think I've got a brother I don't know about or something?"

"A brother? Oh. I hadn't thought of that."

"Or do you think Anna's paintings are coming to life?" He said it in a teasing way, and then was sorry, for Maggie's shoulders tensed.

"What do *you* think?"

"Me? Well shoot, I don't know," he said lightly, trying to smooth the tension away. "You're the one who's supposed to be making sense of Cooper. So you tell me when you find out."

She was silent then, her face serious, lost in private thoughts of her own.

Fox flipped the Desert Wind tape over. The music began with a whisper of flute—the copal flute he'd had from Tomás. And then the low chanting of Begay's Navajo uncles singing pow-wow songs. It made for a peaceful sound: the flute, voices, percussion like the rattle of stones. The moan of the didjeridoo was the rising wind just before a storm.

Fox raised the volume, for it filled the silence between them as they travelled back to town.

That night she slipped through the shadows of the bedroom, making no noise with her bare human feet. Her heart was beating rapidly. She wished once again that the Spine Witch was here. But this was her task alone tonight, to retrieve that single copper band that had left the mountain for so many years and now had come back again. She could see it on the night table, glowing in the darkness like a star.

She crept up to the head of the bed. She cast a nervous glance at the sleeping woman, and slowly slid her hand to the table. She reached for the band, her fingers closing on it. Then her wrist was pinned. A light went on.

"I've got you," the woman said, looking at her. Her eyes widened when she saw what she had caught.

The little one cringed against the side of the bed, covering her face with long jackrabbit ears.

"Oh good heavens. You're trembling. And you're such a little bit of a thing, now aren't you?" The woman's voice grew softer. "Come on now, I'm not going to hurt you. I just want to know who you are. What you are. And what are you doing with all my things?"

She lifted one ear and peeked up with one eye. She whispered the woman's name—"Black Maggie."

"That's right," the woman said to her. "But who are you, little darlin'?"

"I have no name." Her human voice was both whispery and gravelly. She'd never tried it out before. She said hopefully, "You can call me what you like." She felt a flutter of excitement in her chest. Was she about to get a name at last?

The woman smiled. "All right then. But what shall I call you? How about . . . Thumper?" She laughed, a husky sound. "You've probably never heard of *Bambi*, have you?"

"Thumper." She lifted her other ear, and grinned, exposing little teeth.

"Thumper, if I let you go, are you going to disappear on me?"

Her smile left and she gravely shook her head.

"All right, I'm going to trust you then. But I want you to let go of the bracelet first. That's Anna's bracelet and I'm not going to give it to you, understand?"

Thumper shook her head again, and she let go of the copper band.

Crow would not be happy. But what could she do? The woman had caught her fairly. There were rules about these things, of course. Even Crow was bound by that, although it was true he wasn't bound by much. Not like the rest of them. Not like her, with the animal self always tugging at her, overwhelming her other senses. Not like the Spine Witch, bound to the cactus in which her magic was housed; or the Nightmage whose soul had been plucked from the wood like a bean popped from a mesquite pod and put only Earth knew where.

Black Maggie let go of her wrist. Thumper stood, legs splayed, her hands on her belly, waiting to see what would happen next. Then the fur rose on the back of her neck. Thumper began to tremble again. Outside, the Hounds had begun to bay. They sounded very close, and she was afraid. If she left this house they would find her, and now that she had failed him she doubted that Crow would give her any protection.

But Black Maggie couldn't hear the Hounds. "You're cold," she said as Thumper stood shivering. "Here, come have a blanket then."

She climbed up on old Cooper's bed. She was less than half the size of the woman, and thinner, more loosely stitched together. Her long, boney limbs were human in shape but covered with a pelt of soft grey fur. The bed was warm where the woman had slept. She took the blanket and curled at its foot, her head nestled up against Black Maggie's knees. She sighed deeply. Tonight she'd sleep safe. Perhaps she did well to be caught after all. She had safe haven, she had a name, she had a bit of warmth in the dark. She smiled then and she closed her eyes. In an instant, she was fast asleep.

DAVIS COOPER
Redwater Road
Tucson, Arizona

Anaïs Nin Guiler
Acapulco, Mexico

August 2, 1949

Dear Anaïs,

I knew you of all people would understand that the line between dream and reality is a thin one, a fragile membrane easily ruptured by a poet, a painter, or a drunk's clumsy hand. Yes, I am drunk. It doesn't matter. The edges of the world are softer this way—for life has been sharp as a cactus spine since Anna fled back to the family bosom and refuses to see any of us again.

I am learning patience. It is only a matter of time before she returns. It is not possible, it is not conceivable that she will stay away for good. Anna loves these hills, this sky, this house. She'll come back for the land if not for me.

In the meantime, I am gathering her paintings, or at least as many as I can reach. I know that this is important to her—I don't know why, but I will honor her wish. She was buying back every canvas she could from the Rincon series painted in the last two years. Will you part with the one she gave to you, for Anna's sake if not for mine? I can send you one of the earlier pieces instead—*The Highwayman* or *The Star Blower*, which I know you have always liked.

The one you own now, *The Trickster*, is a portrait of one of the creatures I told you about. Anna calls him Crow. I don't trust him. They were often in the hills together in the days just before everything went wrong. You've asked me what these creatures are, and I must admit, I do not know. Spirits, phantastes, fairies, ghosts ... no single word seems adequate. They are not supernatural beings, they are as natural as the land itself. I believe them to be an essence, a rhythm, a language, a color beyond the spectrum of our sight. They appear in the shapes we clothe them with—and at first I thought it was only Anna who had the power to do this, but now I've seen creatures from my own recent poems, flickering like moths in the mesquite groves. Perhaps it is art that gives them these shapes, or belief, or our own expectations. You once told me that art is a mirror, reflecting each new face that we wear. So are these creatures. Right now the faces that they show me are of my loneliness.

I am pathetically grateful for your words about the new poems I am writing. My agent hates them, the idiot. He says if I want to write fairy tales I should stick to children's books. Pat at Scribner's is telling anyone who'll listen that I drink too much, I've lost my edge, I'll never write another Exile Songs. He is right of course—but that doesn't mean the poems I'm writing now are no good. Pat will publish them regardless of his doubts—the Pulitzer has earned me that at least, even if I still have a readership that can be counted on the fingers of one hand. The hell with Pat, and Frank, and the critics. The hell with the entire literary world. I am writing down the language of this land as I hear it, and what poet can do more?

So how is Hugo's film coming? Your own new story is enchanting and strange and I am disgusted you can't find a publisher. If my name counted for anything these days I would tell you to go ahead and use it—but then your own name would be tarred with the same sour brush that Pat uses on mine. The critical avant-garde insists that there are no boundaries that the artist may not cross, yet it seems the mythic world is as taboo to our colleagues as the sexual world is to the censors. Look at how Richard St. Johns savaged Anna in his last review, as though she were some idiot savant painting "an unfortunate choice of subject" (I quote), "albeit with consummate skill."

Outside, the coyotes are howling in the hills. I shall finish this bottle and howl myself. I hope you will send The Trickster soon. And one more favor: this is between you and me, this is not for the damn diary.

Yours as ever,
Cooper

eight

The Drowned Girl leaves wet footprints,
plaits her hair with pond weed, fingers
white as milk, as death, as loneliness,
upon root, wood, black stone. . . .
   —The Wood Wife, *Davis Cooper*

When Maggie awoke she was alone in the bed. But she did not for a moment think that she had merely dreamed. The girl, the creature, whatever she was, had left the room not long before. The featherbed still held the indentation where she had lay sleeping, curled against the back of Maggie's knees the way her cat once had.

Maggie dressed, made herself toast and coffee, and eagerly got back to work, sitting in the little studio with her feet propped on Anna's table. There were references to a Jackrabbit Girl in Cooper's notes, she remembered. She flipped through the computer files, cross-checking. Yes. He had used the image seven different times in the rough drafts of the *Saguaro Forest* poems. And once even in the *Wood Wife* poems; a rabbit-child. She'd forgotten about that. Maggie looked it up.

   . . . curled in a twist of root,
   the face of a girl, the long limbs pelted,
   the rabbit-child lies dead
   or sleeping
   dreaming this day into nonexistence.

Maggie sat back and sipped her coffee, thinking about the night, about Thumper's pointed face, those wide eyes dark against the soft fur of her pelt. As supernatural visitations go, it had been about as frightening as taking in a stray pussycat; and like a cat, Thumper had left fleas behind her when she went. Maggie would have to do something about that. She'd been scratching ever since she got up.

It was curious to her that it didn't alarm her more to have her vision of reality so abruptly expanded to include the surreal, the supernatural—although it now seemed the most natural thing of all. But it was the only thing that made sense of it all, the notes, the poems, the packet of letters from Anna to Maisie Tippetts. Thumper. Crow. There were probably more of them, out there on the mountainside.

She found that it neither frightened nor unnerved her to think of Cooper's images walking the hills. Anna's images, she corrected herself. Perhaps because she'd lived with those images for years—ever since she'd been at university in England, reading *The Wood Wife* and walking in the Devon woods for the first time. Such was the power of Cooper's language that his world was already real to her; she'd always half-expected to glimpse it in the mossy hollows of Dartmoor. It was not hard now to abandon more rational solutions to the puzzle of Cooper's life in favor of the mythic, the surrealism that had tinged his life, and his later work, with the colors of Anna Naverra's palette.

She felt a rush of excitement as she finished her coffee and got back to work. At last she felt she was getting somewhere with the thorny mystery of Cooper—even if the path that had opened before her was not one she would have predicted. She smiled to herself, thinking about Nigel and his film sales and his six-figure deals. Nobody was going to publish this story, unless she gave herself a Brazilian name and called it magical realist fiction. It didn't matter. It wasn't pursuit of a big book deal that had brought her up here. It was the chance to finally have what Cooper had long denied her, the chance to really know him and his work.

She wished she could talk to Dora about this—it was a pity the other woman had become so uncomfortable when Maggie had broached the subject. But perhaps if Dora read Anna's letters she would begin to understand what was happening here.

Maggie flipped through the letters once again, postmarked half a century before. Anna had met the young Maisie Tippetts at Cafe Jazz in Mexico City, a favorite haunt of European exiles, just down the street from her school. Maisie had introduced Anna to Cooper, confiding his romantic story to her: he'd fled from a French detention camp to New York, marrying a wealthy young socialite there; then he had fled to Mexico City to run from the disastrous marriage.

At Cafe Jazz, Anna found herself surrounded by artists she'd only read about before—including a group of women Surrealists who encouraged her desire to paint. In one short year she had gone from being a good Catholic girl in a well-to-do family, to living with Cooper, a married man, and moving in avant-garde circles. By the time Maisie left for New York and the steady correspondence between them began, Anna's family had already disowned her—a situation she referred to with humor as dry and as sharp as the desert.

But scratch the surface of the bohemian young woman, and a proper Catholic schoolgirl still lay beneath. There was pain beneath the protective wit, and a desperate dependency on Cooper, who was required, it seemed, to fill up the space where an entire extended family used to be. And yet to go back to her family, Anna had written Maisie with heartbreaking simplicity, would require that she give up painting. And that she could never do.

So many people lost family during the war that Anna Naverra did not consider her own loss to be exceptional. But her letters were tinged with unhappiness that never lifted during the rest of her brief life. Maggie's picture of Naverra had always been of the strong-willed, fiery, creatively fecund woman that Davis Cooper's reminiscences portrayed; and she was those things, but those qualities were increasingly cloaked by a veil of depression. By the time she and Cooper left Mexico City and settled here in the United States, she had turned her back on the rest of the world, retreating into her own private place of myth, symbolism, and dream.

September 9, 1947

Dearest M.,

    I have had another visitation. You'll laugh again at my "stories." Very well. You may call them my stories if you wish, but one day you'll come west once again and then, my dear, you'll see. I've been experimenting. It has been my theory that I have been creating these ethereal beings. Yes, how very arrogant of me. I am not God. Now I believe I merely create the shape they wear, like clothes, which they put on in deference for my modesty, not theirs. They have no modesty. They do not think like us. They are clearly amoral beings. I do not yet know where they fit in the heavenly hierarchy I was taught as a child. They are somewhere between us and the angels, I think. Or perhaps between us and el diablo.

    Cooper's cold has not gone away. That horrid man brought it here with him, that hard little journalist friend of Henry Miller's, with a hard little heart in his hard little breast. He pestered Cooper for an interview and finally Cooper gave in to him. It was a mistake. Now he's lost a whole week of work on Exile Songs. *Ah, but the card from you has cheered us up. Sweet Maisie, you will still be welcome here even when we build a wall of sparkling quartz eight million, trillion, zillion feet tall to shut out the rest of the world.*

October 23, 1947

Dearest M.,

    My experiments continue, with intermittent success. I've learned I can paint these creatures now if I paint in a particular way, and that seems to bind them more securely to this earth—or at least to the forms they wear. When I walk in the hills I often see them. They seem to be growing more solid. But sometimes I am frightened by what I call up, and then the paintings must be destroyed. Cooper doesn't like this. He wants to preserve all of my work, the dark and the light. He says that one must balance the other, but I don't think that can be right. I think the dark will overwhelm the light if I give it half the chance. Look what has happened in Europe after all. I have learned to fear the dark.

Cooper is often far away, deep within the poems now. Exile Songs is nearly done and I hate the book with a savagery I'd feel for a rival of the heart. Now I know how Cooper feels when he loses me to the paint and the hills. But the place where he goes—into the past, the land of memory, war, regret—is a place I cannot follow him. That dead world is more real to Cooper right now than the mountains. Or me.

March 20, 1948

Dear Maisie,

I wish you wouldn't encourage Cooper with this mad idea of a trip to New York. He says that I should come with him, but I can't leave the mountains now. There are too many paintings still unfinished. Sometimes I feel there's not enough time, I shan't be able to capture them all. My skill feels like a finite thing—the well will run dry and then what will I be? Just an empty woman, searching in these hills for a vision I can no longer see.

Cooper is recovering his mind again now that Exile Songs *is done. I've only just gotten him back, Maisie. Don't take my Cooper away to New York. New York doesn't need him as I do.*

June 29, 1948

My dearest M.,

Thank you for the books, mi corazón. *How did you know that we have developed an interest in Trickster legends? One of the creatures here is a Trickster. I have named him Crow. He amuses me, but sometimes he can be very trying. . . . And thank you indeed for finding* The Moon Wife *by Rosa Bete, you have made Cooper happy. He read the book as a child, you see, and has been longing to read her tales again. Fairy tales and myth and legends—they are the meat of his diet now. He has become quite the expert on the subject, dear Maisie—now, aren't you surprised?*

Our days out here are quiet ones. The harsh summer heat fills the valley below and reaches us even here. The paints have failed me, the images fled, Crow and the others, all disappeared. Or perhaps the heat has driven them away, pushed them farther up into the hills along with the wolves, the coyotes, and the deer. I am lonely without them. I was lonelier still when Cooper was far away from me. I was afraid New York would steal him back—but he belongs to the mountain after all.

We are together here, and yet we are alone. No one else lives in the canyon now. At night, the desert air is soft. The tall saguaro are crowned with fruit, and the birds pick at the sweet red pulp until it runs like blood. In the hills of Mexico, my grandmother's people are busy turning it into wine.

I often think of Mexico. Of my family. Of my sisters, married women now, with growing children of their own. The paintings will be my children since we have decided I shall not bear ones of the flesh. Perhaps this sounds paltry to you, but when they leave me, those children, then I know I am a mother indeed, for it feels as though my heart will break.

Perhaps I will have to tell Riddley that I simply can't exhibit anymore.

September 10, 1948

My dearest M.,

I have been thinking of you all day. I am sending you kisses and bottles of champagne and a chariot pulled through the New York sky by six white birds and a seventh of black, taking you to your opening night in a dress the color of the Rincons. I know it will be wonderful. You must send us all the reviews—as well as a picture of this new man of yours. He'd better love you as much as we do or I shall place a hex upon him! I could do it. My mother's mother was a witch, although no one ever liked to speak of that. She was a small fierce Indian woman, from one of the Northern desert tribes. But no one liked to speak of that either.

I have no news to match your own. My life is quiet, the hours slow. Some days I do not speak at all, at least with the voice you know. I have learned to speak with chalk and paint, to listen to the wood and stone. When you and Richard come at Christmas, you'll see the paintings, *and then you'll understand. Then we'll talk about real things, true things—all the things I cannot speak of here. Then Time will be our pathway, Maisie, and Distance shall never come between us.*

November 9, 1948

My dearest M.,

I have learned so much. I have learned at last how to talk to the paint, and through the paint to the fire, the water, the stones, the wind in the mesquite. There are seven paintings that must be done, and yet I only know six of them:

The Windmage
The Rootmage
The Floodmage
The Woodmage
The Stonemage
The Nightmage

Those are their names. I have not discovered who the Seventh is, or even if the Six are true images, or merely the reflection of my own ideas. But I work hard every day. I am thin and strong. I can walk for hours into the hills. I will learn to walk the spiral path and when I do, ah, then how I shall paint!

Can you send more of those brushes I like? Riddley will give you a check.

December 4, 1948

My dearest, dearest M.,

I am sorry about Richard. You say you are past tears now, but I would still give you this shoulder to cry on, or even just to lean on, if only I could step from Here to There, walking on the spiral path. I came across this in a book yesterday, by Dorothy Sayers, and I thought of you:

'The best remedy for a bruised heart is not, as so many people seem to think, repose upon a manly bosom. Much more efficacious are honest work, physical activity, and the sudden acquisition of wealth.'

The first two I know you have in abundance, so I am sending you a wishing stone for the third, this little desert quartz wrapped up in silk. And the turquoise stone is for protection, of your heart, of your precious self. Cooper and I send all our love. If you took ten Mr. Richard St. Johns and stacked them all together end to end, you would still be worth more than all of them. I still can't believe he already had a wife. Was he going to tell you at the altar?

December 20, 1948

My dearest M.,

Enclosed are two Christmas presents for you—I wish that they were better ones. I wish I could give you all the magic in the world filled into a great copper tub. Then you could warm it and step inside and have yourself a luxurious soak.

Yet in this simple copper band is more magic than most of our kind will ever see. You must not wear it, but keep it close. Someday it will want to return to the mountains, but now I think you must have it. Keep it close, and I will be close too.

The other gift I have drawn for you. I am sorry it is not a painting, as you'd have liked. I feel the new paintings must not leave the mountains, but I wish to give you something of mine. And so I send this sketch, this child of mine, and ask that you please give it a home, as skinny and ragged and humble as it is. I send this parcel with my love, and Cooper would surely send his as well, if he were speaking today.

March 3, 1949

Sweet Maisie,

How is it I have a friend who is so strong and brave and vital as you? I would hide at home by my nice, warm fire, but there you are, speaking out from the stage, the street corner, the lecture room—and now you are ready to go before Congress and speak out for Women once again. Surely Injustice must tremble in his boots when he hears that Maisie Tippetts has come in. You are trying to change the world, my dear, and I but to understand my little piece of it. It is good of you to love me anyway, foolish little dreamer that I am.

And I cannot even claim that I am succeeding in my own small task. The land baffles me, showing me a strange new face every time I walk it. But this is one thing I have discovered to be true: the land will mirror back at you whatever it is that you most expect to see. Whether that be good or ill. When I look in that mirror, I see images in oil paint, spirals, feathers, creatures metamorphosizing from leaf to flesh and back again. Cooper, of course, sees language in the mirror of the stones, the sky, the trees. And you, what will you see, my Maisie? You must come, please—come and tell me.

April 20, 1949

My dear,

I am sorry. I know you must be hurt, or angry. I don't know what I can say to explain. I only know you mustn't come. It is because I love you that I keep you away. Can you understand? It is difficult now. I fear that I have made a terrible, terrible mistake. I keep thinking back to the years of my girlhood, before I lost the state of Grace. I have no such protection here, no holy water, no penitence. Only a stone, that crumbles in my hand like my hopes, my work, our future.

I set pen to paper in order to explain, and now I give you riddles, like Cooper. Let me be clear then. I found myself pregnant with Cooper's child. I am no longer pregnant. There. The words are said.

Maisie, I am not a good woman. I have done things no one should do. I've loved these paintings, these breathing images, more than any flesh and blood, more than anyone but Cooper, maybe even more than him. And the God that I knew as a child would surely Damn me now for that.

Please understand, I couldn't bear for you to see me now, like this. I must be still, regain my strength. And then, my dear, I must paint.

April 24, 1949

Dearest M.,

As you see, I have sent you a canvas. It is my final painting: The Nightmage. *The other paintings must remain on the mountain, but this one, my dear, you must promise me to keep safe in New York, far from here.*

It is the finest I have ever done, this stagman with his horns of flames. He is a master of fire, and an artist himself. He was my muse, but no longer. I have been his creature, while I thought he was mine. I have been his canvas, his chalk and his paint. I know I will not paint again. I am emptied out. I am hollow inside. The land mirrors my nightmares now and I cannot bear this emptiness. Worst of all, I can not answer the questions I see in Cooper's eyes.

He doesn't know there was a child, Maisie. I cannot tell him. I cannot tell him.

Now I want only peace, silence, empty white walls around me. I don't want to see these colors, these spirals, these lines, this terrible beauty anymore. And so I entrust my work, my muse, my passion for the land, my love for Cooper into your strong and capable hands, where I know they will find safe haven.

A.N.

Maggie held Anna's last letter in her hand, staring out at the mesquite wood that lay beyond the window glass. Anna may have sat in this very same spot when she wrote the letter to Maisie. Never dreaming that half a century later a stranger would read those anguished words. She felt again that pang of conscience that made her wonder if she was even cut out for the role of biographer. It was different than journalism, different than interviewing a living and willing subject.

Cooper must have wanted this, or he'd never have left his papers to her. Maisie must approve as well, or she wouldn't have sent Anna's letters. But what about Anna Naverra herself? Maggie sighed. She knew what the answer would be. And she didn't know if she had it in her to ignore it, to publish these letters anyway. But she also could not simply abandon the work, and leave the riddle of Cooper unsolved.

At the very least she wanted to find, or reconstruct, *The Sagauro Forest*. She owed him that, for bringing her here to this land that was stealing her heart.

Dora put on a silk chemise, a man's vest, and a long bright skirt—a full one, good for dancing, with a lace petticoat of Anna Naverra's peeking out from underneath. She tied back her hair, and put on earrings of dangling Mexican *milagros*. Around her neck she wound the strands of a Zuni necklace: silver beads and malachite. She pulled on her scuffed green cowboy boots, and smiled at herself in the bedroom mirror. It had been too long since she and Juan had gone out on a date and enjoyed themselves. Juan hadn't been off the mountain in weeks. A night on the town would do them good—and their marriage good as well.

The barrio bar where Fox played tonight used to be one of their favorite haunts, just down the street from the little house they'd rented when they first got to Tucson. The music would be loud, the beer would be cold; she wanted to dance until the place closed down. "What do you think, Bandido?" she asked, attempting a Cajun two-step, the move made awkward by the piles of clothes, books, and lumber underfoot. "How do you think I look, old boy?" The dog yawned hugely, rolled over on his back, and closed his eyes, ignoring her.

The light was still on in Juan's studio. She checked her watch. They ought to leave soon. She left the house, whistling zydeco tunes as she crossed the stable yard. "Juan?" she said, pushing open the door.

He sat on a stool in front of his easel, his dark hair paint-streaked and tousled, sticking up in an endearing way.

"Juan?" she said again, smiling. "It's eight o'clock. Hello, Mr. del Río? Anyone home?"

He pulled his eyes away from the canvas with effort, and focused on her. "Dora," he said, naming her. Looking dazed. "What is it? What's wrong? What do you want?"

"Nothing's wrong, love. It's just getting on time to go to the Hole, or we'll miss the first set. Are you going to want to clean up first? Mind you, I think the dishevelled-painter look is rather sexy," she added as she came up behind him and put her arms around his waist. "Eau de Turpentine. My favorite." She kissed him behind one ear.

He sat stiffly in her embrace, still looking at his work. The canvas had dark shapes blocked out, images slowly emerging from the paint. He moved away from her and took off his glasses, rubbing his eyes with the heels of his hands. "Oh lord, Dora. Sorry. I forgot."

She shrugged, wounded, but she gave him a bright smile. "That's all right. We still have time to get there. Let's take your jeep, okay?"

He lowered his hands and looked at her. "I've just gotten going with this," he explained, "and I can't really leave it now. Oil paint dries too damn fast out here in the desert—I need to work while it's still wet." He put on his work glasses again. "I'll tell you what, we'll go out tomorrow night instead. I promise."

Dora swallowed. "I'm at the hotel tomorrow night. And it's tonight that Fox is playing. Juan, we made these plans days ago. We never go out anymore."

He gave a short, explosive sigh, and paced over to his worktable. He picked up a paint-soaked rag and a clean bristle brush, and he turned to face her. "Dora. Honey," he said to her with a visible attempt at patience, "I'm in the middle of my *work*. We can always go out another night but this . . . this is important to me. And this isn't going to wait."

She took a deep breath, and conceded, "Yes, of course. I know your work is important." And not me, she added silently. Then she winced at the petty sound of that. Disappointment was a stone she swallowed, lodged inside her throat.

"That's my girl. I knew you'd understand." He smiled as he stepped back to the canvas, patting her shoulder as he passed. Exactly the way he patted Bandido or the cats. Absently. Dismissing her.

The gesture undid her. "Actually, Juan," she said more sharply, "I don't understand. I don't see why this is more important than a promise you've made to your wife."

He shot her a puzzled look. "Come on, you're being melodramatic.

It's only one night out, after all. We'll do it again. We'll go dancing next weekend." She stared at him stonily. He sighed again. "Look, I'm right in the middle of things here, so if you really need to argue about this, we're just going to have to do it later." He turned decisively back to the canvas, adding rusty color on the left side of it with wide, cross-hatching strokes.

"We need to talk about this, Juan," she persisted, stepping toward him. "It's not just tonight. It's too many nights of broken promises, all adding up. It's you sleeping on the sofa now. It's the fact that you won't even talk to me anymore—goddamn it, put the brushes down and talk to me for once."

He shook off the hand she had put on his arm. "This is not a good time for a therapy session. I need to capture this image while it's fresh—and if you keep on like this, I'm going to lose it." He ran his paint-stained fingers through his hair, looking harried. "Why are you doing this now? Why does this have to be a big deal? We can talk about it later, all right? We'll talk about it tomorrow."

"No, we won't," she said quietly, close to tears. "You won't want to talk tomorrow either."

He turned on her then, anger in his eyes. "Don't play the martyr here, Dora. It's not attractive. It doesn't work on me." Juan stabbed the brush into the paint on the palette. "You married a painter, you want me to be good. You're always on at me about bringing in more money—so for god's sake, let me do my job."

She paled and backed off. "All right," she said. Her voice was high and tremulous. Exasperation crossed his face.

"Oh for heaven's sake, don't start crying now. Why is everything such a drama with you these days? If you wanted a man who worked nine-to-five, you should have married a banker, not me. You know I can't predict when a painting is going to happen. Why is this such a problem all of a sudden?"

Dora took another steadying breath. She wasn't going to cry. She wasn't going to stand there like a fool. "I'm still going out tonight," she told him. "Even if you're not coming. I need time off the moun-tain, Juan."

He shrugged. "Fine. I hope you have a good time." He bent over his painting again, blending the rusty tones into the browns. He gave her one last glance over his shoulder. "Tell Fox I'll catch him next time."

"You tell him yourself," she snapped.

She left the barn, closing the door behind her—although her impulse was to slam it. She was torn between anger with him, and guilt. Was she indeed being ridiculous? Weighing a night out in a bar over art? Only, sometimes it seemed inspiration only struck when he was supposed to be doing something else, something for her, or their marriage—and right now that excuse was wearing thin. She went into the kitchen, picked up the phone, and angrily punched in Maggie's number.

"This is Dora," she said. Her voice still wavered. She cleared her throat and tried again. "I know this is short notice, but you wouldn't happen to feel like going out, would you? Right now, I mean. To a bar called the Hole. I'm all dressed up and ready to go, but I've lost my dancing partner. . . . You would? Hot damn, I'll be right over." She hung up the phone and picked up her purse. She was going to have a good time tonight, she told herself firmly, Juan or no Juan.

Dora fetched the keys. She'd take Juan's jeep. He was like a kid with a new toy with the thing; he still didn't like anyone else to drive it. She backed from the yard, grinding the gears and aware that her husband would hear the sound. She gunned the engine and sped from the drive, kicking gravel into the yard.

When she turned onto the road, her headlights picked out three shadows approaching from across the wash. The Foxxe sisters. And Angela's boyfriend, Pepe Hernández. They waved at her to stop, and she did.

"Are you going to hear my brother play?" Isabella asked her.

"That's right." She made herself smile, blinking back an onslaught of angry tears. "Do you want to come along?"

"Can we?"

"You'll have to squeeze together in back, because Maggie is coming."

The Foxxe sisters climbed into the jeep, with Pepe wedged between them. He was a skinny young man, with a sweet brown face and black hair falling to the collar of his T-shirt. He wore an eyepatch over one eye, and always looked to Dora like an underfed pirate. His T-shirt read SAVE OUR DESERT on the front, and on the back, VOTE NO TO THE ROCKING K DEVELOPMENT. It was an old T-shirt and a lost cause; that old ranch would soon be history.

"Strap yourselves in and hold on tight," Dora warned them as she pulled the jeep into Cooper's yard. "I don't quite have the hang of driving this thing." She leaned on the horn and Maggie stepped out onto the porch, looking dashing in her black L.A. suit. She locked her door and came over.

"Maggie, you know Angela and Isabella. And this is Pepe. They're coming with us."

"Great, it's a party." She climbed into the jeep. "Dora, I'm glad you called. I was just about to go out to the U., to hear a chamber quartet. But I'd much rather dance. I definitely need a night out on the town."

"Not half as much as I do," Dora wagered, flooring the gas, speeding down Cooper's driveway and trailing clouds of dust behind. She steered the jeep through the dry wash bed and out to the graded dirt road of Reddington Pass. Then she turned the radio to a salsa station, and headed for the lights of Tucson.

The Hole was officially The Hole in the Wall, but no one used that cutesy name. The place itself was not cutesy, it was a bit of a dive, southwestern style. Located downtown in an old adobe building at the edge of the Barrio Histórico, it had remnants of a past glory in its saguaro rib ceilings, carved oak doors, thick adobe walls, and weathered wood plank floors. There were bullet holes in one smoke-stained wall from bandidos back in 1912.

Maggie stopped and read the sign on the door: BIG BAD BAYOU RATTLER BOYS. "Is that the band? What kind of a name is that?"

Dora laughed at her expression. "There are musicians out of four different bands jamming together tonight. Bayou Brew is a Cajun band. Diamondback Rattlers are Tex-Mex, mostly. Big Bad Wolf plays Celtic punk and the Momba Rhomba Boys are reggae. Fox has played with all of them at one time or another."

"Fox is playing?"

"You bet he is. Fox miss a jam like this?" Dora said, and behind her the Foxxe sisters giggled.

"What kind of music will it be tonight then?"

"*Loud* music," Dora answered. "This isn't exactly Estampie, honey. Anything goes in a jam like this, so long as it's danceable."

She took Maggie's arm and steered her through the door. Inside, the rambling rooms of the bar were already growing crowded. Dora recognized some familiar faces from when she used to live down here: Mexican couples from old barrio families; Anglo yuppies bent on renovating the neighborhood; Little Bob, the hotshot environmental writer; Big Jon, the folklorist, sitting in the corner with his banjo in his lap. Aging hippies and Earth First types in faded clothes from Guatemala mixed with U-of-A students in bright gym clothes that exposed a lot of suntanned flesh. Urban cowboys were propping up the bar, tossing back double shots of tequila.

Dora threaded through the hot, smokey rooms, Maggie and the others trailing behind her. She greeted a woman who used to be a neighbor; nodded at a customer from the gallery; kissed the cheek of a young Apache man she'd met in her bookmaking class. Beyond the maze of little inner rooms was a central courtyard open to the stars. Clematis flowers, big as saucers, covered the vines that choked the walls. Mismatched tables had been pushed back to make room for dancing on the cracked tile floor. The band was setting up on a stage built under the limbs of a mesquite tree. Fox was bent over a tangle of wires; he looked up, saw her, and pointed left.

"Fox has saved us a table," Dora reported. It was close to the stage, with a RESERVED sign on it. Pepe went looking for another chair, Maggie for a pitcher of beer, and Dora sat down with the Foxxe sisters, who were quiet, wary of the crowd.

Maggie came back with a tray loaded down with a sweating pitcher of Dos Equis and bowls of white tortilla chips and green chili salsa, blistering hot. She sat beside Dora and said to her, "Just go ahead and have a good time. You look like you could use it. I'll have one beer then switch to tonic, so I can drive us home."

Dora opened her mouth to protest, then she shut it. Maggie was right. She needed this. If Juan had been here, she would have stayed sober to drive home and even that would have provoked an argument. He would never admit when he was drunk, even when he could barely stand. The hell with that. The hell with Juan, she told herself as she knocked back a beer. She was going to let down her hair tonight, and she wasn't going to think about her husband.

Fox came over to their table, an electric cable looped over his arm. "Howdy. Where's Juan?" he said to Dora, his eyes flickering pointedly to Maggie and back.

"Painting," Dora answered flatly.

Fox looked at her closely, his eyes narrowed. Then he turned to the others at the table. "Hi, Maggie. Hey, Pepe," Fox said, and he gave each of his sisters a kiss on the cheek. "We're starting here in just a few minutes. We've been waiting for Angel, as usual." He nodded at the notoriously spacey drummer, who was still unpacking his gear. "I'd better go help or we'll be here all night. And the natives are getting restless."

The crowd was indeed a rowdy one, which boded well for the dancing. Dora poured herself another beer, amazed at how the first had disappeared. Maggie touched her arm. "Why are some of the band members wearing masks?" she said.

Dora followed her gaze. Two tall black men with long rasta hair had half-masks on with beaky noses; the punky bass player had a mask of rhinestones pushed to the top of her head. "It's Halloween in a couple of days," Dora said. "Guess they're celebrating early."

"Halloween already? Boy, this month passed fast. It doesn't feel like October here in the desert, when it's still so warm."

"Is this your first night out since you got here?" Dora asked.

"I hate to admit it, but it is." Maggie smiled a guilty smile, rolling up the sleeves of her Armani jacket. Dora thought she looked very glamorous tonight, and she'd bet good money Fox thought so too. "I'm turning into a hermit up there in the canyon, just like Cooper."

"Cut yourself some slack. It's only been a month, and you don't even know the town yet."

"I'm not going to get to know it if I shut myself away in Cooper's house. But you know, it helps me to understand why Cooper was the way he was. I've been in the mountains such a short time, and already it's a shock whenever I come back down. It takes a definite mental adjustment to get used to being around the traffic and the noise."

"Now you sound like One of Us," Dora said with satisfaction, sitting back in her chair with her feet propped up on the edge of Pepe's. "But it was different down here for most of Cooper's life. The city didn't gobble up the whole valley until, oh, maybe twenty years ago. I wish that we could go back in time and live in the town he and Anna knew, when more of it was like this neighborhood—a homegrown, desert kind of place. And less of it full of shopping malls like Anywhere, America."

"Didn't you live near here?" Maggie asked her.

"Yeah, when we first moved down from Vermont. I was too homesick to appreciate it though. Which was the last thing I ever expected to be—after encouraging Juan to move back near his family just so I could get away from mine."

Maggie smiled. "Was yours so awful then? I thought you liked your family."

"I do. Particularly with a continent between us. I'm serious! They're sweet people, my parents, I love 'em to death. But they're completely hopeless. They're still flower children and they're pushing fifty now. Did I tell you I was raised on a commune?"

"For real?"

"For real. Until I was twelve, anyway. Then they built their own place—a log cabin with a woodstove that always smoked and a wretched freezing outhouse in the back. All terribly PC and organic, of course." Dora rolled her eyes.

"There were other kids, right? You said it was a big family. All boys but you, do I have that right?"

"Yep. I'm the oldest. Can't you tell? The practical, responsible type—that's me. I pretty much raised the other five kids. Seven if you include my parents." Dora sighed. "I'll tell you, I'm getting tired of it. Of being sensible. Paying the bills. Wearing fruit on my head in a stupid hotel bar." She poured more beer, took another hit, and wiped her mouth on the back of her hand. "If I stop being the practical one, what do you suppose will happen then? We can all sit around and paint while they turn off the lights and the water, and the bank takes the house."

Maggie looked at her closely. "I thought you seemed a little tense tonight. Is that what this is about? Did you and Juan have a fight?"

"A fight? It takes two to fight. And that would take too much time away from Juan's precious paintings." Dora flushed. She had meant to say the words lightly, as a joke, not in a burst of temper.

Maggie leaned forward and touched her hand. "Do you know that you are repeating one of Cooper's letters, practically word for word?"

"Cooper?" Dora said, surprised.

"That's right. Complaining about Anna. When she painted, she didn't care about anything else—not Cooper, not their friends, not the house, not anything."

"That's interesting." She was embarrassed by her outburst and glad to share the problem with Cooper. "I thought this was an exclusively female dilemma I was having. I thought I was turning into one of those horrible women whining: 'Honey, pay attention to me.'"

"Well, it usually is a female problem," said Maggie; "and not a unique one either, so don't be so hard on yourself. How many men do you know who wear fruit on their heads so their wives can paint? I don't mean the ones who already have a good living and can afford to be magnanimous," she added quickly. "But someone who's working hard, scrimping, saving, making sacrifices for a woman's art."

Dora shook her head. She couldn't think of anyone who fit Maggie's description. And like Maggie, she could think of half a dozen of her girlfriends in that position.

"Now Anna," said Maggie, in between munching on hot salsa and tortilla chips, "she lived a fairly privileged life. She grew up in a time and place where it was expected that a man would support her. Cooper had an inheritance, so it wasn't a financial sacrifice for him—but he went to the mountains for the sake of Anna's work, even when he'd have rather gone back to New York. He always took Anna seriously, as an artist of equal calibre. There weren't many women of her time—or even of ours—who could say as much."

"But his support wasn't enough, was it? Look at what happened to Anna in the end. She was only my age when she killed herself."

Maggie shook her head. "No, it wasn't enough. Cooper couldn't stand against the entire weight of her family, her culture, her religious upbringing. Or of all the critics," she added drily, "who dismissed her work as derivative of any male painter within five hundred miles."

"Well then, you've got to give old Cooper credit. He really believed in Anna." Dora frowned again. "And I believe in Juan. It's just . . . I don't know. I'm just tired, I guess. I get tired of being a wife sometimes. I want someone to be a wife for me."

"Don't we all," said Maggie with a rueful smile.

On stage, the music was starting up, amplified and cutting short any possibility of conversation. Dora didn't know whether to feel sorry or grateful for the interruption. It might be helpful to talk to Maggie about Juan, and yet she was hesitant, and not only because Isabella, Angela and Pepe were sharing the small outdoor table. She hesitated to talk to Maggie because she didn't quite know what the problem was, or even where her loyalties should lie; she only knew that something had happened out in the desert, the night that Cooper died. Since then, Juan had been a different man. And Dora was going to have to find out why.

She topped up her glass, emptying the pitcher, sending Pepe to the bar for another one. Dangblast it, girl, she scolded herself, you're not supposed to be thinking about Juan. She lifted her glass as the music began, knowing she was well on her way to getting thoroughly soused tonight.

The band started out with a Celtic reel, electrified and bone-shaking. Angel, the drummer, was hot tonight, moving smoothly between a bodhran, a dubek, a water drum, and a congo set. Fox was on accordion, a man from Bayou Brew on fiddle. The spikey-haired girl from Big Bad Wolf belted out rude Irish lyrics. They slid from one reel into another, the second as raucous as the first. Then the addition of a bass and a reggae beat turned the reel into something rather dif-

ferent. One of the tall Jamaican men took over the vocals, backed up
by the other. Dancers were spilling onto the dance floor, and Dora felt
the music's pull.

"Can I borrow your boyfriend, Angela?" she shouted over the bass.
Angela smiled. Dora knew from past experience that she would not
dance in a place like this, not even before the injury that had crippled
her right leg. Fox's sisters came for the music, and were content to sit
and quietly listen. But Pepe was a different matter. Get a single beer
into Pepe and the boy started howling at the moon.

She took Pepe's hand and pulled him into the crowd. Then she lost
herself for a good long while, existing only in the beat of the drum,
the quicksilver fiddle, the throb of the bass. She was sweating when
the set came to a stop, her face flushed hot and strands of hair escaping from her velvet hair band, but Pepe was not even breathing hard.
He gave Dora a grin turned rakish by the eye patch over one eye.

They returned to the table and she gulped down some beer, wiping
her brow with the back of her hand. "Aren't you going to dance?" she
said to Maggie as she stood, panting, catching her breath.

"Might do," Maggie said.

Dora took her by the arm. "Atta girl. Come on. You too, Pepe?"

Pepe shook his head, looking at the dance floor longingly, but hov-
ering close to the sisters.

The next set had a salsa beat, with didjeridoo thrown in for good
measure. Halfway through Maggie took off her black suit jacket and
threw it back to the table. Underneath she wore a man's sleeveless
undershirt—cooler, and rather sexy, Dora thought. Then Dora closed
her eyes again, and gave herself to the music.

They sat out the next set. Dora retied her damp hair back from
her neck, then poured another beer. She put her head close to Maggie's ear and said, "So what do you think of the band?"

Maggie gave Dora a thumbs-up sign. Her cheeks were flushed, her
sleek European haircut tousled and spikey with sweat. Dora sat back
and followed Maggie's gaze. The other woman was watching Fox. He
stood beating out the time with his boot heels, fingers flying across
the accordion keys, and it seemed remarkable to Dora that he could

make even that maligned instrument sexy. Though he'd only dressed as he always dressed—ripped jeans, flannel shirt, the inevitable cowboy boots—he had a presence on stage that drew more women's eyes than Maggie's tonight. If Fox spent his time alone these days, it was by choice, not necessity. For the next tune Fox picked up his flute, leaning close into the microphone. The sound trembled over the wailing guitars, bluesy, throaty and compelling.

Dora leaned over to Maggie again. "Our Johnny Foxxe is good, isn't he? I mean, maybe not quite like your ex-husband, but . . ."

Maggie shook her head. "So what? You can't compare them. Nigel is utterly sublime; he's in another league altogether. But Nige," she told Dora, "needs to be at the top. He's more businessman than musician now. When I met him, he'd play for the sheer pleasure of it." She made a face. "Now it's only for a crowd."

"They can give him a crowd here at the Hole," Dora teased, "and all the free beer he can drink."

Maggie laughed. "You know, it might do him a world of good. I worry about Nige. He's brilliant, successful—but he never seems to be very *happy* to me."

"Happiness is a talent like any other," Dora told her. "It's another art form. Some people are good at it, some people aren't."

Maggie looked at her thoughtfully. "Neither Cooper nor Anna were very good at it. They had a lot of talents between them, but not that one."

"Honey," said Dora with exasperation, "I think you ought to give that book a rest tonight."

"Am I sounding as single-minded as Nigel?" Maggie asked her, looking up with a guilty expression.

Dora decided not to answer that question. She gestured to the stage instead. "Now, look at Fox," she said to Maggie. "He's got the talent for happiness in spades."

Fox was completely absorbed in the music, the rhythm, the give-and-take of the session, playing with the calm and steady concentration that he gave to everything he did. The band had launched into an old Billie Holiday number, the lyrics sung in Spanish. The combination of instruments was bizarre, but its quirky energy won the crowd. The musicians were skilled, the jam was surprisingly tight and completely infectious.

The song ended, and Dora drained her beer, looking at the empty pitcher on the table. "It's a good thing you're driving," she said to Maggie. "I think I'm getting a bit drunk."

"Slow down, okay? You're going to get sick."

"You're right," she replied as the band struck up a fairly straight-forward Cajun tune. The accordion player from Bayou Brew took over for the set, giving Fox a break. Dora said, "I think I'll dance again. Want to come?"

"I don't know how to dance to this."

"Fox will teach you. He's the one who taught me and Juan how to two-step. It's not so hard."

"I don't think—"

Dora turned to Fox as he came over to their table. "Johnny, teach Maggie to two-step, will you?"

He blinked at Dora. "All right," he said, taking Maggie by the hand. She could see Maggie still protesting as he pulled her onto the dance floor.

Dora smiled to herself as she watched them together, moving across the crowded floor. Maggie was having a good time out there—tripping over her feet, laughing hard, her hazel eyes very bright. Then someone touched Dora on the shoulder. Matt Romero, from her bookmaking class.

"Do you want to dance, Dora?"

"You bet I do." She smiled up at the young Apache man, feeling slightly giddy as he swung her into the crowd.

She was feeling more than slightly giddy by the late hour when the music stopped. The last remaining dancers stumbled out of the bar to the sidewalk, reeking of beer and smoke. The electric signs in the window switched off. The musicians were hauling equipment to their trucks. The sky was clear in the valley tonight, but the stars seemed distant compared to the canyon's stars. She'd be glad to get back home to the Rincons now, and gulp down that bracing mountain air.

She was feeling rather dizzy. She leaned on Matt as she followed the others to the parking lot. "Good night," she told him. "Great to see you again."

He leaned down and kissed her lightly on the lips. "So call me," he said. "We'll do it again."

She shook her head. "I'm a married woman."

"Not so very married tonight," he pointed out.

"I know. But this is an exception."

"Too bad," he said softly, looking disappointed. As he walked away, he said over his shoulder, "But call me anyway, Dora, okay?"

She smiled at him, knowing she wouldn't, unless it was to talk about bindings and type. She'd had four good years of marriage with Juan; he was her lover, her family, her best friend. She wasn't going to throw it all over because things had gotten rough these last months. Not without a fight, she wasn't, she decided as she climbed into the jeep.

Maggie drove them home, and the ride went fast, for the traffic had thinned on the city streets. In the back seat, Angela and Isabella were singing Billie Holiday songs, in Spanish, the way the band had played them—their lovely voices too soft, too ethereal to do justice to the blues. When they reached the eastern part of town, the roads grew dark and quiet at last. They turned up the dirt road into the mountains. The Foxxe sisters were singing songs now in a language Dora didn't know—low, haunting songs, like a Navajo flute given voice, or the songs a saguaro might sing; or perhaps it was just that Dora was very drunk. She groaned and closed her eyes.

Maggie parked the jeep at Dora's house. "Good night, everybody. Good night, Dora. Are you sure you'll be all right?"

"Just fine," Dora reassured her as Isabella, Angela, and Pepe disappeared down the road.

"All right then. I'll see you tomorrow," Maggie said, and she followed after the Foxxe sisters.

Dora turned to the house. The lights were still on in the house and the studio; Juan was still up. She went inside through the kitchen door. She could smell smoke as she entered the house. Juan had a roaring fire going; he was standing by the hearth looking red-eyed and haggard. There were pieces of dismantled frames strewn around him. His pictures were gone from the wall.

"What are you doing?" Dora demanded.

"I'm burning shit," he said tightly. "Don't start on me, Dora. These are my paintings. I can't stand them any longer."

"Those are *our* paintings. That's *our* life you're burning. Our old life back in Vermont. Goddamn you Juan," she said, her voice breaking as she crossed the room.

He looked at her flatly. "You're drunk."

"And you're a bastard. How dare you burn all that beautiful work?"

"They're bad. They're all wrong. I don't want them anymore."

"Well, I do. I loved those paintings," she said, furious. She'd worked hard for those paintings, too. She shoved past him and reached into the fire to pull a canvas out.

He snatched it away and she reached for another. It was their marriage that was going up in the flames. He grabbed her, pulled her away from the fire. She struggled with him, clutching the charred painting. He shook her, struck her, but she wouldn't let it go.

"Those are shit, don't you see that?" he said, wild-eyed. He hit her again, harder this time. She dropped the canvas, stunned by pain, reeling, falling against the couch. "They're shit, they're all shit. I'm not that man anymore. Stop making me be that man. I want to be good. I will be good. I won't let you stop me. All this, this goddamn money-guzzling house, all this stuff, it's all shit, why can't you see that?" She huddled on the floor, her arms protecting her face, as he crossed the room grabbing objects, books, art from the walls, tossing them all to the flames. "We think we're so great," he railed at her. A book sailed past her, grazing her arm. "These stupid paintings, your little stories, our little lives—we don't hold a candle to *them*. They laugh at us. They think we're pathetic. And we are. They're the ones who are beautiful. Anna understood. Why can't you understand?"

He pulled her up, and shook her, hard, his voice worn raw and ragged. "Why can't you just understand, Dora? Why does it have to be like this?"

She bit down on his arm; when he jerked in surprise she was able to break from his bruising hold. "Leave me the hell alone. It's you. It's not me. Don't you put this on me."

She ran for the bedroom and locked the oak door, hearing things crashing heavily behind her. The cats had retreated to this room, and the dog was cowering on the floor in the corner. Dora slid to the rug beside Bandido, and buried her face in his rough black fur. Tears burned her eyes but they did not fall as she heard things smashing, his voice still railing. She prayed the place didn't burn down around them. She ought to call someone. Maybe his parents. Maybe even the police. But how could she do that to him? This was Juan, her husband, not some redneck wife-beater. That didn't happen to people like them. She sat holding tightly onto Bandido, feeling sober, and sick, and frightened now.

After a while she heard a door slam. And then there was silence. She waited. But Juan did not return—he had probably gone to the hills, to wherever it was that he went. This time she was glad; she wanted him gone. She stood, shaking. She would lock up the house. When he returned, if he returned, he could spend the night out in the barn. When this madness passed, she would let him back in. And then they would talk. Or else she'd leave.

She opened the bedroom door cautiously, feeling heartsick as she surveyed the damage. She was a wreck, one eye swelling shut. The big room was a wreck as well. And nothing remained on the walls now but the picture by Anna Naverra. Dora crossed over to it, hating it now. She took it down. It ought to burn too. But no, none of this was Anna's fault. She'd give the painting back to Maggie; she didn't care what Juan would think of that. She looked down at the ghostly white "Mage" in distaste. She didn't want it anymore.

She put it on the floor, faced against the wall. Then she gave a small cry as she looked into the hearth. Her copies of *The Spine Witch* were smouldering there along with Juan's old paintings and drawings—every single painstakingly handmade copy of the little book that Dora had. She felt her legs give way beneath her, and she sank to her knees on the cold slate floor. She pulled a charred page from the fire and ran her fingers across the unburned edge, a scrap of back type on thick cover stock embedded with cactus spines, mesquite leaves. She watched as the flames turned the rest into ash. And then, finally, the tears fell.

The boy sat still, perched on one of the granite boulders that had tumbled into Redwater Creek when the One-Who-Sleeps last stirred, or stretched, or turned in his dream of stone.

The boy's body was formed of human flesh, but his two arms were a white owl's wings. He closed his eyes and concentrated, and then he was even more human still, with arms that ended in perfect human hands, and the smooth, hairless groin of a young boy. He wore only a mask of feathers that covered and formed part of his face, and a necklace with a turquoise stone set into a thin piece of copper.

He looked down into the dark water. In the thin light of the waxing moon he could see the Drowned Girl lying there beneath the creek's black surface. He called to her in words for which there was no human translation.

"Mage," the girl acknowledged him. She opened her eyes. The water rippled.

"Mage," he acknowledged the other in turn. "It is the midnight hour. And I have come."

"So I see." She rose from the cold creek bed, silt and small fish streaming from her hair. She rubbed her eyes as though she had just woken up, although she never slept. She was mimicking some human or another; she glanced at him to see if he had guessed. Then she waded from the cold creek water and up onto the stoney bank.

Her dress was wet, mud-stained, and torn; he could see through the fabric to the white flesh beneath. Her feet were bare; she was oblivious of the cactus spines, the brambles and thorns. She tossed her head, and fire smoked, and then her cloud of white hair was dry, crackling like static on shoulders so thin and pale they were almost transparent. Her bloodless skin was of a white shading on blue; her slanted eyes were black as coal. And yet she was terribly beautiful; she pulsed hot and cold, like a star.

"The painter is coming," the Owl Boy told her.

"Juan," she said, tasting the name. "I am almost finished with this one, which is a pity. He is exquisite."

"You are driving him mad."

She acknowledged this with a nod, tilting her lovely head.

"But will he do what needs to be done? Will he hunt? Will he kill, this painter of yours?"

The girl smiled, a sharp little smile.

"And what will you give him in return?" he asked. "What is it he wants?"

"The usual. His dreams are of wealth and fame. He has asked to paint Great paintings."

He yawned. "How dull. He should learn from Anna. He should ask to paint true paintings instead."

"Ah, but then he would be dangerous." She stroked his back, and the boy sprouted feathers beneath the soft pressure of her touch. "And Anna is dead. He'll learn nothing from her. He does not walk the spiral path."

The Owl Boy laughed.

She cocked her head. "Now he is climbing up the hill. Come, and you can watch me work," she invited her partner and her rival.

He flung himself back into the white owl shape, and followed after her.

DAVIS COOPER
Redwater Road
Tucson, Arizona

Sisters of Mercy Convent
Mexico City

October 1, 1949

My beloved Anna,

    Yes, I am writing again. Do you even get these letters, I wonder? Or does someone stop them, your mother perhaps, or the sisters at the convent? I send them out into your silence, still hoping for one small word in return. Can you hear me? Can you see me? Can you forgive me for whatever it is I might have done to drive you away?

    The sycamore leaves are turning to gold along the banks of Redwater Creek. The late summer rains have given us a season of flowers— they are covering the hills now. Pink lantana, lush orange mallows, carpets of deep purple verbena and those yellow, fragile-looking things whose name I can never remember and now you are no longer here to remind me. How is it that a land that grieves for you can look so beautiful? For I can feel its grief, a murmur in the stones, a sigh in the wind through the mesquite wood—or perhaps it is my own grief, heavy as granite in the hollows of my heart.

    Even your creatures sigh and droop and look to me less substantial now, shimmering in the desert heat. Yes I know, you will say they are not "yours" at all, but they wear the shapes you gave to them. They hover in the trees beyond the house seeming puzzled and perturbed by your absence. The Spine Witch peers in the studio window, hissing and bristling, like an angry cat, when she sees my face and not yours through the glass. The rootmegs gather in the mesquite wood; they no longer flee when I walk by, but simply sit in the shadows of the trees, watching me with wide, dark eyes. What would you have me tell them, Anna? And what should I say to Maisie? Or to Riddley Wallace when he writes to ask when you will send him paintings again?

    Forgive me. I will not pressure you. Take what time you need to think, to mend, to do whatever it is you have to do—just so long as you come home again to this sad, drunk poet who needs you. The Rincons need you. The coyotes and the deer and the jackrabbits all need you. I can't bear to think of you in the flatlands where the stones do not whisper your name. Come home, or let me come to you.

With my heart in my hands,
your Cooper

nine

The Spine Witch searches the soil
for grubs and beetles, the skeletons of birds
and discarded poems, their bones
as weightless as breath. Or prayer.
—**The Wood Wife,** *Davis Cooper*

The sun was already high above the mountains when Maggie rose the next morning. She rubbed her eyes, disoriented. The day had started without her. Thumper lay at the foot of the bed, curled into a ball of fur. She'd been there when Maggie had returned last night, snoring softly in the nest of quilts. Maggie slid carefully out from under the blankets, careful not to wake the girl.

The day was hot, the sky cloudless, as Maggie stepped onto the porch to retrieve the pile of morning mail, including the letters that still came for Cooper, and a thick envelope from London. Beyond the porch were a dozen fat quail, their topknots bobbing like question marks as they searched out a breakfast of seeds and bugs from the dry and dusty soil. A sidewinder snake divided the group as it undulated across the yard, moving through the sage and the brittlebush with a sideways motion. The quail scattered apart suddenly, and the snake lifted an inquisitive head. The skinny coyote had come into the yard, trotting briskly from the mesquite wood. He ignored the snake but eyed the fat grey birds, licking his chops.

"Good morning," Maggie called.

The coyote cocked his head and looked at her through his one good eye. His long pink tongue was visible, hanging comically to one side.

Then he came toward her, approaching slowly, moving in a strange, stiff way. His back was arched aggressively, but he held his head tucked low in submission. His mouth gaped in a snarl, or a smile, exposing long rows of canine teeth. She had read about this in the books she'd borrowed from John. This was how coyotes made friends, or communicated peaceful intentions. But nothing she'd read indicated they would do this with humans, only other coyotes.

Inch by inch the coyote crossed the yard, bowing and bobbing as he came, till he stood just at the edge of the porch by the step where Maggie sat. He turned his head, looking through the good eye. He made a sound deep in his throat. Then he bussed her hand with his long cold nose, gave a bark, and dashed away.

She waited on the porch a while longer, but the one-eyed coyote did not return. The quail came back to finish their meal. A spotted roadrunner appeared in the yard; it stopped for a moment, raising and lowering its long tail, then it turned and raced on.

Maggie took the pile of mail inside. She put the teakettle on the stove. The house was quiet. Thumper was still sleeping when she went into the bedroom to grab some clothes. It wasn't until Maggie sat down to breakfast along with the latest letter from Tat and a copy of last week's *Village Voice* that she heard the bedsprings squeak in the other room and a flurry of footsteps.

Thumper appeared in the kitchen doorway, one ear standing straight and stiff, the other angled down over one eye. She stood and blinked, her eyes very dark, her hands spread over her belly.

Maggie swallowed, staring at the girl, who was very real, very dirty, and smelled rather strong as she stood barefoot on the kitchen floor.

"Are you hungry?" Maggie asked. "I've got cereal here. Muesli. You can have some."

The girl nodded and came into the kitchen, pelted feet padding softly across the floor. Maggie continued to stare at her. She needed more coffee, no doubt about it.

Maggie dished muesli into a second bowl, poured milk over it, and placed it on the table. She sat down and gestured to another chair.

Thumper looked at it. She climbed over the chair and sat hunched on the tabletop. With small, agile fingers, she fished the oats and nuts from the milk and popped them in her mouth. Maggie watched the girl eat, then she went to the sink and ran tap water into a glass. She passed it to Thumper, who took hold of it, her expression intent, almost reverent. She dipped her tongue into it three times, and then she passed it back to Maggie.

"No, that's for you," Maggie told the girl, and Thumper's eyes grew even wider. Of course, Maggie realized, water would be precious to a creature of this land. "But let me put it in a bowl for you instead. I think you'll find it easier that way."

The girl emptied the bowl, lapping at the water delicately with her small pink tongue. She looked amazed when Maggie filled the bowl again from the tap at the sink. She said, distressed, in her soft, gravelly voice, "But I mustn't. I don't have anything to give to you."

"That's all right," Maggie told her.

Thumper shook her head. It wasn't all right.

"Well then," said Maggie, sitting down again, "I'll tell you what you can give me. I'd like you to answer some questions for me."

The girl looked at her warily.

"Is that the rule," Maggie asked her, remembering Cooper's notes about gifts and exchange, "that when you receive something, you must give something back?"

Thumper nodded, looking down at her toes.

"But you've taken things from this house before. My stones. My Celtic broach."

"The Spine Witch took the stones," she whispered. "And then she gave you Sight."

"Sight?"

"So you could See the desert."

"She did? Well now, that's interesting. Why did the Spine Witch want the stones?"

"For protection." Thumper lifted her eyes.

"Protection from what?"

The Rabbit Girl frowned. "I don't remember," she admitted.

Maggie smiled, trying to put them both at ease. "What about my silver broach then?"

Thumper hung her head. "I wanted it. It was pretty," she told Maggie.

"And what did you give back for it?"

Thumper swallowed. "Nothing. I forgot."

"What happens if you forget?" asked Maggie.

The girl looked perplexed. "Nothing happens."

"Then why is it a rule?"

Thumper shrugged, a very human gesture. "It's just a rule. That's all. It's *dammas*. It's . . . it's what you do."

"Dah-maz? What's that?"

The girl flushed red, two spots of color beneath the downy cheeks. "Beauty. Motion. That-Which-Moves." She made a spiral movement with her hands. "I can't tell you. I don't have the words. . . . Or maybe I forgot them."

"Then who has the words? Who can answer my question?"

Relief flooded the Rabbit Girl's face. "A mage. A witch. Or a shape-shifter."

Maggie said, "And what are you, then?"

"A shifter. But only a very little one. I don't know very many shapes. I always forget them," Thumper admitted. She held out her hand, so Maggie could see the spiral pattern marked on her wrist.

Maggie was reminded of Crow's spiral tattoos. "Is Crow also a shape-shifter? Is he the one I should take my questions to?"

"Uh-huh. To Crow, or else the One-Who-Sleeps—only you mustn't wake him up. But not the Drowned Girl. She scares me." Thumper shivered. "Only I forget why."

"All right," Maggie said, "I'll ask Crow then. I won't ask you anything more; I can see my questions distress you. But thank you for trying to answer anyway."

Thumper squirmed and ducked her head. "Don't thank me."

"Why not?"

"It's just another rule. I think it is. But—"

"You forget," Maggie said. She sighed.

She rose from the kitchen table and took the empty bowls to the sink. She heard the scrapping of a chair, and when she turned around, Thumper had left the room. Maggie went to the door. The girl was running through Cooper's front yard, laughing now, pleased with herself.

"Hey!" Maggie called. "Come back tonight. You're welcome here. Remember that."

"Thumper, Thumper, Thumper," said the girl. She chanted, almost sang the name. Then she dropped to the ground and rolled in the sandy soil, covering her soft grey pelt with a layer of fine sepia-colored dust.

Maggie watched her as she rolled and scratched and stretched, and curled into a ball. When the girl uncurled, she had been transformed, or else she had transformed herself, into a grey hare, a desert jackrabbit, covered with a layer of dust. Then the jackrabbit rolled, exuberantly, somersaulting across the sun-baked earth. It turned into a blur of light, a shimmer of heat on the golden stones, and then the creature was gone.

The yard was empty. The hare, the quail, the skinny coyote—they had all disappeared. Maggie lingered in the doorway nonetheless, admiring the deep lapis blue of the sky, the wind in the trees, the sun on the stones. It took her a while to realize that behind her the phone had begun to ring.

It was her daily call from her ex-husband. "Nigel," she said, "isn't there anything I can say that will persuade you to call me later in the day?"

"This *is* later," Nigel protested.

"Oh. You're right. Sorry, Nige. I got up late this morning."

"So where were you last night then? Had a hot date, did you?"

"None of your business," she told him in a bantering tone. But in fact it was none of his business. "Nigel, what is it you want?"

"Go get your copy of today's *New York Times*. There's something I want you to see."

"I don't have today's *Times*. I get it by post, so it comes a day late up here."

"God, you are in the boonies. All right, I'll read it to you."

Maggie sat down, cradling the phone, to listen patiently to a long article on medieval music, Estampie, and the fabulous life of Nigel Vanderlin.

She was pleased for him, and gratified that those long years of work had come to fruition—even if she didn't really need to hear the whole thing right now, word for word, long distance. But the words he read seemed unreal to her as she sat in Cooper's dusty house. There was no hint of the Nigel she knew: those Amsterdam kitchens, underpaid gigs, rooms without heat, months of cabbage soup. In the *Times* version of Nigel's history, Estampie was the labor of one brilliant man. Never mind the group, much less the network of people who stood behind the group, who had formed the safety net beneath the high-wire rope of success Nigel walked. It wasn't Nigel's fault really; this was the mold their culture fit heroes in. The independent man, the solitary cowboy striding into town at high noon.

Halfway through the *Times* article, Maggie found herself tuning out Nigel's voice. Her thoughts had strayed many miles away, following Thumper into blue-grey hills, when the words in her ear came to a halt, and then Nigel asked, "Aren't you pleased?"

"Yes, I'm pleased," she fudged and wondered what exactly she was claiming to be pleased about—the article? Or perhaps something Nigel had said. She'd have to read it tomorrow.

"But enough about me," said Nigel. "I want to talk about this filmscript of yours. I've got a meeting with Harvey next Friday. He's certain he can set it up at Tristar."

"Earth to Nigel," Maggie said, "listen to me for once. There is no filmscript. There won't be a filmscript. I'm not even sure there will be a book."

"Now Mags, you can't be serious."

"I am. Dead serious. Are you really listening? I don't want to write a film about Cooper—"

"Look, you don't even have to write it, although you'd make a hell of a lot more money if you did. Just give me a treatment. I know you can do it. They'll probably want a real writer on the script anyway."

"A real writer?"

"I don't mean that. You know what I mean. A scriptwriter. Harvey represents Desmond Cappell."

"Who's he?"

"He wrote all the Deadly Touch movies."

"You want *him* to write about Davis Cooper? You want to make a horror film?"

"Mags, calm down. Cappell is good, and those films made a lot of money. If you want to try screenwriting yourself—"

"This is a completely absurd conversation." Maggie paced across the room as far as the cord for the phone would allow. "Cooper was my friend. I'm not going to exploit his life—"

"What do you think a biography is?"

"I thought it would be a testament to Cooper. Done right, that's what it would be. But I'm not even sure I can do that now. Cooper put his life into his poems; maybe we should all be satisfied with that."

"You can't film a bloody poem. You've got a great story here, why waste it?"

"Give it up, Nigel. I don't really believe Desmond Cappell wants to write about an elderly poet anyway."

"A poet, no. But a *murdered* poet, that's a whole other kettle of fowl. Have the police found out who did it yet?"

"Fish. And no."

"That's good," he said. "That leaves us more room."

"More room?"

"For telling a good story. We can decide who we want to have done it. We're not bound by the facts."

"Nigel, you've been in L.A. too long," Maggie snarled, and she hung up on him.

The phone rang again immediately. She sighed and picked it up.

"Don't speak. Don't hang up. Just let me apologize first," Nigel said in his best contrite-Nigel voice. "I see that I'm being insensitive here. I realize Cooper was a friend of yours, so of course you're still touchy about his death. It's just that I want to see you do well, Puck, that's all. And there you are, sitting on Cooper's estate—you said yourself you thought he wanted you to write about him. Why else would he have given it to you?"

Why else? How could she begin to explain about the land, about Anna, about Thumper and Crow?

"Apology accepted, Nigel," she said. "But look, you've got to back off. Off of Cooper's life, and off of mine. I'm a big girl. I'll make my own decisions."

"You always were stubborn," Nigel said, exasperated, and with a grudging admiration.

"And you're not?" Maggie countered.

"I miss you, Maggie," he said suddenly. "Let's not sell the house. Not yet."

She blinked at this sudden change of subject. "I want to sell it. I need the money. I paid for most of that mortgage, remember, and I'd like to get my money back out."

Nigel made an impatient sound. "I'll send you money."

"Don't. I'd rather have my own. I'd rather sell. You're hanging on to something that's passed. Let's let go and move on."

"I'll think about it," he said reluctantly. "Look, I'll call you to-morrow."

"I know you will." She smiled. "And Nigel?"

"Yeah?" he said.

"Cancel Harvey's meeting."

She put down the phone, and picked up Tat's letter. The morning was very nearly gone and she hadn't even made it through the mail. She wandered over to the sink with it, and ran more water into the kettle. She heard a loud crack as she set the kettle on the stove and lit a flame beneath. She frowned at the stove. She heard it again; the sound was coming from somewhere outside. Maggie peered through the kitchen window and saw that the skinny coyote had come back again, running hard in the direction of the house. She heard a third crack. It was gunshot. Maggie ran for the door, and flung it open.

"This way," she called to the animal.

He actually came. He hurled himself through the open door and collapsed, panting, in the hallway.

"Oh god. Are you hit?" She saw no blood. "You stay there. Don't leave the house." She shut the door tightly behind her, and then she strode across the yard in the direction of the wash. A man was there, tall and sunbrowned, dressed like he'd stepped from a Marlboro ad. He had a shotgun in his hands, and he was following the coyote's tracks.

"What are you doing here?" she demanded. "This is private land."

"Not the wash. This here's a public right of way."

"But it's posted. No hunting," she told him flatly.

He took off his hat and smiled at her. He was Anglo, and young— maybe twenty years old. "I'm not hunting, ma'am," he said politely. "I'm not after the deer; just keeping the pest population down. I almost had that sonuvabitch coyote. He must have cut through your yard."

"That 'sonuvabitch' belongs to me," she lied. "That's a tame coyote, a family pet. You hurt him, and I'll see you in court."

His friendly smile disappeared. "You got no business keeping coyotes."

"And you've got no business coming up here with a shotgun."

"The hell I don't," he disagreed. "We've got a place down there in the foothills, and those coyotes are pestering our horses. A pack of them took down our best mare. They're predators. They need to be controlled."

"You're lying," Maggie said.

His eyes narrowed, but he said mildly, "Now how do you figure that?"

"Coyotes live on mice, rabbits, carrion," she informed him coldly. "They're not going to mess with an animal that big, unless there's something already wrong with it. You haven't got a dead horse, buster. You're shooting coyotes for the sport."

He laughed without humor. "I should've known. You're one of them bleedin'-heart treehuggers. You think coyotes are cute li'l pups and you don't give a damn what they cost a working man."

"I want you off our land. Now. If I see you here again, I'll call the cops."

"Well now, lady, you just go ahead." He put his hat back on, still smiling. "I'm not doing anything illegal. There's no law says I can't shoot coyotes."

"Not here, you can't," Maggie insisted, without even knowing if this was true. "Are you leaving or should I dial that number?"

"Listen, bitch," he said suddenly, "if that's a pet, you keep him on a chain. Or I'll have his ass next time I see him. And you can count on it."

He spat in the sand and stalked away. When he reached the bend in the wash, he turned and levelled the shotgun in her direction. His face was blank of all emotion. She heard the click of the safety's release. *He's trying to scare you,* she told herself, standing her ground though the blood drained from her face.

He lowered the gun with a boyish grin. "Have a nice day," he said pleasantly, then disappeared through the cottonwood trees. Maggie watched him go, her heart pounding. Then she heard a shot. And another one.

He's trying to scare you, she repeated to herself, tension and fear crystallizing into anger. She heard the sound of a truck start up and move away down Redwater Road. She ran back to the house, grateful that the coyote was safely inside.

Damn, she cursed. If only she had gotten the license plate number, she could file a complaint. When she reached the porch, she saw that the blue front door was hanging open. The hall was empty, the coyote gone. She cursed again. Then she jumped, nerves raw, as she heard the sound of someone moving in her kitchen. But it wasn't the poacher in her house, or even the one-eyed coyote. It was sweet Pepe Hernández, gulping down water from the tap cupped between his two brown hands.

"Pepe," she said, relieved to see him. "Where's the coyote? Did you see him? Is he gone?"

Pepe looked up, wiping water from his chin.

"Come with me. And hurry," she said.

She ran outside and down the road with Pepe loping along beside her, and found the tire tracks where the poacher had parked his truck by the side of the wash. There were no other tracks besides his; the coyote had not come back this way. Maggie breathed a deep sigh of relief. A single quail lay dead in the wash, its blood bright on the silvery sand. The poacher hadn't bothered to claim the body. He had left it there for her to find.

She turned to Pepe to tell him what had happened. But Pepe was gone and the one-eyed coyote sat in the sand close by her heels, breathing with a labored breath. She stared at him with new understanding. The animal—Pepe—stared back at her out of his one undamaged eye. Then he stood and quickly crossed the wash, scooping up the dead bird in his mouth, crunching down on thin, brittle bones as Maggie watched, trying not to feel sick. This was how they lived, after all. They killed so that they could feed themselves, their mates, their children—so that life could go on. They didn't kill out of sheer cussed spite like that poacher, like her own kind did.

When he'd finished his meal, he looked back at Maggie. Then he climbed up the other bank of the wash, disappearing into the creosote beyond. A moment later, she heard the coyote howl, and then an answering song.

Maggie listened to the wild duet. Then she slowly walked back to the house, her thin shirt drenched with salty sweat, the fierce sun beating down. She went into the house, dialed Fox's number, distressed to find he wasn't there. She dialed his workshop, then Juan and Dora's number, but still no answer. She didn't know the Alders' number. She picked up her knapsack, her hat and her keys, and carefully locked the blue front door—for all the good that lock ever did her. She paused at the door of the rental car. Maggie doubted it would make it up the Alders' drive. She sighed and headed up the road on foot, past stands of tall saguaro cactus and green paloverde trees, and down the rutted drive that led over Coyote Creek to the Alders' ranch.

She rang the bell at the outer gate, and let herself into the quiet courtyard. A wind chime rang in the willow's branches. The sun beat down on sand and stones. The big front door stood open and Maggie crossed the yard to the porch.

"Hello?" she called.

A small girl appeared, dark-haired, dark-eyed, her thumb in her mouth, dragging an old stuffed rabbit across the floor by one frayed ear. She wore a Star Wars pajama top, and nothing at all from the waist down.

"Hello there," Maggie said. "I'm looking for John or Lillian. Are they inside?"

"My *abuelita*'s out back," said the little girl without removing her thumb.

"Can you take me to your *abuelita*?"

The child nodded. She led Maggie through the passageway to the back of the ranch, past the horse stables, out to the fenced runs where the wild creatures were housed. Lillian was coming out of a cage, a fat bundle of fur in her hands. "Maggie," she said. "You've come just in time. I've got this poor doped-up critter here and I want to change his bandage. I can use an extra pair of hands. Come on. I'm headed for the kitchen."

"Let me see," said the child, reaching up one hand to grab a fist-ful of fur. Lillian held the animal above the girl's reach. "He's sick, sweetie pie. You can't touch him. He's a real wild critter, not a stuffed animal like old Jack Rabbit there." Lillian looked at Maggie and winked. "This is my granddaughter Mahina. She's my son J.J.'s little girl—the exhibitionist of the family."

"So I see," said Maggie as she followed the older woman into the house. She asked, "Is John home?"

"Nope. He's out on a Search and Rescue call. They've got the horse posse out for some hiker missing on the Rincon Peak trail."

"Is Fox with him then?" Maggie's heart sunk. She had hoped she'd find Fox over here.

"Could be. No, now that I think of it, probably not. John only took one horse." The old woman turned to Mahina. "Spread that towel there across the table, honey. Thatta girl." Then she put the animal down. It looked like a cross between a raccoon and a cat, with a long body, large round ears, a pointed nose and a striped, bushy tail.

"What is it?" said Maggie.

"He's a ringtail cat—but they're not cats at all. Cousin to the 'coons. This here's another leg-trap accident. He's a bit mangled, but we're going to save the foot. Here, hold the leg out for me like this. Don't worry, he's fast asleep."

The little girl, watching, grew distinctly pale as her grandmother unwound the bloody bandage. "Mahina, I think we can finish up without you—don't you, Maggie?"

The girl left the room without argument, dragging her bunny behind her. From the other room came the sound of a Roadrunner cartoon on the television.

Maggie made herself watch as Lillian carefully washed out the ugly wound. It could have been Pepe lying there, if the poacher had been any quicker. She could feel a faint pulse beating beneath the fur of the damaged limb she held. "What are these traps supposed to be catching, when ringtail cats aren't falling into them?"

"Coyotes," said Lillian. "The traps are set on leased public lands down south of here. PRC lets us take these little guys away. They're no threat to anyone."

"And the coyotes?"

"They're shot. That is, if they haven't starved to death in the leg-trap first."

Maggie frowned. "I've been reading those books John gave me. Coyotes are smart. Surely by now they have learned to avoid the traps."

"Well, yes. So they use bait to attract them." She did not look up at Maggie as she worked.

"But I read coyotes learn to avoid meat they haven't killed themselves. . . ."

"There's other kinds of bait," Lillian said tersely, applying medication to the ringtail's wound. The animal remained quite still. "Let me tell you how coyote bait is made—it's your tax money paying for it, after all. First thing you do, you string up live coyotes—hang 'em upside down by their legs and wire their mouths shut. Terror makes them pump adrenaline into their systems. Then you cut the bladder from the live animal and use the scent of it as 'passion' bait. Works like a charm."

Maggie stared at Lillian. "And John used to do that?" She felt distinctly sick.

Lillian looked up and shook her head. "The day he found out what coyote bait was made from he resigned from PRC. Went back to school and studied wildlife behavior. And became the kind of man I'd want to marry." She wrapped fresh gauze around the ringtail's leg and taped it firmly. "There we go. Pretty as a picture. Let's put the little fellow back in his bed."

She picked him up gently, nested in the towel. Maggie stared at the creature. She saw human arms; small human hands; bony little legs, one crushed and bandaged. The pointed face had a ringtail's eyes, a human chin, and cactus spines instead of hair.

Lillian seemed to find nothing amiss with the creature in her arms, but she stared at Maggie. "What is it? What's wrong?"

Maggie swallowed, searching for her voice. She could see the creature both ways—as a ringtail cat, and as something else from Cooper's poems, or Anna's paintings, or the lands of a surrealist's dreams.

"Actually," she said, her voice husky, "I came over here to tell you and John that there was a man shooting at coyotes in the wash, right near my house. He was after that skinny one-eyed fellow, but I don't think he actually hit him."

"Tell me what happened," Lillian said. Her voice was clipped and angry. Maggie did so, following the older woman outside to put the ringtail back into its cage. Then Lillian turned to Maggie, eyes narrowed. "That's the one who shot Cody. Same description. Same nasty disposition. I want you to tell John about this. It sounds like it's time to call the sheriff."

"He told me there's no law against shooting coyotes."

"He was bluffing you. He's got no right to shoot a gun in this canyon at all. Not even in the wash."

"I was hoping that you'd say that," Maggie told her, relieved.

"Doesn't mean that'll stop him."

"But at least we can report him to the cops."

"Darn right we can," said Lillian decisively. "It's even conceivable that he had something to do with Cooper's death. Cooper wouldn't have reacted kindly if he'd caught him shooting coyotes either."

Maggie swallowed. "That hadn't occurred to me."

"It might not be connected at all, of course. But I think we should mention it to the sheriff's office. *And* about the time that those hunting dogs went and made a mess of Cooper's house. The sheriff will put more enthusiasm into looking for a murder suspect than for a poacher. The point here is to scare this guy off, keep him out of the canyon."

"Whatever happened with that sample of animal scat John took? Did the lab confirm that it was from dogs?"

Lillian frowned. "Now that was peculiar. I reckon Fox didn't get a proper sample after all. The lab technician told John there was only leaf mold in the container. But it must have been dogs. What else could it have been, making that kind of mischief?" She turned, shading her eyes from the sun, and looked the younger woman up and down. "Maggie, why don't you come back to the house and I'll rustle up something to eat. I don't know when John's going to get back and, darlin', you look tuckered out."

"Thanks," said Maggie gratefully. "I'd rather wait here than go home right now."

"Let me just finish up the feeding here. You go sit down. Go on."

Maggie sat down heavily on a bale of hay as the old woman tended to her other animals. While she worked, Maggie peered into the surrounding runs—but the animals there were just animals, and nothing more mysterious than that. The bobcat kittens had gotten quite large, wrestling each other in their small fenced yard. The cast had come off of the kit fox's foot. The antelope had gone back to the wild and a pregnant mule deer was in his run now, one leg thickly bandaged. Maggie looked down to the end of the row where Cody's run stood empty.

"Still no Cody?" she asked Lillian.

"We've seen her, twice," Lillian replied as she filled up the eagle's water trough. "She's let us know that she's still around, but she's not going to come back now. I reckon that even with that bad leg, she's happier in the wild."

"Provided we can keep that fool with the gun away from her," Maggie muttered.

"Amen to that," said Lillian. "Cody was with that one-eyed coyote both times that we spotted her—as well as that other female she runs with. John thinks Cody and One-Eye have mated, and that's why she left us so suddenly."

Maggie swallowed. Was Pepe running with Cody? And did that mean Cody was one of them too? Her eyes widened suddenly, thinking about Pepe Hernández and the Foxxe sisters. Cody had disappeared about the same time that Fox had told her his sisters had come home. Angela walked with a limp, as Cody did. Isabella could be the second female. Was she totally loco now, or were the Foxxe sisters like Crow, like Pepe, like Thumper? And if they were, then what did that say about Johnny Foxxe himself?

She pulled her hat brim down against the sun, watching Lillian in the kit fox's cage. She remembered what Lillian had said about the painting of Crow, naming him Mr. Foxxe, the father of María Rosa's children. Yet Johnny Foxxe was a man of flesh and blood; Maggie would stake her life on that. He had none of the glamour of the other-world around him, not like Crow or Thumper, or even his two sisters. And he'd seemed as baffled by the painting of Crow as Maggie herself had been.

Was it even possible for a creature like Crow to father children on a human woman? Old folktales recorded such occurrences of fairies impregnating human women, and creating changeling children. She found she could easily imagine that the shy Foxxe sisters had parentage that was only half human. But then she thought of Fox himself, sunbrowned, lean, and . . . *solid,* was the word she came up with. She thought of him swinging a hammer on Cooper's roof, and playing the accordion last night, and putting away ten of Dora's enormous pancakes in one sitting. She shook her head. No, she just couldn't see it. Unlike his sisters, Fox was one of the most down-to-earth people she'd ever met.

Maggie sighed deeply, thoroughly confused, as Lillian finished in the last cage.

"Honey," said Lillian, "you're white as a sheet. Let's get out of this sun and get some grub into you before you faint clean away on me."

As Maggie followed her to the house, she paused beside the ringtail's cage. The plump animal was still curled up asleep, his sides heaving with labored breaths. She closed her eyes and then looked again. One almost human arm was tucked around skinny knees, the other pillowed his cheek. His flesh was the silvery green of cholla cactus, and cactus spines circled his head. Pale rays of light streamed from his shoulders. They looked for all the world like wings.

Fox scraped the knife across the stone. He tested the blade. It was very sharp. Then he stripped the bark from the thin willow poles he had brought to the edge of Redwater Creek. He placed the poles into the ground, bending them into a circular shape; he lashed them together, using the long strips of bark and lengths of rough twine. When he was finished he had a low hut standing barely waist high, circular in shape. He covered this frame with a heavy green tarp, blocking out the afternoon sun.

When the inside of the round structure was completely sealed against the light, Fox raised a flap and went back out. The sun was riding lower on the distant hills, casting long, cool shadows. He dug a firepit and gathered deadfall, sycamore and cottonwood. Adding this to his pile of dry mesquite logs, he began to build the fire. Fox spoke to it softly as he did so, talking to the wood, to the smooth round stones placed inside the circle of the kindling and soon covered by the leaping flames.

As the fire grew, he stopped talking and he listened, the way Tomás had taught him. He heard only the crackle of the fire, the snap of the dry wood, the hiss of the green. The music of the water. The whisper of the wind. A single coyote in the hills. He frowned, knowing that if Tomás had been here, the other man would have heard more.

Fox knew that there were creatures in these mountains, even if he still couldn't hear them speak. Spirits of the rocks, the trees, the

water; they'd been his playmates as a child. He had lived out-of-doors
so much back then he could have almost been a mountain spirit himself; but then he'd grown up, and gone down to the valley. He had not
had such visitations since. It wasn't until Tomás came to the upper
cabin, with his drums, his songs, his spirit-fires, that Fox had begun
to realize there was more to those old visions of his than a lonely
child's imagination, steeped in too much poetry.

He loved this desert. He wanted to know it, to See it with more
than simple human sight. He knew that Tomás could teach him how.
He had worked with the older man for several years, and still he
could not hear the voices in the flame. He could not See as a child
Sees. But he was a patient man. These things took time. And Fox had
all the time in the world.

He sat beside the fire, waiting for the sun to set, the moon to appear. He placed his deerskin drum beside him, where the skin would
tighten from the heat of the flames. Next to it was an Irish penny
whistle, an Indian flute, and a western one. He took a small pouch
from the pocket of his jeans and poured tobacco into his palm. He
held it for a moment, then he gave it to the fire with a prayer for all of
his ancestors . . . whoever they might have been.

Mr. Foxxe. María Rosa. He had no certain knowledge of their history. He could only guess by the lines of his face what lineage was in
him: Anglo blood, by the color of his eyes; something else by the light
brown color of his skin. Hispanic? Indian? Did it matter? He was of
this land, whatever it had been. He was born here. Eaten its food,
drunk its water, sweated under its hot, hot sun; he had taken the land
into his body. His blood and bones were formed of it. He belonged
here, as nowhere else.

Tonight he would ask the land for blessing, and protection, as he
had that night six months before. He frowned, remembering his fire
by Deer Springs on the night he'd come back to the mountains. He'd
been traveling down in Mexico, and he'd felt such joy by the fire that
night, to be back home in his Rincons again. But that was the night
that Cooper was killed, as he'd discovered on the very next day. He'd

been the one to find Cooper's body, in a wash bed, miles from the canyon.

Fox added more wood to the fire, his heart heavy. The old man drove him crazy, but he missed him. If only he had thought to ask for Cooper's protection that night by Deer Springs as well. . . . But he hadn't. Maybe it wouldn't have mattered. He wished he could know that for sure.

He had learned from this. Tonight he had come not to ask for the land's protection for himself, but for the ones he loved in this place: for his sisters, his mother, the Alders and del Ríos. For Tomás, and the wild ones in the hills. And most of all, for Maggie Black.

While Fox waited for the sun to set, he picked up the flute of copal wood. The courting flute. He blew a soft note on it and adjusted the slide. Then he sat and he played, for the spirits of the hills, and for Maggie, wherever she was tonight: a Navajo song, an Irish song, a Spanish song, and a song of his own. He gave his music to the wind, the water, the stones, the yellow and crimson flames. Soon he would give them tobacco smoke, cedar, sage, and sweat as well. And then he would ask what he'd come to ask. He'd speak, and then he would listen. And this time, if he listened hard, he might finally hear an answering voice.

The sun was sinking in the hills by the time the men from the sheriff's office left. Maggie declined Lillian's offer of supper; she'd spent half the day at the Alders' already. Maybe Fox would be home by the time she got back, although he still wasn't answering his phone. She said good night to Lillian and John, and hiked down the driveway to the road. The track joined the road at the posted entrance to the Red Springs trailhead. Maggie hesitated, and then she turned onto the trail instead of heading home.

The evening air was crisp and dry. The light was tinged with violet and the saguaro cactus cast long purple shadows across the winding trail. The pathway led through staghorn cholla, teddy bear cholla and prickly pear. She could hear the sound of the creek in the distance. A coyote loped across the hill. It was not an animal she recognized, but she said, "Tell Crow I'm looking for him," as he dashed through the brush toward Redwater Creek, his white, bushy tail held high.

She continued on until she reached the creek at a place where it formed deep bathing pools. The trail merged with the path that climbed the hill along the water's edge. The path led to Red Springs in one direction, to the Foxxe sisters' house in the other. Perhaps the white stag was at the springs tonight, Maggie thought as she chose the uphill path. And perhaps he wasn't a stag at all, but another shape-shifter like Crow.

Maggie found herself looking twice at every bird, every lizard, every rock and creosote bush, wondering which was real and which was . . . what? Unreal? Or *surreal,* as Anna Naverra would say? It was all real. It was the magic, the pulse, the heartbeat at the center of the world. She wanted to know it better. She wanted to learn the secrets of the desert, Cooper's "language of the earth." If she listened hard she could almost hear it, a thread of flute song above the wind.

And when you learn its language, what then? said a dry voice in her head, a Cooper voice. Well then, maybe she'd start writing poems again, Maggie told it. Not like Cooper's poems, of course. Her own poems, her own exploration of the desert. She frowned. But how could she render this place better than Cooper, or even half as well? Those old doubts rose to the surface again, the ones that always chased her away from making poems. Journalism was easier—if only because she didn't care so much.

"So," came the sound of a voice, amused, "you have decided you can answer my question after all."

Above her, Crow was sitting on a ledge of stone jutting over the creek's other bank. He wore only his copper bands, and the feathers braided into his black hair. His body was marked with spiral tattoos, as it had been in her dreams.

"What question is that?" Maggie tilted her head back to look up at the shape-shifter. The dying sun turned his skin to gold and she shaded her eyes from the light.

He said, like a teacher repeating a lesson, "You have asked me twice, now, who I am. I told you that you could ask me a third time only if you could answer that same question. And now you've come to look for me. Have you discovered the answer then?"

"I've always known the answer," Maggie said. She crossed the creek, leaping from stone to stone, clambering across a sycamore's root. "Give me a hand. Help me up there."

Crow grasped her wrist and pulled her up. She sat on the rock ledge next to him, dangling her boot heels over the side. The water flowed swiftly below, carving waterfalls from the smooth white stone. She could barely hear the music of the flute above the water's song.

Crow grinned at her, and she wondered why she never noticed before that his teeth were so sharp, canine and predatory. *Grandmother, what big teeth you have. . . . The better to gobble you up.*

"Then tell me who you are," Crow said, "and why you have come to this land of mine."

"That's two questions," Maggie pointed out.

He ignored this. "Quick now. Who are you?"

Maggie shrugged. "I'm many different people," she said. "So I guess I'm a bit of a shape-shifter too. In West Virginia, I'm Emil Black's granddaughter. In L.A., I'm Nigel Vanderlin's ex-wife; in London, I'm Tatiana Ludvik's crazy friend. I'm a vagabond writer to my friends in Holland; a sweet summer affair to a sculptor in Florence; a hopeless klutz to every gym teacher I've ever had—do you want me to go on?"

"Those are just the shapes. What's underneath? The essence, that doesn't change from shape to shape. That's what a shape-shifter has to know, or you lose yourself. You can't get back. You're trapped in one shape, and you can't get out."

She frowned, thinking about this.

"What are you at the core, Black Maggie?" He smiled viciously. "I don't believe you know."

She said, hesitantly, "At the core, at the very center, I think I'm still a poet."

He shook his head. "I don't believe that. You don't even believe it yourself. You might have been once. What are you now?"

She was growing irritated with Crow. "Once a poet, always a poet; it's in the hardwiring, like breathing," she said, aware that she was paraphrasing Lillian Alder and hoping that she did indeed believe it. "Look, I've answered your question, so I think you should answer mine."

"Why should I?" he said smoothly. "You haven't given me a true answer. Why should I give one to you?"

"Because I'll give you something else back for it," she offered. "I'll give you one of my poems."

He laughed at her. "What makes you think I want your poems? I've had Cooper's. Why would I want yours? You'll have to do better than that. Give me something else."

"What do you want?"

He placed his hand over her heart and pushed her back against the stone. "I want your pulse, your breath, your voice. I want everything."

She said, "No."

He wrapped his other hand into her hair. "What makes you think I can't just take it?"

"You can, but you won't," she told him, and she prayed that this was true.

"Oh no? And why not?"

"Dah-maz," she said.

Crow smiled, a cold, inhuman smile that made her shiver under his gaze. Then he pressed his lips to the top of her head, almost tenderly. He let her go.

"*Dammas*," he said, correcting her pronunciation. He narrowed his eyes. "When you can give me a true answer to my question, then come find me again."

He stood. He flung himself into the air, changing form and taking flight. Maggie caught her breath as a huge black bird climbed the wind and soared into the darkening sky.

She found herself alone by the stream as the waxing moon rose over the hills. Maggie inched down from the ledge with effort, and started across Redwater Creek. A flat stone shifted underfoot and she scrambled for another stone; she was soaked to the shins, her boots leaking water, by the time she reached the other bank.

She shivered. As the sun disappeared, it took all the warmth of the desert with it. She should not have stayed outdoors this late without clothes warmer than one thin shirt. The night was closing in on her. The path was dark and difficult. She no longer heard a distant flute song; now it was the low beat of a drum.

She climbed with care over tumbled gold rock as she descended on the narrow path, passing by the trail that led to the Alders' and continuing downhill along the creek. The creek broadened out, white sycamore trees and small cottonwoods hugging the rocky banks. The roots of the sycamores twined and knotted over stone, like the trees in Arthur Rackham paintings. Tall saguaro populated the hills on either side, watching her pass.

At a place where the land leveled out below, a bonfire blazed in a small clearing. The steady sound of a drum was louder now. It came from a low circular structure built beneath a sycamore's crooked limbs. Maggie stepped into the light of the fire, drawn by the heat and the rhythm of the drum. As she sat, shivering, grateful for the warmth, she saw Fox's flutes, his boots, and his silver Hopi bracelet lying on the ground.

Something that had been tense in her all day relaxed now. Fox was here. She'd been needing his solidity on this day when the ground underfoot kept shifting. And there was something more she needed, or wanted—perhaps it was just to talk to him, to see what shape Thumper and Crow and Pepe would take in his clear grey eyes. Fox was a man, Maggie reflected, who would know just what was at his core. Love for the desert, compassion for its creatures—that's what she'd guess his essence would be; that and an ability to truly *listen*. Why had it taken her forty years to understand how valuable that was?

She fed more kindling into the fire. Overhead, the stars arced over a sky more vast than she'd ever known skies could be. She breathed in the desert, the smells of creosote, sage, dry sand, and burning mesquite. A dark shape crept out of the night. One-Eye, Pepe, in his four-footed form. In this shape, he was more coyote than human, creeping toward her with a wild creature's wariness. Then he lay beside her, resting his chin on Maggie's knees as she sat staring into the flames.

Much later, when the drumbeat stopped and the night was still but for the small bats overhead, Maggie fed the last piece of wood into the fire, feeling herself content, at peace, at rest, *at home*. It was an odd sensation. One-Eye slept; her leg was numb where the animal rested his heavy head. His tawny fur was soft beneath her hand, warm against her thigh.

The tarp was thrown back from the circular hut and Fox emerged, limned by firelight, on his knees on the cold, dry ground with clouds of steam billowing around him. As the smoke escaped into the night, it was lit by a silvery luminescence, and in the smoke, she could see pale figures crowding the doorway behind him. They seemed to be made of smoke and light, vaguely human in shape, but no more than that. They lifted into the clear night sky on wings trailing steam and spiraling stars. Then they faded, with the smoke, beyond human sight. Fox looked up at her with wonder.

"Did you see?" he asked. There were tears on his face, or perhaps just steam on his hot red cheeks. She looked at him, speechless, and inclined her head. Fox stood, and he came close to the fire. He wore only jeans; his chest was bare and his skin smoked where the gleam of sweat met the chill of the cold night air. He sat down beside her, smiling at the sight of the coyote asleep between them.

"You're out of wood," she said finally. The fire was burning down.

"That's all right. We'll let it burn out soon." He picked up a pouch, drew out a handful of something and tossed it onto the embers. A sharp, sweet fragrance filled the air.

"Am I allowed to ask what it is you're doing?"

"A lot of sweating." He laughed suddenly. "The stone people were very hot tonight. This is cedar I'm putting on the flames, to thank them." He showed her the dried green leaves in his palm, then tossed another handful.

"Why was there smoke inside the hut?"

"In the willow lodge? It was from the stones." He wiped sweat from his face and said, "The stones are from the mountainside. So is the willow, and so is the wood that fuels the fire, heating the stones until they glow red hot. Then I took the stones inside, and poured water from Red Springs on them."

"Like a sauna," she said.

He nodded. "Like a sauna. Like a sweat lodge. Like many other rituals from cultures all around the world. It's one way I know of to talk to the land. And to let the land talk to me."

"And do *they* always come when you do this?"

"They never have before. They may never again. But they did tonight, and that's enough." He looked at her, his eyes full of shadows. "I'm glad you were here," he said.

Maggie was silent, watching the dying flames. After a while she told him, "I needed to see you. To talk to you."

"What about?"

"About *them*."

He looked at her closely. He said, "I'm going to wait here until the fire goes out. Then I'm going to go home, make some tea, and eat— I've been fasting all day. Why don't you come back with me, have some tea and some food, and then we'll talk?"

"All right," she said. Beside her, One-Eye stirred in some coyote dream. The night was still as the fire burned low; she could hear the distant cry of an owl, the bark of a fox, the chatter of the stream, but the coyotes were silent in the hills and the night air seemed empty without them. This would be what every night would sound like if the poacher and others like him had their way. The world would be a tamer place. And that, Maggie thought, would be a loss.

Fox rose and put on warm, dry clothes, unself-conscious as she watched him dress. Then he pulled the tarp from its circular frame. Underneath were stripped willow boughs lashed together. He carefully untied them, and soon all that was left was a pile of long, thin poles. He broke them up and fed them to the fire. The wood was green and it hissed as it burned. Fox kneeled down, and picked up the tin whistle. "This one is Irish," he said to her. Maggie didn't know if he meant the whistle, or the song he played as the willow burned.

When the fire grew low, he played another song. The fire burned down to embers again, and then to hot ash that he covered with sand. By the time they left the clearing, carrying the tarp, a bucket, and Fox's bulky pack, it was as though nothing had ever been in the clearing that night at all.

When they reached Fox's cabin the place was cold, but a fire in the hearth began to heat it up. He tossed her a shirt. "Here, put this on. You're going to freeze in your own."

The shirt was wool flannel, a red plaid faded from many washings, and it smelled like Fox. "Ummm. Nice and soft. Look out," she warned him, "or you might not get it back."

"But it's not black," Fox teased her. "I don't think I've ever seen you in color before."

"Neither has half of the western world," said Maggie as she buttoned it up.

He put a pot of water on the stove. "Look, I'm afraid it's just pasta tonight, and sauce from a jar. I'm not much of a cook."

Maggie went over. "Let me see what's in your fridge. We can always doctor the sauce."

"Be my guest. I'll brew the tea," he said. "I think I can handle that."

As she sauteed garlic in olive oil with slices of fresh green Mexican chilis, she began to tell Fox everything she knew about Anna Naverra and Davis Cooper. And about the creatures Naverra had painted, still haunting the mountainside. She told him about Thumper, and her meetings with Crow. Then she looked at him closely, eyes narrowed. "You believe me. I can see it in your face. Nigel would have had me committed by now."

"Nigel doesn't live on this mountain," he said. "Nigel wasn't in that lodge tonight."

Maggie smiled at the incongruous mental picture of Nigel by that fire in his Armani suit. But then, she thought, looking down at Fox's red shirt and her jeans, torn and streaked with ash, she wasn't exactly the same woman who'd first come to this mountain herself.

Fox said, "So Anna didn't believe that her paintings had somehow created these creatures?"

Maggie shook her head. "Anna believed that all she was doing was creating shapes for them to wear. Like clothes, she said, that they put on for our sake, not for theirs. I think maybe they've always been here."

"They seem to be part of the land," he said. "They're probably as old as it is—assuming time even works the same for them as it does for us."

"Why do you say that?" she asked.

He shrugged. "Because of Cooper, and that '*Time is a spiral*' business of his that I never understood."

Maggie sighed. "I sure wish Cooper were here. I've got about a million questions to ask him."

"And what makes you think he'd answer them?" Fox asked her drily.

"You've got a point." She tossed the contents of the frying pan into the steaming pasta. "Have you got some plates?"

He produced two and they took the food over to the fire, sitting on the Mexican rug with the plates held in their laps.

"This tastes good." He glared at her. "Is there anything that you don't do well?"

"Are you kidding? I can't do much of anything at all except write— and I'm not always so sure about that. I can't paint, or speak Spanish, or balance my checkbook. . . ."

Fox grinned. "You can do a mean Cajun two-step."

"That's because I have a good teacher." She took another bite of pasta, then she said, "Now Nigel, he was Mr. Perfect. For years I felt like a bumbling incompetent—it didn't matter what it was, Nigel did it all well."

"Not everything," said Fox. "He lost you, didn't he? I can't think of a stupider move than that."

Fox held Maggie's eyes for a long moment, and she felt her cheeks burn. She looked away. She looked into the flames instead. She hadn't felt this way in a long, long time—not even with Crow, for that had been madness. She hadn't felt this way with anyone in all the years since she'd left Nigel. And she wondered if she was really ready to feel this way again.

Fox broke the silence. "You know, Maggie, there's one thing you still haven't told me."

She glanced at him warily.

He said, "How is it you can charm coyotes into your lap? I want your secret. I've been trying to make friends with them all my life, and only Cody lets me near."

Maggie bit her lip. She hadn't told him about Pepe, or her thoughts about his own sisters. Now she took a deep breath and she told him about One-Eye, and the poacher, and Lillian's comments about Cody. She watched as his face flushed with anger over the poacher, and then as it paled when he drew the same conclusions. He was silent when she finished. Then Fox rose and went outside; he closed the door behind him. He stayed out there for a long while. When he came back in, he brought more firewood. He put a thick log onto the flames, then he sat back down, his arms around his knees.

"Of course," she said, tentatively, "this is only speculation."

"Is it?" He sighed and rubbed his face with his hands. "I don't know what to say. I wish I could tell you that you're out of your mind. But I can't. I can't pretend that I've never thought there was something . . . unusual . . . about my sisters. I'm going to need more time to think about this." He looked up at Maggie suddenly. "Does that mean you think I'm one of them too?"

"I thought about it. But no, I don't."

He attempted a smile. "Because if I am . . . well, hell, it's news to me."

"You want to know what I think?"

He nodded cautiously.

"I think your mother told you the truth: your father was some sweet-talking Tucson cowboy who probably split when she got pregnant. She had the twins ten years later, right? Maybe that's when she met Crow."

He nodded slowly. "Could be. It makes sense," he admitted. "At least, as much as any of this does."

"Maybe we could talk to your sisters tomorrow?"

He groaned. "They're as bad as Mama."

"Then maybe I should try to talk to Crow again. He still owes me an answer or two."

Fox looked at her sharply. "I don't trust this Crow. I think you should stay away from him."

"Cooper didn't trust him either," Maggie said. "He had something to do with what happened to Anna."

Fox frowned. "Then promise me you'll stay away from him."

Maggie shook her head. "I can't do that."

"All right, stubborn woman—how about promising that you'll please be careful if you see him again?"

"I think I can manage that," she said. "I promise."

"I'll hold you to it."

Fox rose and took the plates away. She heard dishes clattering in the sink. "Do you want another cup of tea?" he asked.

"Sure," Maggie said. Then she got up herself, and followed him over to the small kitchen. He was up to his elbows in soapy water, and it made an endearingly domestic picture. When he reached for the kettle, there were suds dripping from the glint of silver on his wrist.

"Do you want herb tea or black? Or coffee?"

Maggie picked up a towel and began to dry a plate. "Actually," she said, not looking at him, "I don't really want any tea at all. I just wanted an excuse not to go home yet."

"Then don't go home. Spend the night with me."

She swallowed. The room was warm, and something was melting inside of her—it felt like her bones. She looked at him and he turned from the stove and gave her an apologetic smile. "I didn't mean that the way it sounded. The sofa folds out into another bed if you don't want to be alone tonight."

Maggie looked down, embarrassed, and overwhelmed by the weight of her own disappointment. If her mind had decided she wasn't ready to fall in love, her body had clearly decided something different. "Thanks," she said, her voice husky, "but I think I should go on home after all. It's getting late—and I don't think there's really anything out there to be frightened of."

"Except the poacher," Fox pointed out. "And whoever, or whatever, killed old man Cooper. At least let me walk you home, Maggie. Completely unnecessary I'm sure—but humor me anyway, okay?"

Fox turned off the flame under the kettle, screened the fire in the hearth, and loaned her his denim jacket against the cold. The wind had risen. Clouds blocked the stars, and the temperature had dropped several more degrees. Coyotes were hunting farther up the canyon, quite a few of them by the sound of their cries. Crossing the yard to the mesquite wood, Maggie wondered where One-Eye had gone to now. Back to Angela and Isabella? Or perhaps into the midnight hills where coyotes who were only coyotes roamed and nothing more alarming than that.

Maggie and Fox were silent as they followed the path through the mesquite trees. Hagstones rattled by the wind made a dry, lonely sound overhead. Her earlier ease with Fox was gone and Maggie felt a certain sadness for that; she was too aware of him now for ease, too conscious of his presence at her side. He also seemed nervous. Perhaps he could tell what she'd been thinking about him. Perhaps she had ruined their friendship now, and just when it had come to matter to her. As they left the wood and crossed the yard, Maggie silently cursed herself; she should have kept that vow she'd made to Tat about men, and stayed away from Johnny Foxxe.

They reached the house, passing beneath the raised arms of the Three Graces. She climbed onto the porch and turned to Fox. "See?" she said. "No bogeys in the dark. Not even little Thumper tonight."

"How do you know?" he asked her curiously.

"The door's still shut and locked for once," she told him as she fished out her key and flipped the deadbolt open.

"Well, goodnight, then." Fox hesitated.

She waited. He stood frowning at the door, as though something about it disturbed him.

"What is it?" she asked him.

"Well—" he said. He looked at his boots, and then looked up. "I don't suppose you've got a cup of tea?"

She looked at him, startled. "You really want some tea?"

"No," Fox said, with a sheepish look. "I want an excuse not to go home."

She stared at him. Their eyes were on a level. She stepped closer to him, shivering. "Don't go home, Fox. And don't suggest sleeping on the goddamn sofa either."

As Fox put his arms around her, he said, "I think I can manage to promise that."

He smelled of fire, of mesquite smoke; he tasted of clear, sweet creek water; the touch of his skin was as hot as the desert sun as he gathered her close.

Crow stopped on the trail to Rincon Peak, closed his eyes, and shifted shape. He was human now, but he no longer wore the face Maggie Black had found so compelling, or Anna Naverra before her. Now his face was thinner, longer, the tattoo markings more pronounced. He was half-ugly and half-beautiful, mirroring the duality at his core.

He looked down the trail the way he had come, annoyed by points of light far below. At the midnight hour, the land should be still but for the movement of the night creatures, the owls, the bats, the mountain lions, and the smaller creatures that they hunted in the shadows of the waxing moon. But here were humans spread across the hill, searching the mountain for one of their own kind. If he cared to do so, Crow could tell them that the hiker they sought, a college student, lay at the bottom of a small ravine, thirsty, delirious, swollen and dreaming a rattlesnake's poisonous dreams. He would probably die before the searchers found him. This meant nothing at all to Crow. The boy would survive; or the boy would die, gifting the carrion eaters with life. Either way, it was *dammas*, that-which-moved. Crow continued to climb.

When he reached the peak, he sat cross-legged in the dirt. The mountains spread below him, as far as human eyes could see, and farther, to the edges of the world. He sat and he waited. He did not wait long. The others came, as come they must. The calendar drew them— toward the one night in all human Time that belonged to them.

He shifted into another of his many Trickster shapes: his Laughing Coyote shape now, wearing a coyote's tawny head on the lean, brown body of a man. Bells were tied around his shins; he held seed rattles in his lap. He'd play the clown, the fool, tonight. He did not belong in their mage-circle. They would tolerate his presence here, for Tricksters were outside the rules, outside all of the things that bind, and thus both above and beneath them. Crow's coyote mouth gaped in a smile, the pink tongue hanging to one side, as they gathered on the mountaintop. Amused, he watched them come:

The Windmage arrived from the sky, trailing storm clouds in his wake. The boy settled on a perch of stone, his owl wings lightly fanning the air, his face masked by white feathers.

The Floodmage arrived from the south and sat down at the Owl Boy's feet. The Drowned Girl wore a thin, wet dress, her bright hair knotted up with weeds. Beads of moisture seeped from her white skin and puddled on the ground.

The Rootmage arrived from below and stood, patient, immovable. A plump creature with a wrinkled green face, eyes like pebbles and a toothless smile, she had hagstones hanging from the rags of her clothes and a white stone strapped onto her back.

The Woodmage arrived from the west, wearing a mask of white sycamore bark. Her cloak was stitched from the small brown leaves of acacia, ironwood, and mesquite; the long, twiggy sticks of her hair rattled lightly in the wind, and her dry limbs creaked.

The Stonemage dreamed this gathering from his rocky bed in the mountains to the north. He was the One-Who-Sleeps, a mage of granite, volcanic ash, and quartz. When he turned in his sleep, rock slides filled the canyons; if he woke, the mountains would fall.

It took six mages to form the circle: earth, sky, the four directions. Within that circle was the spirit, the mystery, the wild beauty of the land it enclosed. But the Nightmage, of the eastern hills, was missing from his midnight haunts—missing now for many years, as humans reckoned Time. A seventh mage had replaced the missing one, to keep the circle whole: a Spiritmage. A human mage. And now that seventh mage was missing too—or not missing, precisely, for they knew exactly where he was. He was dead. The earth cradled his bones. His spirit was beyond the spiral path.

The Floodmage stood. She was the Dark Hunter who wore the shape of a pale young girl. This paradox was pleasing to Crow, and he listened closely as she spoke. "Tomorrow I shall loose my Hounds again and they shall hunt. Do any here dispute this?"

The wind groaned as it crossed the peak. It tugged at the girl's white hair, the Owl Boy's feathers, the leaves of the Woodmage's cloak. The Rootmage braced herself against it and she said in a voice not unlike the call of the wind, "No, but is that wise?"

The girl smiled. "What has that to do with me? Wisdom belongs to you, Grandmother. Wisdom belongs to the soil, not the flood. I have spent many months in preparation. I will now set things in motion, that's all."

"Things you cannot control," said the old woman. "You run with the Hounds but you have not mastered them. The Hounds will hunt as they wish to hunt."

"Take care, water witch," the Owl Boy hissed, "or the hunter will be the hunted."

She shrugged, unconcerned. "Then a man will die. They die anyway, sooner or later."

He said, "Your tender concern for that little painter of yours is touching."

The girl shrugged again. "And is he concerned for the paint and the canvas? He is a tool, nothing more."

Crow barked in laughter. "You foolish creatures. Kill a man, kill a hundred of them if you can—but it won't bring your Nightmage back. What makes you think he can come back? What makes you think that he wants to?"

They ignored him. The Woodmage spoke, her voice so low that Crow had to strain to hear it. "There is another way. Another could be found, a new Nightmage perhaps—"

"Ridiculous," Crow commented. "You'd have to wake the One-Who-Sleeps."

"—or else," the Woodmage continued, "another Spiritmage to stand in the east."

The Drowned Girl spat into the sand. "You've been with humankind too long, wood wife. A Spiritmage is no mage at all. Humans can't be true mages. They live, they eat, they fornicate, they die."

"They create," said the Woodmage calmly.

"They destroy," the Floodmage countered.

"They exist," said Crow conversationally, "so it's no use pretending they don't, or that they're simply going to go away."

The Floodmage turned black eyes on him before she remembered that *he* didn't exist, not here, not in this circle with them. She turned away, ignoring his laughter, the jingle of bells, the rattle of seeds.

"I hunt," the Floodmage announced. "The moon will be full; the Hounds will rise. I hunt tomorrow. Will anyone stop me?"

The mountain was silent. The wind died down.

The Floodmage bowed her lovely head, a cold smile on her pale, young face. "Pity. It might have been amusing."

Crow laughed again, delighted now.

"Poof, go away," he said to them. And they did, disappearing in a flash of light. Thunder cracked loudly in the sky above. Lightning danced, and the rain began to fall. He jumped to his feet, threw back his head, and he howled as the rain came down.

The Riddley Wallace Gallery
New York City

December 3, 1950

Dear Riddley,

I apologize. I suppose I was drunk when I wrote you last. These past months since the news of Anna's death came to me—well, they've been hard. You caught me on a bad day. I confess I can't remember what I wrote.

Today I am sober and contrite. You were always good to Anna in your way, and so of course I know you are not capitalizing on her death by planning a retrospective now. And you are right, it is more important than ever that Anna's work be exhibited. But you can't have the Rincon series for the show. You can have all the work through '47, but the other canvases must remain here. Those creatures belong to the mountain, Riddley. Don't ask me about them again.

Your words of concern were kindly meant, old boy, but don't waste time worrying about me. Yes, I drink, so what? Half the poets I've known have been drunks, and the other half are dead. I'm doing fine, or at least as well as a man in my position can do. The light has left my world with Anna, and I am learning now to see in the dark. I'm at work on a new collection of poems. I plan to call it The Wood Wife.

Thanks for the tip about Jack's place but I don't intend to come back to New York. I have my work. I have the mountain, and solitude. It's enough. It's everything now.

Yours as ever,
Davis Cooper

Rain and sun shall feed me now,
and roots, and nuts, and wild things,
and rustlings in the midnight wood,
half-mad, like Myrddin, wandering.
 —The Wood Wife, *Davis Cooper*

There were rocks, trees, water, wind, words, the rise and fall of breath, of sounds, of language, of poetry as she crossed the wash of dreams, and climbed up the banks of wakefulness. . . .

Cooper's bedroom was dark when she opened her eyes. The dream slowly faded. Rain tapped on the roof. The featherbed was warm around her, and someone was whispering in her ear.

"At night I dream that you and I are two plants that grew together, roots entwined, and that you know the earth and the rain like my mouth, since we are made of earth and rain."

"Ummm, Neruda," Maggie murmured. She pulled Fox closer around her, curled into the warmth of him. She could feel his breath on the back of her neck. He whispered,

"How shall I touch you unless it is everywhere? I begin here and there, finding you, the heart within you, and the animal, and the voice; I ask over and over for your whereabouts, trekking wherever you take me, the boughs of your body leading deeper into the trees. . . ."

She placed her hand over his on her belly. "Are you quoting Neruda again?" she asked him softly.

"No. Mary Oliver," he whispered. He kissed her down the curve of a shoulder blade. "I want to seduce you with language, but I don't

have any words of my own. My language, my skill, is all in my hands.
A working man's hands."

"A craftman's hands, a musician's hands," she murmured, feeling
the warmth of his rough, calloused fingers against her softer skin.

"So let me speak to you in my own language," he said. And then
he was silent as he did so, creating poems with touch, and taste, and
breath, and his desire.

The second time Maggie woke that morning, the sky had turned a
pale peach color, bathing the room in silver light. Her body felt warm,
luxurious, every part of it relaxed, in tune. She became aware that
Fox was awake beside her. "Have you slept at all?"

"Not much," he admitted. "I'm too . . . full? Content? Surprised? I
don't have a word for what I feel."

She looked at him in the thick morning light. She felt the same.
And a little terrified. Of all the things she had come to search for in
the desert, on Cooper's mountain, Fox was the very last thing she had
ever expected to find.

She sat up suddenly, startling him. "I think I'll go make some coffee," she said. "Don't get up. I'll bring it in when it's done."

"I can make it," he offered, his hand on her wrist. She shook her
head.

"Make it for me when I'm at your house. Let me treat you to coffee
in bed when you're here."

Fox grinned, and Maggie realized the unspoken assumption that
lay beneath that statement. Her pale cheeks flushing, she belted Nigel's robe around her and escaped into the kitchen.

As she set the kettle on the stove, she thought about Thumper, and
hoped the girl had found a warm, dry place to sleep. Would she come
only when Maggie was alone? Or would Thumper permit Johnny
Foxxe to see her? Maggie stepped outside onto the front porch. Her
feet were bare on the rough wood floor; the morning air was dry and
unusually warm for the end of October. The rain had stopped. The
desert smelled fresh, spicy, extraordinary. She felt her heart swell like
the tall saguaro, filled with wonder like they filled with rain. In the

early light, the land was rich with color, the sandy soil pink against the silvery cactus green. Slate-blue hills rose behind the wash, loud with the sounds of the desert birds.

A horrible sound came from Cooper's side yard, shrieks and growls, the crash of trash cans falling. She edged around the corner of the porch, and stared. Then Maggie ran into the house.

"Fox. Come, quickly," she said. "But be quiet, or we might scare them away."

He threw on his jeans and followed her. "What is it?"

"More of *them*, I think," she said. "Shhh. Come out and look."

She took him to the porch. They were still out there, seven of them, with big bristly heads, long snouts, standing as tall as her knee. Their bodies were thick, but they moved on tiny feet, delicate little fairy hooves; their rough fur was a salt-and-pepper color, and emitted a sharp, musky scent.

Fox began to laugh. He could not stop laughing. He put his arm around her shoulders. "Maggie," he said, catching his breath, "you *are* a city girl, aren't you? That's a javalina herd. They're wild pigs. And they'll go for your garbage cans if you haven't got your lids on nice and tight."

"Pigs? There are wild *pigs* around here? I give up. That's too bizarre for me." She was laughing now herself. "What the hell are they doing?"

"Fighting over your old apple cores. Look at this one, old Tusk Face there. She wants it, but the younger one won't give it up."

Maggie listened to their loud snarlings and snortings and snappings, and poked Fox in the ribs. "That's a 'he.' That's male territorial posturing."

"Nope. These critters are matriarchal. That's a Big Mama running the herd. Wait 'til you see their litters in the spring—the little ones are so damn ugly that they're cute." Then his smile slipped. Maggie knew what Fox was thinking. He was wondering if she'd be here in the spring.

She didn't know the answer to that one herself. She said, "I'm sorry I got you out of bed. I guess I'll go make that coffee."

He followed her. "I don't mind getting up. It's a beautiful morning out here today. I love the desert after the rain."

"It smells like heaven," she agreed.

They came back out to the porch with their coffee just in time to see the departure of the javalina herd, trotting briskly across the yard, big Tusk Face in the lead. Maggie peered through the cottonwood trees and spotted One-Eye in the wash. She called to him, but he dashed away, shy of her this morning.

"He's gone to tell my sisters where I spent the night, I reckon," Fox said drily.

"Wait, he's coming back. No, that's not him. That's Dora coming down the wash."

Fox rolled his eyes. "At this rate, half of Tucson will know where I spent the night." He stood up. "I think I'm going to go put on more clothes. I'll be right back."

"Fox, wait. There's something wrong." She could see it in the set of Dora's shoulders, even before the woman got close and they could see the black eye and the cut beneath her lip. She carried a painting under her arm, and wore an embarrassed expression.

"It's not as bad as it looks," she said quickly.

"My god, Dora, what happened?" asked Maggie.

Dora swallowed. "Juan and I had a fight."

"Juan did this?" Fox said, startled.

Dora winced. "It's partly my fault, I guess. I was drunk, and I got angry with him."

"But that's no excuse for hitting you," Maggie said firmly, horrified. "Come sit down. I'll get you a cup of coffee."

The younger woman gave her a smile that was both grateful and apologetic. "I know it's a bit early. But I didn't sleep last night, and I remembered that you always get up early. . . ."

"For heaven's sake, it's fine. Sit down. I'll be back in a minute."

As Maggie slipped into the kitchen, she heard Fox ask, "Did this happen last night?"

"Night before," Dora told him. "And Juan hasn't come back since.

He didn't take the truck or the jeep. I'm beginning to get real worried about him."

"Night before last?" Maggie repeated as she came back out with a mug for Dora. "Honey, why didn't you call us? Have you been all alone in the house since then?"

Dora nodded her head. "I called in sick to work. It's just . . . well, I'm embarrassed. And I thought Juan would come back home by now."

"Why are *you* embarrassed?" Fox said angrily. "It's Juan who should be embarrassed. Or appalled. Preferably both."

Dora colored, and Maggie put her hand on Fox's arm. Her glance said: *Take it easy.*

Maggie said to Dora, "Do you want to tell us what happened? Do you mind talking about it?"

Dora looked up, tossing back her bright hair. "No," she said decisively. "I came over here to talk to you. I should have done it before."

"I can go," said Fox, "if you'd rather just talk to Maggie."

Dora slipped her hand into his. "No, don't, Johnny. Stay here and hold my hand. I want something solid to hold on to right now." Then she told them about her fight with Juan, and the half-fights that had preceded it, and of Juan's increasingly strange, obsessive behavior over the last several months.

Maggie asked, "What is it that happened several months ago that started all this? Do you know?"

"Cooper died," Dora said softly.

Maggie stared. "You think that's related somehow?"

"I know it is. The night Cooper died was the first night Juan disappeared into the hills. I went looking for him. I found him near dawn, lying on the stones by Redwater Creek. He had taken off his clothes . . ." Dora hesitated, cheeks burning with embarrassment. ". . . and covered his skin with oil paint. Zigzags and spirals—crazy stuff." She shot Fox a defensive look. "I know, I didn't tell the sheriff that when they were investigating Cooper's death. I guess I was afraid they'd decide that Juan was involved in it somehow."

"You're certain he's not?" Fox asked carefully.

"Of course not!"

"Dora, how can you know that for sure?"

"I can't," she admitted. "I can't prove it. Only, Juan just isn't that kind of man. You know him, Johnny. You know how special, how good he really is."

He touched her bruised cheek gently. "But the Juan I thought I knew, he wouldn't have done this."

"Spirals, jagged lines," Maggie mused. They both looked up at her, puzzled. "That's like Anna's paintings—"

"Yeah, I know," Dora interrupted. "Juan is completely obsessed with Anna Naverra. That's why I've brought her painting back. I don't want it in my house anymore."

Maggie leaned down and picked up the canvas that rested against the front porch steps. *"The Mage and the Midnight Hour,"* she read. "Dora, how long have you had this?"

"Since my birthday, last March."

"Right before Cooper died? Which was when Juan's behavior began to change?"

Fox said, "I know what you're thinking, Maggie; but the old man gave away other paintings—to Tomás, to the Alders. There's one hanging in my cabin. And no one else has been acting noticeably different than they ever do."

Maggie frowned. "Okay. But," she turned to Dora, "did Cooper say anything about this *particular* painting?"

Dora hesitated. "Well, he always called it *'The Drowned Girl'* like his poem, instead of Anna's title. And he said a kind of funny thing. He said Juan and I were the nicest people he knew, so he thought that he could trust us with it. And not to give it to anyone else, because the Drowned Girl was . . . something. Headstrong, maybe? Something like that. He said it might be dangerous if we gave it to someone who wasn't so sweet as us. It was crazy talk, the way he got when he was drunk. Flattering, but crazy. I just told him I wouldn't ever sell it. He seemed to be content with that."

Maggie looked at Fox. "Thumper also said that the Drowned Girl is dangerous. I don't know who this Drowned Girl is—a mage,

according to this painting. I don't know what a mage is either. But
something about the word is familiar."

Fox was silent, considering this. Then he said, "What's interesting
to me is that Cooper thought the quality of 'goodness' mattered here.
Remember what you told me Anna said about the land mirroring
back at you whatever was inside of you?"

"Sure. What are you thinking?"

"That Anna Naverra had it figured out, way back in forty-eight.
That the land and its creatures appear in different guises depending
on what expectations we bring to the encounter. . . . In which case,
'goodness' would be important, right? It would render any encounter
harmless. Whereas fear would be mirrored by something fearsome,
violence by something violent."

Dora looked back and forth between them. "Would you please tell
me what you're talking about?"

Fox said, "We will. But can you answer me one question first? Are
you certain Juan was never obsessive, or angry, or violent before?"

"No," Dora said definitely. "Not in all the time I've known him.
He had a temper when he was younger, that's what broke up his
first marriage—but he went through therapy after his divorce. He
changed. He wasn't like that anymore; I wouldn't have married him if
he had been. He's always been an angel to me." She sighed heavily. "I
mean, he was before all of this."

Fox met Maggie's eyes over Dora's head. She knew what he was
thinking. Juan had encountered the Drowned Girl, perhaps because
he'd gotten so entranced by Anna's paintings. And the girl was drawing out something at the core of Juan that he'd thought was dead and
buried.

"Look, you've got to tell me what's going on," Dora said with
mounting irritation.

Maggie looked at the younger woman squarely. "I believe the creatures Anna painted are real, Dora. I've actually seen some of them.
I've never seen a girl like the one in this painting; but I think it's very
likely that she's out there, somewhere, in the hills, and that Juan has
gotten . . . involved with her."

Dora looked at her sharply. "They're real? You've actually seen them?"

Maggie nodded. "Real enough to touch. I fed one breakfast in my kitchen—and that's pretty real, wouldn't you say?"

Dora looked at Maggie, her eyes narrowed. "All right. If *you* say so, I believe you. I can't believe you'd lie to me. I've never seen anything like that myself; but yes, I've always *felt* something in these hills. Something . . . I don't know, more like Cooper's poems, or Froud's paintings . . . that's how I'd imagined it. Not like Anna's paintings. I don't love Anna's work like the rest of you. Her vision is too somber for me; I just don't see the world like that." She shivered, letting go of Fox's hand, wrapping her arms around herself as though the morning air had turned cold.

"And that," said Fox softly to Maggie, "is why Dora's okay, and Juan is not."

Maggie met Fox's eyes. He might be right. Then she thought about her encounter with Crow, when the face he'd shown back to her had been her own. She wondered what she should make of that, and what that meant about her own psyche.

Dora was shaken, but there was color in her cheeks and a spark of life coming back to her eyes, replacing that dull, defeated look that she'd worn when she first came up the wash, alarming Maggie more than the bruises.

Maggie said, "How long has Juan been gone now?"

"We fought just after I got home from the bar with you, night before last. Then he walked out and he hasn't been back."

Fox asked, "Did he take anything with him? Camping gear, anything like that?"

Dora shook her head.

"Then I think we should call out Search and Rescue," Fox said.

Maggie protested. "If the mountain is crawling with people, it's going to scare off Crow and the others. And they may be the only ones who know where Juan is now."

Fox considered this. "You're right," he said, "but we've still got to go out there and find him. Juan is completely unequipped for the desert.

He's got no water if he strays from the creek; he's got no protection from exposure. There are mountain lions, and rattlesnakes—yes, I know I'm scaring you, Dora, and I mean to. This is serious."

"John and Lillian will help us look, won't they?" said Dora anxiously.

"And Tomás," Fox said, "if he's home. I'll call him. But we can't go off half-cocked, like Juan. That means hiking boots, water, food, sunscreen, and first-aid supplies." He ticked these items off on his fingers. "I'll bring my Search and Rescue pack; some climbing gear; cedar and sage. . . ." His eyes met Maggie's. "We don't know what we're going to find out in those hills."

She suspected finding Juan would have more to do with Crow and his kind than it would with mountaineering. Yet she found Fox's physical competence and knowledge of the desert comforting nonetheless. She said, "I'll go get dressed. Then I'm going to scramble up some eggs—I think we should eat before we go. Dora, try to think if there is anything that Juan has mentioned that might be useful. Or anything that Cooper might have told you, for that matter. Anything at all."

"I'll try," she said.

Fox went home to get his gear and Dora stepped into Cooper's kitchen to put in a call to the Alders. She came into the bedroom and reported, "They're expecting us over there within the hour. I told them we'd explain it all then."

She sat down on the bed while Maggie dressed, her eyes lingering on Fox's silver bracelet resting on the bedside table. She gave Maggie a speculative look, but when she spoke it was about the Alders.

"What are we going to tell them?" she asked.

"That Juan is missing in the hills. It's up to you how you want to account for that black eye—but if it were me, I'd tell the truth."

"I meant about the Drowned Girl and the rest."

Maggie sighed. "As little as possible, I reckon. At least for now, anyway. You believed me, and Fox believed me. I'm not sure I want to push my luck."

Dora put her arms around her knees. "Are they beautiful?" she asked wistfully. "Juan said that they're much more beautiful than us."

"Did he? Crow is beautiful. And Thumper—"

"Thumper?"

Maggie smiled. "That's my name for her. She's beautiful like wild animals are, or else like the trees and cactus are. They look just like they *should* look. No more, no less than that."

Dora herself looked rather forlorn. "Juan said that we're pathetic next to them."

"Well now, if Fox's theory is right, that's how Juan is feeling about himself—not about you." Maggie sat down on the bed and put her arm around the smaller woman. "Look, Dora, we'll find him." At least she hoped they would; and if they did, that he'd want to return. Old folktales were running through her head, about men entranced by beautiful fairy women, spirited away into the fairylands for seven years . . . or the rest of their mortal lives.

Dora leaned her head against Maggie's shoulder. Then the phone began to ring.

"Oh god, that's probably Nigel," Maggie said. She sighed deeply; she didn't want to answer it.

Dora sat up. "I'll get it," she said. "I'll tell him that you can't talk now."

"God bless you, dear," said Maggie gratefully.

She followed Dora into the kitchen. It took the other woman a while to get back off the phone again.

"Nice voice," said Dora as she hung up the receiver. "But he's persistent, isn't he? He kept saying he just had one little itty bitty question. Something about a guy named Harvey? He didn't want to take 'no' for an answer."

"That sounds like Nigel all right," Maggie said.

"He's always like that? No wonder you left," Dora muttered, rolling her eyes.

Maggie took out eggs, peppers, tortillas. She heated oil in a frying pan. Something was nagging at the back of her brain. Something about that familiar word, "mage." She thought about where she'd heard it before. . . . Thumper had said she could ask her questions of "a mage, a witch, a shape-shifter." Lines from *The Wood Wife* drifted into her head; she repeated them silently as she broke the eggs:

. . . and the mages gathering,
a crescent moon,
the land stretched taut between them, between
tree and stone; west and south;
north, the solemn slumbering rock;
east, there is only poetry,
the poet stumbling, the broken moonlight.

Mages. The word was plural there. Were there other mages in Anna's paintings? She stopped suddenly, remembering Anna's letters. Mages. That's where she'd heard the word before. She turned the flame off under the frying pan just as Fox came through the door.

"What is it?" said Fox when he saw her expression.

"I'm not sure," Maggie admitted. "But come back to Anna's room with me."

In the small studio, she took out the packet of letters and explained what they were to Fox and Dora. She shuffled through them, and found the one she wanted. It was dated November 9, 1948. She sat on the table, her boots resting on the seat of the chair, and read the letter aloud.

"*My dearest M.,*" she read to them, "*I have learned so much. I have learned at last how to talk to the paint, and through the paint to the fire, the water, the stones, the wind in the mesquite. There are seven paintings that must be done, and yet I only know six of them:*

The Windmage
The Rootmage
The Floodmage
The Woodmage
The Stonemage
The Nightmage.

Those are their names. I have not discovered who the Seventh is, or even if the Six are true images, or merely the reflection of my own ideas. But I work hard every day. I am thin and strong. I can walk for hours into the hills. I will learn to walk the spiral path and when I do, ah, then how I shall paint! . . ."

Maggie looked up them.

Fox said, "See? This fits. She's worried that her own ideas might shape who they are—and it sounds like she wants to get beneath the shapes she created, down to the 'true' essence."

Dora's eyes were narrowed with concentration. "Where have you put those journals, Maggie, that I was looking at the first day we came in here?"

Maggie pointed to the shelf beside the desk. Dora knelt down and began to pull them out. "I'm trying to find the one that I was looking through that day," she explained. "Remember I said there were notes for paintings in there? Well, this is all beginning to sound familiar: the Nightmage, the Stonemage. . . ." She flipped through the pages of a journal, then pulled another out. "No, these are Mexico City journals . . . wait. Here we are. The Rincons." She bit her lip as she turned the pages. She stood and brought the journal over to the others. "Here it is. See?" She set the book down on the table, and they looked at it together.

The pages were filled with thumbnail sketches for paintings Maggie recognized: the white girl of Dora's canvas; a tree woman like the one in Fox's cabin; a sleeping figure made of stones like the painting up at Tomás's place; and a stag man like the pencil sketch that Tomás also owned. Maggie pointed to an owl-feathered boy. "That one's in here," she said to them.

Fox nodded. "Cooper used to have that one hanging in the living room."

"I've got it back here, in storage. As well as the one of Crow." Then Maggie pointed to the sketch of the Stag Man. "Tomás has a larger sketch of this. But where is the painting now?"

Fox shook his head. "I've never seen one. It's not here?"

"No, definitely not," she said. She pointed to another sketch of a bright-eyed, wrinkled woman with a stone tied to her back. "I haven't seen this one before either."

"Cooper gave that to the Alders," Dora told her. "Anna called it

The Root Mother. He said it reminded him of Lillian, since she's a botanist and all—and then Lillian pretended to be offended, saying she
wasn't that old and wrinkled yet." She smiled. "I've always liked that
one. It's not so dark or sad as the others."

Maggie turned the page. There were notes printed in Anna's neat
handwriting and, unlike the titles under the sketches, they were written in her own language. "Can you translate?" she asked Dora.

"Yes, but Fox's Spanish is better than mine."

He frowned down at the journal. "Can you give me a pen and
some paper? I'll copy out the list she's made." He took a notebook
from Maggie and wrote:

The Guardians

Windmage/Owl Boy: Sky
Rootmage/Root Mother: Earth
Floodmage/Drowned Girl: South
Woodmage/Wood Wife: West
Stonemage/the One-Who-Sleeps: North
Nightmage/Stag Man: East
Seventh mage: ???

Fox pointed to a note in Anna's margin, next to the name of the
mage of the east, the Stag Man.

"What does that say?" Maggie asked him.

"It says: *The Muse. Guardian of our hills.*"

"Well, we're in the east here in the Rincons," Dora pointed out.
"East of Tucson anyway."

"Anna calls them guardians?" said Maggie.

"*Ángel de la guarda* is the term that she uses."

"Guardian angels?" Maggie said, and he shrugged.

"She was Spanish Catholic, right?" said Fox. "So she's put a Catholic spin on it. If she'd been Irish, she probably would have called them
fairies. And Tomás would call them spirits, I reckon."

"Tomás? Has he ever seen them?"

Fox smiled drily. "You ask him," he told Maggie. "Maybe he'll give *you* a straight answer." He looked down at the page again. "This reminds me of something he told me once. He said there are seven directions. North, south, east, west. The sky. The earth."

"Then what's the seventh?"

"The seventh lies within the heart. He says that we carry it inside of us."

Maggie met Fox's eyes, his clear grey gaze. She said, "Let's go find Tomás."

"Breakfast first, remember?" said Dora. "And John and Lillian are waiting for us."

"Breakfast first," Maggie agreed, closing the studio door behind them.

When the meal was finished, Maggie put on her English walking boots and one of Cooper's hats. She filled up a knapsack with apples, chocolate, a bottle of water, Fox's warm shirt, a flashlight, a trail map of the Rincons. She handed Fox his silver bracelet, and she put Anna's bracelet on her own wrist. "Are you wearing any turquoise?" she said to them.

"There are turquoise beads on my choker," Dora answered.

"I'm not wearing any," said Fox. "Does it matter?"

"They say turquoise is for protection. Even Tomás told me that." Maggie handed him a small turquoise stud. "If you wear this earring, I'll wear the other one. Maybe it won't do anything at all . . . but you never know, do you?"

Fox took the stud from her hand, and replaced his gold earring with it. "Look out," he teased her, repeating her own words to her, "you might not get it back."

Maggie smiled, meeting his warm grey eyes. "I can live with that."

While Fox climbed the hill to look for Tomás, she followed Dora over to her house, standing in the doorway as Dora fetched her hiking boots. Maggie gazed around the big room with surprise. It was remarkably neat and tidy now. But all the long walls were bare.

They left the house with Bandido between them, catching up with Fox by Coyote Creek. Tomás Yazzie was with him, and Maggie gave the mechanic a timid smile. There was something about the older man's quiet self-assurance that always made her feel a bit shy. His fierce, broad face turned gentle when he answered her smile with a smile of his own. He had a blue bandana tied around his brow, and his black hair hung in two long braids. He reached out and touched the copper band on Maggie's wrist. She saw that he wore one too.

"This is Anna Naverra's," Maggie explained to him.

He nodded. "May I see it?"

She took it off and gave it to him. He looked at it closely. "Yes, they are the same."

"Can I ask where you got yours?" she said as he handed Anna's back to her.

"From my spirit-brother," he answered her, but he volunteered no more than that.

At the Alders' ranch, Lillian and John were waiting for them anxiously; and as Fox had predicted, their reaction to the news of Juan's disappearance was to insist on calling Search and Rescue.

"Juan may have hitched a ride down the mountain," Fox extemporized, his eyes flickering to Maggie's. "Maybe he just needed to get away for a while, and he's down the valley with a friend. Let's not put the alarm out until we know that there's a reason to be alarmed."

John fetched his pack. "All right," he said dubiously, "we'll begin the search ourselves—I appreciate that it's a delicate situation, and you want to keep it in the family. But if he's not been heard from by tonight, then I'm going to let the sheriff know."

Maggie watched Dora carefully as the six of them left the Big House together, heading down the long drive again and into the Rincon hills. Dora's mouth was set in a thin white line, her face was bloodless, her shoulders tensed, and Maggie prayed that they'd find Juan on the mountain long before nightfall. They stopped at the Red Springs trailhead, and agreed to split the group into three. John and Lillian hiked to the north, on the ridge that ran above Coyote Creek. Dora wanted Fox as her partner—his presence seemed to give her strength. The two headed south on the lower path, Bandido following behind them. Maggie and Tomás took the Red Springs trail, running east along Redwater Creek. They would cover familiar ground until the Springs, and then Tomás would lead the way as they climbed higher, farther back into the wilds of the mountain.

As they started up the path, he touched Maggie's arm and stopped her, pointing to the left. Behind a stand of paloverde trees, a white Ford truck had been parked off of the road. "I know that truck," she said to him.

"The poacher," Tomás guessed accurately. "John told me you had a run-in with him."

"He's after the coyotes."

"No, he's after the deer. He'll shoot coyotes if he's a mind to, but it's that white stag he's after."

"How do you know that?"

The older man shrugged. "I've talked to the stones, the wind. They know. That big white buck's a rare prize."

Maggie frowned. "Should we go back and call the sheriff's office? They're supposed to be looking for him."

Tomás shook his head. "The poacher can wait. The stag never shows himself before sundown. He's quick, he's smart, and he's no fool. He's more than a match for that one. Right now, we need to find Dora's husband."

"All right, let's go," said Maggie. She muttered under her breath, "Damn hunters."

"I hunt," said Tomás, in a soft, almost conversational tone, as if he'd said: *The sun is hot.* Then he added, in the same uninflected voice, "But I wouldn't hunt that big white buck. I look for the lame, the weak; I hunt as coyotes hunt. For food, and not for sport."

"We're not coyotes. We can get our food from farms and grocery stores," she said flatly.

"From farms? From factories, that's where it comes from. Tell me why such a death is better than a clean kill, with respect and prayers?"

"Why kill at all?" she challenged him back.

He turned his stern, chiselled face to her. "Life feeds on life. We are part of that circle. Two-legged, four-legged, the green nation of the trees and plants; it is all the same."

Then he was silent, his face expressionless, as they followed the winding trail through the tall saguaro, the creosote scrub, spiney green cholla, and thorny sticks of ocotillo. The mountains embraced them, the Rincons to the east folding into the rugged Catalinas to the north. The sun beat down. Maggie angled her hat to shade her eyes from its fierce white glare. A jackrabbit darted across the path. Maggie called to it. It ignored her. It was browner, larger, than Thumper had been, and probably just a jackrabbit after all. But Maggie thought about Thumper, and Crow, hoping that thought, desire, expectation, might draw her closer to them.

They followed the creek to the circle of stone and white sycamore that surrounded Red Springs. It was empty, as Tomás had predicted. Maggie hoped that it would stay empty, that the big white buck would not appear—not as long as the poacher was out today, wandering the beautiful Rincon hills with the ugly weapon he carried. They sat by the springs to catch their breath, refilling their bottles with clear, fresh water. Maggie thought that no other water had ever tasted so good and so sweet.

"Tell me about this buck," she said to Tomás. His silence made her nervous. "How long has it been coming around here?"

"There's been a white stag in these hills," he said, "for nearly fifty years, according to Cooper."

"But not the same one," said Maggie. "That would be impossible."

Tomás's lips quirked in a smile. "Black Maggie, you're still talking about what is possible and impossible, even now?"

She shivered. "Why did you call me that?"

"That's what the stones and the wind call you."

"You've heard the stones and the wind speak my name? Are you one of them too? Like Crow and the others?"

He laughed; he seemed to find this hilarious. "No," he said finally, "I'm just a man. And I'm partial to this old shape I wear."

She refused to let herself feel embarrassed. It had been a reasonable question. She asked him another. "What about this stag, then? He's fifty years old, he sheds turquoise stones where he walks. He's surely of their world, not ours."

"Their world *is* our world," Tomás told her. "They're born of this earth, and so are we."

"The stag," she persisted, "is it a shape-shifter like Crow? Or maybe a mage?" she added, trying out the word.

He laughed again. She wasn't quite sure why Tomás found her so amusing. "You're like Fox. You want some Big Wise Man to come along and give you all the answers. What makes you think that I know more than you? Or that my answers will be the same as yours? You tell me, what do *you* know about this stag, Black Maggie?"

She considered the question. "I know that there's a stag man in the hills. Anna called him the Nightmage, the 'guardian of the east'— which I assume is here in the Rincons. You have a drawing of the creature. Juan has made a sculpture of him, and that sculpture feels . . . *true* to me. There must be a painting of him as well, but no one knows where that is now. . . . No wait, I think I do know where it is. In her journal, Anna called the stag man her muse. And she once sent a painting that she said was of her muse to a woman named Maisie Tippetts, in New York. It was the last painting she ever painted, and she told Maisie not to let it ever come back to the mountains again."

Tomás was staring at her, his eyes intent. "You see, you do know more than I do. Even Cooper didn't know where that painting was. Cooper died still wondering."

"Is it important?"

"Yes," Tomás said simply. He did not offer to tell her why. He looked at Maggie sternly, or perhaps his fierce brown face made it seem that way. "If you make a gift of that information again, make sure it is to someone you trust."

She nodded. "Like I did this time," she said.

He gave her that wonderful smile of his. He stood. Then he turned to her suddenly. "You've given me a gift of information. I should give you a gift as well, and so I'll tell you that it's not just the painting of the Nightmage that is missing. It's the mage himself, the guardian of this place. The stones, the fire, the water—I've heard them calling him. And no one answers."

"How long has he been missing?" Maggie asked.

"I don't know," said Tomás as he started up the trail. "It's diffi-cult to tell. Time works differently for them—and for us, when we're around them."

As she followed behind him, climbing up the steep path that led to the next rocky ridge, she said, "May I ask you one more question?" He did not answer yes or no, so Maggie pressed on. "Have you told me this because it is *dammas* to give something back again?"

"*Dammas?* What is that?" the older man said, pronouncing it cor-rectly.

"Beauty, motion, that-which-moves."

"Ah. That's what my Dineh relatives would call *hohzo:* walking in beauty. That is how a man should live his life. If he doesn't, he sickens and dies." He reached down, offering his hand to pull her up over the lip of the ridge. *"Dammas,"* he mused, pondering the word as they continued down the trail together.

At the foot of the next ridge, the path grew narrower and Tomás took the lead once more. The trail was even steeper here, and they needed both hands and feet to climb. She moved warily over the rock, avoiding cactus spines, loose stones, the shadows where snakes or scorpions might hide. Tomás soon outdistanced her, although even he was working at the climb. The sun was fierce. Maggie stopped once again and gulped down more spring water.

She was breathing hard by the time she reached the edge of the ridge above her. Here the land leveled out into a broad saddle that was filled with tall old saguaro and boulders twice her height. Tomás was somewhere far ahead; Maggie couldn't see him on the trail. She continued on, feeling light-headed up here. The sky was close, and very blue. The rocks were golden, capturing the light, and she could almost hear them speaking to her, a low sound, a sigh, a murmuring. She began to understand what Tomás meant; there were words in the rocks underfoot and the wind overhead—where had she heard them before? She had a half-memory of a dream she'd dreamt last night, and then that memory was gone. But the words remained. They were poetry, filling her like the thin mountain air she gulped down, trying to catch her breath.

Overhead, a bird called raucously. It was huge and black, circling the cliffs. It swooped down on her like a hawk on its prey. Maggie flinched and the bird's raucous cry turned to laughter. Crow was standing before her.

She looked behind him for Tomás. The trail was empty. "Oh, he's not here," said Crow. "I've led him astray on an animal path. Now why do you look alarmed? I thought you wanted me to come? Oh dear, you've hurt my feelings now," the shape-shifter told her, laughing at her.

Maggie laughed suddenly herself. She said, "You *have* no feelings, Crow."

"None that you would recognize as such," Crow agreed. He climbed a pillar of rock, and when he perched there looking down on her, it was the face of a grey desert fox he wore over the muscular figure of a man. He was singing to her, his voice lower and raspier in his throat: *"Sun and dark she followed him, his teeth so bright did shine— and he led her over the mountains, that sly bold Reynardine. . . ."*

"Reynardine, the were-fox," Maggie said.

"Very good," Crow growled at her, gaping his mouth of canine teeth in something that might have passed for a smile. "You remember your English folklore."

"Yes, I do. But why do you? We're an ocean away from England."

"True fact," he said. "Why do you think?"

She frowned. "You're taking things from my head."

"Wrong. I took that one from Cooper's, so don't give yourself airs, my dear. Have you come to answer my question again?"

"Well now, can't you just take the answer from my head?"

He growled, a low rumble in his throat. "I want you to *give* it to me."

She looked up at him, squinting against the sun, and said with exasperation, "I've only got the answer you've already dismissed. At the core, I still feel like a poet—that's just how the world looks to me. I've tried to think of something else clever to tell you, but I haven't come up with anything."

He cocked his head and looked at her. "I accept that answer," he growled. He snapped his jaws as if he had gobbled it up, and licked his chops.

Maggie glared at him. "Why will you accept it now? Why wouldn't you accept it before?"

He shrugged. "It's true now. It wasn't true yesterday." He scrambled halfway down the rock and peered at her with interest. "What's changed? What's different about you today?" He sniffed her with his pointed canine nose. Maggie pushed the nose away. "Besides, of course, the fact that you have lost your maidenly virtue."

"I lost my maidenly virtue over twenty years ago," she snapped. "And I'm not here to discuss my sex life. If you've accepted my answer now, then you owe me some answers yourself."

He slid off the rock and stood beside her, his arm around her shoulders. He smelled wild—musky and rank; and Maggie tried not to inhale. "I want to know what's different now," he persisted. "Then you can ask me all your little questions."

"I don't know what's different. But last night, today, I hear language in the stones below. I find that I want to write poems again," she said, and realized that this was true. "I can feel them bubbling up in me. I've not felt that way in years."

He sniffed her again, closely, intimately, making her cheeks flush red with heat. He narrowed his foxy eyes at her. "I'll be careful of you from now on."

He dropped to the dirt, and sat there, cross-legged. She sat down and faced him, crossed-legged as well. A small fire burned between them, with no source of fuel that Maggie could see. She took the knapsack off of her shoulder, and pulled out two small bundles of cloth. She unwrapped them. Inside one was cedar and sage; the other contained tobacco. Fox had given them to her, and now she was glad that he had.

Crow watched, slit-eyed, as Maggie poured a small palmful of tobacco into the fire. A flat stone rolled out of the flames toward her. The stone was glowing red with heat. She covered it with cedar and dried white sage; their smoke and scent billowed into the air. In the smoke, she could almost make out the pale forms of the creatures in the fire last night.

Crow sat and watched her, silent for once, an expression of interest on his pointed face.

"How many questions may I ask?"

Crow said, "I have promised you only one. After that, as long as you amuse me, I will answer. When you stop amusing me, I shall go away."

"All right, but the one you've promised me I already know the answer to. I know who you are."

"Today I'll stew and then I'll bake, tomorrow I shall the Queen's child take: Ah! how famous is the game; there's nobody here who knows my name. . . ."

"It's *not* Rumplestiltskin. You are a creature of this land, a Trickster and a shape-shifter. When I met you, you were wearing a shape that Anna Naverra gave to you."

Crow inclined his head in assent. His eyes were very wide and dark, reflecting the flames of the fire.

"I also believe that you are Mr. Foxxe, and that you fathered Angela and Isabella, but not Johnny. Am I right about that?"

"Wrong," he said with evident satisfaction.

"Wrong about it all? Or wrong in part?"

"There is no Mr. Foxxe. Angela and Isabella have no father but the sky, no mother but the earth."

"Then where did they get the shapes they wear? From Anna? From Cooper?"

"Wrong and wrong again! Their shapes come from a painter from New York City, a children's book illustrator. He came to the desert on vacation and he hiked into the canyon to sketch. One of his drawings was a true drawing. He never knew what he'd left behind."

"But Johnny Foxxe is different. He's human," she persisted.

"As you are in a position to know," he said lewdly.

She ignored this. "Then who is his father? Cooper?"

"Ask his mother," said Crow, and he laughed.

"All right," Maggie said, "I will do that. Maybe she'll even answer."

Crow narrowed his eyes. "If you can do that, I shall be careful of you indeed."

"What about Juan? Where is he now? Is he all right?"

Crow cocked his head, as though he listened for something. He sniffed the air. And then he told her, "He is sitting on the banks of Redwater Creek. It is a wonder you didn't trip over him as you came up the hill just now."

"He's all right then," Maggie said with relief.

"He's alive," Crow amended. He yawned. "This begins to grow tedious." He made a gesture and the fire, the scented smoke, all disappeared.

"No, wait," Maggie said. "Tell me about Cooper. Tell me how Davis Cooper died."

Crow got to his feet. "Ask Cooper," he said. "I think you've asked enough questions now."

"One more," Maggie said, rather desperately. He paused, half-turned away from her, and she ran through all the questions that had been building up inside her these last several weeks. She grabbed one, almost at random, and said, "So what is the 'spiral path'?"

"Ah," he said, turning back again, "now you begin to interest me. Do you wish to walk the spiral path?"

"Perhaps," she equivocated warily.

"Davis Cooper is there," he told her.

That sounded rather sinister to her. "If death is the spiral path, then no thank you."

He barked with laughter. "You need not die. The dead walk on the path, it's true; but the place where they walk, no living man can reach." He offered his hand to pull her to her feet. She took it, and rose. "Come, walk with me," Crow said, and now his face was shaped as a man's—beautiful, and lightly drawn with spiral tattoos across the cheeks. She was glad to see that face again. The fox face had been too unnerving. "Come, and I will show you the path. Then you can decide for yourself whether you wish to follow where it leads."

He took her to the mountain's edge. The city sprawled in the valley below, surrounded by mountains, half hidden by long plumes of

clouds drifting past the ridge where they stood. Crow waved his hand
and spoke a word in a strange tongue. The clouds moved with his
movement, creating a straight and unnatural line that ran from the
mountains on the northern horizon to the Santa Rita range in the
south.

He said, "That's the path that you humans walk, from the moment
of birth until the moment of death. You think that every year, every
step, is a progression from the one that fell before it to the one that
follows after. You call it Time. It makes no sense to us." He waved his
hand and the line disappeared. The clouds broke up. He waved, spoke
a word, and then he spun them into a perfect circle.

"This is also Time. It is the cycle of the seasons, the harvests, of a
woman's blood moon, of birth and death. The circle is a true shape; it
has beauty in it. Yet it's still a human Truth, not one of ours. It is not
dammas," he told her. He dismissed it, waving. The circle dispersed,
the clouds scattering across the wide valley, casting patterns of shadows that drifted across the lower mountain slopes.

Crow spoke another word. He made a stirring motion, as though
he stirred a great cauldron of soup. The clouds below them spun and
roiled, then formed the shape of a white spiral that seemed to be
made out of fine spun sugar. It covered the valley, blocking it from
sight, and unlike the other cloud forms, it moved—a slow, barely per-
ceptible movement, steady as the orbit of the earth.

"This is our path, the spiral path. This is how the world looks to
us. We have no Time, as you know Time. We know only that-which-
moves. On the spiral path, the past and the future are simply two different directions. I stand in the present, at the center of the spiral, and
I can walk as easily to one as to the other."

Maggie stared at the cloud form before her, shaped like the patterns on the bracelet she wore, like the spirals in Anna Naverra's
paintings. She tried to grasp what Crow was telling her; but it felt exactly like stepping off the side of the cliff. She shuddered. "Did Anna
walk the spiral path?"

"She tried," Crow said. "And she failed."

Maggie looked at the white cloud shape before her, the great unknown spreading at her feet. She could understand why Anna had failed. It was not a human path at all; it was neither rational nor safe. It threatened her whole understanding of the world, and her place in that world, in Time, in history. It was beautiful and terrible. Maggie looked away, feeling dizzy.

"What about Cooper, then?" she questioned Crow. "Did he try to walk the path?"

"Maybe he did and maybe he didn't." The smile Crow gave to her was sly. "If you really want to know, I suggest that you go and ask Cooper yourself."

She stared at him. "I could do that?" she said, her husky voice breaking. "I could talk to Cooper?"

"Of course. On that path, you could walk into any of the years when Cooper was alive on this mountain."

Maggie stood, overwhelmed, understanding the true seduction of what he offered. For all of the years of her adult life she had wanted to talk face-to-face with the man whose words had opened poetry to her, and unlocked the poet within herself. Fox, Dora, Tomás, the Alders—they had all had, all taken for granted, the very thing that she had been denied, and had thought she had lost forever. Crow smiled a small, self-satisfied smile, knowing that he had found the one desire buried in Maggie's heart that would lead her to walk off a cliff.

Crow said, *"One road lies to wickedness; one road lies to righteousness; and the third road—"*

"—lies to fair Elfland, where thou and I must go," said Maggie, finishing the line from an old folksong. She hesitated, remembered her promise to Fox, to be careful around this man. She looked at him. "What's the price? What does one have to give up to do this?"

He crossed his arms. "That's negotiable," he said with that smile she knew better than to trust. "Tell me, Black Maggie. What will you give me?"

"What did Anna give you?"

He shrugged. "Something she wanted to be rid of. Something she came to regret."

"Her art," said Maggie.

"Wrong," said Crow, amused. "Try again."

Her eyes widened. "The pregnancy," she guessed, and she could see by his face that she'd guessed correctly. "You took the baby, didn't you?"

"Baby? There was no baby," Crow said. "There was only the idea, the glimmer of one. She was six weeks pregnant. She would have miscarried in another three weeks anyway."

"But you took it."

"That's right. I took it from her belly as a stone—a stone in the palm of my hand."

"The Night of the Dark Stone. . . ."

The sly smile returned. "How quick you are after all, Black Maggie. It took Cooper forty years to discover that."

"Why? Why didn't you tell him?"

Crow cocked his head. "Because it amused me not to."

"And did it *amuse* you not to tell Anna that she would have miscarried anyway? Did it *amuse* you to watch her eat her heart out with guilt and sorrow afterwards?"

The smile never wavered. "The deed was done. The bargain was kept." He sounded truly puzzled, and Maggie began to grasp just how far from humankind this creature was.

"Where is the stone now?" she asked, eyes narrowed.

His expression grew shifty. "I gave it away."

"To whom?" she persisted, asking the questions rapidly so that he wouldn't grow bored.

"To a mage," he answered.

"Which one?" she shot back.

"You know there's more than one? Very good. I gave it to the mage who stands in the west."

Maggie did a quick mental calculation. "That's the Woodmage, if I remember right."

His eyes brightened with surprise that she knew this. Good. He wasn't bored now. He was staring at her with great interest.

"And what did the Woodmage do with the stone?" she asked, the words sounding like a riddle from a folktale, as did his answer.

"She swallowed it," said Crow.

Maggie blinked. "And that was that?"

"And it grew, and it grew."

"And then what?"

"She gave birth, in a dry wash bed, nine years later."

"Nine *years*?"

Crow gave a bark of fox laughter. "Time is different for us than for you."

Maggie sat down suddenly, feeling dizzy again, aware that she stood at a cliff's sharp edge. "She gave birth in a wash bed. Cooper was there. She wouldn't name the child, or tell him the father's name, and so he called it after Johnny Gutiérrez," she said, more to herself than to Crow.

"And I know the story is true for I danced at their wedding and drank at their feast," said Crow, repeating a line that often ended the folktales of old Europe.

She looked at him sharply. "You told me Johnny Foxxe was human," she accused.

"But he is. He's Anna's and Cooper's child. It was only his birth that was . . . unusual."

"Then María is the foster mother. The Woodmage."

"The wood wife," Crow agreed.

"From Cooper's poems," Maggie said, understanding at last. "He gave her that shape in his poems. An almost-human shape. She gave birth, she aged—she even loved him in her way," she added, remembering the tender look on María's face when she'd showed the old woman Cooper's journal. "Did Cooper ever know who the child was?"

Crow yawned elaborately. "Cooper, Cooper, Cooper. Always Cooper. Ask him yourself if you want to know."

"Perhaps I will. If I walked on the spiral path, would I be able to return?"

"If I showed you how."

"Will you show me how?"

"And what will you give me?" he said. "Now tell me quick!"

She frowned. "What do you want?"

"Your firstborn, the donkey who shits coins of gold, the thing that stands behind your house," he said.

"No, no, and no. What else do you want?"

"Your poems, your passion, your heat."

"No," said Maggie. "What else?"

"Johnny Foxxe."

"He's not mine to give," she said flatly.

"You think not? Well then, Black Maggie, you must make an offer to me."

"The first poem I write, or the last one."

"It's not enough. Quick! Make another."

"My mother's ring, that I've worn all my life."

"Almost enough. Quick, quick! Make another."

Maggie bit her lip, thinking hard. She had information that Tomás Yazzie had said was important—Crow might think so too. But Tomás had also said not to give that information to anyone she didn't trust.

She said, "All right, here's my final offer. Take it or leave it."

"You're bluffing."

"Am I?"

"What is it then?" he said, his eyes bright with interest.

"I'll give you my friendship. Besides poetry, it's the only thing I've ever been good at. Tell me, quick, quick! Do you want it?"

"Interesting. No one's ever offered that before." He looked her up and down, eyes narrowed. "But is it worth it?"

She rose to her feet. "Davis Cooper thought so. And Tatiana Ludvic. And Johnny Foxxe."

Crow smiled a feral and sharp-toothed smile. "I accept your bargain," he said.

"Then we're agreed," Maggie told him. She'd worry later about what she'd just agreed to. Her head was spinning with riddles and answers . . . and the riddles that the answers posed in turn.

"Come," said Crow, "we'll prepare you for the journey. The path is not easy for one of your kind. You must become as One of Us."

"And if I do, will you promise that I'll return home safe, to my own human shape?"

"No. I make bargains, not promises. It's not in my nature. I am what I am. But I will hold your essence here like a rock in my hand while your shape walks the past," Crow told her. "Others have walked on the spiral path and come home again." The shape-shifter's face was serious now, and she found that for once she believed him.

She said, "If I walk into the past and talk to Cooper there, what if I say something or do something that changes what happened back then?"

He shrugged, unconcerned. "Then the present is changed, and the future shall be changed as well."

"Could it change so much that I never came here? Or never even knew Cooper? Or Fox?"

"It could. But what does that matter? It is all what it is. It is all *dammas.*"

"It matters to me," Maggie told him firmly. "I want the life I have, not another."

"Those of your kind who would say that are rare indeed; that's why you interest me." Then he advised, "When you find Cooper, say little and listen much. Small changes are only ripples in Time—it is only the big ones you need fear."

She nodded. "I'll be careful."

Crow cupped his hands, and she saw water in them. He let the water pour down to the earth. When it touched the ground, it burst into flame. The flames died out, leaving reddish-brown dust. Crow dribbled more water from the palm of one hand, and stirred the dust into a thin paint. He dipped one finger into it, and beckoned for Maggie to step closer.

He painted spiral lines on her cheeks and intricate knotwork patterns around each slim wrist. He unbuttoned her shirt, and painted more lines on her belly, and in the hollow between her breasts. He took off her boots, and painted jags of lightning on the soles of her feet. He untied a string of small bells from his ankle, and wound it around one of hers.

He said, "You must hold on tightly to the image of the place and the time where you wish to go. The spiral keeps turning; the motion will pull you into other directions. Don't let it, or you may not be able to return. Stay clear. Stay focused. Don't let your fear distract you. Think about Cooper in that house you know so well."

"And when I want to return?" she asked.

"Then you must think of the mountain, and of me. I'll hear the bells. I'll know where you are." He untied a white feather from a braid in his hair, and knotted it into Maggie's. Then he held her wrist lightly, and led her to the edge of the cliff, where the path was waiting.

The midday air seemed to shimmer around her. The clouds looked almost solid underfoot. She said, "Why wasn't Anna able to walk it? She knew so much. She had worked so hard."

"She couldn't take this next step," he told her. "Anna lived a protected life. In her parents' house. In Cooper's house. And then in the house of her Christian God. This is a solitary path. She wished to walk it. She could not."

"I'm not sure that I can either," said Maggie, looking down at the valley far below. And yet she'd had a lifetime's practice of stepping out into the great unknown. She thought of the day that she'd left West Virginia. She thought of the day she'd left Nigel.

Crow said, "Cooper did it. He walked the path. And you are no less than Cooper."

She met his eyes. "Thank you for saying that."

"Don't thank me," Crow growled back at her.

Maggie took a breath. She looked straight ahead. And she stepped into the sky.

The clouds held firm under her feet. The sky grew dark around her. Absurdly, the images from old Roadrunner cartoons were running through her head: Coyotes spinning in the air; coyotes hurtling to the ground. *Don't look down,* she told herself. *Don't think about that now.* She thought about Cooper; she pictured his house; she pictured the man from the photographs stepping through a freshly painted blue door and onto the wooden porch. Around her the sky darkened into

black; the spiral was a pathway of stars underfoot. It moved. It carried her, spun her into motion. She herself was *dammas,* that-which-
moves. She heard a low humming, a soft, steady whisper, chanting in
the language of the stars.

She thought about Cooper. She could see the house, a glimmer of
light through the mesquite trees . . . but the stars spun her past it. She
couldn't get back. There was somewhere else that they wanted to go,
pulling her to an image even more integral to the core of her being
than Cooper's.

She felt mud underfoot. The stars hung overhead. The night was
cold, with a winter's bite. Rain was sleeting down, drenching her unbuttoned shirt, gleaming on the black surface of a road. Where was
she? The smell of the place was familiar. It made something ache deep
inside of her bones. Then she saw the car come. A white Oldsmo-
bile. She knew that car, and what it would look like the next morning
when they dredged it from the silted riverbed. She watched it skid,
flip over onto its roof, slice sideways through the thin guardrail to the
steep bank of the river beyond, the faces of her parents both looking
so pale, so small, so very young. . . .

"No," she whispered, staring at them. Time stopped. Collapsed.
It was not *dammas,* this emptiness, this horrible stillness, frozen between one moment and the next. She pushed against it. Time moved,
and its grinding motion pulled Maggie back to the path, her heart
pounding, the blood roaring in her ears, spinning her away from that
terrible place as she reached for something solid to hang onto.

It was the railing of a stairway. The stairwell was dark; the bulb
was busted overhead. She knew this smell too: cigarette smoke, turpentine, rain on the London streets outside. She climbed steel stairs
to a warehouse landing and stood before a familiar red door, her
heart swelling with a thousand memories she'd thought she'd long
forgotten. The door was plastered with postcards, smudges of color, a
painter's fingerprints.

In her hand was a key, and with it she opened the door. Inside,
the huge half-empty loft was covered with dust. She looked slowly
around the room at industrial windows, Tat's bright monoprints, her

own old desk, their jerry-rigged kitchen. Two women sat in some battered chairs, Tat, and herself, so young, so young, looking up at her in surprise. She started to speak—the spiral pulled, and she clung to the door, but it pulled her away. It flung her back into the night sky, away from the girl she'd once been.

Cooper, Maggie told herself, *concentrate on Cooper and the mountain.* Or she would drown in the past, the path like a flood of water, pushing her under. *Concentrate.* That light. The blue door. The black trees of the mesquite wood. She breathed in; she breathed out. The whispers, the chanting, they rose and they fell with the rhythm of her breath. She saw the blue door. She walked toward it, ignoring the grey-and-white images flickering past: her grandfather in that awful coat he loved and always used to wear; a sculptor walking the streets of Florence, looking like he'd lost something precious; Nigel, in a crowded room, his movements eloquent of great weariness. . . . At the sound of her footsteps Nigel turned; she saw that his face was lined, his hair thinning, his blue eyes wide with fear or wonder. . . . *No, not that way; don't get pulled into Nigel's future. Think of Cooper, of walking to Cooper, and that light, that dusky, silver light.* . . .

She felt solid, sandy ground underfoot. The mountain smelled fresh, as it did after the rains. Dusk had fallen. A lantern was lit on the porch, where Davis Cooper sat. He stared, as though Maggie were a ghost, which she was, coming out of the wood.

She crossed beneath the Three Graces and stopped just short of the front porch steps. His eyes were wide. The clean lines of his face had started to weather into cragginess from the Arizona sun, alcohol, and grief. He might have been Maggie's age, not much older, yet he put down his glass with a shaking hand, and his voice was the gruff voice of an old man. "Are you one of Anna's, or are you one of mine?"

She swallowed. "I'm neither. I'm Marguerita Black, and I'm as human as you are, Cooper. I've come from . . . a long way away. Another point in time. On the spiral path."

He took this information with equanimity. Maggie realized the man was very drunk. "Where are my manners?" Cooper said to her. "Sit down. Can I get you a cup of tea, or some gin?"

Maggie smiled, for Dora had been right—even on this mountain, he was still an Englishman. She shook her head. She could feel the spiral's pull. "I don't think I'll be here long."

"Why have you come then?" He sat very still, as if she might disappear if he moved.

She dropped her eyes, feeling suddenly shy of the stranger before her. "I came because you've been good to me. *Will* be good to me, years from now. And I never had the chance to meet you face-to-face while—" She stopped abruptly, but he finished the sentence for her.

"While I was alive?"

She nodded silently.

"How very interesting. You walked here on the spiral path. And you say that you are not a mage, a shape-shifter, or a witch?"

"I'm a poet," she told him.

"Ah, now, that explains it," Cooper said. She felt the ground shift underfoot.

"No, not yet," she cried aloud, but the earth heaved, flinging her sideways, sending her rolling across the hard stones of the yard; the wind pulled at her, pulling her back to the roiling clouds and the stars.

Cooper, she chanted silently, over the song of the stars in her ears, *Cooper, let me stay here with Cooper.*

But the stars kept turning, the wind kept blowing; Time moved again, and the earth spun below. She stood at the center of the great spiral, the stars pulsing hot and cold around her, the lights of the valley spread beneath her, cradled by the dark mountain slopes. She thought about what Crow had told her: *On the spiral path, the past and the future are simply two different directions. I stand in the present, and I can walk as easily to one as to the other of them.*

The Cooper that Maggie needed to talk to was the man he had been these last twenty years, the man she had known, just before his death. She concentrated on that point in time, on a blue front door, more weathered now, and the old house as she knew it. She took a breath. *Breathe in; breathe out.* She breathed to the rhythm of the pulsing stars. She took several steps. She walked from *here* to *there,* and stood in the mesquite wood. She crossed over Cooper's yard again, following the path she had taken before.

She saw lights inside, heard movement, and she went right in through the blue front door. Cooper was in the living room, taking paintings down from the adobe walls. He looked up in anger as Maggie walked in, then his face softened with his surprise.

"Marguerita," he said, his voice as full of wonder as a child's on Christmas morning.

"Cooper," she said, feeling even more shy than last time, if that were possible—for this was a Cooper to whom she was real, and not just a ghost from the wood.

"You've come to me on the path again, after all these years," the old man said.

"Yes." She stood and just looked at him, the Cooper she'd wanted to see for so long, the face of the man who had been her mentor—and more than that, her friend. Then she roused herself. "But I don't know how long I'll be able to stay this time either."

He frowned. "All right, then, my dear. Why don't you come into my study? We'll talk for as long as we can."

Maggie followed him and was startled by the change in the room where the poet worked. The place was a flood of papers and books, dirty dishes, laundry, stale pipe smoke. Cooper sat down in the middle of the chaos, and pushed books off of another chair for her.

He reached out, gently touching her cheek. "It's you, in the flesh. I'm not drunk, and you're here."

"Goddamn it, Cooper," Maggie said to him, "I would have come anytime, if you'd have let me."

"How could I?" he said. "When you appeared on this mountain, when I was forty-two years old, you said that we'd never met in my lifetime. And so I dared not let you come."

"Oh," she said, startled laughter breaking from her. A broken piece of herself began to knit. It wasn't that he hadn't wanted her here. The look on his face was proof of that.

"If we only have a little time," said Cooper, "then let us speak frankly. The Nightmage is still missing, I presume, and that's why *they* have sent you here?"

"The Nightmage? Do you mean the stag man himself, or the painting of the stag man?"

"Both. For if the painting is found, surely the other will be found as well."

"I know where the painting is," she said carefully, without naming the place. "But that's not why I've come. I don't know why the painting is so important."

"You don't?" he said, puzzled. "Then why are you here? I thought *they* would have sent you on the path in order to search for it again. That's why they come, when they come to me. Several times their Hounds have searched this house, but the scent of the stag eludes them. They don't believe me when I tell them that I don't have Anna's painting, or know where it is." He frowned. "Yet you say the painting has been found. Then why have they let you come here?"

She hesitated. She couldn't begin to guess why Crow did anything he did. And she didn't want to admit to him that she'd come to learn the reason for his death.

She looked away, and her eyes rested on the bulletin board above Cooper's desk. The envelope was there, the letter to her, jutting out from the picture by Brian Froud.

Cooper followed Maggie's gaze, and he paled. "You recognize that letter, don't you? Then that means that I will fail." He bowed his head. "I knew that was a risk. That's why I was locking up the paintings, to keep them safe, just in case."

"My reading that letter is inconclusive," Maggie told the old man quickly, "for you still don't know what circumstances I found it under. Perhaps it was after your death at the age of one hundred and three; I'm not going to say. Only now you must be certain to leave it there, for someday I must indeed read it."

Color came back into the poet's face again. "Yes, of course. Yes. Yes, I will." He smiled. "My letter worked, then. It intrigued you enough to stay in the canyon. To meet *them*, and walk the path."

"You and your damn riddles, Cooper," she said with exasperation.

"Why couldn't you have written me something a bit clearer? Why can't you even be clear with me now?"

He rubbed his face with one hand, looking every bit his age. "I've been around *them* too long."

She sat down again, her knees close to his, and took his two thin hands in her own. "Tell me about the Nightmage," she said. "Explain it to me. No riddles this time."

"No riddles," Cooper agreed. His hands were trembling. "I'm afraid I need a drink."

"All right." Maggie rose. "I'll get it. I know where you keep it, after all."

She came back with a bottle of Jack Daniel's and two glasses. She poured, and handed one to Cooper.

"The Nightmage was Anna's muse," Cooper told her, his eyes narrowing with distaste for the creature. "He was the first of these fairies to—"

"Fairies?" Maggie interrupted him.

"I'm an Englishman, and my mother was a Celt. That's what I've decided to call them. To Anna they were angels . . . until the end, when she thought them no better than the devil himself. What do you call them, Black Maggie?"

"I don't know. Spirits of the mountain, of the land?"

"That will do. The names, like the shapes, are ones that they wear for us. They don't much matter to them."

Maggie thought of Thumper, joyfully chanting out her name. In this, at least, he was wrong.

"The Nightmage was the first of them for Anna," he continued, "and he gave her the Sight to see the rest. Under his influence, Anna began to paint the paintings in this house. It is the best work she's ever done; true work, and they all know it. . . ."

Maggie didn't know if he referred to the critics who ignored it, or to the creatures on the mountain.

". . . But what she didn't understand is that *they* have artists among them too. They call them mages. And for some of them, we are the materials they use. Our lives are their raw canvas; our emotions are the paints. We're the clay: they push a little here, they prod a little there, till the work is done. If they drive a man or woman insane in the process, it matters little to them. They are amoral beings, Anna told me. They are neither good nor bad, Marguerita; those concepts mean nothing at all to them. The Nightmage was an artist, like Anna. And she was the work that he was creating. When she was strong in herself and in her art, the work they created of each other was good. But later, when Anna was frightened, and a bit unstable . . . then it all went wrong."

"And the land mirrored Anna's nightmares," Maggie said, remembering the last letter to Maisie.

"That's right. So she stopped it. She stopped *him,* and proved herself to be the stronger artist after all. Perhaps he didn't know that she was granddaughter to a Mexican *bruja,* a witch woman. Anna bound her muse into a painting, into a shape where he could do her no harm. You've seen him, the white stag in the hills? She trapped him in that shape, that animal form, by putting the essence of him somewhere else. In the painting. And that's why *they* want the painting back again so badly." He gave Maggie a haunted look. "If I had it, I'd give it to them now."

"So what was it that happened to frighten Anna?" she asked, although she already knew the answer. But how much did Cooper know, she wondered? He hesitated before he spoke.

"She became pregnant," Cooper told her frankly, his blue eyes holding shadows of the past. "She never wanted children—she wanted to paint. Art was everything to her. I confess I never wanted them either. Poems and paintings were enough for us both.

"Anna never told me when she conceived. *They* helped her to end the pregnancy before it had gotten very far along. But it turns out the little Catholic girl was strong in Anna after all. It was an impossible situation for her; she saw it as a choice between being a mother and a painter. That's a choice no one should have to make. Afterwards, it haunted her—she lost her faith in her art, in the mountains, and even her faith in me. She replaced it with her childhood faith . . . and once that came back into her life, then the rest of us were damned to hell."

He poured himself another shot of whiskey, the wound as raw as it had been decades before.

"How did you find all this out," Maggie said, "if Anna never told you?"

"The stones, the water told me. Tomás has taught me to listen to them. It took me many years to learn, but I'm a stubborn old man."

"They told you what happened to the child?" she said carefully.

"There was no child. I told you, she ended the pregnancy. Afterwards, she suffered. And then she made that last painting."

Maggie frowned. Something was bothering her. "Why," she asked, "do these creatures come to ask you where the painting is? Why not go back and ask Anna herself?"

He smiled. "Because that clever witch woman made herself, and the painting, invisible to them. They can't find her on the spiral path. It's as if she never existed at all. But I can find her. I know I can. I can find her in hell itself if I have to."

She looked at him, alarmed. "What are you planning, Cooper?"

He leaned forward, and confided to her, "Tomorrow I'm going to walk the spiral path. It's because of you that I know it can be done. Tomorrow night is April sixteenth. I'm going to return to that night so many years ago, when it all fell apart. But this time, I'll be with Anna. This time she'll keep the child."

"You can't," said Maggie, suddenly cold. "You can't, Cooper. That will change everything." *And Anna Naverra would miscarry. And Fox would never have been.*

"Exactly," he said to her. "Look at me. I'm a drunk, a recluse, an unfashionable poet. I'm an old and broken man. This is not the future I wanted."

"*I'm* in this future, Cooper. And Johnny Foxxe. Tomás Yazzie. Juan and Dora. What's going to happen to us if you do this?"

"Maybe we'll know each other anyway. Or maybe not. That can't be helped. Don't judge me harshly, Marguerita. You'll still be a fine poet without me—remember that, my dear, if you can. Somewhere at the core of your being. Try to understand. I'd give the sun and moon themselves to be with Anna again."

She looked at the old man's ruined face, and saw that this simple statement was true. Yet she knew what would happen tomorrow night. He would join his lover, but not by walking into the past on a pathway of stars. She swallowed hard, knowing that he was going to his death, and that she must not stop him.

She stood, averting her face from Cooper so that he wouldn't see the sorrow written on it. She walked to his desk. She could feel the floorboards swaying gently underfoot; she could hear the distant song of the stars; and she wondered how much longer she would be able to stay here with him. She leaned against the poet's desk, bracing herself against the shifting of the room. Her eyes resting on the list of her own poems pinned to his bulletin board.

"What is this?" she asked, pointing at it.

"Your essence, my dear. As clear a portrait as any photograph could be. Those poems are the reason I knew that you could learn the language of this place—even if you'd never walked the spiral path and come from the wood that night. Are you writing poems?" His voice became stern. "Or are you still running away from your true nature, Marguerita Black?"

She turned back to him. "I'm hearing them again; I can feel them growing inside of me. You were right to bring me here, Cooper. This *is* the land of poetry. And you, you've been writing poems yourself. Why didn't you bloody tell me?"

His smile was rueful. "I would have, my dear. As soon as *The Saguaro Forest* was complete. But now, I'm afraid, I've bargained them away. The poems will go to the mage who will set me on the spiral path."

Maggie looked at him sharply. "A mage? It isn't Crow who is taking you?"

"Crow? That creature? Heavens, no. It's the one I call the Drowned Girl. An enchanting little fairy, she is. And yet she drives a hard bargain."

"All your poems, Cooper? You've given them all away?"

"Yes. But don't look so sad, my dear. They were for the mountain. And for the wood wife, who's been good to me for all these years. Perhaps they were never meant for the world. No great loss. The world doesn't want them."

"And is that why you've kept Anna's paintings here? Do they belong to the mountain too?"

He frowned. "No, I think I was wrong about them. They should have been exhibited. It was not *dammas* to keep them here; they need to move out into the world. Anna couldn't let go of them. They were precious to her, our only children. I couldn't let them go either. But you, you should exhibit them." Then Cooper looked up at her and smiled. "Yet, what does any of this matter now? After tomorrow night, all this will change, and Anna will exhibit them herself." He raised his glass. "Come now, let's drink a toast to you, Black Maggie. And to poetry. If we meet again, it will be in your future, not in mine."

"That sounds like a farewell. I'm not going yet."

"I think you are. I can see the desk right through your hand, my dear. Tell me something, quick, before you go. Do you like the ninth of the 'Wood Wife' poems?"

"I like all your poems, Cooper, you know that."

"But that one, Marguerita—what about that one?"

The floor slipped sideways, the stars swirled around her shoulders, and she could not answer him. Time was pulling at her again. She was not One of Them, she could not ignore it. Time, to her, moved in only one way—to stay in this place was to swim against floodwater running in the opposite direction. Her strength was ebbing, but still she swam, hanging on to that place, that time, trying to find a solid foothold that would keep her there, if only long enough to say goodbye.

She found it, climbing with great effort from the stream of Time to the banks of a wash. The wash was dry, the sand turned to silver by the light of the round moon overhead. She was in the desert, her desert. But the place was not familiar to her. She stumbled up the wash, heading east, judging by the shapes of the Rincons' dark slopes. She stopped abruptly. There was a body there—a dead man lying face down in the dirt. She did not need to roll the body over to know it was Davis Cooper.

She looked down at him, her eyes burning and yet dry, as terribly dry as the land. She heard the sound of coyotes calling, grieving—there must have been hundreds of them. Then she felt the pull, and she gave in to it, grateful to let it spin her away from that night, that wash, leaving a single set of footprints behind her in the sand.

As she gave up her resistance to it, the pull of the path seemed to lessen. The moonlit desert stretched below her as she stood in the very center of the spiral. The mountains surrounded her, spreading out to the edges of the earth. She could see with a sight that was not human sight. She could see Johnny Foxxe build a willow lodge by Deer Head Springs, and a fire that would not speak. Above him, in the trees, a white owl hovered who was not a white owl but a mage. She could see a fire in Red Springs Canyon, and Tomás Yazzie's stern face by its light. These flames murmured softly, and the man gifted them with tobacco, listening with rapt attention.

She could see the Alders, nursing three tiny fox pups who would not make it through the night. She could see the ghostly stag by Red Springs, glowing like candle flame in the dark. She could see Juan del Río, marked with paint, marked as though he were One of Them, waiting in vain for the beautiful mage who had deserted him by Redwater Creek.

And she could see that mage, the Drowned Girl, standing in a dry wash bed running south of the canyon. Cooper was with her. He had brought the package of poems. The Floodmage looked at him with cold, black eyes. She had painted his flesh with red spiral marks. Now she pointed a finger and spoke a word, and the wash bed slowly twisted. It sparkled like coins in the light of the moon, and Cooper put one foot upon the spiral.

"Imagine this place, these hills, this land, in that moment in Time where you wish to be," the girl whispered in the old man's ear. "I'll take you there. I'll hang on to your hand. It's as easy as stepping from one stone to another."

She smiled an innocent, young girl's smile. Cooper stepped upon the path. He stepped through Time. Maggie could *see* it swirl and turn around him, she could *hear* the song of the stars and the flood as he stepped on the path, stepped into the past, stepped into 1948 . . . into the deadly embrace of the water that had flooded the wash bed back then.

The Floodmage was as good as her word. She didn't let go of the old man's hand. She was still holding tight when she stepped back through Time to return to the dry riverbed.

"You see, Cooper," she said, amused, as she picked up the package he'd left in the sand, "I took you there. I didn't let go. I kept my side of the bargain."

But now another being stood on the banks of the wash, looking down on the translucent girl. She was a woman in a carved wooden mask, wearing only a cloak made of dried brown leaves. Beneath the cloak, her skin was tattooed with lines like the grain of polished oak. When she spoke, her voice was soft as the whisper of wind in a mesquite grove. "And what will you give to *me,* water witch, for taking my man away from me?"

"Your freedom, wood wife," said the girl. "You've been with humankind too long. You are as One of Them and not One of Us. Now his poems will bind you no more."

"It was never a poem that bound me," said the other, her voice low and fierce.

"What do you want then?" the girl said lightly.

"Give me his poems," said the masked woman.

"Take them." The girl crossed the wash and climbed the bank, her white feet leaving no tracks. She handed the package to the woman, bowed, and then faded like mist on the stones. She sunk back into the cracks of the land, to the water coursing far underground.

The Woodmage tore the brown paper wrapping, and uncovered the precious pages within. She held them to her breast for a long, silent moment—then she threw them into the sky. The pages came down, falling as rain. Where they fell, tall cactus sprang up and took root: a forest of mature saguaro turned to silver by the light of the moon.

Maggie watched as the Woodmage turned in the direction of Red Springs Canyon, shaped as María Rosa now: a small, old woman in a shapeless dress, passing beneath the saguaro's outstretched arms. It was then that coyotes began to gather, moving through cactus and creosote, called to the side of the dry wash bed by the echoing cries of their shape-shifting kin: Crow, in his swift coyote-shape; Angela and Isabella Foxxe; Pepe and his littermates—the seven Hernández brothers. They sang for the passing of a Spiritmage, of the one who had stood watching over the east through the years when the Nightmage no longer could—although Davis Cooper had never even known that a mage was what he had become.

As she listened to the coyotes' ghostly cries, Time and the rising wind moved faster, pulling, spinning Maggie into the stars that hung low over the desert. "Crow," she called out, trying to picture the mountain, the cliff, his hand, his sly face. Where was he? Why did he not pull her back? What foolish bargain had Maggie made that would now prove to be her own undoing? She could hear the bells on her ankles jingle as Time dropped her into a funnel of stars, a bottomless well down which she was falling, and would fall forever, the past in her throat, the future in her teeth, the death song in her ears. The song of the coyotes . . . the song of the stars . . . the deep bass song of the mountains below. . . .

She panicked, and flailed, looking for something solid to hang on to. Her hand met flesh, and she grabbed for it, falling heavily to the hard, unyielding ground. Pain exploded as her shins met rock, and the skin of her cheek scraped across loose stone. Arms closed around her. "Crow," she gasped.

"Good god, Maggie," Fox answered her.

"Don't let me go," she said to him.

"I won't." And he held her tight.

Crow lifted his head and sniffed the air. The wind carried the sound of bells. Black Maggie was now down by Redwater Creek; she'd returned from the path without his help, and of all the ways the woman had surprised him, this one surprised him the most.

Good. Crow liked surprises. It made the world a more interesting place. And the night promised many more to come; this night, of all

the nights in the wheel of human Time: the 31st of October. *Samhain.*
Cooper called it Allhallows' Eve. The next morning, to Anna, was
the Day of the Dead. Crow smiled a wolfish smile, anticipating the
night ahead. It was the night that *they* rose from the earth, the trees,
the water, the roots of the wood—rose and rode the Rincon hills, and
marked the land as their own.

Crow climbed to his feet on the sharp rock ledge where he had
been sitting the whole day long, waiting for Black Maggie to call to
him from the silt of the past's floodwaters. Many hours had passed
while she was in that place—where Time moved faster, and slower,
than here. Now the moon had risen. The Star Maker flung jewels
across a black sky. Crow shaped himself into coyote form, sniffed the
air, and followed Maggie's trail. He leapt down the dark, steep mountain slopes to the canyon below, howling as he ran. All around him,
his kin in the midnight hills lifted their voices in answer.

He found the woman at the edge of the creek in the place where the
water formed deep bathing pools. He waited in the shadows, coyote
ears cocked forward, and watched her curiously. How had she gotten back again? She was white as bone and breathing hard; her chest
rose and fell beneath the spiral marks he had painted on her. Crow
narrowed his eyes, watching Johnny Foxxe wash the blood from her
cheek with a bright red cloth. The one called Dora stood nearby, her
unbound hair the copper color of the moon. A black dog caught the
scent of Crow and growled, his hackles rising.

"What is it, Bandido?" Dora said. "What is it you see out there,
boy?"

As Dora peered into the darkness, Crow studied this second
woman with interest. Her husband was the young painter that the
Floodmage claimed as her masterpiece. The mage had made a Hunter
of the man, and tonight he'd run with her spectral Hounds. If he
survived that hunt, then he would win the skill with paint he'd bargained for. But the Hounds would hunt what they wished to hunt—
perhaps the white stag, perhaps the man.

There were many in the shadows of the hills who wagered now on
the outcome of that hunt: would the painter and the Hounds draw

blood that night? Or would the poacher reach the white stag first, led to his prey by the Owl Boy, the Windmage, who had taunted him with it for months? Or perhaps the stag himself might prevail, as he had before, to run another year—wild, wily, beautiful, shedding turquoise stones across the mountain slopes.

Crow's bet was on the stag. The beast was canny, quick, and powerful. Crow's kind would not kill one such as that; no one of them would take down a creature in its prime. A bullet to the heart, a knife to the throat: a human hand must do that work. Crow wagered that the painter's hand would falter. But the poacher was an unknown factor, and that made it more interesting to him.

Crow heard gunshot crack through the hills: two quick shots, in rapid succession. The Owl Boy's pet must be close by. Crow sniffed the air with his pointed nose. There was no scent of magic or the stag. The man was hunting other game now. Practicing the art of death.

"It's that poacher out there," Black Maggie was saying to the others. "The one who shot at Cody, and Pepe. I saw his truck parked off the road. Tomás says he's out to hunt the white stag." Her face was grim as she rose to her feet. "The stag is One of Them. The Nightmage. Anna's 'guardian angel of the east.'"

"In that case, can it be killed?" Fox asked her.

"In that shape, yes, I think it can. Look at the damage a gun did to Cody; and what happens to the ones caught in animal traps. I don't know what will happen if a guardian dies. I don't think I want to find out."

Dora looked troubled. "You know, Juan has taken up an interest in deer hunting lately."

"*Juan?*" said Fox. "He's got to be the least violent person—" Fox stopped abruptly, looking uneasily at Dora's black eye.

"Yes, I know," said Dora, "but he's been asking Tomás all about it. He even bought a hunting knife. I thought it was weird—but then so much has been weird about Juan these last few months."

Fox and Maggie exchanged a look. "I don't like the sound of any of this," she muttered.

Fox said, "All right, here's what I think. You and Dora should hike back to the Alders' house and phone the sheriff's office. We've got to get this trigger-happy young fool out of the canyon, particularly with Juan still out there. We don't know where Tomás is now either, and this poacher could mistake either one for a deer. My sisters are out there somewhere too. They weren't at the house when we stopped by."

"What exactly do you plan to do here alone?" said Maggie. "Threaten the guy with your flashlight, maybe? I say we stick together."

Dora agreed. "The Alders are bound to be calling the sheriff by now anyway. I don't want to go back, not while Juan is still in the hills."

Fox sighed. "All right. I'm overruled. But I don't like it. I'd feel better if the two of you would go back."

"Stop playing the cowboy," Maggie said drily. "Three of us will be more intimidating than one, and I don't really believe he'd shoot at us. It's the stag he wants, not the law on his heels."

"I reckon you're right about that," Fox conceded. "All right, then, let's head for the springs. That's where Tomás has seen the stag; that's where the poacher will be."

Crow crept quietly after them on the path that ran along Redwater Creek. Their trail was lit by the copper glow of the huge, round moon hanging overhead. The moon was high. The air was sharp. An owl hooted somewhere in the night. Soon the Hounds would reach Red Springs Canyon, and then the hunt would begin.

The three ahead were silent on the trail, oblivious to the changes in the desert around them. Rootmegs had begun to gather beneath the mesquites' gnarled black limbs. The willow witch was braiding her long green hair by the rocky edge of the creek; the three passed right by her, seeing only a willow sapling clinging to the rocks. The rocks themselves shifted and groaned, exposing wrinkled faces shaped of granite, veined with quartz, their blind eyes flashing silver mica. Overhead, the winged ones hovered, wearing shapes of mist and dust and light, leaking trails of color behind them onto the stones of the desert floor. In the thorny green cholla, a pale face lifted to drink that color down like rain, while the purple staghorn cholla tied on their staghorn caps over their spiney little heads.

They gathered, the thornwights, the tumbleweeds, the fierce devil's claws, and the tiny fairy dusters. The witches, the mages, the shape-shifters. Phantasms, fairies, spirits, and ghosts. To Maggie and the others it was just rising mist, inexplicably covering the dry, stony soil. Soon the moon would reach its peak. And then, yes, the hunt would begin.

Crow's coyote mouth gaped wide in a smile of anticipation. He sniffed the air. The stag was still distant. The poacher waited at the canyon's heart; his blood lust had a distinct, acrid smell. Crow could also smell blood. The scent of death. He recalled those two shots that had rung through the night. The Owl Boy's pet had killed once already, preparing for the prize to come. Whatever it was he had killed lay somewhere ahead, near the circle of the springs.

Then Crow heard a thin cry, a wailing, a howling more eerie than the coyotes' song. The Hounds were loose, coming over the hills, driving the stag before them. The Floodmage ran in the wake of the Hounds, limned by the light of the copper moon. An owl called again, the Windmage, her rival. Crow shifted into a bird shape himself, rising into the clear night sky above the trail by Redwater Creek. Enough of Black Maggie and her foolish companions. They were slow. They were growing tedious. They were going to miss the hunt.

Crow soared, and circled, and settled on the limb of a sycamore tree arched over the springs. The spring water was hot tonight, steaming in the cold night air. The water ran red, the heart-blood of the mountain, pumping through the land's dry veins. The white trees, the white tumbled stone glowed luminescent in the full moon's light. From that perch, Crow could see the approach of the spectral Hounds, and the Drowned Girl with them, her white hair streaming behind her, her small white feet pounding over the stones.

The Hounds glowed golden, ghostly, formed of moonlight turned to flesh and bone. Their bodies were thin and skeletal, whipcord muscles rippling under the fur. Their eyes were red, their jaws enormous—too large for the rest of them, grotesque, crowded with long, sharp teeth and lolling crimson tongues. The earth was scorched where they passed by, howling in their bloodlust.

But where was the stag? Ah, there he was. The Hounds had split
into two packs, herding the wild-eyed animal between them. In one
pack was the Bright Hunter, the painter, marked as One of Them. His
breath was labored; as was the stag's. They had harried the beast for
some distance. The Hounds breathed smoke in the cold desert air,
their eyes were flames, their teeth like knives. The stag could be hurt,
but not killed by them. He was bound as tightly with protection from
the Hounds as the witch woman, Anna Naverra, had been. The stag
knew the man was the danger here, on this night of all nights in
human Time.

The Hounds herded him to the circle of the springs, the land rising steep around them here, trying to drive the stag to exhaustion
and to bring him down, so the man could strike. Crow rocked on his
perch with his amusement. The little Floodmage claimed to disdain
all of humankind, and yet she overestimated them. That man was
no match for the big white stag, even when the Hounds had done
with it. The man was a painter, not a hunter; a creator, not a killer.
The stag would win, and then the Hounds would feed on the man
instead.

The stag wheeled, chunks of turquoise flying where his hooves
hit the rock of the canyon's floor. The Floodmage's pack was closing
in. But where had the Windmage's poacher gone? Crow lifted lightly
into the sky, circled the clearing and found the man at the edge of
the trailhead, waiting there. Waiting for what? This was interesting.
Crow fluttered and settled on a rock ledge above, where the Owl Boy
sat, his masked face intent. Crow fanned his black wings, startling
the boy. "And what are you up to, my pretty?"

The Windmage put a finger to his lips. "Be quiet, Fool, and you
shall see."

Crow surveyed the night: the stag, the Hounds, the man with the
knife, the man with the gun. Black Maggie was coming up the trail,
the witch woman's son close at her heels. She spied the poacher, just
as the poacher spied the stag bounding up the hill. The Hounds drove
the stag up toward the springs. The stag wheeled. Then the animal
gathered himself, to bound through the clearing and up the steep

slope, toward the east, toward escape, away from the Hounds. He ran, made the leap. He folded in midair, and fell heavily to the hard ground.

Crow shifted to his true shape, his dual horned-man shape, where his quick eyes were the sharpest. Then he saw the cold, metallic gleam of a wire stretched across the clearing. A trap, a poacher's dirty trick. He looked at the Windmage with sharp disapproval. "That is not well done. There's no beauty in it."

The boy shrugged. "The man's doing, not mine," he said. "And I'll still win the wager."

The stag climbed slowly to his feet, moving with effort, with great heaving breaths. One leg bone had snapped, another fractured. The Hounds surrounded him, holding off now. The poacher smiled, and came out from the rocks. He lifted his gun up to his shoulder, the smile wide on his red, flushed face. Behind him, Black Maggie snarled like an animal herself and launched into the man.

Gunshot cracked, ricocheting on rock. A tall sagauro was hit and one long green arm fell heavily to the ground, pinning the leg of the poacher, piercing through flesh with its hundreds of razor-sharp spines. The young man howled in agony. Crow laughed aloud on his ledge of stone. The boy hissed, "You brought that woman here! She's spoiling the hunt! She'll change everything."

"Look there," said Crow. "At the Floodmage's pet."

The painter was stalking the white stag now, his hand trembling, his shoulders tensed. Even with the Floodmage's glamour on him, he was thinking twice of this work tonight. He was a sorry sight for a hunter, and the Owl Boy smiled wickedly.

Crow made an elaborate show of yawning. "The hunt is almost over now, before it's even truly begun. That puppy won't strike. The stag has won. Now all that remains to be seen is whom the Hounds choose as their consolation prize."

The Windmage shrugged. "It could be your own pet, Fool. Look, the woman has broken herself. How will she run from the Hounds?"

Crow frowned. Black Maggie was climbing to her feet, braced by Fox, her face tight with pain, cradling one arm against her. Beside her, the poacher lay flat on the ground, leaking tears into the dry soil. Crow pointed, and said, "She carries turquoise—"

"That will protect her from glamour, not the Hounds."

"—and she wears a white feather in her hair. That feather is one of yours, pretty boy. She's under *your* protection now. The Hounds aren't going to touch her."

The boy shrugged. "In that case they'll take her friends."

"What is that to me?" Crow answered him, but he knew the words were false as he said them. The witch woman's son was of interest to him; it would be a great pity to lose him now. And little Dora had taken his fancy. He watched as she ran across the clearing to her husband, calling out his name.

The Floodmage reached the painter first, her eyes like burning coals, her hair streaming smoke and fire behind her. "Strike! Strike! Why do you not strike?"

Juan swallowed. "I can't. He's so beautiful. . . ."

"You must!" she shrieked. "You must! Or the bargain's off, and I shall take something else! Your limbs, your life! Your work, your wife! Strike, or you will owe me one of them!"

"What fun!" said the Windmage.

Dora reached Juan, her hair as wild and as bright as the mage's. She grabbed his arm, but he wheeled away, holding the knife between them. "Don't listen," said Dora. "Don't do it. Don't listen. Just give me the knife, dear heart."

"I can't," Juan said, his voice breaking. "I made a bargain. I promised to hunt the stag. I can't back out."

"You're hunting an angel, not a stag," said Johnny Foxxe, coming up behind Dora. He looked warily at the knife held between them. His eyes flickered to the Floodmage and back.

The painter's face twisted with some strong emotion. Crow couldn't begin to imagine what it was. "The stag will die anyway," the young man said. "It can't survive crippled in the wild. It would be a mercy to finish it off."

"No," said Fox. "You know that's not true. The Alders can look after him. Give me the knife, Juan. It's over now. Just call the bargain off."

"He can't," hissed the Floodmage.

"I can't," said Juan. "Something is going to die tonight. The Hounds are loose and they'll have to feed now."

"Put down the knife, boy. The Hounds will feed," said another voice altogether.

Tomás Yazzie appeared on the rock ridge above him. He jumped the last drop to the canyon floor, breathing hard, his brown face stern.

"What's this? What's this?" the Owl Boy hissed. The Hounds growled, and the trapped beast trembled.

"Give me the knife. You're no hunter, boy," Tomás said. He took it from the startled painter's hand.

"Thank God," said Fox, closing his eyes as he breathed out one long sigh of relief.

"No!" Maggie screamed from behind him.

Fox's eyes snapped open. Tomás approached the stag, wading through the unresistant Hounds, the knife held in a hunter's grip.

"What the hell are you doing?" Fox yelled, running after the other man. The Hounds turned, snarling, snapping at him, separating him from Tomás and the stag.

"I've said the prayers," Tomás said to the stag. The stag attempted to back away, moving awkwardly, painfully. Tomás said, "I've burned tobacco. I've said the prayers. Gift me with your life, my brother."

The stag attempted one last lunge, one desperate leap to break free of the Hounds, the man, the walls that encircled him. Tomás ran, flung one arm around its neck, snapping back the great stag's head, plunging the knife behind the jawbone, as Maggie screamed again: *"No!"*

The stag slumped to the ground, and the man fell with him heavily. "Go with the wind, brother," Crow heard him tell the stag.

Crow leapt from the ledge on a black crow's wings, and landed behind Tomás, shaped as a man. "Take the skin," he urged him. "Quick! Or else he'll be trapped in the white stag's death, as he was trapped in its life."

Tomás slowly stood and turned to the Floodmage, who was watching him with bright-eyed interest. "Call off your dogs, girl."

"I cannot," she said.

He looked at her sternly. "Then you don't deserve to run them."

Anger crossed the lovely young face. "Give me the blood, and I'll call them off." She gathered a handful of sandy soil, and fire blossomed in her hand. The flames died, and she held a large earthenware bowl. She tossed the bowl to Crow.

Crow held the bowl as Tomás bled the stag. Then the Drowned Girl took the bowl from him, a trail of hot blood staining her thin white dress. "Come," she said to her terrible Hounds. "You will feed soon, my beautiful ones."

When the Hounds had turned from the stag's body, moving like water through the circle of stones, Fox approached Tomás and Crow, Black Maggie close behind. Fox took the leather pouch from his belt and spilled tobacco into his palm. He knelt before the stag's great head, and he poured the offering to the ground.

Tomás bent over the stag's body, the hunting knife clutched in his hand. Then he gutted the beast, pulling the blade from the chest, down the length of the smooth white belly. As the body opened, the entrails steamed hot as a fire to warm the ones gathered round. Steam billowed in the cold desert air, rising as smoke to the clear night sky, forming the shape of a man made out of mist and stars, crowned with horns. His face was narrow, his nose was hooked; the great horns lifted from the curve of his brow. He stepped from the broken body of the stag, pulling himself from the shape beneath. When his feet touched ground, he solidified; the mist became flesh, but just barely so. Crow could still see the night sky through him, the stars and the round copper moon.

The Floodmage looked up from her Hounds, and smiled at Crow smugly. "You see, I was right. I knew that he was trapped somewhere here on the mountain—and not in that witch woman's painting at all. I told you even *she* would not send his essence away from the land."

The girl had been right, Crow would give her that. The Nightmage had been here all along. They'd known the stag was one of his creatures. They'd not known he'd been bound inside it, bound so deep in the animal-self that not one of them *saw* him there.

Crow rose from the carcass and stared at the mage. But the Stag Man who stared back at him was not the creature that he remembered; the arrogance, the intelligence, the sly wit of the mage were gone now. The Stag Man stood and he looked at them all with an animal's wild-eyed wariness. He was panting, his thin chest rising and falling. Crow began to laugh.

"Why do you laugh?" hissed the Owl Boy from the trees.

"Because *I* was right as well. You can't have your Nightmage back again—this one is a mage no longer. Look at him! He's been in the animal shape too long. He's forgotten what he is."

"That's impossible," said the Floodmage sharply, leaving her Hounds to come stand with them. "This land is alive. It would taste ugly and dead if there was no guardian here."

Crow smiled at her, enjoying this game. "Then there must be another guardian. A Spiritmage watching over the east. A *human* mage, my dear."

"Cooper is dead," said the Drowned Girl, glaring darkly at the Trickster.

"Then a new Spiritmage has taken his place." Crow's wolfish smile grew wider.

"Impossible," the girl said again. "This painter of mine is no Spiritmage. And your little poet hasn't been here long enough."

"Then I think it is neither a painter nor poet," said Crow. "Am I right, Tomás Yazzie?"

Tomás inclined his head. "I look after this land as best I know how. I listen to it with respect. Mage, shaman—those are just words. Call me what you will, spirit-brother."

"You can't be a mage," the girl spat out. The ends of her white hair smouldered. "You have no mastery, no artistry. There is nothing about you that is beautiful."

Tomás gave the girl a charming smile. "No mastery? No artistry? You've never looked at my garden, then, have you? My beans, my corn, my big gourd vines—they are beautiful indeed."

The girl's pale face grew paler still. Her eyes were wide and black as the sky.

But Tomás turned his back on her. "I need your help," he said to Fox. "You too, boy," he called to Juan.

He lifted the entrails from the stag's body and left them steaming on the cold ground. Together, they roped the body, lifted and hung it from a sycamore's strong limb. Crow watched with interest as Tomás expertly flayed the skin from the warm flesh beneath. Black Maggie also watched, sitting by the springs until the long job was done. The Nightmage just stood. His eyes never left Tomás, or the gleam of the knife.

When he was finished, Tomás folded the heavy white deerskin into his arms. "Cut the body down," he said to Juan. "Let the Hounds feed and be done." He turned to Crow, and gave him the skin. "Do what must be done with this. No tricks. No games tonight."

Crow barked with laughter, barely conscious of having shifted to half-coyote form now. His arms were still man-shaped. He held the skin, and presented it to the Stag Man.

"Your freedom," Crow said. "Take it. Go on and take it. It's a gift."

The Stag Man took the soiled white skin. He wrapped it around his shoulders. As he did so, he solidified farther, a creature now of true flesh and blood, the great horns on his head forked into points that glowed like flame. His cheeks were drawn with lines and spirals; he wore six copper bands on his wrist. He removed one band and awkwardly tossed it to the ground at Tomás's feet. He gazed long at the seventh mage, his animal eyes unreadable. Then he shifted back into his stag-shape, whole now, and unbloodied. This time it was only one shape among many, a shape to carry him away from the springs, from the canyon, out into the night. The Hounds ignored him, letting him pass, his hooves striking sparks from the rocky ground. And when he left, no turquoise marked the trail that he had taken.

Tomás knelt down by the edge of Red Springs to wash the blood of the stag from his hands. The spring water ran clear and cold. The moon was sinking into the west.

"How did you know?" Black Maggie asked him. "You told me you'd never hunt the white stag. How did you know what had to be done?"

Crow drew close to hear his answer.

"I got lost in the hills. . . . No. Led astray. And so I lit a fire. I listened to the flames, the wood, the wind. They told me on this night the stag would die, and by my hand."

"I see. And can you teach me how to listen to the fire, the wood, and the wind?"

"You already know. You're a poet," he said. "I'll teach you something better."

"What's that?"

"How to grow beans and corn and squash in the middle of the desert."

"All right. It's a deal," Black Maggie agreed, smiling at the hunter.

Crow frowned. She hadn't even asked the man what he wanted in return.

Crow cocked his head and looked at Maggie out of dark coyote eyes; and then at Dora, quiet, shivering, leaning against her husband. The painter was fey and wild-eyed; the glamour was still upon him. By morning it would fade away; he would not remember the work of this night. He might not remember the Drowned Girl at all. Crow turned suddenly to the Floodmage.

"Release this man from your bargain. The terms are met. The stag was killed."

"But not by his hand," the Drowned Girl said.

Crow wrinkled his coyote nose. "The shape you have made him is not beautiful. Nor is it amusing. Let him go back to his true shape now; it was more interesting than this one."

She smiled at him, a cold little smile. "He'll never be a great painter without me. He'll only be good. Content, nothing more."

Crow shrugged. "And what does that matter to me?"

"Then what will you give me if I do?"

"What do you want?" he bargained.

"Give me lightning, thunder and storms. I'll flood Tanque Verde Falls this year."

His own smile was sly. "You'll have it," he said. "Yes. That will be amusing."

When the Hounds had fed, they followed the Drowned Girl back into the Rincon hills, growing more indistinct with every step, turning back into moonlight. The Owl Boy leapt into the sky, careful to leave no feathers behind. The coyotes crawled from the shadows then, and one black dog followed after them, trying to pretend they had never hidden there, never been afraid of the Hounds. Their song echoed through the canyon once more, along with the song that Crow alone could hear: the rootmegs singing, the water chanting, the mountains humming in their deep baritone. Spirits returned to rock, root, and thorn; ghosts drifted back to the dry, sandy soil. The night would end, day could come, and That-Which-Moved kept on turning.

"Look Fox, there's One-Eye," said Maggie as a small black shape came trotting up Red Springs Trail, two coyotes trailing behind him, one limping as she walked.

"Thank heavens," breathed Fox, rubbing weary eyes, leaving a smear of blood on his cheek. The three coyotes surrounded him; he knelt down by the largest. "Pepe, please go find the Alders. Have them call out Search and Rescue, if they haven't called them already. We're going to need a medic back here, and a stretcher. As quick as you can."

Fox rose, crossed the clearing, and squatted on his heels beside the poacher. He took the water bottle from his pack and persuaded the whimpering man to drink. "We can't move you yet. The medics will have to pry you loose from those cactus spines; we'll hurt you more if we move you ourselves. Just hang on. Help's on its way."

"Goddamn cactus," the young man muttered weakly. "Worse than goddamn coyotes."

Fox looked up. "Go on, Pepe. Hurry." But One-Eye had stopped at the head of the trail, nosing something in the shadows beyond. Crow stepped behind him, wearing his man-shape, and peered into the darkness.

"What is it?" said Maggie. She switched on her flashlight. And then she dropped it with a hoarse, abrupt sound. She dropped to her knees, and gathered the shape of the Rabbit Girl into her arms. "Get John and Lillian here quick, Pepe."

It would not be quick enough. The creature was dead. Crow knew that even before he squatted down beside her and put one hand upon the Rabbit Girl's chest. Gunshot. She had been target practice for the poacher, grown bored while he waited by the springs. The girl had shifted into her almost-human form some time after the fatal bullet had struck, shattering one skinny rib, piercing the flimsy tissue of a lung. Crow closed his eyes, and he shifted her back to her core, made of wind, earth, bone, and fur; the grey not-quite-a-jackrabbit shape; something more and something less than all that.

"Come away, Black Maggie," Crow said to her with a gentleness that surprised even him. "It is finished here. It is *dammas*."

Tears ran down the woman's face, floodwater in a wash, spilling over its banks. She cried with the awkward heavings of someone who had long forgotten how to cry. In the anguish on her face, Crow could almost glimpse what it was that human anguish was. Johnny Foxxe came up behind her, bracing her with his arms, his presence, looking warily at the shape-shifter beside her.

She said finally, "We can't just leave her here."

"You must," Crow said, taking the body from her and laying it out on the ground." Another will eat, and live another day. The gift of life passes on. It is *dammas*," he repeated, helpless, perplexed, unable to understand the emotions that pulled the woman as strongly as the winds of the mountain pulled on him. "Come away now," he said again.

She turned her stricken face to him. "I can't do it. We can't just leave her here."

"Maggie, look," Fox said to her. He pointed to the slope beyond, where the Spine Witch climbed through the prickly pear, barefoot on the sharp cactus thorns, her pointed face expressionless, thoroughly ignoring them all. Her tattered wings dragged on the ground as she crossed over cactus, sage and stone. She stood looking down at the jackrabbit's body. Then she lifted it gently in her arms. She cradled the furry creature to her breast, and started back the way she had come.

"Where is she going?" Maggie asked Crow, her eyes wide and dark with wonder.

"To sing the death song."

"Will we hear it?" Maggie whispered, wiping the tears from her hot, red cheeks.

"If you wish to, yes." The shape-shifter leaned over and kissed the woman behind her left ear.

In the hills, the coyotes were singing.

This time, she knew the language of their song.

DAVIS COOPER
Redwater Road
Tucson, Arizona

Marguerita Black
London, U.K.

September 22, 1979

Dear Ms. Black,

In response to your letter of September 1, which Maisie Tippets has passed on to me, I regret to tell you that I am not prepared to authorize a biography of my life; in fact, it would be exceedingly against my wishes for any such endeavor to begin. Obscurity has few rewards, Ms. Black, but privacy is one of them, and I value it. Maisie tells me you are a sensible woman; I trust you will respect my wishes.

She has also given me a copy of your thesis regarding my 'Wood Wife' poems. I never read such things. There is little that can be said about them, good or bad, that hasn't been said before, usually at ridiculous length; and I put little stock in the writings of theorists. A theorist is not a poet.

I would far rather you had sent me your poems. As it happens, I am familiar with your work and have followed your career since your first publication, The Coalminer's Tale. *The Harper's article on Tippetts was very good, very facile—but you are a poet. And poems are the language of the gods, not magazine reportage. Perhaps you would indulge a cranky old man and permit me to read what you have written since your last publication (the collection from Bank Street Press, I believe, or have I missed one?). You interest me greatly, Marguerita Black. I remain*

Yours truly,
Davis Cooper

chapter eleven

Twined together, root to root,
sap seeping from flesh,
the Wood Wife plants me in the soil
and gives me language once again.
—The Wood Wife, *Davis Cooper*

Maggie looked out the window at the London sky. Low, grey, and oppressive. Threatening to rain again. She let the curtain fall back over the window, preferring the brightness and the warmth of Tat's loft: the big monoprints with their planes of color, and the furniture that Tat had painted yellow, purple, indigo blue, and apple green, like the colors from a crayon box. The industrial walls had been softened with a wash of paint the color of milk in tea, reminding her of Cooper's walls, the mottled tones of old adobe.

Maggie shut her eyes and sighed. It seemed that everything conspired to remind her of Cooper and the mountain.

"Are you okay?" Tat said, looking up from the floor where she was framing a print. The English woman was as tall as Maggie, but in every other way she was the reverse of her American friend. Where Maggie dressed only in men's clothing, Tat favored long, loose dresses, albeit worn over army boots. Where Maggie's hair was dark and sleek, Tat's was an unusual silver-white, quite short, and raggedly cut. Tatiana had been diagnosed with multiple sclerosis some years before; the illness had stolen the prettiness from her face, and given her back something more compelling. She was frowning now, looking up at Maggie with worry in her shadowed eyes. "You've been sighing all day," she pointed out.

"It's just the weather," Maggie assured her. "The sky looks so small and closed-in here, after those big, blue desert skies."

"Welcome to London." Tat gave Maggie a wry look as she screwed the frame together. She used the screwdriver carefully, slowly. Such things gave her trouble now. "I, for one, am glad you made it back in time for the Private View of my show. Even if you don't seem so certain that you want to be here yourself. . . ."

"Of course I'm glad I'm here for your show," Maggie said. And then she sighed again. "I just don't know where I want to be after that. And that's the problem."

She got up and went into the bedroom that Tat had built at the end of the loft. She still wasn't ready to talk to her friend about what exactly had happened in Arizona. She would—she didn't keep secrets from Tat. But the words to explain it all hadn't come yet. She felt empty of language, for once in her life. Empty of everything except confusion. She had run from the desert like she had run from everything that had ever sought to bind her. But she couldn't seem to run far enough. It was all she could think about here.

She picked up her bag and sat on the futon mattress, emptying the bag beside her. She was getting good at doing things one-handed, but it would be a relief when the cast came off her arm and she could have her normal life back again. Whatever that was, she thought, and a sour look crossed over Maggie's face. She wasn't sure she knew anymore. She had thought coming back to safe, familiar ground would begin to make things clear again. She had thought she could find the shape of the woman she'd been, before she'd gone to Cooper's mountain.

She looked at the objects spread on the quilt: a single white feather, a string of bells, chunks of raw turquoise, a silver Hopi bracelet. Cloth-wrapped bundles of cedar, sage, and tobacco. Cooper's edition of *The Wood Wife*. She picked up the sage and inhaled it, breathing the scent of another world altogether, another life, another Maggie Black, another shape over the essence beneath. She didn't know if it was a true shape, or if the land had overwhelmed her with one of its own. Perhaps in this place, where the land did not sing beneath her, she'd be able to tell. And when she finally knew the answer to that riddle, she'd write to Fox, as she had promised.

She picked up *The Wood Wife* and opened it. Several of Cooper's letters and an old bill for his dry cleaning were stuck inside its pages. She opened one of the letters and read, "I'll tell you, after arguing with Anna about coming to New York, I find I don't want to be here after all. . . . I want silence again, and vast blue skies. I want the heat, honest earth underfoot. I can't sleep here. I don't think I'll sleep till I reach the mountains, and Anna."

She read another. ". . . . It is not possible, it is not conceivable that she will stay away for good. Anna loves these hills, this sky, this house. She'll come back for the land, if not for me."

And another. "I can't bear to think of you in the flatlands, where the stones do not whisper your name."

Maggie put the letters down. Here in the city, the stones below were mercifully silent. She could understand why there may have come a time when Anna Naverra needed that. She sat now and listened. Outside the bedroom door was a steady hammering, a muttered curse, and the music of the Desert Winds tape she'd brought to London for her friend, filling the loft with Indian flute and the whisper of another land. Beyond that was the sound of London traffic, someone shouting in an Asian tongue, trucks rattling over the cobbled stone of the alley below the warehouse windows: sounds less beautiful to her than the desert's, but just as dear.

Maggie opened *The Wood Wife*, and she looked down at the ninth of Davis Cooper's poems. She read:

The ghost comes from the wood holding
the future, not the past, a fragile gift
as weightless as the smoke
that rises where she steps. . . .

She read it slowly, haltingly, as though translating from a foreign tongue. Her eyes skimmed down the rest of the page. She turned it, and she read:

> . . . the night visitors, three women, three Fates,
> three Graces, the ghosts who haunt me here;
> the painter who stands behind me; and
> the poet who stands before me; and
> the wood wife, silent at my side,
> rooting me to this earth. . . .

She looked at the words. Type on a page. Runic shapes in black, black ink. Words were chunks of turquoise in her hand; words were what protected her. Only right now she couldn't remember just what it was they protected her from.

She closed the book and swept the desert back into her leather bag. She went to the kitchen. She switched the electric kettle on, and spooned black tea into Tat's china pot, thinking of another poem. This one was by Michael Hannon:

> Work with words cannot save us.
> Nothing can do that,
> but perhaps to be saved is not salvation.

> I see the trees along this road
> turn into smoke at sundown,
> and know them for the very ones
> I was meant to see.

When the tea was made, she balanced a tray with her good arm and carried it over to Tat. Then she sat down on the floor beside her, resting her back against a flat file painted the red of an ocotillo bloom.

"Girl," said Tat, reaching for the cup, "do you want my opinion?"

Maggie looked at her best friend warily. She wasn't sure whether she wanted it or not; Tat's perceptions could cut close to the bone. They'd known each other so long now, the other woman could probably read her mind.

"All right," she said, "what's your opinion?"

"I think you done fell in love on me," Tat said, mimicking her

American drawl. "You've got that lovesick look on you. Aren't you even going to tell me his name?"

"Johnny Foxxe," she said, looking down at her knees. "Johnny Foxxe Cooper," she amended.

"Cooper as in Davis?"

Maggie nodded glumly. "Cooper's son by Anna Naverra."

Tat narrowed her eyes, looking thoughtful now. "So they had a child, did they? Back in the forties, it must have been. Hmmm. You've fallen for an older man."

"Not exactly," said Maggie vaguely.

"Then what exactly?" Tat prodded her, nudging Maggie's foot with the toe of her boot. "And what exactly are you doing here in London, if that's the case? Not that it's not fantastic to have you, sweet Magpie. But what are you running from this time?"

Maggie bit her lip, and did not answer her.

"You're always running from something," Tat persisted with the brutal honesty that only she could get away with. "You're always up and gone before your heart can engage—with a place, with a man. Even with writing poems again. Girl, if love outran you this time, I'm not sure that's so bad."

Maggie bowed her head and considered Tat's question. What exactly was she running from? Not Fox. Well, not precisely. And not from the spirits of the mountain. She frowned. "Look, I never imagined ending up in Tuscon, of all places. Loving this man could change my whole life. I'm just not sure I'm ready for that."

Tat put down the teacup and flashed her a grin of commiseration. "Girlfriend, no one's ever ready for that. But life changes on us anyway. And I'm not convinced we get to choose who we love, or when it would be most convenient."

"Now that's a comforting thought," Maggie muttered.

"Well, if you're just going to sit and mope, how about giving me some help here? I have to haul this piece downstairs, and I'm having trouble lifting. Think you can lend me the one good hand you've got? Between us we almost make one normal person."

"Honey, there's no way either of us is going to make a normal person. But I'll help. Is this for the show? I thought it was hung? It opens tonight, for gawd's sake."

"When have you ever known me to do anything before the last possible minute? Yann and Larry are over at the gallery now, making sure it's all properly hung."

"Together?" Maggie asked. Her friend merely shrugged. Only Tat could pull off having two different men in her life, and have both get along.

"I promised them they'd have the last piece by five, which gives us . . ." Tat consulted her watch. "Bloody hell, we'd better get a move on it. I hope you don't mind leaving early? I promised them Indian takeout for dinner."

"How are we supposed to get the print over there? It's not going to fit in your Morris, you know."

"I've got Yann's van."

"The new one? And you're doing the driving?" Maggie said skeptically, rising to her feet. Tat's bad driving was notorious, even before the MS. "He's going to want it back in one piece."

"What do you suggest? That *you* drive? What are you going to shift with, your feet?" she growled, grinning at her girlfriend. She picked up one end of the frame. "See if you can lift that side."

The phone began to ring before they made it out the door. Tat put the print down. "You get it. That's Nigel," she predicted. "I'd know that imperious ring anywhere."

It was indeed Nigel; his third call that week. She hadn't even told him she was coming to London, and he'd tracked her down within twenty-four hours. She still couldn't decide if she thought this was endearing, or just annoying.

"Hi," she said now. "Where are you today? Atlanta? D.C.?"

"Back home in L.A. Atlanta was last week, don't you remember? The tour is over, thank God. My percussionist's wife has left him for the soundman, and it's all a bloody mess."

He sighed, and Maggie frowned. He sounded genuinely troubled. She knew him too well not to hear it in his voice. Something was wrong besides a colleague's marriage, and she wondered what it was. But she resisted her old, habitual reaction: to ask, to jump in, to soothe, to help. Whatever it was, it was Nigel's problem, not hers, she reminded herself firmly.

"Well," she said simply, "get some rest now that you're home. See a movie. Go hear a new band. Do something fun, Nige—something that hasn't got anything at all to do with Estampie."

He sighed again, waiting for her to pick up the cue and ask him what was wrong. Transatlantic silence stretched between them. Finally Nigel said, "Look, Puck. Well. I've got some news."

He sounded unusually hesitant, and Maggie was suddenly wary. "It's not about Harvey, is it? Promise me you didn't sign anything."

"Harvey?" he said as though he couldn't place the name. "Oh, no. Not that. It's about Nicole."

"What about Nicole?"

He was silent again. It was very unlike him, and Maggie's mind was racing. Had Nicole left him? Were all the Estampie wives suddenly defecting at once? Would Nigel be a free man again? And if he was, did that even matter to her?

"Come on, Nigel, what is it?"

"Good news, actually. Nicole's . . ." He cleared his throat, sounding as if he wasn't quite certain if it was good news at all. "It seems we're going to have a baby. It's due in the middle of June."

"Oh. Good heavens. That's great news," she said. And found, to her relief, that she meant it.

"Yes, great," he repeated tentatively.

"Nigel, are you happy about this?" she asked her ex-husband with concern. "You always expected to have kids some day, and you're not getting any younger, dear." She smiled drily as she said it. It was only his lovers that were getting younger.

"Of course I'm happy. Certainly. Well. It's just . . . I hadn't planned on a baby. It's totally fantastic, of course. But. Well. It's going to change things here."

"Life changes anyway," she told him. Tat was smirking at her in the doorway. Maggie picked up a book and threw it at her.

"Nicole is thrilled. She'll have to stop modeling for a while. I don't think she cares. I think she'd rather be home; the traditional wife. She's not much like you are, Maggie."

"No, she's not. And that's why you married her, remember?"

"Damn straight," he shot back, teasing her, but his voice still sounded distracted.

Silence stretched again. Tat was looking at her watch, a worried expression on her face. "Nige, I've got to go. But I'm really glad that you called to tell me the news."

"Okay, then. I'll ring you tomorrow. How long are you going to be in London?"

"I haven't the foggiest idea."

"Well, just make sure you're back in L.A. by June," Nigel commanded.

Why? she thought, as she hung up the phone. This was their baby, not Maggie's. It was Nicole who mattered now, not her. The Nigel part of her life was finally ending—and something new could begin. She was startled, and a little abashed, by the feeling of liberation that washed over her.

She turned to Tat. "It looks like our Nigel's going to be a daddy."

Tat's eyes grew bright. Her grin was wicked. "Now won't that be a sight. Nigel changing nappies. Babies drooling on his posh designer suits."

"No way," wagered Maggie as she lifted the end of Tat's big print with her one good arm. "He'll have Nicole and nannies to do the work."

"Until it's old enough to boss around; then the kid will be working for Nigel," Tat agreed. She picked up the other end of the frame, and they hauled it to the freight elevator. Tat lowered them down to a loading dock, and they packed the piece up in Yann's big van.

"Brilliant," said Tat, with satisfaction. "Now come upstairs and tell me what to wear."

"That's easy," said Maggie, following her. "Wear that black dress that barely covers your bum."

"The one that gives Larry apoplexy?"

"The very one," said Maggie.

Tat disappeared into the bathroom, and reappeared in a skintight dress that exposed a lot of long white leg, spotted with streaks of paint. She glared at Maggie. "Do I look like an artist or a prostitute?" she demanded.

Maggie laughed. "Honey, in those army boots, nobody's going to mistake you for a hooker, don't you worry."

Tat continued to frown. "Do my eyes deceive me, or have you let a bit of c-o-l-o-r actually come in contact with your virgin flesh?"

Maggie flushed. She wore Fox's shirt under her black Armani jacket. "Big deal," she mumbled. "Life changes, right?"

"Will wonders never cease?" said Tat, putting her arm through Maggie's as they headed for the elevator.

The traffic was heavy as Tat drove from her loft in the industrial streets of Spittalfields to the gallery in the West End where her show would open that evening. Tat's sweet French lover, Yann Kerjean, looked relieved when the two women finally arrived, glad to get the last of the prints and to see that his van was still intact. Maggie left Tat in Yann's capable hands, and went off in search of dinner.

She eyed the sky suspiciously as she stepped back out onto the street. The rain was holding off, but it wouldn't hold off for very much longer. Tat had said a good Indian place was up the street and to the left. Maggie passed trendy dress shops, other galleries, a noisy pub . . . no Indian food. She felt a drop of rain on her face, and then another. She walked another block. She passed a Greek restaurant, a leather shop, then a gallery window that stopped her in her tracks. She looked at the exhibition sign again. The show was of work by Brian Froud, Cooper's friend, and Dora's favorite painter. She looked at her watch. There wasn't much time, but she went inside anyway.

The gallery was long, narrow, and well-lit. Maggie barely noticed any of these things. Her eyes were caught and held by the paintings themselves, glowing on the gallery walls as though all the color that was missing from the grey London sky was captured here. The paintings were of fairy creatures drawn from shapes of brown oak leaves, of moss on stone, of water and wood, of light and wind and stars. She knew these creatures. Or if not precisely these, then their kin, born from the dry desert soil. Looking at those haunted faces made something ache deep down inside her.

It was a low, dull pain, both bitter and sweet. It was homesickness, she realized; a feeling she'd never once felt before. She missed the desert. She missed its colors, its spirits, its scent after the rain. She missed Johnny Foxxe. Maggie closed her eyes, and took a steadying breath.

She stayed in that gallery for a long time. When she finally left, it was raining in earnest. She fumbled left-handed with her small and useless umbrella, hurried up the darkened street, and found Tat's takeout place up the block on the right, not the left. Good old Tat.

There was a phone booth just beyond the restaurant. Maggie stopped and looked at it. The wind snapped her umbrella inside out, breaking its brittle, cheaply made spines. The rain drenched her as she stood, indecisive. She ran to the booth, closed the door. Water pounded overhead as she slid her credit card into the machine with cold, numb fingers. She punched in the long transatlantic number and waited, wet and shivering.

The connection was made, but just as the phone began to ring, she slammed the receiver down. What on earth was she doing? It was still early on the mountain—half a day and half a world away. And what would she have said to Fox? She was just as confused as when she left. She stepped outside, her heart heavy, her fleeting connection to the desert soon washed away by the cold London rain.

She purchased curries, rice and naan and hurried back through the flooded streets. By the time she reached the door that led to the gallery on the floor above, she was thoroughly drenched. There was water in her boots. Her hair dripped rainwater down her neck. She had spent so much time in the other gallery that Tat's Private View had already begun. Maggie sidled into the artsy crowd, embarrassed, feeling like a drowned rat.

She handed the sodden bag to Tat. "Dinner," she said with an apologetic smile.

"Put it in back. We'll eat it later. Go towel off in the loo or something."

Maggie did as she was told, grimacing at her bedraggled reflection in the bathroom mirror. She dried her face and slicked back her wet hair before returning to the crowd.

A blues trio played in one corner: a tiny, wrinkled black man on guitar, an Irish woman she knew on bass, and long, lean Larry Bone, Tat's other lover, on harmonica. Tat was on the other side of the room, talking with a man Maggie recognized as a journalist who worked for *Time Out*. Yann was cornered by a woman in spandex and spike heels, looking rather alarmed.

The gallery owner was fluttering around the room. He'd make few sales tonight. There were too many other artists here, with barely a quid between them. They'd come for Tat, and the free champagne; the art itself was mostly ignored. Maggie gazed around the room, nodding at old friends and pleased by the good turnout. Then she saw another face she recognized. Standing over by the windows.

She stared at him. Then she crossed the room, oblivious to the greetings that followed her. When she stood before Fox, she just looked at him. She was silent. She had no words at all. She wondered how he had found her.

He held up the invitation to Tat's show. "This was on your refrigerator," he said to her with a sheepish grin. Then he looked at her warily. "I'm not like Nigel. If you don't want me here, I won't bother you again. It's just . . ."

His voice trailed off, and she continued to look at him silently.

"It's just," he said, "that you once told me that if I wanted something, I should go after it. And you were right. That's why I'm here."

He watched her with that wary expression.

"Say something. What do you reckon, Maggie? Do you want me to go away again?"

Maggie swallowed. She took hold of Fox's hand, feeling the warmth and strength of it. He carried the scent of the desert with him, in his clothes, in his hair, in the wind of his breath. But words had utterly deserted her. His question had too many others crowded beneath. One thing at a time, she told herself. She swallowed again, raised her eyes to his. One thing at a time, one step at a time; everything changed, it was all *dammas*.

"What I reckon," she said, reaching for the only words she could seem to find right now, "is that when I go home to the mountain, I'm going to have to get me a truck."

"Home?" Fox smiled, relief in his eyes. "You know, I think that's the word I came across an entire ocean to hear."

She gripped his hand, feeling confusion and indecision draining away. Drying up like water in the hot desert sun that he carried. Language was slowly returning to her, a foreign tongue that she remembered after all.

She said, "There's something I'd like to do here. Before heading back to Tucson again." She looked up at him, at the question in his eyes. "I'd like to take you out to Dartmoor. Where Cooper was born. Where I went to school. I'd like to show you my Wood Wife. The English one. Will you go with me?"

"You bet. It's a deal."

She smiled at Fox, reminded of Crow and his bargains. "And what do you want in return?"

He considered the bargain carefully. "I want to meet Tat, your mysterious best friend."

"My other best friend," she corrected him. She tugged at his hand. "Come with me," she said. And then the bargain was sealed.

epilogue

On the night that the Trickster returned to the Rincon Mountains, the coyotes began to sing. Not as they sang most other nights: to hunt, to make love, to cherish the moon; on that night they sang as the angels sing, filling the valley with one great song that rang from the mountains east, west, north and south, to the city below.

He had wandered far in the form of a wolf, a coyote, a fox, a crow, and a man. The Sonoran land that formed Crow's bones stretched from Arizona into Mexico, but his heart was baked from the Rincon clay and it was there that he always returned.

Now he sat on Rincon Peak, the stars around him like a cloak. He listened to the song of his four-legged kin; then he threw back his head and he answered them. He laughed, the wind whipping back his black hair, delighted with the night, and with himself.

In Red Springs Canyon, the Alders watched as a lame mule deer gave birth to a fawn. The little one stepped into the dark world on wobbley legs, its black eyes wide, trusting the hands that held him, trusting that the night meant him no harm.

In the old ranch stable, Dora del Río did not wake, but Juan listened to the nightsong from his lonely bed on the living-room couch. The coyotes sang, and Bandido howled. Something frozen inside Juan seemed to melt. He missed his wife. He had her love, but he needed more, to earn back her trust. He lay there and prayed that the wounds would heal from a night he still couldn't remember.

Up the hill, Tomás heard the nightsong. He stood in his garden for a long while, listening to those voices and the others that came on the wind. Then he smiled and closed the cabin door. Spencer Tracy was on

*the movie that night. He was a man like any other, and he turned on
the television.*

*The old Foxxe house was empty now. Dust lay on the pots and pans,
on the table Johnny Foxxe had built. Pepe ran the hills with his kind,
adding his voice to the midnight song, but Angela and Isabella were
clothed in their slender human forms. In the circle of stones surrounding Red Springs, the Foxxe sisters were dancing.*

*Far to the west, the wood wife sat by her trailer and smoked an-
other cigarette. When it was done, she shook off the shapeless dress, the
folds of woman-flesh; she put on her cloak of leaves and slowly walked
through that land, humming as she went. Where she passed, saplings
of ironwood and mesquite rooted in the dry soil.*

*In Cooper's house, Maggie stood at the window, Fox behind her, lis-
tening.*

*"This is the kind of night," Fox said, "when I think my mother was
right after all: that the cactus run away and waltz together as soon as
we're not looking. The coyotes are making the music for them. What
are they singing for now, I wonder?"*

"For joy," she said. "Listen. Can't you hear it?"

"It's not a death song?"

"It's a life song. But I think they might be the same thing."

*Fox put his arms around her. He whispered into Maggie's ear, "To
feel that waking is another sleep that dreams it does not sleep and that
death, which our flesh dreads, is that very death of every night which
we call sleep.... To transform the outrage of the years into a music, a
rumor, a symbol ... of such is Poetry, immortal and a pauper."*

She leaned back against him, her eyes thoughtful. "Is that Cooper?"

*"No, it's Borges," he told her. He pointed. "Look. That's poetry too.
The moon. And the color of that sky. The Three Graces in the yard. The
mountains looking like one of Anna's paintings come to life."*

*"Those are gemstone colors, not paintbox colors," she said. She whis-
pered into his ear, "The night, blue lapis. The mountain, onyx. Saguaro, verdigris within a copper dish of moon. The wind rustles dry
mesquite. A coyote howls. A star falls. And the night cracks me open,*

with beauty sharp and poignant as grief. The night cracks me open, like a geode, exposing the crystal veins of God."

"Is that Cooper then?" Fox asked.

She shook her head. "Only Maggie Black."

Fox smiled and kissed her bare shoulder. "Come away from the window, Only-Maggie-Black. The saguaro won't move while we're watching them—and look, you can see they're all ready to dance."

She looked out the window one last time, and saw that they were indeed.

author's note

The story of *The Wood Wife* was originally conceived for a series of novellas based on the magical artwork of British painter Brian Froud; over time, the original tale shape-shifted and became the novel herein. Despite the many changes since the story's earliest conception, Brian's beautiful art remains a strong influence throughout the text. I am grateful for his vision, his generosity, and his friendship.

I am also grateful to Patrick Nielsen Hayden, John Jarrold, Ellen Steiber, and Delia Sherman for their insightful comments on the text; to my agent, Julie Fallowfield, and legal counsel, Mimi Panitch; to Robert Gould for conversations that sparked the character of Maggie Black; to Leigh Grossman and Keith Decandido for early encouragement; and to the following people who helped with fact-checking: Midori Snyder, Tania Yatskievyick, Dhevdhas Nair, Ian Brackenbury, Russell Stevens, and Ray Pepes. In addition, I owe deep thanks to the following people who—in various ways—opened my eyes to the beauty of the Sonoran desert: Beth Meacham and Tappan King, the Harlan family, Jim and Loma Griffith, Dick Laws and Marie Rogier, Jodi and Rupert Encinas, Elisabeth Roberts, and Munro Sickafoose, and, as always, my thanks to Thomas Canty for his faith.

I'm a newcomer to the Sonora, and only a part-time desert dweller at that. I strongly recommend the works of the Southwestern writers who know this beautiful region best, such as Edward Abbey, Charles Bowden, James Griffith, Janice Emily Bowers, and Gary Nabhan—as well as Hope Ryden's extensive study of coyotes in the wild: *God's Dog*.

—Terri Windling
Tucson, Arizona and Devon, England

And it was at that age . . . Poetry arrived
in search of me. I don't know, I don't know where
it came from. . . .

—**Pablo Neruda**